The Extraordinary Visit
of
Benjamin True

The State of the Union as no one else would tell it

By Jack Pelham

Dedication

To all who would make a difference

if they could figure out how.

Contents

Prologue

It was beautiful; the chance to speak the truth to people long in need of hearing it was simply beautiful. And then, as if that weren't treasure enough, there was the near-certain expectation that at least a few of them would take it to heart and heal themselves—because that's just what some people choose to do when they hear the truth. For those, my message would be a gift—a blessing. And it was my joy to bring it.

~Benjamin True

Chapter 1

Nine O'Clock

"Mister Speaker,...," rang out the Sergeant at Arms of the House of Representatives in a commanding tone. "...The President of the United States!"

It was precisely 9:00 p.m. Eastern Standard Time when this announcement roused all those who had not already been standing inside the Chamber of the United States House of Representatives. President Rafael Hernandez had been waiting for just a moment outside the recently-closed Chamber door as the clock drew down to the appointed hour. He confidently anticipated the pomp and circumstance that awaited him just inside, and was confident that he knew exactly what to expect at this, his third speech to Congress. He was, after all, the most powerful man in the world, and as he stepped across the threshold into the House, this was, in his mind, another grand opportunity to remind the world of that fact.

He had no idea.

Cheers and applause quickly filled the room as President Hernandez began the tiresome photo-op parade from the double doors at the northern center of the House, down the royal-blue-carpeted center aisle that led southward to the Speaker's rostrum. It wasn't supposed to *look* tiresome, mind you. Rather, it was an opportunity to give the impression that the President was both wildly popular and deeply respected by the Members of Congress who had arrived hours earlier just to get a seat near enough to the aisle to have a chance at catching his attention. Some had been planted here by Party leadership, of course, to shake his hand or pat him on the back—whatever would give the impression that the State of the Union under his leadership was strong.

One couple had striven for a seat near this aisle in hopes of getting in a one-liner proposal of some sort as President Hernandez passed by. It was hard to get a meeting with him, naturally, and this was a chance, they thought, to put a bug in his ear in hopes of being granted a proper meeting in the near future. To most of them, however, whatever their other motives may have been, this was also an opportunity to be seen with the president for their own political benefit.

President Hernandez had been the first Hispanic elected to the Oval Office, and was in the third year of his first term. He had been fairly popular so far, and largely on account of his Latino heritage, for Americans had become increasingly generous in their attitudes about such things, and now somewhat fancied the idea of electing individuals from ethnic groups that had not yet had a representative serve in the White House. Indeed, Hernandez had a lot going for him as far as many voters were concerned, beyond being from the right heritage at the right time. He was a commanding figure, and had had a respectable two terms as the governor of Florida before ascending to the presidency.

Critics, however, accused Hernandez of not being the sharpest tool in the shed. He was a "driver", one had said, and owed his success to bullying people until they gave in. Others suspected that he might have been a puppet for behind-the-scenes money interests, and they argued that he simply couldn't have gotten here on his own devices. Still others, while proud to have a Latino in the White House finally, were disappointed that that particular Latino had to be Hernandez. There were surely other Hispanics who were wiser and more qualified, they argued, but Hernandez had been in the right spot at the right time. And so it was he to whom the honor fell on this special annual event; he was the one touted as "the most powerful man on Earth" and as "the leader of the free world". And whether any particular person liked him or not, he would forever hold the title as having been the first Latino President of the United States.

As Hernandez inched along the aisle, the opportunists awaiting him at that aisle could each be observed, along with their various idiosyncrasies of character. Some would settle for the benefits of whatever video footage might make it to TV media and other social media, such as

Facebook and YouTube, but many had their own smart phones in hand, and if they had the chance, would shamelessly pose for "selfies" with the President of the United States—or "POTUS", if you like the insider acronym. These new photographic treasures would stay tucked away safely in their phones until their owners could get home and post them on their own Facebook pages. Some, of course, would see no need to wait at all, and would post them immediately where they stood, as soon as their brief time with the President had ended. A few even "went live" on Facebook, streaming video as they shot it.

And so they waited along that aisle, most of them silently rehearsing their planned utterances while trying to look as unrehearsed as possible as President Hernandez inched along the aisle. The entire Congress, of course—House and Senate alike—were all present on the House floor, along with those justices of the Supreme Court who had cared to come, the members of the Executive Cabinet, the Joint Chiefs of Staff, and a few other dignitaries of various sorts. All of them were awaiting Hernandez's address, along with over 60 million TV viewers around the world. And wait they would because this ritual was simply more important in President Hernandez's eyes, and no one dared challenge him on the rudeness of it all, just as they had tolerated the previous presidents who had done the same.

The Chamber, appointed in federal style with dark walnut wall panels, was decorated as it always was, except that a scattering of small furniture at the lowest floor level, which was normally front and center of the rostrum, had been removed to afford both a less-cluttered view of the President for the TV cameras, and extra floor space for the additional chairs needed to seat all in attendance. Besides that, little else was unusual but a pair of teleprompters that had been set in front and to each side of the second-tier lectern, which was normal for the President's annual State of the Union Address.

The Members of Congress had long since stopped dividing up into their political parties for this annual event. They used to sit with the Republicans on the right side of the house and Democrats on the left. In what they now jokingly called "Date Night", they would mix it up and sit in no particular partisan arrangement. There was, however, one noteworthy remaining custom with regard to the seating. The first two to four rows of the permanent seats were reserved for the Members of the US Senate, who also were visitors in the House Chamber. This hall was much bigger than their own, making it the obvious place to meet for joint sessions of the Congress. Bringing in 100 extra legislators had the undesirable consequence, however, of requiring that extra chairs be brought in to the rear of the hall for the displaced Members of the House to sit. The Chamber was tightly packed, such that it would make a fire marshal nervous had it been in any other town. But in this town, where prudence often takes a backseat to political expediency, this was business as usual.

The Speaker's rostrum consisted of three tiers of counter-like desks, each tier longer than the tier above. At the top stood Speaker of the House William DuBois, along with his guest for the evening, Vice President Linda Surgeon. Few Americans knew it anymore, but the Vice President's role, according to the Constitution, included duty as the President—that is, the presiding officer—of the Senate. As both houses were meeting together and officially convened in a joint session, the presiding officer of each house shared the place of honor at the highest tier of the rostrum. Even so, the Speaker of the House was still in charge as it was his House.

As always, President Hernandez was to speak at the Clerk's lectern on the middle tier, just in front of and below the Speaker's desk. Speaker DuBois was all too aware of the significance of this. This was *his* house, and the President of the United States was not allowed to set foot in it without an invitation from the Speaker. He had invited Hernandez by letter about a month before, as was the custom, and POTUS was not allowed to be here without his say-so. Even the high and mighty Secret Service, he beamed silently, had to yield to the authority of his Capitol Police for this event. They were merely bodyguards for the president, but it was DuBois' police force, or at least he liked to think of it that way, that was in charge tonight. They numbered 1,700 officers and 350 other staff, if all the shifts are counted together. And for once, DuBois thought, the Executive Branch was in its rightful place—below the Legislative Branch, and reporting for duty. *If only*, he thought, *it were like this all the time!*

It was in the Constitution, after all, that the President...

> ...*shall from time to time give to Congress information of the State of the Union and recommend to their Consideration such measures as he shall judge necessary and expedient.*[1]

And so here he was, President Rafael Hernandez, oozing down DuBois' House aisle on his third annual visit for such an address.

Vice President Linda Surgeon's attitude about the President was somewhat softer. She sat in that unique role of being the Vice President of the Executive Branch, having been chosen primarily for the same reason that most vice presidents are—because it was believed she would bring votes from her home "swing state" to the Party's ticket. But she also sat as the presiding officer over the "upper house" of the Legislative Branch, the Senate, and had the power of being able to cast the deciding vote in the case of a tie among the 100 senators. For Surgeon, the man walking her direction down the aisle was something of a mixed bag. On the one hand, she wasn't fond of him and found him hypocritical and moderately irritating, but on the other, he had made her name a household word, and if his presidency could stay popular, she had a shot at the Oval Office herself, albeit another five years down the road. So, it wasn't all that hard for her to smile cordially as POTUS made his way southward toward her position. It was business as usual.

Having at length exhausted his course down the aisle, President Hernandez finally approached the clerk's lectern, where an aide handed him two black, leather-bound copies of his speech. No one was behind the middle-tier desk for this event, even though it would normally seat several employees of the Clerk of the House during regular sessions of the House. At the wider first-tier desk, however, seven were seated, including a court reporter, who sat with his stenotype machine, just off center in front of and to the left of the lectern above, from which the president would be speaking. On this same first row sat a few other employees of the Clerk. Neither their names nor faces were known to the public, and curiosity about whom they must be rarely lasted beyond the opening moments of the event, during which the TV cameras were much more apt to be showing a wider view of things.

Meanwhile, applause had gone on now for nearly sixteen minutes, and weary individuals could be seen to pause from clapping, and then to resume just seconds later for the embarrassment of appearing not to be either enthusiastic, if they were from the same party as the President, or professionally gracious, if they were not. Hernandez made his way to the second tier, where he reached over the Speaker's desk to hand the Speaker and Vice President each a copy of his speech. Then followed cordial handshakes with the two for the cameras, along with the obligatory-and-cordial greetings between him and each of the two presiding officers.

As much as he hated the feigned pleasantries, Speaker DuBois was at least glad that in a minute or so more, his most unsavory task of the evening would be over and done with.

As President Hernandez turned around to face the assembled Congress and other guests, he was stricken by his wide view of the House Gallery above, where several hundred guests were still standing and applauding. *I didn't remember it being so big last year*, he thought. He smiled and nodded graciously, appearing to demur somewhat as he quietly said, "Thank you. Thank you."

Not five seconds of this had passed before the double crack of Speaker DuBois' gavel cut the air and the din of the Chamber came to a near-instant and popularly-welcomed halt. Even those few "true believers"—those whose view of the pomp and circumstance of the evening was inspired by the romance of patriotic idealism, and whose belief was as yet unbesmirched by a knowledge of the *real* goings on in government—even they were tired of clapping, for sixteen minutes is an unnaturally long time to clap, even for a good cause.

As everyone settled down, Speaker DuBois braced himself, took a deep breath, and then commenced with the customary announcement. "Members of Congress, I have the high privilege and distinct honor of presenting to you the President of the United States."

The clapping commenced again, of course, and proper etiquette required that they all give it another go "out of respect for the Office," it was said. DuBois smiled and clapped, of course, while thinking to himself, *"Get on with it, already, you jerk. We've all read your stupid speech already. Just get on with it."* Even with the animus, DuBois fortunately remembered in timely fashion this year to press the switch to make his motorized lectern lower to the height of the desk that supported it. He had forgotten this last year until after the President was well into his speech. When he had realized it, he flipped the switch, not thinking anything of it, but would later be harshly accused of having done it deliberately so as to upstage the President. But that was then. After having pressed the button in plenty of time this night, he also pushed down the microphone's gooseneck, and then he resumed clapping.

"Thank you! Thank you!" glowed the President, waiting for that moment when the applause could be sensed to begin dying out on its own. He would run with it for as long as it lasted, of course. The adoration was politically useful and personally gratifying, but naturally, he didn't want to appear to be encouraging it. His confederates in the audience would take care of that.

As he gazed regally about the floor and gallery, he noticed that the aging Chief Justice of the Supreme Court, who didn't like him very much, had begun the slow, telltale motions of preparing to sit. Chief Justice Wendell Stone was 83 years old, and had the reputation with some of being a Class-A curmudgeon. President Hernandez didn't like him because he had twice ruled with the majority against the administration, and now the old codger was going to sit down early to slight the President. *I don't think so!* thought Hernandez, and he immediately held up his hands, gesturing to all, "Please be seated," before the Chief Justice had barely begun to stoop over.

A palpable wave of relief silently swept over the crowd, who had well earned a chance to rest from their laborious applause. And so sat Vice President Surgeon and Speaker DuBois as well, the latter concerning himself primarily with the task of appearing both stately and mildly interested during the torturous and tired speech to come. *"I hate these things."*

Chapter 2

Mister Speaker

"Mister Speaker," began President Hernandez, "Madam Vice President, Members of Congress, Justices of the Supreme Court, Members of the Cabinet, Joint Chiefs of Staff, our many distinguished guests, and finally, the Citizens of the United States, both in this great hall and at home, it is both my honor and duty to deliver to you this annual State of the Union Address for the third time in my tenure as President of these United States. I am required by our Constitution, as you know, to bring you this address, but it is also my personal joy to do so, for this is the greatest nation on Earth. I am proud to declare that the State of the Union is strong!"

At this, roughly half the room erupted into a standing ovation, while the other half now assumed license to keep their peace. This applause didn't last nearly as long as before. Those clapping from sincere enthusiasm began to die out several seconds before those who were clapping to drive the appearance of enthusiasm finally gave up. By now, the partisan tone of the room was growing obvious, for it was easy to see who in the room would mirror POTUS' enthusiasm, whether sincerely or strategically, and who would not.

"For well over two centuries," Hernandez continued, "we have weathered the storms of democracy and even though we haven't always handled everything perfectly, I think the framers of our government would be very proud of our progress."

POTUS paused, having expected to be interrupted at this point by another round of applause, but getting only a smattering of three or four uncertain claps. *Hmm, did I say something wrong?* he wondered to himself in a split second. But he knew from experience that if he would just move it along without any further pause, it wouldn't seem like such a big deal that there wasn't much applause. He *ad libbed* with a reflective repetition of his last line to the silent hall. "Yes, the framers would be very proud of us."

"I beg to differ," claimed a voice from nowhere. It was as clear as any voice ever heard. *But where did it come from?* many in the House thought to themselves. People stirred and looked about, finding no obvious answer to the question. Speaker DuBois sat forward in his chair, his senses now on alert. He hadn't really been paying attention to the speech, so he didn't notice that the "I beg to differ" had not come from the President, but he noticed the stirring of the crowd, and it piqued his interest. Vice President Linda Surgeon fidgeted, wondering whether she had really heard what she thought she had heard. The crowd was not sure, either, and silence ruled the moment.

Not sure whether to let on that he had heard it, President Hernandez immediately sensed that this was somehow familiar. He couldn't have put it into words in this short a span, because nobody thinks that fast, but he certainly found it familiar somehow. Had he been able to think on it for a few undistracted seconds, what would have come fully to his mind is the famous acoustic anomaly in the Old House Chamber, where a whisper across the room could be heard with perfect clarity if you were in just the right spot. *Some idiot Congressman was speaking out of turn*, he thought. *Just ignore it. Don't want to seem flustered.*

Hernandez continued, "And so we move forward from here, to new frontiers, to new progress—to make the state of the Union even..."

A scream from the floor interrupted and startled President Hernandez. There was a collective gasp, then stirring and murmuring and pointing, and another scream followed in an instant. Only then did he realize that there was someone standing at his right side, not a foot away. The surprise of someone appearing this close to him without any warning was such a shock that it obliterated his habitual awareness of whether he was currently poised or not. Being caught off guard, he defaulted to his natural unfeigned self. He made a quick and wide-eyed turn to his right and took a defensive step back at the same time. "What is this?" he demanded of the figure beside him at the lectern.

"Mr. President," came the calm greeting with a nod and a confident smile. As he opened his mouth to continue speaking, the onslaught of Secret Service agents came like a storm out of nowhere. In a heartbeat, there were seven agents rushing full speed toward the lectern, one down each of the three inner aisles in the room, and two each from the front-most aisles that ran to the left and right of the Speaker's platform. Their pistols were all drawn and angled downward toward the floor as they ran. Meanwhile, two more agents had stood in the Gallery just above the rostrum, one to the left of the white marble facade behind the Speaker, and the other to the right. Both their guns were pointed straight at the intruder just a few feet below, but he had no gun as far as they could see, and he was too close to POTUS for them to shoot safely.

There were screams, of course, which, along with an immediate radio call of "Intruder at the lectern!" from one of the Secret Service agents, alerted the multitude of Capitol Police outside the Chamber that something serious was going on. Those officers had begun their rush to the doors within three seconds of the commotion beginning, and the Secret Service inside the Chamber were already only two seconds away from being near enough to tackle the intruder from multiple sides at once.

Well aware of what was coming, the intruder raised up his arms to each side with palms outward, and gave a sharp push into the air, as if pushing two opposite doors closed at once. "Stop!" he said, and, with this, the room became motionless as his command echoed in the hall with surprising force. The agents at floor level were instantly halted at full sprint, pistols still pointed safely downward in front of them. Capitol Police officers in the halls and foyers were frozen, some just inches away from the doors they were about to enter. Inside the Chamber mouths that were opened and in mid-scream were still opened but silent. Fingers still pointed, and some who had begun to duck for cover were frozen in the beginnings of their crouches.

"Everyone calm down," he instructed them. "No one will be harmed here tonight. No one is in danger," he assured them firmly as he removed his hat and laid it on the desk in front of him. "I come in peace, and I have no weapons." Everyone heard it, but no one could reply. After a brief pause, he said quite calmly to the Secret Service agents, who were all now within fifteen feet of him, "Now, before I let you go, I'm going to put your guns out of reach so that you don't accidentally shoot someone in all the excitement." With this, he waved his left hand across the room from his left to his right, while the crowd watched in petrified and silent disbelief as the pistols of the nine Secret Service agents encircling Hernandez and the intruder left their hands and levitated to a position above the forward-most desk, where they gently settled into a pile on the center of the desk.

This can't be happening! thought one spectator to himself. *Is this for real?* thought another. Others were screaming in their minds, and others still would have been yelling if they could. *Oh, my God! Oh, my God!*

"Now, we'd better have these, also," the intruder said with another wave of his hand, and quite a variety of guns appeared from inside the jackets and pant legs of the nine agents. These guns, too, floated to the pile on the lost desk, along with all their radios, wrist microphones and cords, earpieces, and cell phones. At this point, anyone in the crowd not sure of what he or she had seen on the first occasion of floating guns was now well-enough rehearsed in the procedure to understand it exactly. *This was some sort of magic.*

"I'm going to let you all go now," said the intruder with a warm and jovial tone, "but before I do, I just want you to know that I sincerely hope there'll be no more screaming. It's such a useless activity in situations such as this." And with that, a simple wave of the hand freed everyone from the mannequin-like poses in which they had been involuntarily frozen—all except for President Hernandez, the Vice President and Speaker, the nine Secret Service agents, and the seven employees seated along that lowest and longest desk. There was a bit of rustling from the crowd, who were busy convincing themselves that they were now unpetrified. They were strangely silent, however, without only a low murmur coming from a few here and there. Gesturing to the agents and the others with him at the rostrum, he said, "I'll let you all go shortly, but first, I'm going to tell you who I am and why I am ..."

He was immediately interrupted by a lady screaming in the Gallery behind the speaker's rostrum. She was near the corner to the Speaker's left, only about 30 feet from where the First Lady sat along the adjacent wall. The screaming lady stood in the foremost row of the balcony, just behind the rail. Doing some sort of tiny-stepped jogging in place, as if she had just seen a snake, she screamed again and again, taking breaths periodically, as necessary to keep it going, and pointing at the intruder with a finger that bounced up and down with the panicked footwork.

12

"Ma'am!" spoke the intruder firmly, with a wave of the hand in her direction. She was immediately stilled and silenced, frozen as they had all been before. Her finger still pointed and her mouth was still open. One of her feet was two inches off the floor, and yet she didn't fall over. "Ma'am, I told you that I really don't like screaming," he explained to her. "Do you suppose that you could calm down if I let you go?"

She couldn't reply, of course, but he had asked it rhetorically. "I'm going to let you go, and you can answer me," he said, and with another wave of his hand, she was freed and continued exactly as before with the screaming. "Ma'am!" he said, with another petrifying wave of the hand. When she was silenced, he said to her, "I'm going to sit you down, and then I'm going to keep you frozen there for a while until you have a chance to calm your mind a bit." There was another wave of the hand, and the frozen lady's body sat into her seat, her arms finding their way to the armrests. "Somebody up there remind me to let her go before I leave tonight," he called up to the Gallery. There was no reply. It was a perfectly reasonable and forward-thinking request, and several were willing to comply, but most found themselves still much too overwhelmed to be formulating language at this point. And so they sat, somewhat stunned and hoping for things to start making sense sooner than later.

The intruder's appearance was striking, and doubly surprising since not only had he appeared from thin air, but he seemed to be in costume. He was a handsome white man around seventy years old, it appeared, and in a full Continental Army uniform. He wore a Navy-Blue coat, broadly trimmed in ecru with quarter-sized silver buttons every two and a half inches down the opening and along the cuffs. Under it, he wore ecru nickers and an ecru vest covering a white, collared shirt. White buttoned leggings went from his knees down to the ankles of his black boots. His salt-and-pepper hair was fastened back into a pony tail that nearly reached his shoulders, and on the desk before him sat his black tricorn hat, unadorned except for a brass button half way up the folded brim over his left temple.

His voice was confident, calm, and commanding, and his frame was brimming with energy, defying—many would think—his apparent age. His stance was strong but not threatening and his blue eyes sparkled with life. He had none of the accouterments customary with such uniform. No sword or bayonet, and no musket—neither cartridge box, haversack, canteen, nor bedroll. Few in the crowd would know that this was a private's uniform, and fewer still would be in the least aware that his age was not a good match for such a rank. But there he stood, as bizarre a surprise as anyone might have imagined before it had all begun to unfold.

"My name is Benjamin True. I was born in Massachusetts in 1758, and I fought in the Revolutionary War under General George Washington. I even spent that dreadful winter at Valley Forge and nearly froze to death, along with those many who did. After we had won our independence, I married and lived a good many years, and then I died, at which time I graduated to the next level. Ever since then, for the last couple hundred years, I have watched with great interest and dismay as this country has strayed farther and farther from the extraordinary principles that were agreed upon by those who framed her government.

"Again and again during these two centuries since I left this world, I have said to God that I wish he would send one of his archangels down to straighten out this mess—to get you all back on track—to remind you of your country's philosophical beginnings. But he always told me that in his wisdom, it was best not to intervene in your affairs. And surely, he would know!

"Well, just this morning, I was having yet another of these same discussions with him, and to my great surprise, he looked at me and said, 'Alright, *you* go. You have one night.' So here I am."

He beamed with a smile that would have made most like him instantly, if it hadn't been for the gargantuan distraction around the fact that this was a visit from a supposedly-otherworldly person. Meanwhile, there was some murmuring at his announcement of his schedule. Sensing their uncertainty, he told them, "Now don't worry; I don't plan to keep you all in here all night. With any luck, we'll be out of here in a couple of hours."

"So, you're an angel?" yelled out an incredulous senator from Georgia.

"Yes, you could call me that," said Benjamin True with a sparkle in his eye. "I have come to you today as I used to look when I lived here." He held his arms up in front of himself, looking himself over and said, "I thought the uniform would be a nice touch to help frame my comments."

At this the hum of quiet conversations swept across the House, most of it unintelligible, except for the word "angel," which could be heard many times in the seconds that followed.

"Are you going to kill us?" demanded a male voice from somewhere near the back of the Chamber.

Immediately, there was more screaming. This time it was from the Chamber floor in the first few rows to the right of the Speaker's rostrum. Benjamin True turned in her direction, and this time, without raising his hand, he said firmly, "Ma'am!" She stopped immediately, clamping her hands over her mouth just to be sure. This was funny, of course, and a few laughed out loud.

"Thanks for getting it together," said True, smiling reassuringly at the woman, who was a second-term Representative from Texas. "I really hate screaming," he reminded her.

"Sorry," she said, clutching her hands to her heart and shrugging her shoulders briefly. Her sincerity was obvious.

"It's forgiven," he said with a warm smile and a long nod to her.

"Now, where were we?" said True as he turned and gestured back to the man at the rear of the Chamber. "No, I'm not going to kill you. I just came to talk to you." With this, he waved a hand casually, and freed those few who were still petrified at or near the Speaker's rostrum. To the seven Secret Service agents standing around him, he said, "Why don't you all just step out to the floor there and have a seat on the floor, away from your guns. And please, let's not have any heroics. Nobody is in danger here." The seven men did as he asked, sitting down on the carpet just in front of the semicircular front row of House seats.

True turned around to speak to the two agents in the Gallery at either end of the frontispiece behind the rostrum. "You two can just have a seat where you are, please." They nodded and complied.

To the seven seated at the first-tier desk beneath him, Benjamin True said, "I hate to put you out, but it is a bit crowded up here, and for everyone's safety, I'm going to ask all of you except the court reporter if you would please stand at this time and find some place to stand at the rear of the hall."

As the six stood to comply with his request, he said to the reporter, "You may stay as you are and continue your reporting."

The court reporter, just a few feet from the intruder was a bit bewildered by it all, but kept on pressing the keys on his stenotype machine, feeling strangely calm, given the wildness of the situation that was unfolding.

"This is just some sort of a stunt!" yelled a congressman from his seat near the far right of the hall.

Benjamin True turned in that direction and asked, "Who said that?" The question prompted gasps from a few while Congressman Randy Thomas remained speechless in his chair, uncertain as to whether it was best to answer or not, just in case this really wasn't a stunt. Several who were seated near the Congressman were making the universal "not me!" gesture and shaking their heads, while one of them two rows back from Thomas boldly rose and pointed straight at him.

"He said it," came the shrill and unapologetic voice with a New Jersey accent. "That's Representative Randy Thomas right there, and he said it, sir!" She stood with her arm straight out for a second or two, and staring back at Benjamin True. Then she was suddenly stricken with doubt as to just what she should be doing at that moment. She put her hands on her hips, but that stance didn't seem quite right, so then she folded her arms. Then she simply sat down, not sure whether to be pleased with herself or scared.

"I didn't say it!" pleaded the Congressman. "It was somebody else!"

"You come here," Benjamin True told him. He pointed his finger at the man, and then raised the finger, levitating the Congressman two body heights above his seat, at which point he began to float toward the rostrum where True stood, still beside the President. As the Congressman was floating toward the front of the hall, the angel said, "I'll meet you right down front." Then, still pointing a finger as if to direct the floating politician, True stepped forward, passing through the desk in front of him as if it were made of air. He passed further forward and toward the center, now in front of the lectern where the President stood, and then he walked forward and down again, passing through the pile of Secret Service gear he had previously collected from the agents. Not one piece of all that equipment moved the slightest bit as he passed through it and the desk beneath. As True stepped through that forward-most desk and the equipment on it, the congressman's body turned horizontally like a Superman flying at walking speed. This brought the two face to face, with Benjamin True standing on the blue carpet at floor level, and the Congressman floating in front and above True—his arms shielding his face as if expecting to be beaten by the angel.

"So, you are Congressman Randy Thomas?" asked Benjamin True.

"Yessir," was about all he could manage to say in reply.

"So, we have a doubting Thomas, I see," said True, smiling. "Well, doubting is no sin as long as you'll admit to the truth when it has been proven to you. I trust that this demonstration has been satisfying to you at this point?"

"Yessir, this is no stunt. I'm sorry I said it was." Randy Thomas felt choked up, and would have begun to sob if he had had to speak any further.

"Well, I'll do one more trick for you, but I'd better scoot you back a bit first, so you don't get too scared." True made a slight pushing motion with his right hand, and the congressman floated back another 4 feet or so, still laid out horizontally, as if lying on his stomach on a sofa.

"As you can all see," said Benjamin True to everyone, "I'm not a regular human anymore." As soon as he said it, without any gesture at all, his entire body turned into a body of flames. One could make out that the form was about the same, but the flames rose higher than the form, and looked remarkably like the flames of any common bonfire. They could all see right through him to whatever lay beyond, and while those nearest recoiled to protect themselves, they quickly noticed that there was no wave of heat that went along with the spectacle. He raised his arms out to his sides, and again the people recoiled out of reflex, but quickly relaxed. And just like that, he was back as he had appeared at first—as the Continental soldier.

"So, there you are," said True with his arms still held out to his sides. He turned left and right, looking about the crowd. "This should be enough to convince anyone who doesn't have a motive to deny the obvious. And I must say to you all that I'm pleasantly surprised that there was no further screaming during that trick."

There was some genuine laughter at this from many of those in the audience. It felt good to laugh—sort of—some of them thought.

Turning back to the floating congressman, True asked Randy Thomas, "Shall I assume that you remain convinced?"

Thomas answered, but no sound came out of his mouth at first. He tried again, clearing his throat. "Yes."

"Well, good," True assured him. "Just for the record, there's no shame in voicing your doubts, Randy," he said with a genuine smile. "It gave everyone else the opportunity to assure themselves of the truth of the matter."

Thomas was surprised at this, and found himself smiling before he could finish processing what had just been said to him.

"There is shame, however, in the lie you told. You denied having called out that this was a stunt, yet the truth of the matter is that you were indeed the one who had said it."

Thomas was shocked and felt deep shame for the first time in years. "Yessir," he said weakly, practically in a whisper. "I was wrong to lie." Thomas lowered his face to the floor in shame, averting the gaze of Benjamin True.

"OK, I'm going to set you down and you can walk on back to your seat," said True, and with this, he gave a long, downward nod, in response to which the Congressman's body turned upright as his feet began to descend to the floor.

"OK, I'm going back to my seat now, right?" Randy Thomas was barely audible as he gestured with this thumb to the area from which he had been plucked minutes before.

True reached out to shake his hand, and said, "Right. And thanks again for the conversation."

After the handshake, Congressman Randy Thomas turned to walk back to his seat, and with his first forward step, he felt a rush in his head and then his knees buckled, spilling him into the laps of three of the Joint Chiefs of Staff seated on the front row. They looked to Benjamin True, as if to seek permission to help, and an affirmative nod from him was their answer. They stood him up and walked him back to his seat, the Congressman regaining his strength as he went.

"Does anyone else here still doubt that my powers are real?" asked True, looking about from his position on the floor of the House.

"I don't know if this is real or not, ..." began President Rafael Hernandez, who was now speaking up for the first time since his speech was first interrupted. He had spent the last several minutes clutching the lectern with his hands and nervously trying to figure out what a president would do in such a situation. And now, as he had begun speaking, his

18

frustration began to vent, "...but this is my speech, and I'm in charge here."

"Are you?" questioned True. "The way I see it, you're not standing on the top rung of the ladder here. Isn't that right, Speaker DuBois?

Ordinarily, the Speaker would have been thrilled to see the President being challenged, but given the extreme events of the night, he rather wished not to draw any undue attention to himself. "That's right, Mr. True," he said matter-of-factly, "the President stands below the Speaker's desk, being just a guest in this House."

"So, you're the highest authority here?"

"Normally I am, sir, but tonight, the President of the Senate joins me as an equal, as both houses of Congress are here, jointly assembled," explained Speaker DuBois.

"And there is no one higher still?" probed True.

"No, sir," came the reply, with Vice President Linda Surgeon quietly nodding along.

"Well, while we're on the subject of authority," replied Benjamin True, "I think we should take a few minutes to clarify the matter. Tell me, Mister Speaker, what do you make of that inscription above your head?" True gestured to the inscription in the frontispiece above the Speaker's rostrum. "Does it not say, 'In God We Trust'?"

"It does," explained Speaker DuBois, "but that doesn't mean that God literally has a seat in our government. I mean, obviously, he's not here." It was obvious that DuBois was nervous. He wasn't really taking breaths.

"I'm sure you're nervous," said True, "but please just calm yourself and continue."

DuBois continued, a little calmer simply for trying to calm himself, "That saying is just a political statement that was put up there in the early sixties in response to the Soviet-era Communist threat to our nation."

True questioned him, "So it's just there to pander to the people, as well as to influence them that the Cold War with the Soviets was a righteous cause?"

"I suppose," concluded DuBois.

"Then why do you leave it up there if you know it's not true?" asked

True, getting no response other than a somewhat wilted look from DuBois.

Turning to Vice President Linda Surgeon, True asked, "And what about the house over which *you* preside, Madam Vice President? Don't you have the same inscription in the Senate?"

"We do," she replied in as objective a monotone as she could muster.

"And don't you have another---one in Latin, reading *"Annuit coeptis"*, which when translated means "He smiles on our endeavors"?

"We do," she said again.

"Yes, and this same saying is on the back of your One Dollar Bill, where it is depicted by an image of your unfinished human-built pyramid being topped off and completed by the all-seeing eye of God himself. It is a shameless attempt to declare your nation to be a project of none other than Yahweh himself. But just how do you know that God smiles on your endeavors? Has he told you this?"

"No, sir."

"Well, let me ask you this: is it self-evident that he smiles on *any* of your endeavors?" asked True.

"Self-evident? I suppose not."

"And would you say that the Senate has made any endeavors upon which God does *not* smile?" True continued.

"Well, I don't speak for God, of course." Surgeon was evading.

"I know that you don't speak for God, and I'm glad to hear you admit it. But surely you know *something* about God—enough to render an opinion on whether the more egregious acts of the United States Senate might just displease him or not."

She rolled her eyes a bit and took a deep breath. "I'm sure that God is not thrilled with every act of the Senate."

"Well, how hard do you work in the Senate to ensure that the things you enact are indeed pleasing to God, inasmuch as you understand what is pleasing to him?" True probed.

"The question doesn't really come up in the normal course of business," she admitted.

"So, this saying, then," True concluded, "*Annuit coeptis—He smiles on our endeavors*—is just another bit of propaganda, then."

This time, Surgeon simply nodded in the affirmative, embarrassed.

"Let the record show that the President of the Senate has nodded in the affirmative to the question of propaganda," he announced, having turned toward the court reporter, who honored the request by recording True's words.

Benjamin True then gestured to the members of the Supreme Court, who were sitting in the first two rows to the right of the aisle down which the president had entered the hall. "And what goes on across the street in the Supreme Court, Chief Justice Wendell Stone?" True asked. "Doesn't the Eastern Pediment atop your building feature the biblical figure of Moses front and center, holding the two tablets of stone?"

"It does," replied Stone with a nod.

"But it was not Moses who wrote that law, was it?"

"No, sir."

"Then please tell us, Chief Justice Stone, who did write that law?"

"Well, if you believe the myth," Stone explained, "it was God who wrote it. Yahweh."

"So, you think it might be just a myth?" probed True.

"Yes, I do."

"Then why would you have it front and center on your building if you didn't think it was true?"

"I didn't put it there. Its construction was completed in 1935," defended Stone.

"But you're in charge now, are you not?"

"I am."

"And you let it remain, even though you think it to be a false story?"

Stone gave no response, considering the question to be rhetorical.

"Tell me, Chief Justice," continued True, "don't your morning sessions begin with the crier uttering the prayer, "God save the United States and this Honorable Court!'"?

"They do."

"And do you believe that God exists and that it is by his hand that your court and these United States are saved?"

"No, I don't."

"Then why would your institution continue on in prayer to a God that you believe not to exist?"

"Some of the other justices do in fact believe in God."

"Oh?" questioned True. "Is it, then, the official position of the Supreme Court of the United States that God does in fact exist?"

"We have no such position."

"Except that you pray to him to save you every morning," True fired back. "Indeed, when you take your oath of office, you also say, 'So help me God'. I ask you, sir, how can an oath be worth anything if it is made under false pretenses?"

Stone knew better than to answer.

"I see that you're smart enough not to answer that," said True. "Yet you take that lying oath, just like the Members of Congress also say, 'So help me God', even though most of them have no intention of doing the manner of things that God might possibly be inclined to help a person do."

Benjamin True turned to the President, still standing nervously at the lectern, two tiers above True's position at the floor level. "And that brings me to you, Mister President. Let's talk about the quote from John Adams that adorns the mantel piece in the White House State Dining Room. It says:

> I pray Heaven to bestow the best of blessings on this House, and all that shall hereafter inhabit it. May none but honest and wise men rule under this roof.

"As the current resident of that house, would you care to render an opinion for us all on how that is going, Mister President?"

This drew a few snickers from the House floor and Gallery as well, but Hernandez remained silent.

"Or perhaps we could discuss your oath of office, Mr. President—the one where you swore to 'preserve, protect and defend the Constitution'. Tell us, when you took that oath, did you also include the words 'So help me God' at the end?"

"Yes," snapped Hernandez.

"But those words are not required in that oath. They are not written into the oath prescribed by the Constitution. So why did you say them?"

"It's a tradition going all the way back to George Washington," he replied.

"I see. Well, how's that going? *Is* God helping you to keep your oath?"

President Rafael Hernandez was speechless.

Benjamin True took a few seconds to stare at the president, drawing attention to the president's silence. Then he continued, "All of you—both houses, and in the Court, and in the White House—you all appeal to God in these various ways, yet you do not seem to hold yourselves accountable to him in the least. Did not Jesus once question them saying:

> *Why do you call me, Lord, Lord, and do not do what I say?*[2]"

Again, he took a few seconds to let this one sink in. The entire hall was silent and uncomfortable.

"Almost all of you in this government are inwardly quite detached from what you outwardly claim to be doing," True charged. "You're putting on a show for an audience that desperately wants to believe that something good might actually go on here from time to time."

President Rafael Hernandez could not stand this situation. He knew he was not in control, and he hated that. "I'm not here to banter with you; I'm here to give my speech to the nation," he objected, without having calculated whether he had any chance of getting his way.

"Well, I'm afraid you're going to have to reschedule your speech, Mister President," said the intruder with a sincere tone of apology in his voice, "because I've come to speak, and frankly, what I have to say is far more important than anything you've ever said in your whole life." At this, Benjamin True walked back up to the second tier, walking right through the first and second desks on his way, just as he had done on his way down. He returned to the exact spot at which he had first appeared and stared at President Hernandez, as if to inquire why he might possibly still be standing at the lectern.

"I suppose you want me to yield the floor so that you can give your little speech about winning the nation back for Jesus, right?" Had he thought about it, Hernandez probably would have been surprised at himself, because he was normally much better at keeping his cool under pressure. But this, of course, was not ordinary pressure, and Hernandez was way off his personal map on this one.

"I am not aware that Jesus had ever owned this nation and lost it, sir. No, I'll be talking about reforming the country to the honest, rational, and responsible pursuit of its original ideals—ideals that are still on the record in its official documents, having never been repealed. So, if you'll pardon me, I'll take your place and give my speech now."

President Hernandez didn't comply, but surprised himself again by pushing back in a play to win the public admiration, as if he were back in the presidential debates. "You seem to have a burr under your saddle, Mister True, like you're just bitter and came here to complain about whatever's got you all riled up about this country, but I'll have you know that I believe in American exceptionalism; I believe that America is truly exceptional among the nations of the world. Don't you?" Hernandez cocked his head slightly to one side and raised his eyebrows, calling for a response that he was sure would put Benjamin True in a bad position with this audience.

Benjamin True paused thoughtfully for a second, looking up and to his left, and then he asked, "You're asking me whether I believe that America is exceptional among the nations?"

"That's right," said Hernandez, "and the people have a right to hear your answer. So tell us, do you believe in American exceptionalism?"

True paused again and Hernandez took it as a sign that he had gained the advantage over the angel. He badgered his witness further, this time raising his voice considerably, "Tell us, Mr. True, do you believe in American exceptionalism?"

"No," came the bold reply, "America is not exceptional among the nations; all the other countries have got themselves corrupted governments, too."

This took a couple of seconds to sink in, and eventually, some laughter evolved in the audience. True had beaten President Hernandez in this brief battle of wits. Some in the room did not understand True's joke, and Hernandez was among them. All he knew was that his play didn't seem to work as he had wished. He neither spoke nor moved. He didn't know what to do. He had never been in this situation before, and while he was normally very attentive to looking "presidential" for his fans, he had no concept of what a good president would do in this situation. He felt angry and defiant. Anything he could do here would be weak, so he had no good options. The next thing Hernandez knew, True seemed to be talking to him again.

"If you'd rather not move, I could move you, of course. I believe I have demonstrated that," warned True.

The president was irate. "I'm outta here!" he shouted as he turned a sharp about face and stomped out along the second tier until he had cleared the end of the desk. Visitors were standing all along the wall to the rear of the Speaker's rostrum, so he didn't want to exit through one of the doors there. Nor *could* he have exited, since True had all the doors jammed, but Hernandez didn't know that. Rather, he turned toward the center of the House and began to march toward the aisle, heading toward the door he had entered at nine o'clock. However long ago that was, he had lost all concept of it. He knew he was mad and that it was showing, and he made a deliberate effort not to make eye contact with anyone on his way out, considering it a sign of weakness.

"Not so fast," called Benjamin True. With these words, he raised a finger and the president was stopped in his tracks, mid-stride. "Why don't you just turn around and have a seat right there, because you deserve to hear what I have to say just as much as anyone else here does."

Hernandez did turn around, but he did not sit. Instead, he stared defiantly at True.

"I see that you are not sitting down," observed True. "I must say, Mister President," he continued, shaking his head, "that you seem to be having quite a difficult go of figuring out what time it is." There was some laughter, but Hernandez remained silent and simply held a hateful stare.

"Mark my words, Mister President, you will be seated right there in the aisle, and you will be seated immediately. Will you do it yourself, or do you insist on having me embarrass you?"

"Yes, I do!" Hernandez was screaming now.

"He's lost it," someone whispered.

"As you wish!" said True. And with a stroke of his finger, the president involuntarily flopped down to the floor, sitting "Indian style," as more than one of the various TV reporters covering the event live would describe it.

True shook his head, "You completely had it in your power to avoid this. Perhaps you'll reflect on this later and learn something from it." And then, after a pause, he continued, "Or perhaps not. That is all, of course, a matter of your choice."

"Idiot!" whispered somebody else of Hernandez, shaking their head in the president's direction.

While things were still quite tense in the Chamber, many in the crowded gallery above were starting to warm up to Benjamin True—especially after witnessing his exchange with the president, whose *ad libbed* performance tonight was sure to have a negative effect on his approval ratings.

"I wasn't planning on getting into this tonight," True mused to the crowd, "but before I begin my speech to you all, I'd like to squeeze this in." He looked around at all those he had just challenged in the past few minutes and said, "Every one of you takes an oath to remain true to the Constitution. So, one might assume that you must all be experts on the document, since staying true to it in the course of government business must take a great deal of study. So, let's test your knowledge with one quick question about the Constitution. Nothing difficult, mind you, but just a basic question. Are you all ready?"

There was practically no feedback from the crowd, who were still somewhat stunned by it all.

"OK, then, I see we need a bit of an icebreaker to get things started. So, I'll give you a warm-up question, just so you can see how this works. Quick, you have five seconds to tell me how long it takes to bake a normal cake. Just shout out your answers."

Immediately, there were many speaking out from all quarters of the Chamber. "Thirty minutes," and "half an hour," said many. "Thirty to thirty-five minutes" said another."

"OK, how many of you agree with the 'thirty to thirty-five minutes' answer?" asked True of the crowd.

Well over half the hands went up, including the hands of those who hardly ever bake cakes, but who remembered the answer as being correct once they heard it.

"OK, and does anyone here disagree with that answer?"

There were no responses.

"Alright, then," True said with a smile, "the majority of you seem to understand how long it takes to bake a cake. So that worked out pretty well for a warm-up question. And now I'll get on to the Constitution question I have in mind. Quick, you have five seconds to tell me how long it takes to read the Constitution all the way through."

True began to count on his fingers as the seconds went by, mouthing the numbers silently. The room stayed otherwise silent, although it was obvious from the looks on the faces of many that they were trying to come up with an answer.

"Mmm-hmm. That's what I thought," said True. "Why do none of you know how long it takes to read it? We didn't even have any guesses from the Gallery."

"Uh, two hours?" responded one taker from the East Gallery.

"Four hours!" came another response.

"No," said True. "It takes only thirty minutes for the average reader to read it, or about forty-five minutes to an hour if you really want it to sink in."

There was a collective "Hmmm" that was audible across the audience, as many in the crowd found this new information to be surprising.

"Now, why does nobody here know that? Why is this not common knowledge in this culture? That's less time than it takes you to watch a typical TV show. And even so, nobody knows it. It's almost as if in this culture, reading the Constitution of which so many of you claim to be so proud, and over which you argue so routinely, were simply not an important exercise.

"I'm being sarcastic, of course. But your ignorance in this matter does go to show that your Constitution does not have nearly the respect that you claim to give it. If the Rule of Law under your Constitution were really held dear, you'd know how long it takes to read it, because you'd be regularly teaching it to your kids at home and at school, as well as re-reading it yourselves from time to time. It's *your* Constitution; why won't you just *read* it, America? You should study it like crazy in school, and then read it again once a year to keep yourselves up to speed. Is an hour of your time really too much to ask?" The sincerity of his plea was obvious.

"Well, I'm getting ahead of myself. I guess you can just consider that a little teaser for my speech proper," he said, relaxing his tone and turning a smile.

Benjamin True turned to the third tier behind him, and said to the Speaker and Vice President, "Mister Speaker and Madam Vice President, I apologize that I don't have a copy of my speech to give you tonight. I'm sure, however, that you'll be able to watch it again and again on YouTube if you like." He said this with a grin, and it did strike Linda Surgeon as a bit funny, especially since many in the audience had already gotten out their smart phones, and were holding them out to get video of this spectacle. When True noticed this, he held up a finger to the two, giving the universal "just a minute" signal, and turned around to the second-tier lectern's microphone to address the crowd.

"You'll want to save your phone batteries because you're going to need..." True stopped speaking, having realized that the microphone that was on just moments before was now not working. Peter Willis, the audio technician for the House Chamber was an avid supporter of President Hernandez and had turned off the microphone just to spite Benjamin True.

True turned back to speaker DuBois, and before he could get a word out about the microphone, Dubois was already saying, aloud, "OK, turn the mic back on."

There was a sullen and muffled response from far back in the hall, "It's on."

True nodded in appreciation to Speaker DuBois. "Thanks!"

"No problem, ..." said DuBois somewhat sarcastically.

True was holding up the wait-a-minute finger again so that he could turn back to the microphone, but he noticed that DuBois wasn't finished speaking.

"Yes, Mister Speaker?" he asked.

William DuBois leaned forward and asked quietly, "Are you expecting me to give you the customary introduction?"

"Well, I hadn't thought about that, but it's a nice idea. I'll leave it to you to decide. Now let me finish with the crowd."

True turned back to the mic and said, "As I was saying, you're going to need your smart phones later, so please turn them off for now and save your batteries. This whole thing is being televised live, and I'm sure you'll be able to view it all you want later."

Before he was done saying this, about half of them had already complied, lowering their phones and turning them off. On seeing this, just about everyone else relented within just a few seconds, and turned theirs off, too.

"Thank you." he said to the audience with a small nod. And with this, he turned back to the speaker, saying, "OK, I'm ready."

Speaker DuBois was embarrassed to refuse to introduce Benjamin True. He glanced briefly at Vice President Surgeon, who simply gave a nod. Seeing this, Benjamin True turned back to face the audience and stood quietly. The speaker then pressed the switch to raise his automated lectern to normal speaking height. Then he raised the microphone as he stood to speak. "Members of Congress, I have the high privilege and distinct honor of presenting to you Benjamin True."

This time, there was no applause. There weren't any boos, either. Rather, the crowd simply wasn't thinking about such formalities, but was spellbound as they watched these events unfold. There was silence.

Chapter 3

Dominus

Audra Blake had been monitoring the TV broadcast of the State of the Union Address from her office just off the living room of the fancy K Street House when she saw Benjamin True's spectacular intrusion. She immediately got up from her desk and walked into the adjoining living room to alert the committee of five who sat in the semi-darkened room playing poker with the TV playing softly in the background. They weren't talking much as they played, but they weren't paying that much attention, either, as these things were always so predictable.

"You will all want to see this!" said Audra Blake, rushing for the remote control on a nearby end table to raise the volume.

They knew by her tone that this was serious. The lighting in the room was still dim and they all remained more or less motionless as they watched the first couple of minutes unfold. "Where is this going?" asked one of them rhetorically.

"Who is that, and what's his game?" contributed another. The news station ticker at the bottom of the screen was already reading, "Intruder at State of the Union Address."

"I don't know, but you can't pull off a hoax like this without a pretty sophisticated team," opined a third in a monotone.

One of them looked to Audra and asked, "Dominus, do we have an asset in place in case this gets out of hand?"

"We have one on location. I'll be sure he's in position and awaiting your instructions," she replied.

"Do it," was the command. At this, Audra Blake quickly left the room as she was drawing her cell phone from her pocket.

Chapter 4

Domino's

The whole Capitol Complex was on lockdown by this time, of course. The Capitol Police could not gain entry to the House Chamber as no one could manage even to touch a door from the outside. It was as if some Sci-Fi force field were not letting anyone within a foot of each exterior door. They had tried crowbars, but could not even get them into position to pry against anything. Even a battering ram was ineffective, as the force field simply seemed to absorb all its energy without so much as rattling the door beyond. Yelling through the doors had not yielded even the slightest response from anyone inside, and many people were known to be standing along the interior walls, just a step or so away from each door.

Even though they could not gain access to the House Chamber itself, outside of it, they were ready for World War III. An emergency shift of extra officers had been called in and those who had not yet arrived were expected imminently. Meanwhile, a dozen or more armored personnel carriers with water cannon and heavy machine guns, along with four M1 Abrams main battle tanks had appeared on the Capitol grounds, strategically placed about the campus.

They had had some relayed communications from the Secret Service before the nine Secret Service agents inside had had their communications gear confiscated by Benjamin True, but since then, their intelligence was limited to what could be seen on the House's closed-circuit TV system, which had been installed so that Members could see from the various breakout rooms when a vote was being called. They also had the regular live TV coverage from inside, of course, and what would be seen through the glass panes on some of the Gallery doors above, as well as through the useless cracks between the strangely-locked double doors on the ground level. There was zero evidence anywhere else on the Capitol Grounds that anything else was amiss—except, of course, for the several hundred heavily armed Capitol Police officers and the heavy armor previously mentioned. The actual danger seemed to be localized inside the House Chamber, and they had no idea how to get inside there. There was little they could do but to wait and to be ready for whatever might happen.

They had tried sending text messages to some of the Members of Congress inside, to see what more they could tell them about what was going on, but these failed as everyone had turned off their cell phones at True's request.

On the second floor, outside the Gallery, things were just as tense. The officers were on guard and tended to huddle by twos and threes to whisper their speculations to one another. One such pair was broken up as Lieutenant Dan Harriman's cell phone rang. He looked at the screen to see the incoming call listed as "Domino's".

"Pardon me; I have to take this call." Dan Harriman stepped away from the junior officer to whom he had been speaking and moved a few steps away to the far corner of the hall, where the Northern and Western walls of the Chamber meet.

"Hello?" he spoke softly and coldly into the phone, casually glancing about to be sure that no one was paying too much attention to him.

"Do you know who this is?" asked the female voice on the other end.

"Uh, sure. It's Domino's Pizza, right?"

"Yeah, close enough," she said. Both knew he wasn't speaking with Domino's Pizza. Her code name was Dominus, which is Latin for *master*. The contact name Domino's was just a cover in case anybody ever happened to see it on his screen. This was only the second phone call he had ever received from Dominus. They had never met in person and he had no idea what she looked like.

"Looks like your pizza may be ready for delivery anytime now, and I wanted to double check your address on file to be sure it ends up in the right place. Are you still at 3 Floor Street?" she asked.

"I will be in two minutes," he replied, "I'm just next door at the neighbor's, but I'm leaving right now."

"Great," she said. "We'll text you when the delivery time is certain."

Both hung up without a further word. Lieutenant Harriman stepped back over to the junior officer, a Private First Class who was about 15 feet away, and said, "I'm going to step around the corner and check the service elevators. I'll be back in 15 minutes."

"Roger that, sir. Back in 15," was the reply.

Lieutenant Harriman disappeared around the corner of the hallway, and after a few steps more, stepped through an unmarked door that led to a service elevator. This elevator was used by cleaning and maintenance crews, and it accessed the third floor, from which one could enter the crawl space above the House Chamber for such work as lighting and air conditioning maintenance. Harriman walked down the narrow hallway, immediately above the position where he had just been standing and talking to the other officer. The wall was covered with various pipes and conduits and had several large sheet metal air handler boxes that were four feet across and ran from the floor to the 8-foot ceiling above. At the third of these featureless boxes, Harriman stopped and removed his keyring from his pocket. On the ring, he found the tiny magnet that lived there alongside his other keys. It was about the size of a pencil's eraser and was covered with a white plastic shell that also featured an eyelet by which it could be attached to the keyring.

Harriman glanced both directions down the hall and then listened for any audible signs of other activity. Sensing none, he held the magnet up to the extreme top right corner of the distribution box, touching the box lightly. This produced the expected click of a solenoid, and the entire face of the sheet metal box popped open, revealing that it was actually a door. Harriman stepped inside and pulled the door shut behind him.

The lieutenant found himself in a dark hallway with a modest light emanating from an open slot in the floor about 12 feet in front of him. He removed his service flashlight from its holster and turned it on. This revealed a hard rifle case on the floor, lying against the wall to his left. He knelt and opened the case. In it he found a sniper rifle. Harriman opened the bolt and found the internal magazine unloaded, as expected.

Velcroed around the rifle's stock was an ammunition sleeve filled with eight rounds .308 caliber ammunition. Harriman loaded 4 rounds into the rifle and quietly closed the bolt, chambering a round. He engaged the safety and eased forward to the downward-angling slot in the floor.

From below, inside the House Chamber, Harriman's position looked like one of several huge air vents in the ceiling around the perimeter of the Chamber. His particular vent, however, was not a functioning air vent, but a custom-made shooter's nest designed for just such a purpose. He made sure that his iPhone® ringer was off and that the phone was set to vibrate upon receiving a text or call. He checked the battery's strength, which read 93%. Then he double checked the spare battery-powered phone case that he kept in his trouser cargo pocket, and all four power indicator lights came on.

Harriman sat on the floor with his legs crossed "Indian style" and trained the scope on Benjamin True at the lectern. It was a sharp downward angle, almost 40 degrees, and he couldn't have acquired the target in a more typical prone shooting position. He was careful to sit far enough back that the rifle's barrel would not be seen by anyone who happened to be looking up from the packed hall below.

He had laid his iPhone® face up on the floor beside him so that he could see the flash of light if he should receive any call or text, and now he was ready to report that he was in position and ready. "Arrived at home," he texted to "Domino's". And then he waited for a reply.

Chapter 5

The State of the Union

"Mister Speaker, Madam Vice President...," began Benjamin True, turning slightly to one side to acknowledge respectfully those at the desk behind him. Then he turned back forward and with the slightest smirk and a glance down the center aisle, he continued, "...Mister President...".

President Hernandez was still sitting half way up the aisle in front of the lectern, and, feeling sorry for him, third-term Representative Melanie Parham, who had been sitting along the aisle just three seats back from the humiliated POTUS, stood and walked to the president. "Please take my seat, sir," she said quietly, bending down to his ear. She helped him to his feet and put him in her vacant seat. Then she walked to the rear of the Chamber and stood along the rear wall.

Benjamin True continued, "...Members of Congress, and all the rest of you officials who are here as guests—I have come to speak to you tonight regarding the State of the Union. After I have spoken to you, I'll be addressing the American citizens who are in this hall, and who are watching at home. And when I'm done here, I'm going to float right through that wall over there." He gestured to the wall directly to his left, on the same western side where the First Lady was sitting in the biggest confusion of her life. "I will float from here down Pennsylvania Avenue for as long as there are people who have come out to see me. This way, you who are watching locally on TV can come out with your phones and cameras, and you can get as much video as you want—to prove to yourselves and to everyone else that this is no hoax."

At this announcement, every available news crew within an hour's drive was dispatched immediately to Pennsylvania Avenue, and locals began figuring out how they were going to get out to the street without missing a second of his speech.

Benjamin True continued. "Be advised that I have come here tonight to speak of my own accord—to speak my mind to you. I have *not* come to reveal to you anything that you cannot or should not have known already. The power of my words to you tonight will be because they are true, and not because they are revealing things you could not know or figure out otherwise. And know this also: I have not come to express my opinions about regular partisan issues—things about which reasonable people might reasonably disagree. No, I have come to discuss the corruption of this government and its nearly-complete departure from the founding principles upon which it was chartered.

"Now to the Congress, regarding the State of this Union, I want to start in novel fashion by asking you three questions. And these questions are for all of you here tonight who are elected or appointed members of government. First, I'd like you each to raise your hands if you hate to be lied to."

Those seated on the main level were a bit puzzled at the question. Many of them looked about at each other, as if to find some reason not to comply with the request. Finding none, they began, slowly at first, to raise their hands. Within eight or ten seconds, practically every one of them had their hands up.

"Thank you. You may put your hands down. And now, how many of you hate to be cheated?"

This time, the hands went up almost instantly.

"Alright, and please put them back down for the final question. How many of you hate to be stolen from?"

Again, the response was immediate, and by now, it was unanimous, with whatever few had held out on the first two questions, having now decided that this show-of-hands survey was innocuous enough.

"Thank you for your responses. You may put your hands down," said True. "And I note for the record that the response was practically unanimous on all three questions. So, let's all remember that, and I'll come back to this to make a point later on.

"Now, I have some serious matters to discuss, but no doubt, this will be quite difficult for many of you, for my perspective differs quite considerably from yours. Indeed, if you give proper consideration to where I've been living the last couple hundred years, it shouldn't take long for it to dawn on you that I may see some things differently from how you see them. Now, don't get me wrong; *some* of what I say, you will surely think is pure genius, and some of it, you will think is nothing short of insane—unless you really take the time and care to think it through.

"For this reason, it is important that you know the standard from which I am making judgments about the State of this Union, because my standard is different from your standard. When I consider the state of the United States of America, my primary concerns are not about the state of its economy, or whether you are at war, or how the several states are getting along with one another. Rather, I am concerned about what kind of *people* you are. Now, I'm going to have to say that to you several times before it sinks in. I'm concerned about what kind of people you are. So, with that in mind, let me address this Union's beginnings, where your founders struggled with some really big and important principles that most other countries didn't find all that important at that time in history.

"In my view, this country's formation under the ideals of the Declaration of Independence and its early founding documents was one of the brightest things that has happened in the world since the spectacular events of the First Century AD. The ideas that *'all men are created equal'* and that they hold certain rights merely because they are humans, and not because the government grants them those rights—these are very special ideas indeed. And then, the guarantees of the freedom to criticize the government, and even to elect its officers by voting—this all was a formula for a country such as has never existed on this planet. It was patently good in its design. It was not perfect, mind you, but it was very good.

"It is with this beginning in mind that I find the present to be an utter disappointment and disgrace. Most of you incumbents here will see it differently, of course. You will judge the state of the Union by how the economy is doing, or whether you're at war—and mostly, of course, by what you believe to be your prospects of being re-elected."

39

There was some laughter from the Gallery.

"But the way I see it, it brings to mind the words of Robert Frost:

> *Two roads diverged in a yellow wood,*
> *And sorry I could not travel both*
> *And be one traveler, long I stood*
> *And looked down one as far as I could*
> *To where it bent in the undergrowth;* [3]

"Some of this country's founders were highly-authentic and mighty philosophers, as people go—even with their faults. And all humans have faults, course. Others among them were fools, and others yet were scoundrels or tyrants—or both. All of these men, and the women who had their ears, whatever their motives may have been, agreed on the record to some very lofty principles upon which to build this Union of free and independent States. They could have chosen a monarchy, or some other form of totalitarian government, but they did not. Neither the early Articles of Confederation nor the later Constitution designed the government to serve for the good of the governors, but for the good of the people. It was remarkable; it was the first time anything quite like this had been laid down in a national charter.

"But then came the divergence of the two roads, like in Frost's poem, for there was not just one kind of people among them, but two kinds. Some of those men looked down the road as far as they could see—the road set out for them under the Constitution they had ratified—and they saw a Union where the individual was free to live pretty much as he pleased, as long as he did no harm to anyone and paid the modest taxes necessary to support such government as needed to:

> *...establish Justice, insure domestic Tranquility, provide for the common defence, promote the general Welfare, and secure the Blessings of Liberty to ourselves and our Posterity.* [4]

"In their minds, it would be a constant struggle to keep the government on its leash, but this is what they saw as their jobs. They were willing to act as servants of the public good in the interests of freedom and equality for all. And they also depended on the citizens to keep a viable interest in protecting this new order of things, too. Did you hear me at home?" He leaned forward the slightest bit as he looked up at the main camera directly in front of him in the Gallery. "Maintaining freedom and justice was supposed to be the job of the *citizens*, too.

"In fact, Thomas Jefferson was so convinced of the difficulty of maintaining such a government against tyrants that he wondered whether it would be possible to escape having a rebellion every 20 years to do so.[5] He said:

> The tree of liberty must be refreshed from time to time with the blood of patriots and tyrants.[5]"

He knew from his study of history that tyrants always arise to threaten the freedom of others. So, when he looked down that road, he saw a hard battle that was worth the blood, sweat, and tears that it would take to fend off the tyrants. He looked down that road, and he saw promise in it. He and others like him saw freedom and prosperity and self-determination and lots and lots of hard work.

"But not everyone thought like Jefferson. Others looked down that road as far as they could see, and they did not like their prospects on it. They were not the sort to sacrifice themselves for the good of others, nor even to be content with what they could gain for themselves by fair play. No, when they looked down that road, they saw no way under that Constitution for them to build and maintain the level of riches and power they had in mind for themselves. Sure, they could have worked hard under it and become prosperous, but they were not the sort to be contented with an abundance when it was their true aim to hoard for themselves an overabundance—one that would be gathered from taking unfair advantage of their fellow citizens. In this group, there were mainly three types of interdependent people. First were the tyrants. They are the sort to want to be in charge for their own benefit, and who are willing to oppress, enslave, and kill to have their way. Then come the scoundrels—those willing to tolerate the tyrants, while profiting from the tyranny. They would lie, cheat and steal to have their way. And finally, there were those with the same corruption of morals, but with less ambition than the tyrants and scoundrels. They are the sort who will settle for a salary, but who will take it from the tyrant or scoundrel, who gets it as unjust gain. They are the ones who support the system of tyranny with their labor.

"All these, the tyrant, the scoundrel, and the unjust laborer will flatly reject a system wherein everyone is to be treated fairly and justly, because they make it their ambition to take what is not rightfully theirs—even at the expense of the labors of other people. All three levels of these people are predators. And the workers among them think they are insulated from the immorality of it because they are 'just doing their jobs,' they say. But that is a lie. They are just doing the tyrant's and scoundrel's jobs, making it all possible. They are friends of the tyrant and scoundrel—as far as they are concerned—and the tyrant and scoundrel alike need them, too.

"When this country freed itself from the tyranny of Great Britain, it didn't take long for these people to show themselves for the sort they truly were. Indeed, many who free themselves from tyranny prove that they don't mind tyranny so much, as long as *they* get to be the tyrants. And if not the tyrants themselves, then the *friends* of the tyrants.

"It was these men, and the women who had their ears, who envisioned a fork in that new American road—one that would split off from the new American ideal in favor of something much more like that from which they and their European ancestors had come. Having been freed from it, they wanted to return to it like a washed pig returns to its wallow. They saw no point in the principles of freedom and justice, for all they wanted to do was to suckle at the teats of that great mother sow of the public treasury. This was what kind of people they were, and that is what kind of road they wanted. They shunned the narrow road, where both prosperity *and* hard work live together—and where righteousness and justice rule the day—in favor of the wide road, where one hopes to prosper in a dishonest way from the work of others, easing his own load.

"This is the promise they saw in doing things the old way. Yes, they had struggled under European tyrants, but this was their chance to work under a *new* American tyranny—one they hoped would treat them better because they, themselves, would be in charge of it. So they envisioned that wide, old road, but as if with a new name on it. They envisioned that same old road where the bankers could control the government, and where the laws would benefit and protect the favorites of the bankers at the expense of everyone else.

"That's what kind of people they were. They would be satisfied with putting lipstick on a pig to pretty it up a bit. And that's what kind of road they took. They let the bankers have their way and gave them the support they needed to get it done.

"They rejected Jefferson's ideas—he's the one who wrote most of the Declaration of Independence, by which the colonies seceded from Great Britain's control. Instead, they went with Hamilton, who wanted a king, and if he couldn't have that, a ruling class of bankers. So, it was this road, and not the road laid out by the Constitution, that they favored.

"And so I say to this present Congress, and to the rest in this present government, it is the latter road, and not the former, that you are on tonight. As I said before, the corrupt ones among them won out, and they committed an act of deceit. They chose the older and wider road of corruption, but they put a new name on it. They would not call it what it was. Rather, they pretended that it was indeed a road less taken, and they spoke of it as if to take this weary and worn road were to take the one less traveled. It is as if they snatched the new Constitution off the other path and nailed it up on the corrupt path they preferred. The Constitution would not be for them a guide, but merely an empty symbol—a lie. They would not actually follow it, but would merely *pretend* to follow it. And this would satisfy the ill-informed citizenry enough that they would continue to support the government's efforts.

"So, to you, it's business as usual, and you don't give it a second thought, but to me—having the original vision in mind—what you are doing with this government is not only a travesty but treason! You cannot on the one hand claim that the Constitution is the supreme law of the land, and on the other hand disregard it at will, without proving your own lawlessness.

"The whole point of having a Constitution like yours lies in the wisdom of the Rule of Law. For those of you who don't know—and that's a lot of you—the Rule of Law is a concept that was devised for protecting people from governments and from their fellow citizens alike. The idea is that a people would put themselves and their government under the authority of a just-and-hard-to-change set of laws, so that neither the foolish nor evil whims common to humankind can rule the day. That is what your founders set up for you, but America has corrupted the Rule of Law under this Constitution."

One of the guests in the Gallery to Benjamin True's right leaned and whispered to his son who was with him, "This corruption goes back over a century, to when Woodrow Wilson was president."

"I heard that," said True, turning toward the man who had whispered. You said, "This corruption goes back over a century, to when Woodrow Wilson was president."

The man nodded, affirming that Benjamin True was correct.

"You are right, sir," said True, "but it's much worse than you have been taught; it goes back to when George Washington was president."

A few murmurs could be heard from about the hall, and a few even shifted forward in their seats, so as not to miss a word as True seemed to be about to explain this unsettling assertion.

"You murmur because you have learned to deify certain leaders in the past, as if they were not men such as those still found among you today. Think of his good qualities what you will," continued Benjamin True, "but do not lie to yourselves; General Washington was not infallible in his acts as president. The bankers wanted a central bank from which the government could borrow money. This, of course, was so that the government could also pay it back—with interest. That's what bankers do. But this wasn't a bank for *citizens* who would be free to choose whether to use that bank or not. No, this was a bank that was to be established by law—one that the government would use to conduct its business, and over which the citizens had no direct say.

"Now you need to think about this. Suppose that the three of us up here," he gestured to the Speaker and Vice President sitting behind him, "were all shipwrecked on a deserted island. And suppose that Speaker DuBois were great at gathering food, while Vice President Surgeon were great at building huts. And so, we can imagine that they make a deal with one another; he would gather food for her, and in exchange, she would build him a hut. But now, imagine that I were to step into the middle of their arrangement—as a middle man—demanding that as part of their deal, she builds me an awning on my hut, and he brings me a wild goat to eat. I ask you all, what business would I have being in the middle of their deal? None, I tell you. Absolutely none. But the bankers wanted to push their way into the business of the United States—business between the several states and the central government. And why did they want to do this? It was purely for their own profit. It had nothing to do with righteousness and justice, nor with the equality of people, nor with freedom, nor with honesty or rationality or responsibility. It was all about their lust for money and power."

Chapter 6

Poking the Bear

Dominus stood by quietly as the five committee members watched Benjamin True's speech with rapt attention. It was not her job to decide, but merely to facilitate.

"Is he going to come after us, or is this headed in some other direction?" asked one of the five, a man in his sixties.

"This doesn't look good, but we don't know what he's really pushing for yet. I don't know why this guy is poking the bear. Maybe he's just venting, but I'm worried that he's going to prompt them to do something that may pose a threat to us." This came from a woman of 75, whose voice was smooth and calculating.

"If we take him out now, we won't have to risk him making it to his ultimate play," voiced a younger man around 50. "I know that the intrigue of it all is delicious, but I can live with the disappointment of never knowing in return for the security of neutralizing the risk immediately."

"And what will be the consequences of dropping the hammer on this guy?" asked the fourth. She, too, was in her fifties, and her caution was well respected by the others. "I know we may have to decide quickly, but we need to do our best to avoid any serious backlash that may come. I suggest we keep this keenly in mind as we proceed with our deliberations."

They all looked to the fifth member, who had remained silent so far. He was in his eighties and had the patience to go with the years, yet he still had the energy of a 60-year-old man.

"We will wait," he said. And so ended the discussion as they continued to listen to Benjamin True's speech.

Chapter 7

The Venerated Geo. Washington

Inside the House Chamber, Benjamin True's speech continued.

"It was in 1791, the third year after the new Constitution was ratified, and the second year of the new government that it chartered, that President Washington's Secretary of the Treasury, Alexander Hamilton, introduced to Congress a bill to create what is now known as the First Bank of the United States. The bank would be modeled after the Bank of England, and was to assume the war debts incurred in the Revolutionary War by the individual states that had participated in it. It would pay off the debts and the government would pay back the loan—with interest, of course. The new bank, if created, would also issue some paper money, to be used in the place of gold and silver coins, and it would thus inflate the currency supply.

Now, George Washington, like many others at that time, was rightly skeptical about central banks and fiat currency. Just five years before, he had written to a Rhode Island politician about the toll that such banking had been taking on that state:

> *Paper money has had the effect in your State that it ever will have, to ruin commerce—oppress the honest, and open a door to every species of fraud and injustice.*[6]

"Indeed, he had written against paper money again and again—and from a perspective different from your own, for he lived at a time when there was both paper money and coin of precious metal, so he was in a position to see which was better. Consider his words from another letter:

> The wisdom of man, in my humble opinion, cannot at this time devise a plan by which the credit of Paper money would be long supported[7]

"And a little further down in the same letter, he wrote of paper money that so many people had suffered from its use in the past:

> that, like a burnt child who dreads the fire, no person will touch it who can possibly avoid it.[8]

"Not four years before Alexander Hamilton was calling on President Washington to support his paper-money-issuing central bank, Washington had written to Thomas Jefferson that:

> Some other States are, in my opinion, falling into very foolish & wicked plans of emitting paper money.[9]

"Washington's Attorney General, Edmund Randolf, advised him that the bill was unconstitutional—that is, that the government had no authority under the Constitution to create such a bank. [10] He was right. Then Washington's first Secretary of State, Thomas Jefferson, wrote a lengthy paper for Washington, warning him against the creation of that bank and telling him that it was illegal to do it since it was not authorized in the Constitution. [11] He, too, was right.

"Meanwhile, James Madison, the man who had written the Constitution and had led the creation of the Bill of Rights, gave a speech in Congress against the formation of the Bank of the United States, claiming that Congress had no authority under the Constitution to do so. [12] He, too, was right.

"Even with all this impeccable advice from these three authorities, Washington wasn't completely satisfied as he stood looking down the road of the Constitution that they had all sworn to uphold. So, he did what a lot of people do when they're feeling pinned down by reality. He invited *further* advice from a man of whose corruption he was already well aware. Washington sought out the opinion of Secretary of the Treasury, Alexander Hamilton[13], who submitted to him a 13,000-word paper in support of the Bank[14]. Two days later, Washington signed that

Bank bill into law. That was on Friday, February 25, 1791.

"Now, what would have inspired a president who hated paper money to sign such a bill? Indeed, what would inspire a president who knew full-well that there is no authority in the Constitution to create such a bank to sign it into existence anyway?

"Let me remind you that when General Washington had been inaugurated as President on April 30, 1789, twenty-two months before signing the bank into law. At his inauguration, he gave this oath, which is itself prescribed word for word in the Constitution:

> *I do solemnly swear that I will faithfully execute the office of President of the United States, and will to the best of my ability, preserve, protect and defend the Constitution of the United States.*[15]

"It is obvious, however, that Washington did *not* preserve, protect, and defend the Constitution in this instance. And he certainly had both the ability and authority to do so, not because of popular support, but because of the authority granted him in the Constitution. But he did not look to the Constitution as his master in this matter. Rather, he sought out the counsel of whomever would grant him what he really wanted. Indeed, if he could *defend* the bank on the say-so of Hamilton, he most certainly could have *opposed* it all the more on the say-so of Jefferson, Madison, and Randolf—and indeed, on the authority of the very Constitution itself. So, he definitely had the means and the moral support to do the right thing, had that been what he wanted to do.

"And how easy would it have been for him to veto that treasonous bill? Very easy indeed. But he signed it into law. He facilitated the takeover of federal business by a semi-private bank corporation who would use federal business—the business of the people—as a means to build its own riches and power. This was a flagrant violation of not only the Constitution, and of his oath to preserve it, but also of the very spirit of the thing. He violated not only the letter of the Constitution, but the spirit of it.

"But did he go all the way and declare that obedience to the Constitution was no longer good for America? No, he most certainly did not. Rather, he kept on as before, making grand statements about honor and the Rule of Law and honesty and such, while setting the country on a path down the very road he had fought a war to leave.

"And why did he do it, you might ask. Was this just a lapse in good judgment? Was it a misunderstanding of his role as President, or of the meaning of the Constitution itself? Was he somehow forced to do this against his will?

"Good questions, all. Those of you familiar with the 'General Welfare' clause of the Constitution are certainly aware of the great controversy that has surrounded it in more recent years. Few understand, however, that it seems to have been Hamilton who was the first to invoke that Clause in support of something that was flagrantly unconstitutional. [16] It brought up the whole question of whether the government's powers were expressly enumerated in the Constitution, or if far greater powers were 'implied'. The twisted idea was that if you could argue that this or that was good for the 'general welfare' of the Union, then it was 'constitutional'. This was hogwash, of course, and everyone knew it. Had 'implied powers' been the intent of the Constitution, it would be the equivalent of writing a blank check for the Congress to invent whatever powers it might ever take a notion to grant itself. And not even the King of England had that kind of power at that time in history! No, the bankers were taking advantage of this 'general welfare' language that they had intentionally inserted into the Constitution for this very purpose of exploiting it later. And who was the first to exploit it? A banker! It was all about the money, just as it is today.

"But why did Washington go along with Hamilton? He obviously knew better—both that the Bank of the United States was unconstitutional, and that paper money is a very bad idea because its value is not fixed and certain. So, why did he go along with it? Well, there's more to the story that you need to know, and it involves another first in Washington politics. It involves the first time that the Congress deliberately held up one matter in order to get what it wanted in another. [17]

"As you likely know, the Constitution had called for a federal district, where the business of the federal government would be carried out. The district was to be no more than ten miles squared, and the Congress was to decide where to put it. In July of 1790, seven months before President Washington signed the unconstitutional Bank into existence, Congress passed a bill establishing a location for the federal district. Washington, however, asked them to amend that bill in order to allow him to adjust exactly where that district would sit. If he could move it to the south, it would encompass land that he, Washington, already owned in Falls Church and Alexandria, Virginia. [18,19] An amendment to the bill was drafted and submitted to Congress on December 6th. From then, Congress dragged their feet in complying with the President's request to move the capitol district to include his own land. But then, on Friday, February 25, 1791, Washington signed their Bank bill into law, and hours later, the Senate approved his request to relocate the capitol city, with the House concurring just a week later. [17,20]

"Many had watched in silence as Washington pretended to be objective about where to situate the federal city, but it was obvious that he wanted it to encompass his own land. [21] Indeed, with its proximity to the Potomac—which Washington believed would become the major East-West corridor in the nation, his land there stood to increase considerably in its value. So, Congress granted his wish a week after he granted their wish for the Bank of the United States.

"John Adams wrote to Dr. Benjamin Rush some twenty years later that Washington's deal had:

> raised the value of his property and that of his family a
> thousand percent, at an expense to the Public of more than his
> whole fortune.[22]

"Am I saying that everything about George Washington was bad? By no means. But *this* was bad—bad enough to have him impeached. And lest you think he was the only scoundrel involved, James Madison, the very father of the Constitution, also owned land inside the new district, even while promoting the deal that would move the district there. [23] So did some in Congress—two of whom switched their votes to be in favor of it precisely because the new location would benefit them personally. And this kind of behavior went on and on, with one official after another using the seats of government to serve to their own enrichment. Some for money, some for political gain, and many for both.

"So, President Washington and the others got the desired increase in the value of their land, and the Americans got the First Bank of the United States. And that's not all they got. Because of all the newly available credit, and the deluge of paper money, in the five years from 1791 to 1796, wholesale prices increased 72%!" [24]

This shocking fact finally drew a notable response from the audience, many of whom were wondering where this lesson was going, and when it would be over.

"And that's the kind of results you get, friends, when individuals are allowed to run a government for their own gratification.

"Now, to be perfectly clear, lest you think I'm here to pick only on General Washington for some reason, he was by no means alone among the presidents in his willingness to subvert the Constitution for financial or political gain. The second president, John Adams, supported and signed into law legislation that made it illegal to criticize his government. They were called the Alien and Sedition Acts, and they flagrantly violated the First Amendment's guarantee of the freedom of speech. Cleverly, the law was written to expire on the last day of John Adam's term, in case the other party were to win the White House on the next go-round. Again, this political maneuver was a blatant violation of the very Constitution that Adams had sworn on oath to preserve, protect, and defend. And by supporting this, he violated the wish he had had carved on the mantel of the State Dining Room in the White House.

"Even the noted philosopher, Thomas Jefferson, the one who had warned Washington against enacting the Bank of the United States—he became the third president and initiated the Louisiana Purchase, which doubled the size of the United States territory for only $15,000,000. It was a great idea, by nearly all accounts, and a 'smokin' hot deal,' as one of your car dealers might put it, but it was wholly unauthorized by the Constitution, which gives no such power whatsoever to the government to purchase foreign territories. Thus, did Jefferson also violate his oath of office in grand fashion.

"I could go on and on down the line, even to the current president, and you would not find one of them who did not violate the Constitution. In fact, some of those whom you hold to be your biggest heroes— demigods, practically—were its biggest violators. They all swore to uphold it, and to a man, every one of them violated it.

"Now, don't you think for a second that I am only concerned with the bad behavior of the Executive Branch. Rest assured that I am not, for both the other branches have been about the same bad business since the beginning. And we haven't time to detail the sins of the thousands who have sat in this House and in the Senate.

"And then there's the Supreme Court, who have taken to quoting what the other kids on the playground say as an excuse for their own bad behavior. They frequently do not rule from the actual Constitution and from the laws justly written thereunder. Rather, they rule from what they call 'case law', finding 'precedents' in what other courts before them have decided. They have even cited foreign law from time to time to 'justify' their decisions. And so they have perverted the system to be whatever they want it to be—whatever would profit themselves and their friends the most.

"But even they are under oath. This is what they pledge:

> I ... do solemnly swear that I will support and defend the Constitution of the United States against all enemies, foreign and domestic; that I will bear true faith and allegiance to the same; that I take this obligation freely, without any mental reservation or purpose of evasion; and that I will well and faithfully discharge the duties of the office on which I am about to enter. So help me God.[25]

And as if that weren't enough, they take a second oath, called the Judicial Oath. It says:

> I ... do solemnly swear that I will administer justice without respect to persons, and do equal right to the poor and to the rich, and that I will faithfully and impartially discharge and perform all the duties incumbent upon me as ___ under the Constitution and laws of the United States. So help me God.[26]

"These oaths evoke the Constitution, true faith, allegiance, impartiality, righteousness, justice, and God himself. Yet those who take them violate them again and again. Not one of you justices is pure in your record. Not one. And this line, where you swear to do equal right to the poor and to the rich—can you get any more brazen than that? Who even came up with such a line—as if that court ever had any intention of not stealing from the poor to support the rich?

"Your house—your entire house of government—is broken down, and yet you carry on, pretending that it were not so. You point to buildings and flags and economic profits as signs that the country is alive and well, but it is philosophically dead, having abandoned its founding principles far too many times to have escaped the consequences. The gap between its official principles and its practice is immense, and you don't care. You will not admit that you are lawless and that you care nothing for the Constitution. Rather, you simply make use of it, pretending to abide by it now and again, whenever it happens to suit your selfish purposes.

"There are not five of you in this Congress who have not violated your oath at least once, and for most of you, violation of your oath is your regular business. You are plunderers. Vain plunderers who have no rightful place here. You lie, cheat, and steal as a livelihood. And these are the very things you all said you hated when I had you raise your hands a while ago. And if you don't know what that means, I'll tell you; it means that you are hypocrites. It means that you are breaking the Golden Rule that wise men throughout the ages have recognized as a foundational rule for life. It says:

Do unto others as you would have them do unto you.[27]

"But you hypocrites could not survive if others treated you like you treat them. You are filthy leeches—parasites who will not make their own way in the world anymore, but who profit instead from the labor of others, whom you force to pay out what they do not rightly owe. Your destruction is certain if you do not change your evil ways.

"When I look at you, I am disgusted—not only by your sins, but by the wasting of your lives—by the wasting of your talents and skills and knowledge—by the wasting of your time. Surely, you will all die, and not one of you on his or her death bed will think, 'If only I had lied, cheated, and stolen more often.' Many of you will regret your sins before you die, but will not truly change your ways. Indeed, even at this moment, many of you are feeling the urge to allow the possibility that maybe, just maybe, there's something to what I'm saying here.

"But no matter; you will all be cast aside soon enough." Benjamin True paused for a moment to let that sink in.

Associate Justice Kerwin Johnson stood from his seat on the first row of the House Chamber and raised his hand. "Sir?"

Benjamin True looked his way and say "Yes?"

"Sir," continued Johnson, "when you say that we will all be cast aside soon enough, do you mean to say that Jesus will be returning soon to bring fire upon the Earth?"

Benjamin True rolled his eyes at this question. "Why the sudden interest in such matters, Justice Johnson? You have had years of leisure in which you could have studied the scriptures on this question, yet it is obvious from your question that you have no clue in the matter."

"It is true that I haven't studied it," replied the justice. Then he sat down.

"Well, what *did* you mean by it, then?" It was a woman in the far northwestern corner of the gallery. She had kept her seat, but her voice was loud and clear.

As True was turning to face her, another voice called out from the center of the House floor in front of him. "You're here to kill us, aren't you?"

Benjamin True looked straight at the man, a senator from Vermont, and said, "Do you deserve to die?" The man had stood to ask, and at True's response, he hung his head.

"Tell me, sir," asked True of the same man, "what is the customary penalty for treason?"

"Death," said the man.

"Indeed, it is. But I have not come to execute judgment on anyone here. I already told you that you are all safe, did I not?" reasoned True.

"So, what did you mean when you said that we'd all be cast aside soon enough?" It was the lady in the far corner of the gallery again.

"I did not say that you *all* would be cast aside. I was speaking of those in the seats of government. You should..."

"So, you're leading some sort of coup?" interrupted a representative from California.

"No," replied True sharply. "I'm here to see whether the American people are interested in making a second attempt at establishing righteousness and justice in their country, as it failed the first time. There are still some Americans out there who value honesty, rationality, and responsibility, and who are willing to correct themselves. I'll be..."

"Now you listen here!" It was Senator Bertrand Earhart, standing and pointing an accusing finger at Benjamin True. "I'll have you know that I was seventeen years a minister of the gospel before God called me to this Senate, and I'm here to tell you that there are people right here on the floor of this Chamber who value honesty and—how did you put it? Honesty and responsibility and..."

"I said honesty, rationality, and responsibility," reminded True.

"Right," continued the Senator. "Well, there are people right here who hold those things quite dearly."

"Senator, when I said earlier that there are not five of you in this Congress who have not violated your oath at least once, I was not talking about you. Not only have you lied, cheated, and stolen again and again in your so-called service to the American people, but you do not even know how to give a rational answer to a common problem posed by your own cognitive scientists."

"Sir, I am, by the power and grace of the Almighty, one of the most rational men you will ever meet. If you knew my IQ, you would know that it is very high. I don't say that to boast, of course, but that does happen to be the truth of the matter."

"Rationality and IQ are not the same thing, Senator. You appear to be unaware that standard Intelligence Quotient tests do not measure one's skills in rational thinking—nor one's moral disposition to think rationally."[28]

"I can assure you, sir," boasted Senator Earhart, "that my rationality skills are in fine order!"

"Then prove it," challenged Benjamin True. "Answer me this:

> *A bat and a ball sell together for a dollar and ten cents. The*
> *bat costs a dollar more than the ball. How much is the ball?"*[29]

"That's simple. The ball is ten cents," came the cocky reply. The senator held his head back a bit to look down his nose at Benjamin True.

"And how many of you out there agree with the senator?" asked True.

At this, a veritable sea of hands shot up, and many could be heard saying, "That's right" or "ten cents", and other affirmative things.

"Wait!" came a voice from the northwest corner of the Gallery. "The ball is only five cents!"

"OK, he says it's five cents. How many of you agree with that?" queried True. Somewhere between 50 and 100 hands went up.

The "five cents" answer had come from a boy of fourteen. His name was Tom Peterson and he sat just behind the rail in the northwestern corner of the Gallery above the House floor. He was there with his grandmother Eula Mae Peterson. They had been invited by President Rafael Hernandez, who had planned to mention Tom Peterson in his speech as a fine example of an inner-city youth from a troubled area who was excelling in his studies in spite of the challenging environment in which he lives.

Benjamin True looked up at the boy and said, "Mister Peterson, why don't you stand and explain your answer to everyone?"

The youth was quite surprised at this, but complied quickly. He stood at the rail, and nearly everyone in the audience turned his way to listen. "The first answer I thought of was 'ten cents', just like the senator, but then I thought I had better check my math. So, I figured that if the ball were ten cents like I thought, and if the bat is supposed to be a dollar more than that, like the problem says, then the bat would be a dollar and ten cents. Well, that can't be right, because we know that both the bat and ball sell *together* for that much. So, I knew the ball had to be less than ten cents. I tried five cents and checked my math again, and it worked that time. So, the answer is five cents."

"Thank you, Mister Peterson" said Benjamin True, smiling and obviously proud of the boy.

Tom Peterson sat down and whispered to his grandmother, "How did he know my name?"

Benjamin True said, "I heard that. Mister Tom Peterson asked how I know his name." At this, he looked up at Tom, cocking his head to one side slightly, and holding his arms out with palms up, in a questioning gesture.

Tom Peterson looked puzzled for a couple of seconds, and then a look of understanding washed across his face. "Oh, yeah," he said. "I get it." There was laughter as Tom sat grinning widely and nodding his head in appreciation of Benjamin True's otherworldliness.

"Well, Senator Earhart," said True, "it appears that you are not as rational as you think you are. The boy thought to check his math, but you assumed that your math was up to the challenge.

"I simply misunderstood the question," fired back Earhart.

"Right, you and about 80 percent of the people here. As it happens, when scientists ask this question, about 80 percent of people miss it. And the most common error they make is the exact error you made. Let's try another, shall we?" True did not wait for Senator Earhart to agree. "This time, I'll give you a multiple-choice question:

Jack is looking at Anne, but Anne is looking at George. Jack is married, and George is unmarried. Is a married person looking at an unmarried person? Yes, no, or cannot be determined?[30]

"What do you say, Senator?" asked True.

"Could you, uh, repeat the question?"

"Sure, I'll be glad to repeat it.

> *Jack is looking at Anne, but Anne is looking at George. Jack is married, and George is unmarried. Is a married person looking at an unmarried person? Yes, no, or cannot be determined?[30]"*

"It's the last one. Cannot be determined," answered Bertrand Earhart.

"Is that your final answer?" prodded True.

"Yes, that's my final answer. You didn't tell us if Anne is married, so the answer cannot be determined."

"What do you say on this one, Tom Peterson?" True was once again calling the boy in the back.

"I'm with the Senator on this one, sir. I say it cannot be determined. Am I right?"

Benjamin True paused for a bit and noticed that many were leaning slightly forward in their seats in anticipation of his answer. "Nope," he said, "you're wrong." The Gallery was filled with sighs as many slumped back in their seats, upset that they had missed it, too. For some reason, those seated in the House Chamber below weren't quite as interested in the exercise, though a couple of them could be seen to exhibit the same kind of interest as those in the Gallery above.

"About 80 percent of people miss this question, too," said True. "The most common error on this problem is to answer a question that you were not even asked, rather than the one that you *were* asked. You weren't asked whether Anne's marital status can be determined, yet that's what most of you answered. Rather, you were asked whether a married person is looking at an unmarried person."

Senator Earhart threw up his arms in disgust and said, "Now how in the world are we supposed to figure that out when it's plain as day that you didn't tell us whether Anne is married or not?"

Benjamin True replied, "A highly rational person, given a problem like this one, would pause to consider all the possible scenarios the problem could entail. You are right that Anne's marital status is important, but there are only two possible choices for that status. That is, she is either married, or she is unmarried. So, to solve the problem, you run it both ways to see how it would come out." True paused to check on the Senator, "Are you still with me, Senator?"

"Say on," came the aggravated reply.

"OK, we know that Jack is looking at Anne, but Anne is looking at George. So, let's say for a moment that Anne is married." True held his right hand far out to his side, as if to provide a visual aid to the senator. "If that were the case, then would a married person be looking at an unmarried person?"

"Uh, married Jack is looking at married Anne, so no. Wait, married Anne is looking at unmarried George. So YES!" The senator sounded excited, as if he were getting into the exercise despite himself, but it was more from the desire to avoid even for a second being seen as wrong, than from any particular enjoyment of the exercise itself.

True, still holding out his right hand, continued, "OK, so if Anne is married, then the answer to the problem is 'Yes, a married person is looking at an unmarried person.' So now we need to think through the other possibility. That is, imagine how it would work out if Anne is unmarried." With this, True held out his left hand and put the right one down. He looked at the senator and awaited his reply.

After a couple of seconds, Earhart asked, "Are you waiting on me to answer that?"

"Yes."

"OK, what was the question again?"

"The question was, 'how would it work out if Anne is unmarried?'"

"Well, if she's unmarried, then married Jack is looking at her. So, we'd get a yes again."

"That's it," congratulated True. Either way, it works out where a married person is looking at an unmarried person. So, the answer to the question is 'Yes'." True was smiling, and Earhart seemed to be waiting for the point of all this.

"People make thinking mistakes like this quite a lot. Just think about it. You people sitting right here are supposed to be, some would say, the brightest and best in the country—the most fit for leadership. But about 80% of you missed these two standard rationality problems. And it's not just you; the whole American culture simply doesn't use Reality-Based Thinking [31] very much, so you're not even aware how much you make errors like this. Seriously, you need to study logic and get some basic knowledge of probability—and then there's your very serious problem with cognitive biases."

"I'm not biased," defended the senator, who was still standing. Waving an arm about the room and searching with his eyes, he said, "I *love* black people." There were a few chuckles and snorts from the crowd at this, and others perked up to try to understand what had been funny.

"A cognitive bias," explained Benjamin True, "is not just a prejudicial thought about people of a certain skin color. Rather, it's like a corrupted mini-program of thinking. A bias might be something like, 'All Italians are thieves.' That's messed up because the truth of the matter is that only *some* Italians are thieves, and if you go around thinking that *all* of them are, you're going to be wrong about an awful lot of people.

"Another cognitive bias," he continued" says something like, 'Whatever my preacher says is right.' The fact of the matter is that preachers sometimes say things that are wrong—as we have all witnessed here first-hand tonight. So, anyone who tells himself that his preacher is always right is going to be getting some things predictably wrong. Isn't that right, Senator?"

Earhart did not answer. Some others, however, were quite enjoying the line of questioning.

True went on, "My personal favorite of all the cognitive biases is this one: 'If I were wrong about this, I'd know it.'" This got a few solid laughs across the hall. "This one seems to be the default way of thinking for a lot of you on this House floor tonight—even among those of you who understand this bias well enough to find it funny like I do. You rarely give careful thought to your ways[32], but merely assume that you have got things right. Like in the bat and ball question, you don't check your math, and like in the Jack, Anne, and George question, you don't consider all the possibilities. Also, like in the Jack, Anne, and George question, you often substitute an easier-but-wrong answer for the difficult-but-right answer that you don't want to take the time to figure out.

"You do this frequently. A considerable portion of the population are lazy bums who don't want to work for a living, so what do you do about the problem? You don't teach them to think differently, becoming self-sustaining people, which would truly solve the problem. Rather, you pay them a salary, and say it's for their 'welfare'. This only corrupts them further, but you don't stop to consider the folly of your ways. And you do a great many things like this."

Chapter 8

Accountability

Senator Jeanine Planter interrupted him. "Now you hold on right there, mister!" She was now on her feet. "I'll have you know that not everybody on welfare is a lazy bum. A lot of them are disabled Americans who couldn't work if they wanted to."

"No, *you* wait right there, Senator!" shot back True. "Did I say that *everybody* on welfare is a lazy bum?"

"There are hard times in this country, and these people...." she replied, not answering the question.

True interrupted her with sharp intensity in his voice. "Did I say that *everybody* on welfare is a bum? Answer me yes or no."

Again, she tried to dodge. "You obviously have some sort of prejudice against the poor, and I don't know wh..."

True had frozen her mid-sentence. He spoke in a quiet and measured tone, "Ma'am, I'm going to ask you a direct question one more time, and then I'm going to give you three seconds to answer me honestly, rationally, and responsibly. You're obviously not accustomed to being held accountable, but that's what's going on in your life at this moment, and the sooner you figure it out, the better it will go for you. Now, here's my question for the third and final time: Did I say that everybody on welfare is a lazy bum? Yes or no, please." He waved a hand to set her free.

THE EXTRAORDINARY VISIT OF BENJAMIN TRUE

"No, but y...." He had frozen her again.

"I'm going to disregard that 'but' and just talk about the 'no' for right now. If I did not say that *all* welfare recipients are lazy bums, and a certain person knew that I did not say that *all* welfare recipients are lazy bums, then wouldn't it take a dishonest person to accuse me as if I *had* said that all welfare recipients are lazy bums?" He released her again.

"Yes, I guess so."

"In fact, Senator, wouldn't it take a *very* dishonest person to continue in an accusation that he or she knew to be untrue?"

"Yes."

"Then doesn't that make you a very dishonest person, Senator Jeanine Planter?"

"Yes, I guess it does," she replied.

"Indeed, it does," agreed True. "And yet, you don't seem at all regretful about your compromised moral state."

She didn't really understand the debate she was in. She was simply driven by the habit of pretending to take the moral high road, and bullying her opponents into submission. "I'm just trying to stick up for the poor."

"No," replied True, "you're trying to *use* the poor to defend and maintain a system from which you and your banker friends continue to profit. And you're willing to lie, cheat, and steal to do it."

She cut him a look that left nothing undiscovered about her hatred for him.

"You can stand there with your brazen heart and those dead eyes if you want to, but I'm going to tell you that in all of reality, there are actually some situations in which such a posture is not considered a wise move. No, sometimes, people are actually held *accountable* for their bad acts. It's quite amazing to behold. And when it happens to them, they generally seem to be the most surprised people in the room."

"Oh, so what are you going to do," she fired back, "strike me with leprosy or something?"

"Do you deserve to be stricken with leprosy?"

"Of *course,* I don't deserve to be stricken with leprosy. What kind of a stupid question is that? Nobody deserves that."

"OK, then what punishment *do* you deserve?" asked True.

"For what?"

"For being a low-down liar who would dare to make a false accusation against a fellow being for her own political benefit."

"I was just saying that not all welfare recipients are lazy bums."

"You lie. You were not 'just saying' that. You were suggesting that *I* was saying the opposite, which I was not. You knew I did not say it, and that I did not even believe it. So, you just made it up, as if I were a stupid person, unable to see what you did there. You must be really accustomed to playing before a stupid audience, because where I come from, that kind of trick won't fool anybody."

"Are you done with your little *ad hominem* arguments?" she challenged him snidely. "You've called me stupid and dishonest and brazen and who knows what else, and that's what *some* dull people do when they don't really have an argument; they attack the person rather than the person's arguments. Name calling is a tactic of immature people."

"Is it, now?" True shot back. "Let me get this straight. You just suggested that I am 'dull' and 'immature', all in the same speech where you accuse me of *ad hominem* argumentation?"

"You heard me," she stabbed.

"Well, here's a tip for you. When you use a term—and especially one in Latin, you would be well advised to understand first what it means. So, I'm going to explain to you what *ad hominem* means, and you and several million other Americans really ought to listen up, because this is widely misunderstood, even by people who have graduated from your public schools and colleges.

"*Ad hominem* means 'to the man' or 'about the man'. It's a reference to a dodging tactic in argumentation, by which one person avoids the *argument* in question and attacks the *person* making the argument instead. It generally seeks to jump to the preferred conclusion by way of substituting the supposed faults of one's opponents for the actual substance of the debate. For example, someone might try to cheat in an argument about sports by saying, 'Well, you're fat, so why should we listen to you?' Do you see what they did there? They pretend that the person can't be right about sports because the person is fat. This is a fallacious argument, however, and people who are honest, rational, and responsible won't resort to that.

"What *I* did, however, was nothing of the sort. I called you a liar because you lied, and not because your lying proves you wrong. That is, never did I suggest anything like, 'You are a liar, and therefore, your position is wrong.' *That* would be *ad hominem*, but that's not what I did."

She shot back again, "You don't even know me, and yet here you are making all these judgments about my character."

"Ah, another common tactic. You suggest that since I don't know you, I am unqualified to make any judgments about your public behavior. What you are failing to recognize is that you have voluntarily behaved here tonight in my presence—as well as in the sight of many tens of millions of viewers across the world—and your behavior is self-evident. I do not *need* to know your birthday or your favorite TV show in order to recognize a lie when I hear it."

"Well, you jus..." He froze her again.

"What? You're *still* talking? You seem to be 'identifying' as one who has not just been hanged with her own rope. Your transgression is obvious, your lack of regret for it is obvious, your intent to keep spinning it is obvious, and the moral corruption of your mind is obvious. You, of course, should have been tarred and feathered and run out of town on a rail a long time ago. But you're among friends here. You're in a business where almost every one of your colleagues should have been run out with you. And there aren't nearly enough citizens in this country who hate corruption, so you enjoy great latitude in this career that is almost completely free of accountability. Indeed, God does not strike you people dead when you commit such sins. If it he did, hardly anybody in this room would still be alive.

"Now, personally, I find your ugly heart to be an offense to what is right and true and good. And I take further offense that you would dare to behave in such a way in the people's House, and especially under the banner of 'In God We Trust'. So, I'm going to take it upon myself to give you a little something extra to be thinking about during the rest of my speech. I'm going to free you to move about as you wish, but for the remainder of my time here, you will be mute and blind."

He pointed a finger sharply at her, and immediately she began to grope about. Her mouth was moving, but no sound came out, and it was obvious from her face that she was intending to scream. A couple jumped up to steady and calm her, but she was beside herself. They sat her down just as another from several rows back—a representative—was standing to address Benjamin True.

"Sir, don't you think that you are being rather cruel to this woman?" asked the man respectfully.

"Am I? I have allowed her to keep her hearing, but have prevented her temporarily from seeing and speaking. It is the one thing that she most needs to learn how to do—to listen, and to consider what she hears—to *really* consider it, and not just to be looking to formulate the next line of rebuttal. If she changes her ways, as she should, she will be eternally grateful for this intervention. And if not, she will be bitter about it. I can assure you, sir, that what she has done is worthy of much greater punishment than this. She is in no pain, and her senses will be fully restored when I leave. She has chosen to be morally blind, and I'm giving her a taste of what it means to be literally blind."

The man nodded and sat back down.

"Wait a minute, Representative," said True. "I have a question for you, too. Why did you speak out on this woman's behalf, as if in the interests of seeing justice done, when you did not speak out on *my* behalf when it was clear that she was twisting my words to score her own political points?"

Benjamin True looked across the entire assembled Congress and all those visiting. "Not one of you spoke up on my behalf, yet many of you feel sorry for this snake when she finally gets a little slap on the wrist for her bad behavior. Now, why is that? How did you get this twisted?"

"Sir," an old woman from the Gallery dared to speak up, "you called her a liar, and that is just plain rude. You crossed the line."

"Madam, how is it that it is more tolerable in the eyes of this culture to tell a lie than to call the liar a liar? How is that? If that's not some twisted sense of morality, I don't know what is. You people have got some seriously corrupted thinking! From where I stand, it is exceedingly obvious."

He continued, "I was saying before this argument about welfare broke out that your culture is not nearly as good with logic and probability as you think you are, and that you have many more cognitive biases than you think you do. But that's not your main problem. No, your main problem is that you don't *care* that you are corrupt in your thinking. If you cared, you could learn your way out of most any mess you're in. But you *don't* care. You don't care that you're hypocrites. You don't care that you're dishonest and irrational and irresponsible and ignorant. You don't care that you lie, cheat, and steal. And you are supposed to be the elders of this society? It's no wonder that there's so much corruption across this country."

"Now you listen here," started Senator Bertrand Earhart, shaking a bony finger at Benjamin True.

His neighbor shushed him tugging at his coat sleeve. "You better shut up, Bertrand, or he'll strike you with blindness, too!" came the hissed whisper.

"I don't care if he kills me; I'm going to speak the truth to the man," replied Earhart in his supreme confidence.

Turning back to True, Earhart continued, "I don't know about all these mind games you're wanting to play here tonight, but I can tell you that this country is filled with good people who go to good, Bible-based churches, and you've got a lot of gall to stand up there and criticize these good people like that."

"Don't get me started about the churches!" replied True, shaking his head. "When eighty percent of the people aren't even responsible enough to check their math on a fairly simple problem, what makes you think they're going to be qualified to interpret the Bible correctly? Think about it. It's over eleven hundred pages and was originally written in three now-dead languages, borrowing words from several other now-dead languages—and it was written by multiple authors over a span of many hundreds of years—a span that ended nearly two thousand years ago, and in a culture that's not only quite unlike your own, but that was from many thousands of miles away from here. If you really think about the Bible for long—and if you know *how* to think—it becomes fairly obvious that it was not written to cater to the lazy-minded and incurious person in this present culture. No, that kind of person is quite likely to walk away from the Bible with all manner of misunderstandings about it."

"Excuse me, sir." It was the voice of an elderly man in the center of the

Gallery above the rear wall of the House Chamber. He had stood and was asking quite respectfully, "Do I understand you to be condemning the Christian churches?"

Benjamin True shook his head again and gave a small sigh. He paused, and when he spoke again, his tone was a little softer, almost pleading. "Look, I don't condemn anybody for what they get *right*. It's not what you get right that is the problem; it's what you get *wrong*. And I'm not the judge of mankind, mind you—but I can tell you that what is condemnable is that so very many persist in egregious errors that they could have realized and fixed long, long ago, if only they *cared* about such things. It is a way of life for this culture, and it needn't be that way. Remember, I said my main concern about the state of this Union lies in what kind of people you are.

"Just look at yourselves! You are a society that is stocked with people who still think such stupid and false things as 'war is good for the economy' and that some genetic disposition called 'race' determines what kind of character people have, and that Abraham Lincoln 'saved the Union'. You have far too many people who can't wrap their minds about something as simple as the definition of reality. Reality is the state of things as they actually exist, but you have many who insist on speaking of it as if it were merely a word to name people's *perceptions* about things. They say things that are destructive to the mind—things like 'perception is reality.' This kind of thinking muddies the waters so badly that those who believe such notions lose their bearings. They end up believing some of the most ridiculous things, such as that the reality of their sex depends on what they choose to believe about themselves. They say that they 'identify' as male or female, as if a mere act of mental assent can somehow set aside the obvious reality that their bodily organs are what they are. And even worse, they expect that the world should be forced to pretend alongside them, and to throw off definitions of sex that have existed for eons, simply because such definitions make them feel uncomfortable.

"I could go on and on—far beyond the short time we have here tonight. More and more your culture is filled with insane ideas—rules that break themselves with use, such as 'Stop judging!'" True raised a mocking finger, which he waved in imitation. "They accuse others, saying, 'You're judging me!' yet they have no idea that they themselves are engaged in the act of judging with those very words. See, the 'Stop judging' rule breaks itself the very moment you point a finger at someone and accuse them of breaking it. Do you get that?

"Just look at yourselves. You love to judge yourselves and your country by the outward things. You look at things like technological advances, infrastructure, and the economic markets as a matter of great pride. And it's true that if you were to plot a graph of such advancements in this country since 1776, you'd see a very impressive curve, to be sure. Millions of you are extremely proud of innovations that you personally had nothing to do with—as if you had each actually invented your smart phones or the MRI medical scanner. No, that's the work of other people, and it sure looks good on the graph of progress, so you take pride in it. But that particular line on the graph says very little, indeed, about what kind of people you are. No, if you were going to plot a curve about how good Americans have been over the decades as diligent overseers of their own government, you'd get something awfully close to a flat line, showing now improvement at all. Americans let the bankers run away with the country in the beginning, and they're still doing it today. And even so, they insist on finding ways to be proud of themselves in spite of this major abdication of their civic duty. America has a reality problem.

"And while I'm on that note, I'll give you one more highly-relevant example," said True. "Many of you can be overheard to say things like, 'There are no absolutes.' That sounds good to you—you think it is an enlightened thought and you fancy yourselves to be philosophers—but you don't realize that the statement, 'There are no absolutes,' is itself an absolute statement. An absolute statement, for those of you who don't know, is an assertion that purports to be true at all times and in all circumstances. When you say, 'There are no absolutes,' that doesn't leave room for *any* absolutes in *any* time, place, or situation, yet here you are making an absolute statement, undermining the very rule you wish to promote."

The elderly man in the Gallery spoke up again, "So you're saying that you do believe that there are some absolute truths?"

"Is there any other kind?" replied True. "That's what truth is, people. Truth is—*reality* is—what exists independently of your perceptions and beliefs. It exists whether you perceive it or not, like it or not, or understand it or not.

"What I'm telling you here is as self-evidently true as anything that could be said, and yet your culture is confused about these things. And so, Senator Earhart," said True, turning back to the earlier challenger, "a society of people like that is certainly not equipped to make consistently-good judgments about the Bible. They are ill-equipped even for the simplest task of disengaging from their own points of view in order to survey the subject matter from the authors' points of view. Failure to override this basic my-side bias accounts for a great deal of what ails this country and its churches alike."

"I'd like to add to that list of stupid things that people believe, sir!" It was a new challenger, a senator from Rhode Island, who continued, "I'll have you know that I'm an atheist with a strong background in astrophysics, and I can assure you that belief in God is not only completely unscientific, but also just plain stupid."

"Is it?" True paused for an answer.

"Yes, there's absolutely zero scientific evidence for it," replied the scientist senator.

"Do you mean to suggest that things for which there is no scientific evidence cannot be true?" True's question was not met with an immediate reply, so he continued as the senator seemed to be thinking it over. "If things for which there is no scientific evidence cannot be true, then don't we have to opine that Pluto did not exist until humans discovered it in 1930 by way of scientific evidence? Do you believe, sir, that Pluto just popped into existence at the moment it was first seen, or do you think that it existed even before it became obvious to humankind?"

"Obviously, it was there before it was discovered," said the atheist.

"How, then, can you insist that belief in a God you cannot see is ridiculous? Surely, you don't mean to suggest that you can *prove* that God does not exist?" questioned True.

"You can't prove a negative," the scientist pushed back.

"Pardon me, but would you please repeat that last line?" True asked, having heard it just fine the first time, but wanting the audience to have the benefit of hearing it again.

"You can't prove a negative," the scientist complied.

"You are right that one cannot prove a negative—at least when the thing in question could very well exist outside of the knowledge and

71

view of the observer. So, if you are a true scientist, sir, then, why are you adamant about something you cannot possibly prove? Is this not the behavior that you criticize in those who believe in God? Are you not doing the same thing?"

There was no answer.

True continued, "Isn't yours the same sort of absurd behavior I just criticized in the general public?" True did not wait for an answer. "Indeed, it is. Yet here you are doing it in the name of scientific enlightenment, where some other person does it in the name of religious enlightenment. Both are wrong."

"Tell me," continued True, "isn't the listing of one's assumptions a crucial part of the scientific method?"

The scientist nodded in agreement with a slight rolling of his eyes, as if to ask, *So, what?*

"So, if you were responsible enough to state your assumption," continued True, "then your argument would have sounded something more like this:

'Assuming that God doesn't exist, then God doesn't exist.'

"And that, sir, is a logical fallacy of the first order," True continued. "As you well know, it is called 'begging the question' or 'assuming the initial point'. It is circular reasoning that depends on itself for its own proof. Now, how is it, sir, that you consider yourself to be America's school teacher, and yet you lack the wherewithal to catch yourself in such a fallacious gaff?"

The senator sat down without a word and looked at his cell phone, as if it were not still turned off.

Benjamin True looked over the crowd and invited, "How many of you here are atheists?"

There were about 40 atheists in the hall, but only about half of them dared to raise their hands after what had just happened.

"OK, I have a question for you all," announced True. "If the Bible were true about the existence of God, would you believe it?"

Four of them said "No" at about the same time.

"Thank you for demonstrating your moral disposition," he said to those four. "If you would refuse to believe something you knew to be true, then you would be abusing your own minds, depriving yourself of reality.

"Listen to me, all of you. Dishonesty, irrationality, and irresponsibility are not limited to just one field of human endeavor. It permeates every field. There is not one profession that is uncorrupted by it. You'll find bad behavior in science, religion, government, business, education, marketing, medicine, engineering, and everywhere else. It's what kind of people you are—generally speaking. And in your culture, it's generally not considered desirable to rise above it, though you are certainly able to do so."

"No, sir!" reported Senator Earhart sharply. He was standing again now, and looking fiercely at True as he continued. "The things you are pointing out are the result of the Fall of Man, at which event he turned from sinless to desperately corrupt. Even the great Martin Luther said of his own corruption, 'I am capable of naught but error.'[33]"

"Have you ever stopped to think about the implications of that statement, Senator Earhart?" asked True.

"What do you mean? What implications?"

"Well, if Martin Luther were right, then he couldn't possibly have been right."

"Come again with that," said the senator, confused.

"Luther said that he was incapable of anything but error, right?"

"Right."

"Well, if he was right about that—that is, if his statement were true— then his statement—the very one you are quoting—would have had to be an error, too. There's no other way to take it. It's a self-breaking rule just like the other ones I was talking about a few minutes ago—a rule that breaks itself with use. He might as well have said, in your more modern language, 'Everything I say is wrong'. Well, just how are you supposed to take an idea like that? As the truth? If so, you're disagreeing with the guy who said it."

Benjamin True continued, "This is just another example of the mindlessness of your culture. You go around repeating memes like that that might sound good at first blush, but that can't hold up under examination. And when it comes to understanding human nature, most of the popular theories are just rubbish.

"Ponder this, Senator: Billy gets fired from his job because he shows up three hours late and drunk on a Thursday morning. Larry sees this and says, 'Of course he got drunk; that's his sinful nature.' So, someone might ask Larry how it was that Billy, having his so-called sinful nature and all, managed to show up two hours early just the day before, to help the boss—*off the clock*—to finish a difficult and overdue project that had been holding back the company's production. How does 'sinful nature' explain that? Now, to this question, somebody usually pipes..."

"It was Satan!" came the answer from Earhart. "Satan prompted your Billy guy with false humility—false love."

"How ironic that *you* should be the one to interrupt with this, Senator. Yes, that's exactly the ridiculous idea I was about to mention! You nailed it. Except that you were serious. And here's the problem with your answer: it doesn't fit the rest of your model, for if you had never heard this scenario, and I had asked you whether Satan *ever* wants people to do loving, godly things, you'd have told me 'no'. So, you are cheating your own doctrine in order to avoid having to answer for it.

"Please sit down, Senator. I think we are done," requested True. "You have provided some excellent examples of the kind of wild overestimation of one's own knowledge and cognitive abilities that is so rampant throughout your culture. And it's exactly this sort of thinking error that lies beneath so many of the evil things that are done by this government. You are quite corrupt in many ways, and yet there is still hope for you."

Earhart murmured from his seat, "Yeah, and what's that great hope for us?"

"I heard that," said Benjamin True. You said, 'Yeah, and what's that great hope for us?'"

"Well, Senator, the Three Stooges had it figured out. The skit goes something like this:

> Curly: I can't see! I can't see?
> Moe: What's the matter?
> Curly: I've got my eyes closed![34]

74

"There's only one person in this room who couldn't see if she wanted to, Senator Earhart. Everybody else here who is blind is blind because they choose to be. And that includes you.

"Now, I'd like to move along in my speech in order to address the American citizens, but I want to give all of you in government here a chance to speak up if you believe that I have not proven the vast corruption of this government. Would any one of you care to challenge my assertion as to your corruption?" True looked about the Chamber, not smirking exactly, but rather with a pleased and confident grin on his face.

To the surprise of many, there was one taker to this offer. It was Representative Max Wallace of Tennessee. "Mister True, I just want to point out that we are not 100% corrupt here. Sure, we all have our faults, but there are a lot of good people in this government, trying to do their best to solve the people's problems."

"And are you among them?" True probed.

"I'd like to think that I am," said Wallace.

"I'm sure you would like to think that you are," barbed True, "so, please do go on about the good that you've personally done here."

"Well, just this month, we've funded new scientific research into finding a cure for ADHD, and we've provided funding for relief for the families of veterans who have committed suicide after returning home, we provided funding to help hurricane relief in the mid-Atlantic states, and also, we passed a law strengthening hate crimes legislation." At this, the Representative quietly sat down, hoping to be done with the discussion.

"First of all, Mister Wallace, let me remind you of the principle that the *good* things you do are not your problem. No, it's the *bad* things— the things you get wrong—that are the problem. But you've got things so twisted around that you're not open to seeing what's wrong with *anything* you're doing. Take the four accomplishments you just listed, for example. All four of those measures are outside the authority granted to Congress by the Constitution. And that would be the same Constitution that you vowed to obey in your oath of office. This means that you violated your oath of office to vote for these measures, whether they would be otherwise good ideas or not.

75

"You knew that, of course," Benjamin True continued, "but you chose not to care. You chose to deliberately close your eyes to that fact. It doesn't matter whether these things are actually good deeds or not, in and of themselves; if they exceed your authority, then they are against the law, and you have compromised yourself to do them."

Max Wallace stood back up with a troubled look on his face and began to plead his case. "Mr. True, this country has lots of very serious problems—great needs that aren't being met—and the Constitution is just a piece of paper. We can't let that stand in the way of doing what needs to be done."

"Just a piece of paper, huh?" replied True. "Then why did you take an oath to support and defend 'just a piece of paper'? Why would you possibly do that? This is not your first term in office, so you already knew that the Constitution does not allow you to do the kinds of things you want to do, yet you took a vow to support and defend it when you were re-elected. Why would you do that? Why would you volunteer an oath that makes it impossible to do what you think needs to be done?"

"Well, we all have to take the oath; you can't get in office without doing it."

"So, you just lie, and then get on with business?"

"Yeah, that's pretty much what we all do. But it's not really a lie; it's done with an understanding that our Constitution is outdated, and that we don't really follow it anymore."

"And whose job is it supposed to have been to keep the Constitution updated, Congressman?"

"What do you mean?"

"What do I mean? What do you *think* I mean? It was not a difficult question."

"Well, if you want to update the Constitution, you have to pass an amendment."

"Right. So, you've passed all these bills that are unconstitutional, but you haven't amended the Constitution to grant the Congress the authority to do what the bills call for."

"Do you have any idea how hard it is to get an amendment ratified?"

"Yes," answered True. "It takes three quarters of the states agreeing to its exact wording before it becomes a part of the Constitution."

"Well, that's practically impossible, so that's why we generally don't bother with it. And besides that, the Supreme Court are the ones who rule on whether something is really constitutional or not, and they haven't struck down any of these laws."

"So," True sized up his case, "you're a liar and an oath breaker who ignores the rights of the states to approve of the changes in the rules up here, but this is OK and all is right with the world?"

"I don't want to debate with you, Mister True."

"I'm sure of that, Mister Wallace. People who debate me don't get very far. And do you know why that is?" Benjamin True did not wait for a response, which suited Wallace just fine. "It's because I only say what is true. I only say what fits with fact and logic. But this is not so with you. You are willing to say whatever it takes to get your way—even if it's a lie."

"I never claimed I was perfect, but...."

"No, but you claimed that you would support and defend the Constitution, which is something you had zero intentions of doing. You don't have to claim to be lying in order to be a liar, Mister Wallace."

Wallace rebutted, "You just don't understand how hard this job is."

"Oh, I see. Well, it's true that I have no recent experience with lying. And it's true that I have no experience violating an oath of office, nor violating the Constitution. Are these the things you're claiming are so hard to do?"

"No, sir."

"Then let's have it. What are you talking about?"

"You just don't understand." Wallace was shaking his head back and forth, looking somewhat pitiful.

"What a clever dodge, Mister Wallace. You pretend to have greater knowledge than me, and to be the sole judge of that assertion. And you hope, of course, that someone will have sympathy for you, taking your word in the matter that you are in what is practically an impossible situation. Well, Congressman, one big difference between you and me is that I think that wrongdoing is wrong, even when *you* do it. You, on the other hand, do not. You think that if it's 'for a good cause', you're completely justified in doing whatever you want to do."[35] Wallace was very frustrated, and yet maintained his worried look and his pleading tone. "Sir, we couldn't have passed these bills if we had to amend the Constitution first."

"Exactly. You broke the law and you did it on purpose. You simply crossed the states' approval out of the picture and went ahead as you pleased."

"Do you understand that practically everything we do here is not *technically* authorized by the Constitution?" Wallace asked.

"Yes, I do. And I understand that liars ever since Alexander Hamilton have pretended that the 'general welfare' clause in the Constitution's Preamble authorizes the Congress to do anything it might ever wish to do, so long as they claim that it's necessary for the general welfare of the nation. But everyone knows this is a lie—even the people who continue to tell it."

True went on. "Think about what you're doing, Mister Wallace. Every time you bypass the Constitution, you bypass the states' right to have a say-so in what goes on here. And yet it is the *states* that are the bodies that have united themselves together to make these United States. It is not you, Congressman, who comprise this Union, but the states themselves. If it is anybody's business what you do here, it is *theirs*."

"But the people of my state elected me to come here and represent them," Wallace defended.

"Right. And what do those people know about the wisdom of the Rule of Law? Is it not obvious that they are either ignorant or corrupt, inasmuch as they have sent *you* here? Over half the people in your state, Congressman, cannot name you as their Congressman. They can't even name the Vice President, or the year that America declared its independence from Britain. Like you, they are ignorant that the fundamental idea behind this Union's design would be that it would be run by *law*, and not by the whims of its rulers. You break that law with great regularity in order to pass new laws that you have no authority to pass."

"You yourself said, Mister True, that this is how it has been since the very first Congress. So, I don't see why you're coming down so hard on us."

"Mister Wallace, when the government is in the habit of being unruly, they tend not to take care of important business with diligence. For example, it is very likely that you will not be prosecuted for employing six different prostitutes in this last year."

This revelation prompted widespread murmuring in the hall.

"I most certainly did not!" objected Wallace.

"Tell me, Congressman," questioned True, "is that another one of your lies, or are you telling the truth? See, with your track record of lying when taking your oath of office, we really wouldn't know whether you were lying at any particular time or not, now, would we? Yet you speak up as if you have any shred of credibility left. But it's true about the prostitutes. And it's also true that you took a $150,000 bribe from Lilex Corporation, who wanted you to bury a report on their harmful pharmaceuticals that you had been threatening to expose in a committee meeting. And it's also true that you currently have nearly $300,000 in cash stuffed in the bottom of some Christmas decoration boxes in your attic at home, right next to the dusty exercise bike and the lawn darts."

With each successive revelation, the reaction of the crowd grew louder.

"It's also true that you have traded votes again and again to get the support you needed for your favored legislation. You helped your buddy, Congressman Verma pass a bill that turned out to be actually bad for your own state, but it helped him to get a bribe for $50,000 from Wehmeyer Steel, and in return, he voted for your bill that would fund a new highway in your state, from which your own brother-in-law, who owns an asphalt company, would receive many millions of dollars in profits. And so I ask you, Congressman Wallace, have I begun to get a good grasp on what you meant when you spoke about how hard a job you have here in the House?"

Wallace gave no reply, but lowered his eyes, averting Benjamin True's gaze.

"I see," said True. "And would you care to stand up here and object to any of these further facts I have revealed about your schemes in office?"

Again, there was no reply, as Wallace kept his head down.

"Well," continued True, "fortunately for the rest of you, I don't have the time to go through this room, telling of all your personal misdeeds that could and should be known about you." At this, Benjamin True held up a finger, starting at his extreme left, and pointing directly at those filling the chairs on the floor of the House Chamber. "One by one..." True's finger was pulsing along with his speech now as he pointed directly at those in power, panning from left to right, "...we could go through how you have soiled yourselves by violating your oaths of office. We could talk about the illegal deals you have made, the bribes you have taken, the lies you have told, the blackmail to which you've given in."

In just these few words, True's pointing finger had made it only as far as the middle of the first row of the House seating. It was quite unsettling, and those at whom he had pointed so far could be seen to squirm in their seats. No one dared say a word. No one except the retired preacher, Senator Bertrand Earhart.

"How do we know who you are?" demanded Earhart, standing and pointing accusingly again at Benjamin True. "How do we know that these things you've been doing aren't counterfeit signs, wonders, and miracles? As far as we know, you could be none other than Satan himself!"

Benjamin True looked straight at the senator. "Since when is it anybody's idea of Satan that he would stand up here for half an hour and say nothing but what is true and reasonable and just and righteous? Indeed, Senator, if this is your impression of Satan's qualities, then I dare say that such a Satan as you imagine would have made a much better preacher than you did."

Earhart was dumbfounded. He didn't know what to think, and much less what to say. He just stood pointing, not even sure why he was still doing that.

"I'm going to tell you what the biggest difference is between me and you, Senator. In fact, this is the biggest difference between me and just about everybody in this entire room. So here it is—here's the difference, and it should sound awfully familiar to you, as I just said it to the Congressman a few minutes ago: I think that wrongdoing is wrong, even when *you* do it. *You* think it's wrong when others do it—or at least when they do it to you—but when you do wrong yourselves, you excuse it. And you lie to yourself about how your good qualities supposedly outweigh anything bad that there might be about you.

"Well, I'm going to tell you a story about that," continued True. "It's a story about how you judge people incorrectly and how you don't understand what people are really like. It's a story about Joseph Stalin, whom you hate, and whom your parents' generation knew as 'the Butcher'. The same Stalin who was responsible for the cold-blooded murder of many millions of humans.

"Well, one night Stalin's adult daughter—Svetlana Alliluyeva—was invited, along with her boyfriend, to a small dinner party in America. It was at the house of some patrons of the arts. Among the other guests were Albert Einstein's step-daughter, Margot, and the conductor of the Princeton Symphony Orchestra and his wife, who was a professional singer. During the dinner, Stalin's daughter asked the singer if she knew any of the classic German art songs. The singer replied that she did, and she said that after they were done eating, she'd have the host accompany her on piano as she sang. After the meal, the singer treated Svetlana to a few songs by Schubert and others, and noticed to her surprise that Svetlana was silently mouthing the words along with most of the songs. Afterwards, they asked Svetlana about this, and she went on and on about how much she loved them and how it was that she had learned them. It seems that she and her father, Joseph Stalin, had spent countless evenings when she was a young girl, sitting together in front of the Victrola—a phonograph or record player, for those of you who don't know—and listening again and again to these wonderful works of art. She spoke so warmly, so dearly, of those precious times with her father—with the man known to the rest of the world as a tyrant and a mass murderer.[36]"

And what is the moral of this story? I ask you," said Benjamin True to his audience. "Do you not consider Stalin to have been a bad man? Do you not even use the word 'evil' to describe his terrible deeds? Yes, you do. And yet this story shocks you. It surprises you because you do not understand how evil works. To you, an evil person is all evil, and a good person is all good, more or less. And this is why a story like this surprises you. You do not understand that a person who would do as many evil deeds as Joseph Stalin might just have had some good qualities about him—that he might have had some good times as a father, such that his daughter would still adore those times fondly after many years. Indeed, how many fathers in this world would give their right arm to be cherished by their adult children?

"No, it's easier for you just to label the whole man as "evil", on account of his evil works. And when you hear that there was indeed something good about the man—however small it may have been—you dismiss it. It doesn't fit the model in your minds, and it requires too much thinking, so you simply dismiss it and think nothing more about what it might teach you. You are such cognitive misers, refusing to spend a penny on your thinking that you're not forced to spend. [37]

"*And what might it teach us?* you may be wondering, now that I've asked the question for you. Well, I'll tell you. You judge yourselves by the same bad reasoning as you judge Joseph Stalin—except that you simply flip around the good and evil when you judge yourselves. That is, when you judge him, you judge the whole man for the evil things he did; you ignore the good and focus completely on the bad, so much so that you are shocked to learn that there was indeed something good about the man. But when you judge yourselves, far too many of you do the opposite; you ignore the bad and focus completely on the good. This is how you lie to yourselves; it's how you manage to keep feeling good enough about yourselves so that you don't just fall apart in one guilty mess, admitting all your faults, and laying claim to the responsibility for fixing them.

"Remember what I said earlier about the difference between us. The difference is that I think that wrongdoing is wrong, even when *you* do it. And you think it's only really wrong when others do it. So, you lie, cheat, and steal, hating it when others do it to you. In fact, when they do it to you, you consider them evil for it. But when you do it to them, well, it was 'for a good cause'[15]. Or maybe you'll say, 'nothing personal, it's just business'. Or some of you will say, 'nothing personal; I'm just doing my job' or 'I was just following orders'. However you try to excuse it, it's wrongdoing, and you are denying responsibility for it. And you don't only do this for yourselves, but for the others in your own party, as well as for your heroes in history. You judge Washington and Lincoln by the good stories about them, and you brazenly ignore the bad because it undermines the lore that you profit from promoting. You do this with Hamilton and Jefferson and all the others, if you happen to like them. Meanwhile, those who are your political opponents today, you vilify, as if they could not possibly have a single good thought or deed as long as they oppose you. You are such hypocrites in your behavior.

"As I said before," True continued, "one hand has plenty of fingers to count those of you who have not compromised yourselves in office by lying, cheating, stealing, and murdering. And of those, there is precious little courage to stand up to the wrongdoing of all the others."

Speaker of the House, William DuBois had felt utterly undone inside for the last several minutes. He knew that every word from the visitor was completely true. He surprised himself, for he lacked the will to deny any of it any longer, even after a long career that had been built on exactly the sort of denial of conscience that Benjamin True was talking about. He lacked the words, and didn't know how to formulate them, but he had to get it out.

"I'm guilty!" shouted the Speaker, leaning forward in his chair behind Benjamin True, and reaching out as if to put a pleading hand on True's shoulder in front of him. "I've done all these things." Speaker DuBois was now holding his face in both hands and began to ball. Shaking his head back and forth and rocking to and fro in his seat, he went on. "I've taken money to promote one bill or to kill another. I've made deals to further my own career..." He was nearly yelling at this point, not surprisingly inarticulate in his anguish.

Benjamin True had turned around to listen and stood silently with his hands folded in front of him. It was always painful to see someone wrestle with admitting truths long denied, but there was no possible better thing that Speaker DuBois could be doing for his own soul at this moment—nor for the collective soul of the country—than to be sharing these thoughts aloud. True felt for him, having been no stranger to such moments of realization in his own lifetime.

"I killed them! I killed them!" DuBois was shouting.

Everyone was silent.

"I sent people to do our bidding—just like you said—to force open new markets overseas for American goods—and they killed people—and some of *them* got killed, too. And it's my fault. I killed them," DuBois sobbed, his voice retreating to a whimper. He looked up at Benjamin True, "Can this ever be forgiven?"

"Yes," came True's firm reply.

"What can be done to set it straight? What do I need to do? I'll do whatever it takes." DuBois was surprised at the clarity of conviction in his own mind. He did not remember the last time he had had a moment like this. He had crossed into new territory and could not fathom all the implications and consequences that he was about to set in motion.

Chapter 9

Exposure

Things were tense and nearing panic at the house on K Street as the committee of five and Audra Blake sat staring at the large TV.

"That's it. He's turned the Speaker, and we are as good as dead if this is allowed to continue."

Another one chimed in, "We're too exposed already at this point, and if DuBois is allowed to keep talking, we will never be able to recover from it."

"I say we end it now. Are there any objections?"

"Wait, who are we neutralizing? True, or DuBois?"

"Both" said another.

"Do it," said the eldest to Audra Blake. Seeing that all the others were nodding in the affirmative, she quickly dialed her cell phone.

Lieutenant Dan Harriman had sat awkwardly in his shooting position high above the floor of the House Chamber with his rifle pointed at Benjamin True, but having heard nothing in many minutes, he had lowered the rifle to a more sustainable position. He saw the wash of light from his iPhone's screen and quickly picked it up off the metal floor beneath him before the buzz of the vibrator could make any appreciable racket. The screen said "Domino's."

"Hello," Harrison answered coldly and quietly.

"This is Domino's," came the reply from Dominus. "We're sorry there was a delay with your order, but we've thrown in a second pizza for your troubles. It should be there immediately."

"Wait. *Two* pizzas?"

"Yes, two. Your original order, of course, plus the other special that's really making a splash on TV right now."

"Gotcha. Two pizzas comin'. Thanks for the call."

Harriman and Dominus both hung up.

Harriman raised his rifle and disengaged the safety mechanism. He looked through the scope and aimed it at Benjamin True's head, his finger still off the trigger. "First target," he told himself. Then he swept the rifle upwards and slightly to the right, putting the crosshairs on William DuBois' head. "Second target," he said. Moving his aim back down to Benjamin True, he continued coaching himself. "The soldier first," moved his lips with the faintest of whispers, "then cycle another round, then the Speaker."

The rifle's safety was already disengaged, and now Harriman moved his finger to the trigger. "Finger on the trigger," he said to himself, knowing from years of experience that talking to himself was the best way to keep from messing up. "The soldier, then cycle another round, and then the Speaker," he repeated one last time, envisioning a first shot, and then about two or three seconds until his second shot. This was the end of his routine. Like a pilot coming in for a landing, he knew exactly how to talk himself through it in those last seconds until it was done. "Breathe in..." he told himself, taking a deep breath, "hold it and release a bit..." he said, letting out a bit of the breath he had taken in, so as to better steady his body for a precise shot, "hold six feet high..." he said, raising the rifle's aim six feet over Benjamin True's head, "and send it." At this he squeezed the trigger and the boom of the rifle shattered the near silence of the great hall below.

Chapter 10

Come Down Here!

Before the shot, Speaker DuBois had still been sobbing. He had looked up at Benjamin True and said, "I will do whatever you think is..."

True had turned toward the Speaker to listen to him, but had surprised DuBois when he held up a finger to make DuBois pause. DuBois noticed that True didn't seem to be looking directly at him, but was curiously distant. And then True whispered something that, to DuBois, was the strangest thing: "Hold six feet high..."

A second later came the massive boom that rocked the Chamber and Gallery alike. The .308 caliber bullet had ripped through the air at supersonic speed, not aimed at its intended target, which was Benjamin True's head, but aimed instead at a spot about six feet higher than that. This put the path of the bullet not only over True, but over the head of Speaker William DuBois, who sat behind the desk at the top tier, above the level where True was standing. The bullet ripped through the American flag that hung vertically behind the Speaker's lectern. It cut a pencil-sized hole through the cloth, quite near the center of the third white star from the bottom on the far-right row of stars in the Navy-Blue field. The impact made the flag ripple a bit, but no one noticed, on account of the unsettling recoil from the rifle blast.

There were screams. Lots of screams. Heads had begun to dart about in search of what had made the great noise, and a couple of the Joint Chiefs of Staff, knowing exactly what would cause such a noise had just begun to get down on the floor in front of them so that they could try to locate its source while under some amount of cover. Four of the nine Secret Service agents had already located the source and were pointing to the shooter's nest as they began to stand up.

The shooter, Lieutenant Dan Harriman, was a bit uncertain of what had just happened, but was continuing in his "engagement sequence"— which is precisely why such sequences are rehearsed to the point of mindless habit. He spoke to himself, "Cycle another round," and then lifted the rifle's bolt with his right hand until it was unlocked, and then pulled it backward to expose the weapon's chamber and expel the empty cartridge he had just fired. The brass casing flew out of the chamber, and a fresh cartridge popped into position to be driven forward into the chamber as soon as he would push the bolt forward again. That empty shell casing was still in the air when Harriman found himself suddenly frozen in place. From his position, he couldn't see the casing hit the metal floor on which he was sitting, but in the sudden and utter silence of the House Chamber, he could hear the *tink-tink-tink* of the cartridge it as it came to rest somewhere behind him to his right.

In the Chamber below, everything was deathly quiet except for the metal-on-metal bouncing of that empty shell casing high above the Congress. Benjamin True's hands were up again from where he had silenced and frozen everyone in place to keep them all from hurting one another in a panic.

"Stay calm. Nobody is hurt," True counseled his silenced and frozen audience. Then, looking up at the shooting position above, True spoke in a commanding voice, "Come down here!" Immediately the false air vent on which Dan Harriman was sitting gave way like a very large door hinged into the ceiling. It swung downward, still attached along one edge, quite like the trap door on a hangman's scaffold. This sent Dan Harriman, rifle still in hand, into a freefall toward the Members of Congress seated about 30 feet below. It would take just under a second at freefall to hit the floor from that height, and this gave Harriman no time to do anything but to tense his muscles and to yell.

"AAAAHHH!" he had just begun to scream when another pulse from Benjamin True's hands brought Harriman's progress to a dead stop still half way to the floor. Harriman's scream stopped just as abruptly as he realized he was no longer falling, but was now floating above the crowd, moving toward True's lectern at what seemed to be near jogging speed. The bolt of his rifle was still open from where he had been interrupted, and he now clutched the rifle to his chest with both hands. During the few seconds it took to reach the lectern, Harriman's body turned mostly horizontal, just as Representative Randy Thomas had floated when Benjamin True had transported him down front and center earlier in the evening. The floating Harriman decelerated over the last few feet and came to a stop when his face was about three feet from True's face. Like so many others that night had been, Harriman was terrified, and knew he was unable to process what all was happening as quickly as one needed it processed.

Benjamin True had been staring at Harriman all along his trip from the rear of the hall to the front. When Harriman came to a halt, True looked at him in silence for what seem to Harriman like a very long time. It was actually only two or three seconds, and then True spoke. "Let's see what you've got there," he said, holding out his arms to take the rifle. Harriman paused only a second or so, and then handed it over.

"This is a Remington® 700 SPS Tactical police rifle in .308 caliber," said True, looking it over. "That's a Harris® bipod and an EOTech® Model 552 holographic weapon sight," he said, as he shouldered the weapon and pointed it upward toward the large stained-glass Eagle in the center of the ceiling so that he could look through the site.

"This is a very fine weapon," said True. "Much nicer than what I used to fire, of course," he said sincerely. With that, True unshouldered the rifle and changed his grip on it, moving his left hand to the stock, where his left thumb could depress the bolt stop release button while his right hand moved the bolt upward and then rear, removing it completely from the weapon. Now holding the rifle in his left hand and the bolt in his right, he said, "These can go to the pile with the others," and they floated up and over Harriman, and then behind him, where they gently settled onto the pile of weapons and other gear previously confiscated from the Secret Service agents.

Benjamin True then held out his arms again and addressed the crowd, with Harriman yet unmoved in front of him. "I'm going to let you all go now, and I trust there'll be no screaming. There was never any danger, and there are no more shooters in position. So, I'm going to let you go, and then everybody take a deep breath and get settled down again." A short motion of his arms released everyone as before. The Joint Chiefs and Secret Service agents who had been in the process of moving now gained their balance and sat back down as they had been before. There was murmuring, of course, but no screaming this time. And someone could be heard to say to his neighbor, "What a night!"

From the lectern, Benjamin True looked up at Dan Harriman. He was not angry, exactly, but he was not whimsical, either. "Why did you try to murder me?" he asked.

Harriman gave no reply, but maintained eye contact with True.

"You sat in that false vent up there with every intent of murdering me and Speaker DuBois here. You were repeating your engagement sequence to yourself, including a line that I introduced into it. Did you not say to yourself 'hold six feet high' just before you said 'send it'?"

Harriman was stunned that True could know this. "You heard me whispering?"

"Yes, of course, but I also sent you the words to say—which you faithfully followed to the letter. You fired a shot six feet over your intended target—my head. It should have hit that flag behind me at about the third star from the bottom on your far right."

Benjamin True turned around to face the flag behind him. He stepped slightly to his left so that Harriman could see it, too. "There's the hole," pointed True, "just off center on that third star up." True looked at Speaker DuBois, who, although quiet and still, still had tears on his cheeks. "Mister Speaker, would you please stand up there and stick your pen through that bullet hole so that everyone can see it?"

The Speaker shook his head a bit, as if to bring himself fully into the moment. Then he stood and removed his classic gold Cross® pen from his shirt pocket and reached up to the hole, about a foot above his head, where he easily pushed the pen through it about half way, moving it in and out a couple of times. There was loud murmuring across the Chamber and Gallery, and many of those at the rail of the South side of the Gallery, above the wall on which the punctured flag was hung, were leaning over in hopes of seeing the demonstration—which they could not.

"Thank you, Mister Speaker," said Benjamin True, nodding appreciatively at the Speaker, who then sat back down quite numbly in his chair.

Benjamin True turned forward again to face Harriman directly. He stepped back to his left, to be centered again behind his lectern so that both Vice President Linda Surgeon and Speaker William DuBois could see Harriman's face as he floated there in front of True.

"Tell us, Lieutenant Dan Harriman, why you attempted a double murder tonight." True raised his eyebrows and waited. Harriman knew, of course, that he could say nothing useful. Nothing would get him out of trouble. Nothing would re-send his shot down range to make it hit the first target this time. He was not supposed to be here; he was supposed to have escaped his shooter's nest by now, having wiped his fingerprints off of whatever he had touched, and escaped back into the hordes of Capitol Police officers who were milling about outside the Chamber. From there, he would have left the Capitol Complex altogether, never to be seen again. But he had not anticipated this outcome, and he was on his own now with no plan and little hope of coming up with one.

"Lieutenant Harriman," continued True, "you need to get a hold of yourself and analyze your situation. You are suspended above the well of the United States House of Representatives in front of a Joint Session of the House and Senate, and before most of the Supreme Court, the President and Vice President, the Executive Cabinet and the Joint Chiefs of Staff, and you are being asked to give an account for your lawless and immoral actions."

Harriman cleared his throat. "I invoke my Fifth Amendment right not to speak as a witness against myself," he said in a voice loud enough to be heard by a couple hundred of those present.

"Well," said Benjamin True, "I think you have more immediate problems than whatever criminal proceedings you may have in mind. You failed your assignment, and now you're a substantial liability to those for whom you work."

Linda Surgeon sprang from her seat behind True's right shoulder. "The Capitol Police ordered you to shoot?" she demanded. "We'll get the Chief of Police in here this instant, and we'll get to the bottom of this." She was seething.

"That won't be possible, Madam Vice President," said True. "The doors are all still locked, and no one can come in or go out at this time. But there'll be plenty of time to investigate later, so I beg your indulgence as our time is short." With that, True waved his arm turning Harriman upside down from his mid-air prone position. Harriman's hands were now pinned behind him and one of the many pairs of Secret Service handcuffs floated up from the pile on the first-tier desk, locking itself onto Harriman's wrists.

"We'll just sit Lieutenant Harriman down on the floor with the others, where he can begin to ponder how long he has until his masters send an assassin to eliminate him as a risk to their organization." True motioned, and Harriman's body began to float toward the carpeted area in front of the rostrum, where the seven agents were still sitting.

"You've got to save me! I was just following orders!" shouted Harriman. True whipped him around mid-air and Harriman quickly floated back to where he had been before, this time with his hands cuffed behind his back.

"I've got to save you, huh?" asked True, rhetorically. "Just following orders, eh?" True paused for a moment. "You know, Lieutenant, you are a prime example to what I was just saying before you so rudely interrupted tonight's conversation. I was talking about how great evils are often carried out at the hands of those who were 'just following orders' or 'just doing their job'. And here you are, begging the assistance of someone that you just tried to kill while 'just following orders'. Do you see the irony in that?

"When you tolerate tyranny, Lieutenant, it will eventually come back to bite you on the buttocks. You may think you have got it under control, since you're on the tyrant's team, but sooner or later, you become no longer useful to the tyrant, and he does with you what he does to anyone else that stands in his way.

"How foolish," said True, shaking his head solemnly. "How quickly you have gone from taking great pride in your privileged position to begging for another master to protect you from the one you have just failed. You show no remorse for your actions, but only for your predicament.

"Well, no matter. Your future as a living human is most likely out of your hands now. And while your situation is regrettable, it is not important to our purposes here tonight." True waved an arm again, and off went Harriman toward the royal blue carpeted floor with the others.

"They'll kill me! They're going to kill me!" Harriman pleaded.

"Yes," said True. "That's very likely. Now you just sit there and be quiet. Perhaps it will do you some good to listen now that you have a new perspective on your own life."

Harriman went mute as his body turned from prone to feet-down in mid-air. His feet touched down, and from there, he sank to a position seated on the floor, just in front of the Justice of the Supreme Court.

"Well," said Benjamin True, now addressing the entire Chamber and Gallery, "this has been a dramatic evening to be sure, but let me assure you again that everyone here is safe. So, I'd like your attention again as I shift my focus from speaking to you all to speaking to the citizens at home."

True turned to his left to face Speaker DuBois. "Mister Speaker, I haven't forgotten that we were in the middle of discussing what I think you should do. Well, I have an idea about that, and we're going to get something done before I leave. So just keep listening, and we'll get to all that in time."

DuBois nodded and sat back in his chair.

Chapter 11

To the Citizens

Benjamin True turned forward again at his lectern. "I now speak to the citizens of the United States, who are watching at home, and who will be seeing video of this event from tonight forward. My message to you is, in one sense, hard to deliver. It is difficult because it will be heavy, but it will not be too much for you to bear—provided that you resist the urge to *think* it's too much. For this reason, I want it to be also very encouraging, in order to keep you in the game, so to speak. And indeed, it is for this very hope that I came—that is, for my very belief that even a modest amount of effort from you could make a big difference in the quality of life in your country, and even in the world. And if I could inspire you to fight for change as *I* would fight for change, if I were living in the here and now, practically *nothing* you would want to do would be impossible for you.

"I cannot customize my message for each individual among you, of course—and you all are in different places in your knowledge, wisdom, and maturity. So, I have little choice but to 'let it rip', as you say, and hope that those among you who get it will help the rest in time to get it, too. But I do ask of you this one thing: I'm asking you to trust me when I say that you can indeed bear what I'm going to say tonight—that you can bear up under it and overcome what needs to be overcome. In other words, don't lose hope through my words, but keep trusting that I have come to help you get to a better life than how you have been living."

Those in the Gallery were curious and scared, but one could sense a tone of support from the body language of a fair portion of them. At these opening remarks, one shouted, "You preach it!" and another, "Tell us!" Many had never in their lives paid more rapt attention than at this moment.

"Let me begin with a question that I'd like you all to answer. You citizens here in the Gallery can answer out loud. Now, tonight you've all seen the ugliness and corruption of your government. So I'm going to ask you the question, and I want you to be really careful how you answer it, so right before I ask it, I'm going to freeze everybody in this hall. Then I'll ask the question and give you ten seconds of silence to think through it before I unfreeze you all. Do you understand what's about to happen?"

His question was greeted generally with nods in the affirmative. Benjamin True raised his hands and gave a single pulse, as if pushing slightly against two opposing doors at once. The room went still.

"OK, here's the question: *Is the American citizen responsible for the state of America's government and the actions of that government?*"

He stood silently and patiently for ten seconds, then he said, "Now, remember to be careful how you answer, because it's a tricky question either way you answer it."

He then relaxed his hands and the room sprang back into motion.

"OK, those of you in the gallery, what do you say?"

Several hundred answered all at once. Both "Yes" and "No" were heard, though the "Yes" answer was obviously in the minority.

"It would seem that you are divided as to the answer," True told his audience. So, let's talk about it. If you say, 'No,' then it raises the question of who *is* responsible for the corruption and the misdeeds of this government. That is, who is *funding* it? Who is *electing* it? Who *protects* it as it continues? Who makes *excuses* for it when it is criticized?

"And if you say, 'Yes,' then it raises the question of what you, yourselves, are doing to correct the bad behaviors of this government for whom you are responsible. Either way, you see, this mess points back to you.

"Most Americans answer, 'No,' of course, and feel quite justified doing so. Indeed, many of you are generally disgusted with the bad deeds of this government—and even more so after this evening's demonstration of its corruption. So you distance yourself from this ugly mess and claim that you are not personally responsible for it. But I want you to think really carefully about that. Indeed, if *you citizens* aren't responsible, then who is? France? The Easter Bunny? The Devil?"

These facetious answers each drew a few snickers, though nobody dared to answer the question.

"So, I want to give you a really useful exercise for judging your own personal behavior in your society. Ask yourself this question:

> *What if everybody did this?*

"This question is a great moral test, and it has hundreds of applications for your society. For instance, what if *everyone* cruised in the passing lane on the Interstate, rather than to use it only for passing?"

There was some murmuring in response to this question. Obviously, this was a common problem.

"Or what if *everyone* stood and visited with friends right in the middle of the aisle at the grocery store?"

"Oh, I *hate* that!" said someone from the Gallery. Others agreed heartily.

"Or what if *everyone* tossed his or her trash on the ground? Or what if everybody in the audience talked during a movie? Are you with me here?"

"Yeah!" was the reply from many.

"People can be real jerks, right?" True asked.

"That's right!" someone called out, and was supported with various expressions of agreement, now more enthusiastic than before.

"Well, ask yourself this:

> *What's to keep a guy who wishes that other people would not be jerks from being a jerk himself?*"

The crowd was more subdued as they tried to think through where he was going.

"How many of you disapprove of Congress? Aren't disapproval rates at an all-time high?"

Many answered that they were.

"And don't you wish everybody would vote their bums out of office?" he asked.

Again, many answered that they did.

"OK, but what do *you* do? You personally? You vote your own bum back in."

There was little by way of reply to this.

"Am I right here? Don't most of you vote your own guy back in?"

True got a modest and embarrassed response from a few admitting that he was right.

"It's no secret that incumbents are reelected with amazing predictability. So, what if *everyone* did that? What if practically everyone in this country kept voting for his own incumbents in Congress? Well, if everyone did that, you'd get a government quite like the one you have right here in this room. So maybe you can see the importance of getting the right answer to that question of whether the American citizen is responsible for the state of the American government."

Benjamin True could tell that he was making some progress, but their verbal response was still unimpressive.

"Am I right about this?"

A few answered that he was.

"Come on, folks. Admit the truth here, since it's so obvious. Am I right about this?"

This time the agreement was more robust.

"Now we're getting somewhere," he encouraged them! "I told you you could get through this difficult exercise," he said with a smile.

Some laughed along with this, taking a little comfort in the amiable nature of the dialog, though still wishing to be freed completely from having to think about their own behavior.

"So, if you want to know whether your own behaviors are acceptable, then ask yourself, 'what if everybody did this—what would happen then?'. And here's another good habit for the backside of that same coin. When you find yourself wishing others would change a nasty habit, ask yourself, 'do I do this, too?'. A great many people would be surprised to learn just how often the answer to that question would be 'yes'!

"So, let's get to the real heart of the matter here. Let's examine one of your fundamental ideas about being citizens, and see how it might be spruced up a bit. You have a quotation that is fairly well known among the reformers of various types in this country. Its source is disputed, but it goes something like this:

> *The only thing necessary for the triumph of evil is for good men to do nothing."* [38]

Someone let out a formal, "Hear! Hear!" and there was more than one enthusiastic "Amen!" from the House.

Benjamin True continued, "This quotation is used to goad people into acting—to get them out of their so-called comfort zone and to do something proactive."

"Mmmm-hmmm," came another approving voice from the Gallery, the feel of which was getting more and more like a down-home church revival than like a hall of government.

"But perhaps it will not surprise you to learn that I have given this quotation a lot more thought than most people do, and I find it questionable. Again, it says:

> *The only thing necessary for the triumph of evil is for good men to do nothing.*[38]

"But I question, *do* good men do nothing in the face of evil?"

One could have heard that proverbial pin drop as the stunned audience tried to wrap its mind around what he had just said.

"*Do* good men do nothing?" he repeated. "Or do good men do *something*? Do they tolerate evil, or do they oppose it? Do they sit idly by and watch it develop, or do they exert themselves to nip it in the bud?"

These were good questions, of course—the sort that most people never ponder much for fear that arriving at a resolute answer to such questions might obligate them to a certain lifestyle to which they are afraid to commit themselves. But Benjamin True wasn't like most people in this regard. Nor *had* he been before his death so long before. He had that clarity of character that comes from the courage to consider issues honestly and deeply, and this was at once an intrigue and a terror to others. This single trait of not being afraid to make a sound moral judgment in a matter had set him apart quite profoundly from most others, and the nature of their responses to him depended quite substantially on whatever was the present topic of conversation. In those cases in which they happened to agree with him, they often found themselves quite impressed, for his well-considered reasons for believing certain things had generally proved better than their own reasons for believing them. In such cases, he was a fascination to them, and a ready-made champion of their established causes. But in cases where they disagreed, Benjamin True had proved a considerable irritant to many of his fellow humans, for his reasons were just as sound for those beliefs, too, and being around him tended to expose the chimerical methods by which most people tend to acquire and maintain a good number of their opinions. The difference was that he was constant in his judgments where the others simply weren't concerned with full-time consistency.

He went on. "I submit that this quotation of dubious origin implies the very lie upon which the corruption in your society thrives. I say that it is simply impossible at once to be good and to turn a blind eye to evil, but the quotation seems to suggest that not only is this possible, but that it is common, and that this is the reason that there is so much evil afoot in the world today—that is, that many are 'good', but are, unfortunately, doing nothing. That is a lie. Good men and women do not tolerate evil, but that they expose it and oppose it. They will have nothing to do with it, and they have the courage to call it what it is."

While still speaking, he turned to his right and walked to the end of the second-tier desk behind which he was standing. Few noticed it, but the volume of his voice did not go down as he stepped away from the microphone. Having cleared the end of the desk, he proceeded downward to the floor level and stood at the end of that longest desk, as he continued speaking.

"And with that, I have just disturbed a good fourth fifths of my audience, for you will insist on thinking of yourselves as being good, even though you have done close to nothing to oppose the evils that have been done by this government. Yours is a government that commits many evils in the name of things like *Union*…" He pointed to the word *Union* carved into the far left-hand panel of that first-tier desk. Then he walked across the front, reading the other panels as he went, "…*Justice, Tolerance, Liberty*, and *Peace*. This is a lie, of course, as many of their acts violate these principles in one way or another. Take 'Peace', to give just one example, for we haven't the time to talk about it all. Since America declared independence from Great Britain in 1776, she has been in armed conflict most of that time, with very few years at peace. And such a record hardly classifies a nation as one that loves peace now, does it?" [39]

"Your government also acts in the name of the Rule of Law. That's the idea that your government was to be:

A government of laws, and not of men.[40]

"That's what John Adams called it, and the idea was that Congress was going to pass really great laws that would be just and fair, and that everybody could enjoy equal protection under those laws, so that nobody had an unfair advantage over anybody else—and that in this way, they were going to protect the people from fiat rule, which is what you call it when a government can do anything it wants just by saying so."

He pointed to the ceiling high above, around which were 23 carvings. "See those carvings up there? These are called the 23 lawgivers. They are historical figures, including Hammurabi and Moses—they're the two up there," he said, pointing straight ahead to the northern wall of the Gallery. "That's Moses in the middle, and Hammurabi just to his left." He motioned all around the Chamber as he continued, "All these were famous for writing various laws or systems of law throughout history. And if you follow this on around…" He turned a slow about-face to his right, pointing as he went, "…you get to Thomas Jefferson, who was your third president under the Constitution. He wrote the Declaration of Independence and he wrote the Virginia Statute for Religious Freedom, which was the precursor for the First Amendment to the Constitution. That's that one that guarantees you freedom of speech and of religion.

"This Congress claims to operate under the Rule of Law, and it calls the Constitution 'the supreme law of the land'. As I have already discussed, however, they regularly violate their individual oaths to follow the Constitution. But that doesn't keep the liars from carrying on business in the name of the Rule of Law.

"And then there's that." True pointed once again to the inscription just above the Speaker's chair. "They even carry on business in the name of God." He read the inscription aloud: "'In God We Trust,' it says. And they have a chaplain in each house of Congress who begins each session with a prayer, asking God to give them wisdom and such as needed to serve the people justly and fairly and so forth.

"All of this is done on your watch. And ultimately, it's done in the name of not only these various principles, and of God himself, but also of you, the people. And *you* let it happen. These people strive to use this government for evil, and there are not nearly enough good men and women among you in the public to keep them from doing it. This is your fault. And this is another of the radical differences between the way you think and the way I think. I think that you are responsible for the actions of your government, and most of you do not. Instead, you will adamantly claim that what these people do in these halls of government is not a matter of your responsibility in the least. This view is no mere 'difference of opinion,' as many might try to pass it off. Rather, it is a lie. You elect them and you fund their salaries, as well as the bills they pass. You are responsible.

"And so I ask you, what kind of people would let this happen? A just and righteous people? Surely not. Yet what have *you* done to stop the corruption?"

A voice from Gallery somewhere called out, "Well, we've *voted*."

Benjamin True looked up the direction of the one having said it. "Thanks for piping in with that thought. I'm sure many were thinking the same thing. But let's talk about it. Can you tell me," he asked the woman who had volunteered the statement, "how well the voting is going to stop the common corruption in government?"

The woman was not really excited about being interviewed any further, but she obliged the question. "Not very good, I suppose."

"I agree," said True. "Perhaps you will agree with my observation that the corruption just gets worse and worse with each passing generation."

"Amen to that!" chimed in some other spectator, with a sarcastic tone. This drew a few chuckles.

True continued, "And aren't your freedoms being whittled away more and more each decade?"

"Yes," came from several voices throughout the hall, along with much nodding in agreement.

"And isn't the standard of living going down more and more? And isn't the moral fiber of the people getting worse and worse? Of course it is, and this is no secret. Anybody who pays attention to such things can easily recognize that I'm telling the truth."

"So, what have you done about it?" asked True. "What you have done is to vote—even though you can witness for yourselves that this strategy isn't bringing about any significant improvements. You're like Charlie Brown, trusting Lucy one more time as he tries to kick that football."

Someone from the crowd interrupted, "We *complain*!"

This got lots of laughs, even from Benjamin True, who replied, "Yes, and just for the record, I'd like to point out that complaining is not even remotely the same thing as fixing."

This sobered the mood a bit, and no one could deny its truth, of course.

Then another spoke up, "Sir, we have not only voted, but we have *prayed*—and some of us constantly."

"Oh, thank you so much for mentioning that," said True quite sincerely as he spotted the one speaking from the Gallery. "And I will ask you the same question as before: how's that going? Has it ended the corruption in your government?"

"Well, I'd like to think it has helped, but no, sir, I can't honestly say that it has," came the honest reply.

"Right," said True. "So, here's a really big question to ponder: What if those of you who are praying about politics are actually waiting on God to fix something that he's expecting *you* to fix?"

There was some murmuring at this, as it seems to have been a new thought for many.

True continued, "What if God thinks that your government is *your* business to handle and not his? Can any of you prove that this is not the case? You pray and pray—those of you who do—but do you get answer after answer or miracle after miracle? No, of course you don't, for this current mess of government is by no means the result of a miracle, and its solution won't be, either. So maybe it's time you did some better thinking so as to figure out what time it is here.

"Indeed, the problem here is the way you are thinking—or rather, *not* thinking." Benjamin True went on, "I'm going to ask you a question that will demonstrate what I'm talking about, and I'm hoping a few of you will be good enough sports to answer it out loud, sharing your true responses to it: When you look at the huge mess in Washington, what's the most frequent thing you find yourself wishing for?" True looked about the Gallery, left and right, hoping for someone to answer the question.

One older man in the Gallery raised his hand, and True gestured in his direction. "What about you, sir?"

The man stood slowly, and with an obvious attitude of respect he said, "When I think about the mess we're in, I find myself wishing we could get a good man in the White House—no offense to President Hernandez, of course." This drew a big laugh, during which the man sat down. Those who might have known where to find the president sitting would have seen him mumbling something mockingly at the man.

"Thanks for sharing that, sir. I'm sure that many find themselves thinking the same thing," said Benjamin True. "Who else in the Gallery has thoughts like that—about what good it would do to get a good president in the White House?"

Many hands went up.

"And how many of you have similar thoughts about the value of getting a good representative in the House or Senator in the Senate?" True went on.

Again, a lot of hands went up.

"Exactly. This is how a great many Americans think. But how rational is that? That is, how well does that idea fit with reality? Think about it—the country's a mess, so your first inclination is to get a good president in the White House, as if that's going to be sufficient to turn all this around. But is it?" True paused for them to reflect. "Do you even *know* what it would take to turn it around? Have you ever done the math, so to speak?

"Of course, you haven't. When it comes to politics, Americans generally avoid that kind of analytical thinking, although most are certainly capable of it. You can't resist the idea of a champion in the White House because it's just such a simple scenario. That is, a fairy tale in which a good president shows up to fix everything is just too good to pass up. And I'm not telling you it's a *bad* idea, mind you, but that it's only a fraction of what would have to be done in order to bring this country into a state of being a good representation of the ideals upon which its government was founded. So, this idea of getting a good president in the White House, or of getting a good representative or senator in this Capitol is very appealing to you, but you have no idea just how poor are its chances, and you have zero plans for doing what else needs to be done to fix things. Indeed, you don't even *know* what else needs to be done to fix things. And sadly, you generally don't even care to get into it."

True looked back up at the gentleman who had dared to speak up, and said, "Thank you again sir, for having the courage to share your thoughts. And now I have another question for the citizens. Quick, somebody name a town or a county in the United States that is known for having run the corruption out of its own local government and for keeping it clean thereafter."

The room was silent.

"Is there not one suggestion among you?" goaded True.

He paused. Then, when it was obvious enough to everyone that no answer was forthcoming, he explained, "There are over 3,000 counties and parishes in the US, and roughly 30,000 cities. And not *one* of them has managed to free itself from the typical corruption of government—the lying, cheating, and stealing, the blackmail, the bribery, the graft, and so on. So, what makes you think that you can fix Washington by putting a good president in the White House when you can't even fix the very towns in which you live?" He had spread his arms wide in a questioning pose, where he paused and waited again until it was plain that no good response was to be had.

"Just look at yourselves, my friends. What are you doing? You're pinning your hopes on some fantasy that some superhero of a public official will come down and fix it all for you. And yet you have never had such a superhero in your entire history—not even in a small town. And don't misunderstand me here; I'm not saying you've never had a reformer in public office; I'm saying that you've never had anybody succeed at reforming the government *fully*—to its proper ideals—and certainly not in doing it once and for all—you know, the way you dream of it happening. Yes, yes, if you read the history books they give out at school, you might *think* you have had a superhuman president or two, but I've already demonstrated how even your most lauded heroes were far from perfect in their practice of the founding ideals.

"So, the problem here is that your thinking is unrealistic. It's a beautifully fantastic strategy, to be sure—that someone would come do all the work for you—but as the saying goes:

> However beautiful the strategy, one should occasionally check the results.[41]

"It is simply not working. You can't even fix your own towns and counties, yet you keep this dream alive of being able to fix Washington, and simply by voting every couple of years. Don't get me wrong, you could fix it for sure, but not by such a casual effort. No, you'd have to *want* it fixed a lot more than that.

"And that brings us to your fundamental problem; you simply have not chosen to *care* enough about righteousness and justice to be deeply interested in having the sort of society that your official documents set forth for you. The government that was designed on paper by those who framed the Constitution gave you the opportunity to uphold those ideals much better than normally happens, but as it has turned out, your ancestors and you have generally not thought that it was worth the effort. So, you let the government devolve into the corrupt artifice and scheme that it is today—this dog and pony show that claims to serve all these holy causes, but serves only to the profit of its masters. Simply put, the tyrants in this room have wanted control of this government for their own evil motives more than you, its citizens, have wanted it for the *right* motives.

"And a lot of that has to do with your overzealous adoption of this one particular principle carved on the front of that desk: *Tolerance*. This one is particularly dangerous because of its ambiguity. It raises the question, 'tolerant of what?'. Well, we don't have time to examine the question at length, but you can rest assured that *nothing* good can come from being tolerant of evil. Ever. When left unchecked, evil behavior generally continues, and often expands. So, your woes are generally the result of your own negligence in opposing evil."

A young man from the Gallery raised his hand and stood up, and then he simply began to speak as there was a pause. "Mister True, we can't tell. Are you a Democrat or a Republican?"

"Ha!" said True, surprised somewhat by the question.

"Let me explain my position to you, sir." Benjamin True held up his left hand high above his head, with his palm down, as one does to show how tall someone else might be. "Imagine a line from this hand," he shook his left hand in the air just a bit, "down to this hand." He shook his right hand in front of him, just above his waist. "At the top of this line are the righteous virtues of honesty, rationality, and responsibility. And at the bottom are dishonesty, irrationality, and irresponsibility. Now, the exercise is this. Think about some person, giving careful consideration to their every thought, word, and deed, and then place them on this line between the top and the bottom, according to how often they are honest, rational, and responsible. Only one human ever would have been at the very top, of course, and no person ever has been at the very bottom. That's because nobody is dishonest, irrational, and irresponsible about *everything all the time*. So, the closer you get to the top and the closer you get to the bottom, the fewer people you'll find. Instead, most people belong here in the middle." With this, he raised his right hand and waved it around a bit in front of his face.

"Now, that's how it works with people, and that's how it works with organizations, too, like political parties and churches and governments and charities and so forth. There is no human organization of any size on this planet that lives at the top of this line, where everything is completely honest, rational, and responsible all the time. Even to find an organization that genuinely *wants* to be there would be exceedingly— *exceedingly*—rare. No, they generally gravitate toward the middle, because, for one reason, that's where most people are, and for the other reason, that's where you can lie, cheat and steal sometimes—and these are the things they really want to reserve the latitude for doing from time to time—some more, and some less. If the organization were to cater only to those of the highest ideals in virtue, they would not be attractive to the bulk of people here in the middle, and they could not have as much power as they might like. And, of course, if they were to shoot for the very low end of the morality spectrum, only a few would qualify for that, and they would be greatly outnumbered. So, anyway, for such practical reasons, they don't shoot for the highest standards— which is also quite consistent with the fact that they don't believe in them anyway. And that's where the Republican and Democratic parties live—right here in the middle.

"And so they are locked in an ongoing struggle over which are the best ways to lie, cheat, and steal, and which are the best ways to violate the Constitution and the founding principles. I'm being sarcastic, of course, for they would never put it that way. No, what they want *you* to think is that it's a struggle over the principles that are the most meaningful to you personally. And since most of you choose to be moral specialists rather than moral generalists—that is, since you are so willing to pick one issue to aim for righteousness in, while you wallow in moral compromise on other issues—it's very easy for the cartel to design a system that keeps the membership numbers in both parties fairly even, so that neither side can get much done. If one side gains too much a following, they simply change its priorities, which angers some people, who then leave and vote for somebody else. This way, they can keep *both* sides from having too many people up here in the higher moral zone. They definitely don't want that, because it's dangerous to them if there are too many people who want to do what is morally right in *all* matters. Things would get out of hand very quickly in that case."

Someone called out, but couldn't be seen, "Yeah, but which party *is* higher, the Democrats or the Republicans?"

"Do you mean higher in what they say, or in what they do?" asked Benjamin True.

There was no answer.

"I think we've lost the caller," joked the smiling True. And this got some laughs, although it took most of them a couple of seconds to get it, as they were puzzled that he'd be up on the goings-on of modern talk radio.

"OK, I'll just continue, addressing either case. Both parties *say* a few good things. For example, one claims to be generally against war, the other, generally for more limited government, one for human rights, and the other for fiscal responsibility. But *all* of these particular things, taken at face value, are good things. But what good is that? What good is talk? No, a political party should not be defined by its rhetoric, but by what its members actually *do* when they get elected to office. And when Republicans and Democrats get elected to office, they tend to violate *all* these principles that their parties are supposedly known for—regardless of their party affiliation. Meanwhile, the clueless voters at home are busy believing that the Democratic Party is just what it says it is, or that the Republican Party is what it says *it* is, as opposed to what those parties *actually* do when they get into office.

"This so-called 'two-party system' is not authorized by the Constitution, yet it has a chokehold on the Union. And no matter who makes it into office, certain bad governmental behaviors are sure to keep right on going. Even when a reformer comes in, he or she is simply not going to reform *all* of what goes on here, because some items are simply non-negotiable with the big-money cartel that steers this government and the parties."

Another voice from the Gallery joined the conversation. "But don't you think that the Democrats are more unruly than the Republicans? Don't they cheat more on elections and don't they riot more?"

True looked quite seriously in the direction of the questioner. "Let me guess, sir, that you are a Republican."

There was no reply, but this did get some laughs.

Benjamin True continued. "If the answer to that you were 'no,' sir—that is, if the Democrats are not statistically more corrupt—would you then rout out the corruption in your own party?"

There was no answer, so True continued, "And if the answer were 'yes,' would you rout out the corruption in your own party?"

Still, there was no reply.

"Just as I suspected," concluded True. "You already have plenty of crime statistics, and you can look up which party has more law-breakers in its membership if you want to. And if the evidence shows that one party is statistically more unruly than the other, the ones in the less-unruly party can use that affirm themselves, saying, 'Aha! I *knew* they were worse than us!' Meanwhile, those in the unrulier party will say something like, 'Well, that may be, but it's because we're fighting a corrupt system, and you have to fight fire with fire' So if you really want to know the answer to that, go look it up, and you can be as honest or dishonest as you like with the data you find. But either way, it is doubtful that even one person in a thousand who is curious to know the answer to that question is going to be the sort to be properly embarrassed by the unruliness of his or her *own* party, whether it's worse than the other party or not.

"These parties are designed to keep the nation split into two roughly-equal halves, while keeping both sides corrupt enough so as to be civically dysfunctional. If you will recall, I said that nobody lives at the bottom of the scale, being dishonest, irrational, and irresponsible about everything. There is no person like that, there is no party like that, and there is no media outlet like that. No, everybody needs to get *some* things right just to stay alive, or to stay in business. So, nobody *wants* to be at the bottom of the chart, and everybody sees to it that he or she stays above the bottom of it, because if anybody got *everything* wrong, they'd be dead in very short order. For example, if a person were wrong about everything, they'd be wrong about whether it's safe in any given instant to cross the street, and the moment they tried it, they'd be killed. But again, nobody is wrong about everything, and nobody *wants* to be wrong about everything.

"And neither does the cartel that is steering this government pretty much where it wants. They do not want *everything* to fail here. No, they want to keep the machine running, because they're staying filthy rich from it, and they're enjoying the allure of power, which is never satisfied. But they also don't want this government to operate at the top of the chart, either, because an honest, rational, and responsible government would put them out of business, and would make everybody equal under the law, with no person or corporation having special advantages."

"So, here's how it works—I will tell you even though many of you will indeed strive to misunderstand it: Both parties are designed to jibe with whatever issues mean the most to their members, and then to corrupt those members along the way to ostensibly pursuing those goals. For one, it's the economy that's most important, and for another, it's compassion. And if not that, it may be the Rule of Law or military might or freedom of religion, or even freedom *from* religion. Whatever is your hot topic—and there are indeed many hot topics from which to choose—you are statistically likely to find one of the two major parties giving lip service to it more than the other. And naturally, you're supposed to join that party. And from there, they strive to keep you going as a member, whether they succeed at furthering your favorite cause or not. Meanwhile, they make use of your support, whether in contributions or votes, by pitting you against the other party, who is pretty much doing the same thing on its own side of the aisle.

"Each party is designed to appear at least a little better the other overall—though not in *every* way. It is their job to play the 'good cop' most of the time, to the other party's 'bad cop'. But what they will *never* do is to insist on 100% honesty, rationality, and responsibility. Nor will they ever condemn *all* kinds of injustice, no matter who is doing it. If they were to do either of those things, they'd either be putting themselves out of business, or utterly reforming themselves—neither of which is likely to happen with so many bad agents in play, with so much money being made at it, and with such a pitiful public in charge of overseeing the business.

"And that brings me to the public's job. In the eyes of those who own these parties, it's your job—you in the public—to find this two-party tag-team to be convincing. You're supposed to decide which of the two choices you prefer, and you're not supposed to figure out that they're *not* both being used by the same masters. You're supposed to think that when one party wins control—whichever party is your favorite, that is—that's pretty good, and when the other party wins control, that's pretty bad. But what you don't realize is that the masters—the mega-money interests who hold such decisive influence over the government—they have split their agenda into two parts: a left side and a right side. When the Democrats win, they advance the 'left' side of their agenda. And when the Republicans win, they advance the 'right' side of it. But it's all still the *same* master plan, and you are being played like a fiddle. The members of both sides generally don't ever figure out that they're pretty much supporting the same big-picture agenda. So they keep on being proud about the disunity between the two sides—each considering himself holier than the other. That's how it works. And the willingness of both sides to compromise on honesty, rationality, and responsibility is absolutely crucial to the success of the scheme.

"So, to the question of which party I support, the answer should be fairly obvious by now. I support those people who are sincerely striving to live at the top of the spectrum, where—and you need to be sure not to miss my exact words here--where *everything* is honest, rational, and responsible *all* the time. You won't find people like that supporting either of these parties, for both of the parties are corrupt by design, and their continued corruption is absolutely necessary to support the current artifice and scheme. And if the parties are corrupt by design, you should understand that most of the individuals that comprise the parties are corrupt by *convenience*. That is, they simply don't think it's worth the effort to maintain an impeccable government *all* the time on *every* issue. So they live their lives at whatever level on the corruption scale that they find convenient, comfortable, and sustainable.

"Now, I realize that's a pretty hard teaching for some of you, because you tell yourselves that you're the *real* 'purists' and that you're 'fighting for change' in your parties. But you should take a look at the results once in a while, and see that your efforts are simply not succeeding in bringing about any appreciable reform.

"Here's a really easy way to get a peek behind the curtain of political corruption. Consider the Supreme Court, whose job it is to settle disputes between certain parties, generally with regard to whether the Constitution is being followed or not. If you are honest, rational, and responsible all the time in every way, then you want the Justices of the Supreme Court to abide strictly by the Constitution in all of their rulings on every issue. But it is very rare to have a justice who holds such a strict track record.

"Indeed, if you're a bad guy, and you want to profit from wide-spread corruption in this country, you're going to have to find a way to violate the Constitution regularly. And one of the best ways to do that is to stack the Supreme Court with justices who will cheat the process and render rulings that are not in keeping with the Constitution—even though their oaths promise that they will indeed abide by it.

"So, with that in mind, go back and study the history of the nominees for the Supreme Court. Look how many corrupt ones—those who will give an oath to do the right thing, and then turn around and do the wrong thing—have been nominated, and you'll see that they've been nominated by presidents of *both* parties. And then look at that rare occasion where a straight-shooting, Constitution-following judge is nominated, and look for who is opposing his or her nomination. When a nominee shows every sign of doing his or her job faithfully, as per the oath the justices take, and somebody opposes that nomination, that shows you that the one opposing it is indeed corrupt. In fact, this is one of the most obvious tests for political corruption, because it doesn't involve any gray areas at all. If everybody in government takes pretty much the same oath of office, then everybody in government *should* be completely in favor of everyone *upholding* that oath. When they're not, there's your glimpse into the corruption."

"So, you're saying that the Republicans are better, right? Because they do nominate more of the good justices than the Democrats do, right?" It was one of those still-hidden people in the Gallery.

Benjamin True rolled his eyes in frustration and fired back, "If one of these parties is better than the other, sir, it's better in the same way that one poke in the eye with a sharp stick is better than two pokes in the eye with a sharp stick. What you don't understand is that in the Republican Party—since that seems to be your favorite—there exists plenty of corruption to keep this government corrupt perpetually. If the Democratic Party were to go away suddenly, the Republican Party is already split between those in it who are less corrupt and those who are more corrupt—just like the Democratic Party is. And they would simply carry on in pretty much the same manner as the two-party government carries on today. That system wouldn't be as stable, however, as people would be more likely to revolt against it, whereas the current system gives the cognitive/moral miser the satisfaction of giving him an easier alternative to do-it-yourself reform."

True looked up to the Gallery and said, "You are very zealous to get some sort of endorsement out of me for your favorite party, but only a corrupted mind would do that when I have clearly condemned the corruption on both sides. You're looking for a way to take pride in not being as bad as your opponent. That shows that your focus is competitive in nature, and that you're competing *against* something. But you should be competing, or striving, rather, *for* something. If you're dead-set on competing against somebody, why don't you start a contest to see which party can exercise honesty, rationality, and responsibility in *every* matter, *all* the time?

"Neither party has much interest in reforming itself. No, their members, thinking quite lowly as they do, are quite willing to settle for being better in their own eyes than the other party. Well, you're quibbling over precious little for bragging rights. The one party has cut loose the chains of the Constitution and is rushing headlong downhill into total corruption. And the other party? Is it standing valiantly atop the hill and demanding that the other return to the Rule of Law? No. Where the Democrats are rushing downhill, the Republicans are simply walking behind, saying, 'Could you guys just slow down a little?' That's what you are like. That's what kind of people you are. Were you forced to tell the truth in your boasting, sir, you would have to say it this way: 'I'm very proud to be less enthusiastic about our corruption than are the members of the other party.'"

The room had grown rather quiet and still as True continued.

"The Realitan [42] strives to be as close to perfection as possible—and

113

not for what he or she can get out of it, but because it's simply the right thing to do. That's a far cry from the one who simply strives to be a little better than the next guy so that he can lie to himself about how good he is. One is based in reality, and the other in vanity."

"If you're still so dull as to want to take pride in your various parties—if you're intent on being some sort of political light to the world, then prove it by running the corruption out of your *own* party before you dare to point out the corruption in the other."

Chapter 12

The Gold Bar

"Let's change the pace a bit. Let's have a little *Show and Tell* to help you understand my point about what's going wrong in this country," said Benjamin True. He left the well of the House, and circled around the rostrum until he got back to the second-tier level from where his speech had begun. Facing the audience, he held up his hands in front of him as if to hold something that wasn't there. Then in an instant, there *was* something there. It was a standard 400-troy-ounce gold bar, the sudden appearance of which drew considerable murmuring from the audience.

"This is a standard gold bar," explained True, "and it weighs about 27 pounds. Depending on the price of gold at the time, this bar is worth about half a million US dollars."

"You got any more of those?" came a humorous shout from somehow in the Gallery behind True and to his right. Many laughed at this, and Benjamin True did, too.

"Thanks for helping me make my point, up there," said True. "This is a gold bar, and most everybody wants one." True held it up higher, above his head, and asked, "Raise your hand if you want this."

Nearly everyone in the hall raised a hand, and many did so enthusiastically, being uncertain as to whether he was offering it or was merely asking. The mood was fairly light by now, and one more class clown type spoke up, "I'll take all of those you got!" He got a good laugh and considered it his latest comedic achievement in life to have worked such a large crowd successfully.

True was laughing, too. "OK, you can put your hands down," he said.

"Is that real?" came a query from the House floor.

"Yes, it's quite real," True replied. He stepped to his left, such that the gold bar was no longer above the lectern, but above the flat counter-styled desk beside it. True lowered the bar until it was about one foot above that desk, and then he dropped it. It fell with a bang, which astonished the crowd and set off a bit of feedback in the microphone at the lectern.

Benjamin True left the gold bar where it was and continued to speak. "A great many people don't own a gold bar, of course..."

"You got *that* right!" shouted another spectator, drawing a good number of chuckles herself.

True went on, "...and a few people do. Of those who do own one, there are three groups. The first group is made up of those who actually earned their gold bars fairly by their own work. The second group is of those who received them innocently by way of inheritance or gift. And the third group is made up of those who get their gold bars by lying, cheating, stealing, murdering, and so forth. It's that third group that is heavily represented in this Chamber by those sitting here at the floor level in front of me. Such people as this are generally found in government, as well as in the upper ranks of the larger corporations. Now, don't get me wrong, I'm not saying that everybody who is an officer in government or in a corporation is a crook, but if you wanted to go out in search of one, those would be two really good places to start looking." With this, True himself got some good laughs.

"So, why did I show you this gold bar? It's to set up a point that I will make by way of yet another question: If you had a gold bar like this, would you leave it lying on your doorstep overnight? Anyone?" True looked about for an answer but did not have to wait.

"No way!" came a willing shout from a lady in the Gallery.

"And why not?" replied True.

"Because it be *gooooone* in the mornin'!" She got her own laughs, though her delivery had not been intended to be funny.

"Thank you, ma'am." acknowledged True, nodding with a good-

116

humored smile. "And how many of you here agree with this lady's wisdom?"

It was obvious, and practically everyone raised a hand in agreement.

"Right. It is a well-known fact about humanity that a good number of people will take what is not rightfully theirs. Am I right?"

"Yes" and "Of course" were heard many times across the hall in reply.

"Why, then, do so many of you leave your doormats out all night on your doorsteps?" True asked the audience.

"Who would want to steal a doormat?" argued one voice, which was joined by another: "And even if they do, it's just a few bucks to replace it."

"So, you're saying that a doormat is not as valuable as a gold bar?" posed True.

"Uh, right!" shot back the latter voice from the audience. And again, there was some laughter.

"I agree," said Benjamin True. "Some things may be worth risking, but other things---well, risking those things is just foolish. And this is what I wanted to say to you. Government is like a gold bar; it's just too valuable to leave out on the doorstep. And you can bet that if you leave it there, some tyrants and scoundrels are going to steal it from you. That's what time it is right here and right now. And that's what time it was in 1791 when Hamilton's wish of a central bank came true. It was his big chance for him and his friends to make a personal profit off of the business of the people's government. So, with the help of corrupt people, just like the ones you see before you on the floor of this Chamber today, Hamilton got his way. The Senate passed the Bank Bill of 1791 and sent it on to the House, where it passed by a vote of 39 to 19. That means that two thirds of the representatives voted to exceed their powers of office, violating the very Constitution they had sworn to obey with the oath:

> I, _____ do solemnly swear or affirm (as the case may be)
> that I will support the Constitution of the United States.[43]

"The writing of that oath was the very first act of the very first session of the Congress. It was their first order of business. And before that session was over, many of them had violated it more than once.

They behaved just like every Congress since has behaved, and in the particular case of enacting the First Bank of the United States, President Washington acted just like every president since has acted; he violated the Constitution as it pleased him to so do."

"Excuse me, sir," interrupted a lady from the Gallery, "but why did the people let them get away with starting that central bank?"

"For the same reason that people today let them get away with similar things," answered True. "You've had another central bank, the Federal Reserve Bank, since 1913, and that's over a century ago. Neither you nor your parents nor your grandparents have managed in all that time to care enough about the plundering of your country to put a stop to that bank. Shall you then condemn those who let the First Bank of the United States have its way with the country, just as you yourselves are currently doing? Well, yes, you should disapprove of them, and of yourselves as well.

"And this is what I'm talking about. The bankers, the scoundrels, will always be highly motivated to have control of the government, because they have a great opportunity to use it for their own evil motives. But where can you find enough citizens for whom maintaining righteousness and justice is a big-enough motivation to guard the government from the scoundrels who would steal it? That has been the problem from day one.

"And this problem was no secret. Thomas Jefferson wrote into the Declaration of Independence—that's the letter they sent to King George to tell him that they were seceding from Great Britain's control and declaring themselves to be free and independent states in their own right. In that Declaration, Jefferson wrote something very observant about people. He said that:

> mankind are more disposed to suffer, while evils are sufferable, than to right themselves by abolishing the forms to which they are accustomed.[44]

"That language is somewhat dated to your generation, but what it means is that people tend to put up with things as long as they can stand it before going to the effort to make a change in their governments. Jefferson went on to detail one grievance after another, where King George had refused to do right by the colonists, and he said that all that wrongdoing constituted 'a long train of abuses and *usurpations'*—a usurpation is a seizing of power that one does not and should not rightfully have. And he said that it was obvious that the goal of all that bad behavior by the King was to *'reduce them under absolute despotism'*.

"Now, it's a pity that your schools no longer teach the same language in which the Declaration and the Constitution were written because you've lost touch with the finer points of how to put a sentence together—and how to take one apart. There's some real meat in these words. What he's saying is that it was obvious that the King intended to reduce the American people into a people without any rights and freedoms, and that he was going to do it under *'absolute despotism'*, which means that he would have complete authority to do anything he pleased to do. In other words, he wrote that they could see this coming—that it was obvious that King George did not intend to stop until he had complete control over everything in their lives.

"Now this Thomas Jefferson was pretty radical—and remember, he was not perfect in his acts, for he violated the Constitution himself when he became president later—but he said something in the Declaration—an idea that is flatly rejected by far too many Americans today. He said that when it's obvious that the government is headed toward such total control, the people have both a right and a duty. He wrote:

> *...it is their right, it is their duty, to throw off such government, and to provide new guards for their future security.*[45]

"Did you catch that? It was not only their *right*, but their *duty*, to get rid of that government and to do something that would work better. And that's the part that's so radical today because far too few of you believe that you have any particular duty to maintain your own government. You don't think you're responsible for what they do on your watch, and you don't think you're responsible to replace them with something better. You think it's someone else's job, or even that you are somehow entitled to have someone else do it for you. To you, it's a strange thought that you should have to lift a finger yourselves to such an end. You think that you are *owed* a fair and just government, as if you have either inherited it merely by being born here, or that you have somehow *deserved* it on account of that mere smidgen of effort you put forth to vote every so often. How foolish."

"Jefferson was right about how people tend to tolerate what they find tolerable. But if you had higher principles—a higher way of thinking—

and higher virtues—if you had that, you'd have gotten fed up with it long ago."

Benjamin True continued, "Now, I told you that human behavior was no secret when they were designing the Constitution. No, it was commonly understood in that generation. For example, when considering the Union's first constitution, the Articles of Confederation, John Adams, who would later become your second president under the more recent Constitution, said this:

> The only foundation of a free Constitution is pure Virtue, and if this cannot be inspired into our People in a greater Measure than they have it now, They may change their Rulers and the forms of Government, but they will not obtain a lasting Liberty. They will only exchange Tyrants and Tyrannies.[46]

"He saw it ahead of time—that the success of a Union based on the freedom of the people would come down to whether they would maintain their own virtue and character. And James Madison saw it, too. Twelve years later, when the new Constitution was up for approval from the States, he said:

> To suppose that any form of government will secure liberty or happiness without any virtue in the people, is a chimerical idea.[47]

"That word 'chimerical' refers to an idea that has no basis in reality—so Madison was saying that it was ridiculous to think that any government could succeed in securing and maintaining the freedom of the people unless those people were themselves virtuous enough to maintain such a government. But maintaining things takes work. In fact, one of my favorite quotes from Ben Franklin when I was a boy was this:

> ...it is easier to build two chimneys than to keep one in fuel.[48]

"Any of you who have ever cut and split firewood will have a good idea of what he was saying. A lot of you won't understand this because you don't have fireplaces anymore, but you can build a fireplace and chimney in a couple of days. After it's built, you will spend the rest of your life working to keep enough firewood on hand to burn in that fireplace. And that's how it is with designing a new government. Sure, you can come up with a plan, but if you really want to keep it running according to that plan, it's going to take constant work—far more than it took to build it in the first place.

"Many of you, however, have given yourselves over to that most ridiculous idea that life on this Earth ought to be easy, and ought not require any work. You hate to exert yourselves, and you think that something strange and unfair is happening to you when you find that some situation requires you to do so. This is not the sort of thinking that comes from natural life in the natural world. Rather, this sort of thinking comes from false entitlement, which is a corruption of the human mind. And this was in view even then. Ben Franklin also speculated about what it would be like if the people should become so lacking in virtue that they could not maintain a free government. He bleakly imagined a time...

> ...when the people shall become so corrupted as to need despotic government, being incapable of any other[49]

"Did you catch that? He links the lack of virtue in the people with being *incapable* of running a righteous government. Instead, he suggests that people so lacking in virtue would need rulers of absolute power to control *them*—since they would be unable to control their own behavior.

"Again, John Adams understood that the new Constitution simply lacked the powers to control a people who were, by their own lack of virtue, unruly. He wrote:

> We have no government armed with power capable of contending with human passions unbridled by **morality** and religion. Avarice, ambition, revenge, or gallantry, would break the strongest cords of our Constitution as a whale goes through a net. Our Constitution was made only for a religious and **moral** people. It is wholly inadequate for the government of any other.[50]

"In other words," explained Benjamin True, "if you don't want some king or dictator being in charge of your behavior, you're going to have to be the sort of people who will look after your own behavior. And I think I have demonstrated well enough that this was understood even back then. Of course, today, people would recoil at this latest quote because Adams mentioned not only morality, but religion. It is now generally taboo to mention religion in the political arena, but your generation does not understand that religion was not always a license for a lack of personal discipline—as it seems to be for far too many today. No, there was a time when it was expected that a person claiming to believe in

121

God would take upon him or herself the responsibility for behaving in a godly fashion. Indeed, they were responsible for themselves and for doing what needed to be done. Did the apostle Paul not write to the Thessalonians:

> if a man will not work, he will not eat' ?[51]

"Yet today, you give away food and all manner of other things to those who refuse to work. They make a career out of your so-called charity, which only serves to corrupt them all the more, as well as to plunder the treasury.

"And many of you love to go on and on about what a great country this is, having cut loose from the moorings of morality and self-responsibility, setting yourselves adrift in the ocean of make-believe. You make another error that was also foreseen and is on the record in the words of Ben Franklin, thinking that you can be great without also being good:

> It is a grand mistake to think of being great without goodness and I pronounce it as certain that there was never a truly great man that was not at the same time truly virtuous.[52]

"Again, far too many of you try to take credit just for being a citizen of this country, without adding anything to its aggregate virtue. This is such vanity, and it profits nothing but your imagination. You think this is a great place because it has great roads, or a great military, but if its people are not good these things are worth very little indeed.

"Now, the founders and framers also understood that it was necessary to place the right people in the seats of power. It wasn't just about having virtuous citizens, but about seeing to it that the administration of the government was properly executed. And for this, virtue was also necessary in the leaders. Consider the thoughts of John Witherspoon, one of those who signed the Declaration of Independence:

> Those who wish well to the State ought to choose to places of trust men of inward principle...[53]

"And James Madison, who would become the fourth president under the new Constitution, wrote that:

> The aim of every political constitution is, or ought to be, first to obtain for rulers men who possess most wisdom to discern,

and most virtue to pursue, the common good of the society; and in the next place, to take the most effectual precautions for keeping them virtuous whilst they continue to hold their public trust.[54]

"I'll restate that in case you were confused by the wording. Madison suggested that there was a need to put virtuous people in office, and then to take precautions to *keep* them virtuous while they are there. But this is not what America does. You let the tyrants and scoundrels come up here and have their way, and then when they lie, cheat, and steal, you turn a blind eye to it, and let them stay in office to do more of the same. Generally speaking, you pick corrupt officers, and then you protect their corruption while they're in office. And so I ask you again that most important question: what kind of people are you?"

Benjamin True looked out over the audience, and after a brief pause, he said, "You have forgotten how to feel the appropriate shame for your own failures. And you have dismissed that most obvious of good human habits, self-correction. You have proved quite simply to be not the sort of people who have what it takes to maintain a government of the sort that the framers designed. You and the generations before you have all failed to rise to the challenge. And I hesitate to say that because certain people who are deep in error about the state of humankind, such as Senator Earhart here, will be quick to chalk it all up to what they call 'the Fall' and to what they call man's 'total depravity.' That's a ridiculous explanation for what we see, but it's certainly an easy explanation. And it has the added benefit—for the dishonest person— of tending to excuse humans for their bad behavior. They simply have to claim that they could not help it, and that it is their very nature to fail in such things.

"Well, if you are doomed to live such a sorry existence by your very nature—or by the God who supposedly created that nature—then you are in a sorry state indeed, and ought never bother to try to fix anything. But you all know better. Even the staunchest believer among you in this false notion of involuntary depravity still seeks to exercise his free will to do better in *some* cases. Indeed, who among you, having turned the TV to the wrong channel for the game says to him- or herself, *'Oh well, poor and depraved soul that I am, I shall be resigned to watching this shop-at-home channel instead of the ballgame I wished to watch because my utter and inescapable depravity leaves me powerless to correct my erroneous choice of channels'*? Who is like that? No one!

None of you are quite *that* stupid. You all know that in the real world, an error can be corrected. You know that you can try again and get it right the second time—and if not then, then the third time. To say that you cannot is nothing more—and nothing less—than a lie by which you absolve yourselves of responsibility in this real world."

The mood in the House was now quite somber, and pausing from his speech, Benjamin True stepped back to his right to pick up the gold bar he had previously set on the desk. He held up the gold bar and said, "I have used this gold bar as a symbol for things that must have strong protection if they are to be kept safe. This is somewhat ironic, though, as those from whom such a gold bar would need to be protected are the sort not to have heard or understood a word I've said in this entire demonstration. It is because they are the sort of people who do not value the great principles of life that they lust so much after the gold. They are sadly mistaken in their belief that riches are the highest possible prize in life. And even if they attain to great wealth, they discover that they are no better people than they were before. This floor is nearly filled with such empty as that—chasing after the money and power, as if it really meant something to have it. And they don't care where they get it from. They don't care if they've earned it, or if they've cheated someone else out of it, or if they've stolen it otherwise. They just think that having it is what life is about. And what a terrible miscalculation that is. Such people have no business running a government or a corporation, nor sitting in any seat of public trust. Yet these are the people that typify your culture.

"And it runs through both of your major political parties. Even though most of you pride yourselves that you belong to one party rather than to the other, this much is obvious to any objective observer: Even if the other party were to leave the Planet Earth *en masse*, never to return again, those of your own party who are in such seats of power are so corrupt as to bring about no real change for the better, even if the whole world were left to them. You have got to get rid of such people. And you must guard the government against people of this sort. These things are self-evident."

True's tone suddenly lightened. "So, I'm done with my gold bar demonstration, and I don't need this anymore." He turned to his right, and then to his left. "Who here on the floor of this House Chamber deserves this gold bar tonight?"

The crowd was a little taken back by the question, but the interest of many was quickly piqued and they could be seen to sit forward in their chairs. True repeated his query while glancing about the room, "Who here deserves to have this gold bar?" Those at the floor level were fairly guarded, though many in the Gallery above were fidgeting and some even dared to raise their hands, not understanding that he was not offering it to anyone in the Gallery.

"Surely some among you in government think that your public service is worthy of this reward—that your accomplishments have not been properly rewarded by your salaries, and that you deserve some further compensation for your years of work. So, let's see which of you will stand up to say so—or do you already have plenty of gold bars at home?"

The laughter at this helped to soften the mood of the room even more, and True knew that some of those in government were considering whether they should answer. Of course, they wanted the gold bar, but they had other practical considerations, so this was quite a test of their priorities.

"OK, going once..." said True.

Immediately, Senator Paula Wolfowitz raised her hand from where she sat and exclaimed, "I deserve it!"

She was sitting in the middle of the second row of the section that was the farthest to True's left. He turned her direction and took three steps to where one would step down from the second level of the rostrum to the first. Still holding the gold bar, he was now about 16 feet from the senator and at a position slightly higher than hers.

True addressed the volunteer, "And tell us, Senator, why do you think you deserve it?"

"Well," she replied, "I've been in the Senate for 13 years and have served on several committees during that time. I even served as the Chairman on of one of them. And I have written several successful bills that did a lot of good for the American people."

"I see," said True. So, you deserve some extra compensation for your service?"

"Yes, the salary one gets for being in the Senate may seem large, but it doesn't come close to compensating for the career I left, nor for the family time I have given up as a mother trying to be a public servant."

True examined her a bit, "So when you were elected, what was the salary for a Senator?"

"It was $186,000," she replied, "which is the same as it is for a Representative in the House."

"That's too much money," yelled a voice from the Gallery.

Benjamin True didn't look away from the Senator, but he raised the "wait a minute" finger and said, "I'll speak to that point when we're done here."

Then he continued with the Senator. "So, you took the job at $186,000 per year, and then you came back for more, twice now, at the same rate of pay?"

Wolfowitz was not sure where True was going with this, but she thought she had little choice but to appear forthcoming. "Right."

"Well, if you thought you were being shafted, why did you come back?" he prodded.

"One doesn't just serve for oneself, but for the good of the country," she defended.

"And were the bills you passed good for the country indeed?"

"Of course, they were!" she answered.

"Then you got what you wanted," True said, shortly.

This had puzzled her. "Huh?"

"I asked why you would seek reelection to a job that didn't pay enough and you said that you were doing it in part for the good of the country. Then you told me that you had indeed succeeded in doing what was good for the country. So, the way I see it, you got your $186,000 a year for thirteen years, *plus* the very good of the country that you were striving to accomplish."

True paused to let it be plain that she didn't know how to answer. "I'm a pretty good judge of character, and I still think that you think, deep down in your heart, that you deserve this gold bar for your efforts. Am I not even a teensy bit right about this? Now be honest?"

"Yes." She murmured.

"I doubt many others heard that," said True, "because you were suddenly mumbling for some reason. Would you care to speak up so that everyone can hear you?"

"Yes! I said yes!" she said loudly this time, feigning the confidence that she lacked.

Looking to the crowd, True smiled and said, "OK, I'll tell you what. I'm going to lay this gold bar down right here on this desk. Then I'll give you a thinking problem to solve, and if you get it right, you can have the gold bar. I'll state the problem and you'll have sixty seconds to answer."

True looked out to the rest of the crowd and said, "And just to be sure there's no cheating, I'm going to freeze everybody again so that you can't talk or give signals to the senator." With a wave of his hand, they were all frozen in place and silent, except for Senator Wolfowitz.

"OK, Senator, I'm going to give you what is called the *Linda Problem*. And I'll put it up on the walls, too—and I'll also allow the audience to turn their heads as needed to see it. Here goes:

> *Linda is 31 years old, single, outspoken, and very bright. She majored in philosophy. As a student, she was deeply concerned with issues of discrimination and social justice, and also participated in anti-nuclear demonstrations.*
>
> *Which is more probable?*
>
> *A. Linda is a bank teller.*
>
> *B. Linda is a bank teller and is active in the feminist movement.*"[55]

Having stated the question aloud, True said to the senator, "You have sixty seconds to answer, and you can read the question again for yourself if you need to."

Senator Wolfowitz already had an answer in mind, but she read the problem again for good measure. Her lips were moving, and every once in a while, one of the words slipped out at a whisper.

"B," she answered. "Linda is a bank teller and is active in the feminist movement."

"Is that your final answer?" asked Benjamin True.

"Yes," she replied.

True looked out to the crowd without giving any hint as to whether she was right or wrong. "The senator has answered 'B'. How many of you agree with her? I'll free you all so that you can raise your hands."

There was an audible rush as over eighty percent of those in the room raised their hands.

"Once again, you have answered in a way that is typical of most people. The Senator is wrong. Linda is more likely a bank teller than she is a bank teller who is active in the feminist movement. This is a very common cognitive error called the Conjunction Fallacy. It shows just how poor a grasp most people have on matters of basic probability—that is, on the likelihood that something is true, or that it will happen. The fact of the matter is that meeting one condition is always more likely than meeting two conditions. It just is; that's how reality works. But a lot of people get this wrong. More than four out of five people, in fact. And, as if you aren't bad enough at probability, you get suckered in by the Coherence Bias, where you just can't resist a story that seems to make sense to you, even if it means that you're going to have to ignore some long-established rules of math to believe it. And that's what a lot of you did with this Linda Problem. You were just certain that a woman who meets the description given would also be active in the feminist movement. So, you got it wrong.

"And this is yet another huge problem in your society; you don't even teach the basics of probabilistic thinking to your school students—and even worse, once you become adults, you don't see to it that you learn it for yourselves—even after misjudging situation after situation. In fact, many millions of people, having missed this problem tonight, will likely never look into it any further. And the next time they're faced with a problem of this sort, they'll likely repeat the same errors they made tonight.

"Another huge area of neglect in your learning is logic. You do slightly better at it than you do with probability, but still, a great many people make basic logic errors regularly, and it gets them into trouble. But this simply isn't important enough to your culture to rate more than a six-week module in tenth grade math class. What you don't understand is that humans are built to learn, and that's not supposed to stop when you turn 18 or 22. When you keep running into problems, you're supposed to take that as a cue to stop and figure some things out. What you don't understand is that:

Self-correction is the rightful duty of all humans.[56]

"When you learn that you are wrong about something, you're supposed to correct yourselves. And you're certainly capable of doing it. So really, it comes down to whether you're the sort of person to care about personal authenticity.

"And you, Senator Wolfowitz, could have learned a long time ago that meeting two conditions is less likely than meeting one, but you didn't. So, you just lost yourself a gold bar. But that gives me an opportunity to make just one more point with it."

Turning again to the crowd, True said, "Who in this room deserves this gold bar?"

They were tentative about answering. Many trusted him by now, but were afraid to look foolish. On the other hand, at over half a million dollars, it was quite a big opportunity to let it slip away without trying. But before any of those who were still thinking about it had a chance to decide, he interrupted them.

"*Nobody* in this room deserves this! That's because it has real value, and nobody here has done anything that amounts to an even trade for this gold bar. That's the only way you deserve something; you make an even trade for it. Either you trade your labor for it, or you trade something else of equal value for it—something that is rightfully yours.

"Now, I used this gold bar to serve as a metaphor for your government. I told you that some things are just too valuable to be left unguarded, because they will be stolen by those to whom they do not rightfully belong. And you need to know that it's not just this way with government. There are many other things of very high value that you dare not foolishly entrust to people who are not trustworthy. Education comes to mind. And religion, of course. A fool or a scoundrel in either of those fields can do a lot of harm. And so it is with your food and medicine. You need to be as careful with what goes in your mouths as you should be with what goes into your minds. Yet you have rarely any idea what's in the food you eat and the medicine you take. You trust far too much to people whose motives and qualifications you never examine. And even when you get hints that your trust in them has been poorly invested, you generally continue to suffer under that investment without making a change. Self-correction is not only the rightful duty of all humans, but it is a necessary tactic for guarding what is important in life."

True bent down and picked up the gold bar from the desk in front of him. "And these things I have just said to you—they are worth many times more than this gold bar. It is just a material thing that will never make any person more authentic. And so it is very easy for me—easier than for most of you—to simply let this gold bar go."

With that, Benjamin True shifted the gold bar's mass into both his hands and he tossed it high above him into the air—so high that those in the gallery above could see it at eye level. And then it simply burst into flames and was no more. At this, the audience was visibly disappointed, for the most part, and sighs could be heard all around.

"You have such high hopes for money," he told them all. "Why don't you have high hopes for the treasures you could hold in your own minds? This certainly says a great deal about what kind of people you are."

Chapter 13

How Did You Get That?

Senator Paula Wolfowitz just didn't know when to surrender. She stood up and told True, "I don't think you're all righteous like you think you are. You're obviously here toying with us. These are hard times, and now you're accusing of us wrongdoing for wanting to have what we need."

True looked at her. "It is still true, Senator, that:

> *those who desire to be rich fall into temptation, into a snare,*
> *into many senseless and harmful desires that plunge people*
> *into ruin and destruction?* [57]

Look at you; you're in it. And you just seem to dig yourself in deeper and deeper. You should give some serious thought to changing your ways."

"Changing *what* ways?" she demanded with offense.

"OK, that was a very foolish question, Senator. You'd have done better just to stop where you were, but now you've asked me to address your ways. And I can get a good start on that by asking you one question: How is it, Senator Paula Wolfowitz, that the day you were sworn into office 13 years ago, you had about $750,000 to your name, but today, after 13 years of service at $186,000 per year, you have over $22,000,000 in cash and other holdings?"

The senator had no reply, and had figured out that even if she did, it probably wasn't the best strategy to give it.

"Let's do the math," said True. "And let's make sure that everyone here and at home can follow along." Turning to the crowd, and pointing to the Gallery, he said, "Everyone look to the panels along the walls in the Gallery, and follow my math." Then with a finger, he drew in the air as he spoke aloud. "Dollar sign, one eight six comma zero zero zero…"

As he spoke, each character appeared in blazing white letters like a plasma stream, along each of the many blue-wallpapered panels behind the Gallery seats. Each panel was about fifteen feet squared, and the characters he was writing appeared about eighteen inches high. Interestingly, the crowd was more shocked by this display than by anything that had happened the entire evening, though to Benjamin True, it was merely a utilitarian effort that was not meant to impress.

He continued as he wrote the multiplication problem in standard format for all to see, "…times one three, and the line goes under here." When he had finished writing the problem, he looked up to one of the many panels to examine his work:

$$\begin{array}{r} \$186{,}000 \\ \underline{\times\,13} \end{array}$$

"Have I set up the problem correctly?" he asked aloud.

"Yes," Came the reply from many in the hall.

He went on, "OK, three times zero is zero, which goes down here. And then we do that again with this other zero, and again with this third one. Now, three times six equals eighteen, so we write down the eight and carry the one. Then three times eight…"

Benjamin True knew exactly what he was doing. He was making painstaking work of this ordinary multiplication problem to show how easy it is to prove the senator's corruption. And he knew it was making her quite uncomfortable, along with almost every other person on the floor of the House.

"…is twenty-four, plus the one we carried is twenty-five, so we bring down the two and carry the other two. OK, that's the hard part. And now we multiply that top number by the one here—and I think we can all agree to dispense with the digit-by-digit narration on this one…"

They found this funny enough for a brief chuckle—even some of those who pretty much knew that they themselves were in trouble.

"So down here we write one eight six zero zero zero. And then we add them. Let's see," he said, writing from right to left, "zero, zero, zero. Eight plus zero is eight. Five plus six is eleven, so I write one one down here and carry the other. Now five plus eight is thirteen, plus the one I carried—that's fourteen, so I write down the four and carry the one. And now one plus one is two. OK, this gives us a total of two million, four hundred eighteen thousand dollars. Did I get that right? Somebody check my math."

"It's right!" said one.

"Uh-huh!" chimed in a few more from the Gallery, who seemed to be getting a grip on the level of corruption in play.

"Would anyone care to dispute this answer?" asked True.

There was no reply.

"Well, Senator, it would appear that you should have actually *earned* $2,418,000 during your time here so far---give or take a bit. But your total wealth equals over $22 million. Oh, wait, I shouldn't just *say* that; I should *show* it. Here's your personal financial statement, compiled for you by your accountant just over two weeks ago."

When he said this, the math problem on every other panel in the Gallery disappeared and was replaced with an imagine of the senator's financial document—a one-page document saying "Personal Financial Statement" across the top.

"OK, let's see here," said Benjamin True. "I think we should find the total down at the bottom. Yes, here it is!" He made a circle in the air with his writing finger, and a blazing red circle appeared on each wall panel around the number $22, 361,740.03.

Senator Wolfowitz jumped up, livid. "How did you get that?"

"You know, Senator, since you're quite in the habit of lying for a living, it would have been cleverer for you to jump up and say something like 'That's a lie!' or 'Those aren't my numbers!' But you didn't. Instead, you've practically validated the record as being your actual financial statement. And as to how I got it, you appear to be working under the impression that your secrets are hidden to the entire universe. But as you can see, that is incorrect."

This deeply rattled almost every member of the government present, for it was very rare to be among them and not be taking money under the table in one way or another.

True continued, "What's really noteworthy about you, Senator, is that on top of all this corruption, you had the brazen boldness to speak up and argue that you 'deserve' a gold bar worth another half million or so. And for demonstrating all that to the people who are watching across this world, I thank you dearly, for it means so much more coming from you than it would from me. Did you really think that you could lie to me and have it go undetected?"

She had no reply, of course, and put her forehead down in her hands.

"You know, folks, it's pretty common knowledge that a couple million in the bank is all it takes to live comfortably off the interest for the rest of one's life. Yet here she is with ten times that amount. So, what's she planning on doing with all that extra money? Is she going to feed the poor with it? Pay off the debts of those in need? Is she going to build houses for the poor? Well, perhaps she is, but to date, she has never donated a dime of it to anybody. So, it would be hard to make a case that she intends to do anything with it but to hoard it for herself—as if she can take it with her whenever she dies. And I think that everybody here knows that that's not how it works.

"Now, the more compelling question than what she plans to do with it is the question of how she got it. Most of it came in the same way that most of the rest of you get it—from making deals with big-money interests who would pay her money and other perks if she would help to pass certain legislation that helped them earn more money. And much of this ill-gotten gain comes, of course, at the expense of the taxpaying public. That's you folks at home. You have been robbed, indirectly, to pay this lady so that she can make a show of what a sacrifice she's making to be here getting twenty-two million dollars in thirteen years. And in return for her hard work, those in government who are supposed to prosecute her for this crime turn a blind eye, just as they are manipulated by various means to do. And there you have it—a case study of a Member of Congress."

Benjamin True walked back to the lectern in the center of the second tier and said, "Now as you all know, I don't have all night here, but I do have time to go over the finances of just one or two of the other office holders here tonight. Who should I pick? I know, to save time, let's just ask for volunteers! Anyone? Anyone? Bueller? Anyone?". This was his best imitation of Ben Stein's role in *Ferris Bueller's Day Off*, and it was pretty good. It drew some laughs from the Gallery, but not from the House floor. Even the couple of officials whose finances were actually clean were so nervous that perhaps they had inadvertently done something wrong that they didn't want to be on the hot seat, either.

"OK," continued True, "while you're all thinking about who wants to go next, let me answer the person who shouted out that $186,000 is too much salary for a Member of Congress. A lot of people agree with this, and they're tired of being ripped off by this criminal Congress. But this is the sort of question that deserves some deeper thinking—if you want to get it right. Yes, it would sting this Congress of oath breakers and thieves if you were to lower their salary, but it would also sting you, too. If you lower the salary substantially, then the ordinary man or woman out there who would be willing to come to Washington to serve as a representative or a senator in the interest of righteousness and justice wouldn't be able to do it. Think about it. If you quit your job and leave home for two or six years, what are you going to do when you get back? You'd better have some money saved up to get you through the transition. So, I don't have a problem with the salary like it is. Now, I will agree with many of you that it makes no sense to give them a pension and benefits for life, like they get if they can manage to stay here for five years. No, they ought to have to work for a living like everybody else, and not be sponging off the taxpayers like that. But you can look into that later."

"Now, where were we?" he said as he looked about the government. "I'm going to assume that since no one is raising their hand to go next, that you all would prefer just to dispense with any further finance-exposing sessions. Is that right?"

There was laughter at this, and naturally, lots of relief. But Benjamin True wasn't done making his presence known. He turned to President Hernandez. "How about you, Mister President? Is it OK with you if we don't talk about your finances?" He received no response but a sullen face—just as he expected. Then he turned to Vice President Linda Surgeon, who was still seated at the top tier of the rostrum by Speaker DuBois. "How about you, Madam Vice President?" Again, no response. "And you, Chief Justice Wendell Stone?" he said, pointing to the old man. "Or how about you, Associate Justice Wilkinson?" he said while pointing to another of the black-robed court. "Maybe Senator Earhart, or Admiral Rupert G. Haskins here, or Representative Willie Gutchens over there?"

They all remained expressionless.

"No? None of you? It would be so hard to choose just one, because there are so many very interesting examples of grifters assembled in this room. Just one of you could make it easier on us all by volunteering. How about House Majority Leader Frida Gonzalez, would you like to take a turn, ma'am? Or Minority Leader Thompson Segal?

"I could go on and on," True continued, realizing exactly how agonizingly uncomfortable he was making them all. "I haven't even addressed the Executive Cabinet members. What a pity." He shook his head along with this. "Maybe we'll have time for more later," he said, as he began to step lively back up to his lectern.

When he got there, he bent to whisper to Speaker of the House William DuBois, "Don't lose the conviction you've been feeling, nor the urge to set things right. I'm going to help you do the right thing in just a little bit."

DuBois nodded sincerely.

Turning back to his lectern and its microphone, True continued to speak. "If you recall, I have been generally addressing the American public—and this little session of *Show and Tell* with the finances of the Members of Congress has been primarily for your benefit. You all know it's happening. Even your movies and TV shows are about it. You even have movies about the corruption in the CIA and the FBI, and about political assassinations and such. You all know about it, but almost every single one of you is content to *do* nothing at all about it. This is not good.

"What kind of people are you? And I'm talking to all you Americans listening or watching from wherever you are outside this hall tonight. Contrary to what you might wish to believe, you are responsible for what your government does. You are responsible for this corruption. You fund it, you tolerate it, you sit idly by and watch it happen, and then you turn right around and vote for the same scoundrels to take their same seats again and again."

"And some of you are tied up in it even deeper than that. That's right— and you at home need to brace yourselves because things are about to get uncomfortable again. You have many Federal departments in this government, but only a few are actually authorized under the Constitution. And several millions of you work for those unconstitutional departments. So, you're earning a living off of the lawlessness that earns these tyrants a fortune.

"Then there are those of you who are earning a living off of various unconstitutional government payouts designed to keep you from working. And there are those of you who get unconstitutional grants for this or that purpose—or whose careers are in companies or universities or other institutions that get such illegal grants from the Federal Government. It's like I said earlier about tyranny: Many people, it turns out, don't really object to tyranny after all, as long as they get to be the tyrants—or in your case, as long as they get to profit as servants of the tyrant. That's what you're doing. And what a pity it is, for you are ensnared by it, and you're unlikely to figure that out. You're like the victims of the monkey trade—those small primates who are captured by way of their own cognitive limitations. The monkey trapper makes a trap from a small wooden box or coconut. He bores a small hole in it, big enough for the monkey to get its open hand through, but not its closed fist. The trapper stuffs a piece of fruit in it as bait and attaches the trap firmly to a tree or a post. When the monkey comes and smells the fruit, it reaches in and grabs it, but it can't get its fruit-filled fist back out of the hole. And worse, it lacks the intelligence to figure out that all it has to do is to let go of the fruit so that it can remove its empty hand and free itself. And that's how you trap a monkey.

"And that's how you get trapped, too. But there's a difference between you and those monkeys—a very big difference. In the monkey's case, they simply don't have the intelligence—as a species—to solve that puzzle. But in your case, every single one of you that is of normal brain health could solve that puzzle. This means that in your case, a lack of intelligence is not the problem. Your problem is not that you can't figure it out, but that you don't want to. No, you don't want to think through all this, determining the most honest, rational, and responsible course of action. You prefer instead to engage various cognitive biases—those corrupted mini-programs of thinking that run by habit in your minds. You train yourselves to think things like, 'But I need this job, so it must be OK for me to keep it,' or 'But I need this grant, so it must be OK for me to take it'. Or you think, 'It's not my fault that the government is paying out money to get this job done, so, therefore, I'm not at fault for taking this job.' Or you think, 'Well, that's nice and all, but I have no other choice but to take this money.' No, you always have a choice. You *always*," he stressed, "have a choice."

"That monkey can't get out of the trap because it can't figure out that it has to let go of the fruit to free itself. You, on the other hand, having been granted by nature with more than enough cognitive faculties to figure it out, simply *choose* not to free yourselves from the trap of public corruption because you prefer being corrupt to being honest.

"You live stupidly on purpose because you'd rather have possessions than to have a self that's worth having. And your stupidity is quite obvious. For example, you are always talking about 'conspiracy theory' as if it's some impossible and mythical idea that two bad guys might actually conspire together to do something bad. But if you want to see a real conspiracy at work, all you have to do is to turn on C-SPAN on any day that Congress is in session, and you can watch these people right here conspiring together to violate the very Constitution they *all* took an oath to protect and defend. Rarely does this Congress enact anything that is actually within their lawful and limited powers to enact, and when they do that, it's often for ulterior motives that they do not want you to discover. But really, how hard is that with a public that is intent on keeping its eyes shut?

"So, you and your media continue with this 'conspiracy theory' talk, as if it were absolutely impossible that two or more people or companies might actually conspire together to defraud or abuse the people of the United States. And if you really want to get into some irony about all this, go do your homework, and you'll see that your own CIA coined this term, 'conspiracy theory' in 1967 with a view toward painting any theory about any conspiracy as if it were necessarily some irrational and ridiculous idea. [58] Well, this deceit worked wonderfully on a public that was just looking for an excuse not to have to deal with the ugly realities of the undermining of their own government.

"And so you continue to shut down the ones who want to tell you the truth about things you'd rather not hear. Indeed, is this not the very reason one of your snipers aimed a bullet at my head this very night? Yes, it is.

"Now, I know that not all of you are murderers. Only a few of you are murderers. The rest of you simply conspire to help the murderers, and you enjoy the perks of the job while getting to pretend that your own roles in it simply aren't 'that bad'. And those of you at home, I'm sure you'd rather not be tied into this. I'm sure you'd rather be off the hook, and not held responsible for what goes on here, but this has your names written all over it."

Chapter 14

The Coin of Rights

"I'll show you what kind of people you are." True reached into the pocket of his white knickers, saying, "When I was alive here, I practiced some sleight of hand for fun, and it's much less impressive now that I have superhuman powers. But I want to show you something, and you can figure out whether it's mere trickery or superhuman powers." He pulled from his pocket a thick copper coin and held it up for all to see. "This is big for a coin, but still small for viewing at a distance, so I want you all to look back up on the walls to see what I'm doing."

The crowd shifted as necessary to view those wall-papered panels in the Gallery again. Senator Wolfowitz's personal financial statement and the math problem had since disappeared, and now a moving image of Benjamin True's hand and his coin could be seen quite clearly on each panel. The coin was not quite two inches across in actual size but appeared a few feet across on the wall panels.

"I call this the Coin of Rights," he said, showing the front of the coin to everyone. It had a pyramid centered on its face and was bordered by a circle of stars. Underneath the pyramid in bold letters was the word, "RIGHTS." Beneath that was some much smaller text, which they could not read well yet, since he was still moving about a bit as he spoke.

"America considers her rights with the dull assumption that she has it all figured out, more or less. But she has hardly a clue as to what's on the back side of that coin. She boasts and brags about her rights and how she deserves this and that, yet she never seems to figure out how it is that her rights are eroding generation by generation, decade by decade."

True now held particularly still so that the small words at the bottom of the coin could be read by all. "It says down here...," he said, looking at the coin and pointing with his left hand. He read it aloud:

"A TRIFLE TO CLAIM ~ A FEAT TO MAINTAIN"

He looked forward to the crowd again and said, "Any person can claim that he has rights, but very few know how to preserve them. Indeed, the fool thinks that the most important thing about himself as a citizen is that he has rights. He sees this pyramid as a trophy to boast about, even to wave his flag about, but he has no idea how to secure and to maintain those rights. And he has no idea that he's only seeing part of the picture."

Benjamin True used his left pointer finger to spin the coin like a globe pinched between the forefinger and thumb of his right hand, turning it half way to reveal the back. Centered on the rear was a larger pyramid, with its top missing. And beneath this one was the word, "DUTY."

"This side," he explained, "is where the heart of authentic citizenship lies. That little pyramid of Rights on the front sits atop this big foundation of Duty."

He looked over at the coin again and said, "Look carefully at the base of the pyramid. See the ground beneath it?"

There was a little murmur from the crowd as they noticed what he was pointing out.

"Hardly anybody ever notices that there is no such ground on the front of the coin."

He spun the coin back around to show its front side.

"There is no ground here. No, this pyramid of rights is floating in the air. It is not grounded like real pyramids are. Indeed, I'll venture to say that none of you have ever seen a real pyramid floating in the air, and that's because in this real world, pyramids don't float in the air. But this one does, because the idea of Rights without Duty is not a real-world idea."

He spun the coin once again to show the back.

"And just what is your duty? Read it here."

Pointing to the small words underneath "DUTY", he read:

"REFUSE UNJUST LAW AND LAWLESS RULER ALIKE"

"A lot of you think that your duty is to pay your taxes and to vote. And some of you, in addition to that, think that your duty consists of one thing more: obeying the government like good little girls and boys, even when the government is in the wrong. But this is all very ignorant. In fact, you're so ignorant—and I don't say that to be mean, but to be accurate—that only a few of you in this room understand that I didn't just pull these two words, "RIGHTS" and "DUTY" out of thin air, but that they come right out your founding document. You should know this, but you don't."

He put the coin down on the lectern and continued to speak.

"I'm going to remind you of those highly-principled words that Thomas Jefferson wrote into your Declaration of Independence—the words that were signed by 56 statesmen who knew they were risking their lives merely by signing it, and much more, if they should actually carry

143

out the words written in it. He wrote—and I'll translate because you don't all speak this same language anymore. And I'll put the words up on the walls.

"Now, for those of you who wonder if I'm about to take you to school, I am. So it's time to put on your thinking caps and think through this, because there's not going to be any recess until this lesson is over. So here is a short section from the Declaration of Independence."

As he gestured to the upper walls in the gallery, some words appeared on its panels in a silvery text that glowed steadily. The first was this line, which Benjamin True narrated as it appeared.

> ... *when a long train of abuses and usurpations,*

"OK, a usurpation is a power grab," he explained.

Then more text appeared, and he read:

> ... *when a long train of abuses and usurpations, pursuing invariably the same object...*

"Now," he explained, "object here means goal or objective, so he's saying that when that long train of abuses and power grabs is constantly pursuing the same goal..."

Then another line was added on the walls, and he read aloud the newest addition:

> ... *evinces a design to reduce them under absolute despotism ...*

"This one is packed, so let's work it out. To *evince* is to reveal the evidence of something, or to *be* the evidence of something. And the word *design* here means a plan. So, he's saying that when a long train of abuses and power grabs reveals a plan to reduce them---that's the people he's talking about. And he goes on: to reduce them, the people, under absolute despotism—that means to put them under total governmental rule, where the ruler or rulers have absolute power, and the people have no rights, except whatever may please the rulers. OK, all this so far is just setting the stage for the point that the Declaration is about to make. So, let's review it one last time up to this point to be sure we're ready for the punch line. He's saying that when a long train of abuses and power grabs is always pursuing the same goal of putting the people under total tyranny, then what?"

True paused for effect. "What should the people do when things get this bad?" He paused again for a few seconds. "Let's see what the founders said about it."

Another line appeared on the wall, underneath what was already there. Benjamin True read it:

> it is their right, it is their duty, to throw off such government, and to provide new guards for their future security.

"OK, fortunately, your society still understands the word, 'right'. And you understand the word, 'duty'—at least in theory. But what is this about 'new guards for their future security'? He's saying they need to put new people into power—people who will guard them against such tyranny in the future.

"Now, don't miss this part. He said it was their *right* to put new people in power. This means they are entitled to do it, and nobody can rightly say that they can't. So, this word, *'right'*, is making a very important statement, and you need to notice it for sure."

When he said this, this word grew bolder on the walls, and pulsed a bit.

"And then this other word—this is where it really gets challenging. This other word is *duty*."

Now both words, right and duty, were pulsing in boldface.

"Here's the part that some people really hate. He says it's not only your right to change your government, but your *duty* to do it. This means that you are actually obligated to do something, and that nobody can rightly say that you're not responsible for doing it. This was what they believed, and I'm going to tell you that they were right. Americans—just like all people on the Earth—Americans have a natural duty to establish and keep a just and righteous government."

"So, remember this—and especially those two words, *right* and *duty*, and now I'm going to show you what kind of people you are."

He picked up his Coin of Rights again from the lectern, and said, "Look at this coin. As I showed you, it says on one face, 'Rights', and on the opposite, 'Duty.' Here's what kind of people you are. America—and I'm going to speak of you as a whole here because this is what the great majority of you are like—America loves the Coin of Rights for its front side only, and she begrudges its back side—the side called 'Duty'.

Rights and freedom and such, she thinks, are for herself, and duty is for someone else. Both sides, of course, come on the same coin, but what does she do? America fumbles about with the Coin of Rights, trying to devise a way to tuck the RIGHTS side safely away in her pocket while leaving the DUTY side out. This is why she can never truly have what she wants. Until she can embrace *both* sides, she will never truly own the side she now prefers.

"There's no way around it friends. You can't separate the two—not in the real world. Here, watch this."

Benjamin True held the coin high with the Rights side forward. "Now, suppose I had a magical knife that could slice this coin in half between its two faces—which I do…"

There was some laughter as he produced a knife from thin air. The knife was not unlike a typical steak knife, and he held it in his left hand as he held the coin in his right, with his thumb on the back side and his index and middle fingers on the front.

"If I had such a knife as this, I could slice this coin into two separate disks like this." The knife passed smoothly down the coin, through its center, between the heads and tails, separating the one coin into two, each being half the thickness of the original. Then the knife vanished from his hand and he spread the front and back halves slightly, one going to the right, and the other to the left, until it was plain that the coin now existed in two pieces where there had once been but one.

Many in the audience were impressed with this, forgetting that it might not be a display of sleight of hand skills, after all, but an act of supernatural power.

"See, this is what most of you try to do. You try to separate the rights from the duty—you want the freedom without the responsibility. So you work up some imaginary knife in your minds, by which to separate the two. You cut off the Duty side so that you can throw it away."

With his left thumb and forefinger, he pinched the Duty half of the coin and lifted it straight up above the Rights half. The cut side was facing forward, and it was as smooth as glass, having no words or figures on it. He slowly turned it around to reveal the original Duty side, which all could see clearly on the wall panels, and then he raised it up and gave it a push upwards into the air, where it was immediately consumed in flames.

"You toss it away and pretend yourselves vainly into a world where rights exist without duty. And now, you think, you have what you want—you think you have got a grasp on dutiless rights."

He held the remaining half—the Rights side—forward, and the image that showed on each wall panel zoomed in closely.

"But it's a lie, for you can't have rights without duties—not in the real world. Wherever the one exists, so does the other." With this, he pointed to the word "Rights" on the front side, and slowly turned the coin around, revealing that it did not have a mirror-smooth and blank backside as everyone expected, but that the back appeared exactly as had the back of the original coin. The word Duty was plain for all to see.

"This is why the United States have failed."

This produced an uncomfortable murmur from the audience.

"Yes, it's another radical point—from your perspective—to be sure, but it's the truth. What you currently have in your minds is an imaginary state in which you pretend to have such high ideals, but to have them without having to do anything to maintain them. Don't get me wrong; it's a very real state for these who run it—and their masters, of course. But what you call 'America' doesn't really exist, except in your imaginations.

"The Union has failed on account of a miscalculation in this experiment of government. Nobody had tried this before in this same way. The big question—the big risk—was whether the people could be counted on to uphold the founding principles and to discipline their government as needed to keep it righteous. Obviously, the people did *not* do it, or else the current state of lawlessness in government could not exist. But *could* they have done it? *Could* they have kept it straight if they had thought it was worth the effort? Now *there's* a great question!

"Yes, they most certainly could have," he answered himself. "The only thing that stopped them were their own lack of interest in it, which was compounded by their own lack of learning.

"Even as I am speaking, a few of you listening have it burning inside you right now—the desire to fix things. And many of the rest of you are willing to do *something*, at least, provided someone else will show you how. But think on this: How many of you have actually been *trained* in these things? How many of you were taught from childhood about the

Constitution and the—*accurate*—history of this country? How many of you were taught that the proper maintaining of the government would require both rights *and* duty? How many of you were groomed by your parents for public service? Very few, indeed. And it makes perfect sense because in a culture where few people embrace their natural duty, few people train their children to embrace it.

"But what if they *had*? What if *your* parents had trained you in this way? Would you be a different kind of people than you are? Indeed, you would—many of you. And I can tell you that there are indeed enough of you to make a difference, if you're willing to work, and to work smartly at it. It's up to you to choose what to make of yourselves now—and what to make of your children—at least as far as it is up to you to train them well.

"But mark my words; what lies before you is no small task. You are in a mess that is much bigger than I could define in one evening. But I'll tell you this—and this is good news when you think about it: almost every bit of the mess you are in has to do with the poor use of the brains you have been given. I keep asking what kind of people you are, and if you really want to sum up what a person is like, just look at how he or she habitually uses his or her brain. How many things does a person believe that are not true? How careful is a person to catch the details? How often does the person overgeneralize or oversimplify? How often does the person correct him- or herself when it's obvious that there's an error in play? These are the kinds of habits that show as much as anything else what kind of people you are. These are your core habits— the very basis of your characters. And the chief among them is whether you will base your thinking in reality, or whether you prefer something else as a basis for it—something like wishes, or lies, even—such as this silly notion that rights can thrive when duty is neglected.

"If I were to tell you how many things you have got wrong—how many things you are just plain wrong about—it would blow your minds. But it is not my goal here to blow your minds; it is my goal to goad you into heading the right direction. And so I ask you again to trust me when I say that you can indeed head in that direction and you can get somewhere. So, let me just sum up where you stand, and then we'll get on with beginning to do something about it.

"Here's the quick summary of what goes on in this country. The ideals upon which it was officially founded are high ideals. They are not perfect, but they are superior to the *de facto* ideals upon which

148

it is actually run. And they are indeed attainable, but no generation of Americans yet has done a good job of attaining and maintaining. Instead, each generation hands the country off to its kids a little worse than it was when they got it from their own parents. They each kick the can down the road for the next generation to solve—or not. And when that next generation grows up to be quite like their parents, well, they predictably do the same thing.

"But when is it going to stop? These people in power here are sure not going to stop it, because they're profiting quite richly from the status quo. So, you're fools if you think they're going to volunteer themselves out of this artifice and scheme—and many of you vote as if you are thinking exactly that. But who among you is going to stand up and say 'Enough!'? Who will finally say, 'Not on *my* watch!'?

"You have that same age-old problem:

Quis custodiet ipsos custodes?[59]

"That's Latin for 'Who will guard the guards?' You put people in office to guard those various gold bars—those valuable things that ought not be left unguarded. Maybe it's the running of your cities or counties— but you put them in charge, and then you hope that you can simply leave them there unattended while you go off to entertain yourselves with more enjoyable pursuits. And invariably, those guards you put into office fail to do what is right. They are like the proverbial foxes guarding the henhouse. And that makes you the foolish farmers who *ask* the foxes to guard your henhouse while you sit inside and watch TV or surf the Web.

"You fool yourselves that your so-called 'two-party system' will watch the henhouse for you. You entrust the government to these parties based on their rhetoric, and not the reality of their habitual actions. You take their word for what it means to be a Democrat or a Republican, and you rarely notice that there's often a big difference between the official party platform and what their members actually *do* when they get into office. So, you go around promoting one of these two parties, and the people from the other party—who look past the rhetoric and see what your party members actually do in office—they think you are idiots.

"And you think that you've got the media as a backup to help you guard the guards. But you've just left yet another gold bar on the doorstep with the media. You can't leave the search for truth in somebody else's hands and expect that it's going to be done honestly, rationally, and responsibly. No, if you want that, you're going to have to stay on the media *constantly*. But you are a hearsay culture, and it's simply not worth it to you to check things out before you believe them. And as a result, you believe all manner of false things, and much of it fed to you by the very media whom you trust to tell you the truth.

"And you are so easily distracted that it's no wonder you can't get anything done to fix your government. All it takes is for a 'white' man to shoot a 'black' man, or vice versa, and you're at each other's throats over this most idiotic idea of 'race'. You want so badly to be owed something by those you hate, and you'll charge them all with owing it to you, simply based on the color of their skin. Yet you hate it when they do that very thing to you. This is hypocrisy at its core. Wrongdoing is wrongdoing no matter who does it. You don't get a pass because of the color of your skin, nor on account of whether someone once did something wrong to your great-grandfather. And if all this foolishness weren't bad enough, you have agents provocateurs on both sides—people who are being paid or manipulated to murder and assault and riot. And you love your hatred so much that you are suckers for this every time. Every single time. You don't check it out to see if it's really true. No, you *want* it to be true because it gives you an excuse—you think—to continue on with the hatred."

True paused. He had one more thing to say, and it deserved a clean space all unto itself. He spoke more softly this time, with a tone of shame.

"You've even left what may be the most valuable gold bar of all out on the doorstep: the raising of your very own children. You hand them off as wards of the state, and whatever the state wants to teach them—or not—that's pretty much OK with you. Oh, you might complain now and then, but so few of you ever pull your kids out of government school to raise them yourselves. Like I said, it's pretty much OK with you to let the government have its way with your kids. You have forgotten what can be learned from nature: Governments don't have babies; humans do.

"Children are born to human parents, and not to governments. And it doesn't just stop with childbirth; children are designed to be *raised* by parents, and trained by them in the wisdom of the ages—all the things that humankind has learned in its time here. But that all assumes that the parents haven't trained themselves *not* to care about such things.

It assumes that the parents aren't corrupted by selfishness and self-designed ignorance. It assumes that they haven't squandered those treasures that are their own human minds. Parents who have decided to live mindlessly constitute one of the greatest cruelties a child can ever endure. To be born with curiosity into a household that has shunned curiosity is agonizing and demoralizing. And even though the child can choose to resist the parents' huge moral error and keep its own curious spirit anyway, many will not. They will be influenced to give up their own minds to ignorance and bias, too, just like their parents.

"And what is the result of all this? Well, in time, you will end up with so many in the population who avoid reality, including things like hard work and cognitive diligence and self-sustenance, that they are simply too corrupt for the sort of government that was designed for this country. As Ben Franklin put it, they:

> ...become so corrupt as to need despotic government, being incapable of any other.[60]

"Indeed, too many kids show up at school not knowing how to blow their own noses, for no one has ever taught them. They don't know how to behave responsibly, for they have lacked competent parentage. They don't know how to think or how to communicate, so rather than beginning their formal education at age 5 or so, they begin remedial education at that age. They were designed to be taught these things in the intimacy of the home with two parents, but now they must learn them—if they learn them at all—in a crowded classroom where the teachers are outnumbered 20 to 1. And when they get home? Well, they are handed off from the school to the TV or the Internet or to video games, for the parents, tired from avoiding reality all day, are in no mood to be diligent parents in the evenings, either.

"Each generation of people like this tends—when measured all together as a whole—to do a worse job of parenting than did their own parents. They don't have to, of course, for people can pretty much learn whatever they want to learn. But most have never been taught to want what is good, but only what is easy, and they never rise above that in any full sense at all. Sure, they might learn to work hard at a thing or two, but not at *all* of life's important things. No, you have left far too many of life's most important things out on the doorstep to be stolen away by those who would make sinister use of them. And you wonder why things get worse and worse. That is what kind of people you are.

151

"This," he repeated gloomily, *"is what kind of people you are."*

Benjamin True looked down with a somber expression and a slight shaking of his head. The room was silent.

He looked up again and asked, "Where are the Christians? Did you really learn this notion of irresponsibility from Jesus? You, of all people, should be eager for responsibility and self-sacrifice and diligence and endurance and truth. Do not the words *righteousness* and *justice* appear over 350 times in the Bible? Don't the words *wise* and *wisdom* appear nearly 400 times in the Bible? How is it, then, that you have chosen such darkness and foolishness as a way of life?

"And where are the parents? Do you really want to let this mess fester so that it's even worse for your kids and your grandkids when it's *their* watch?

"And where are the senior citizens? Many of you have more time for getting involved than anybody else, but you have let this society put you out to pasture; you've given into the myth that once you retire, you're of no further use to our culture. On the contrary, you *should* be the elders who are the wisest and most learned. You should be *leading* the efforts at reform.

"Indeed," he continued, "where are those of you—of any age—who know better than all this? You might not catch it all, but you daily see at least the *hints* of the dishonesty, irrationality, and irresponsibility that permeates this culture. And you are either worn out, uncertain, or intimidated, so you—the very people who are best-equipped to make a difference—settle for seeing nothing change at all."

Benjamin True shook his head again. No one said anything. Some were simply numb to it all, and weren't processing anything in their minds, for this is what some people have decided to be like. And a few others—very few—were wrestling to keep a grasp on it all—this flood of truthful talk—and were eager to get busy making changes as soon as they could figure out what should come first, for this is what some people have decided to be like. And in between these two groups were the bulk of those listening to True's speech. Despite his assurances that they could indeed handle it all, they felt overwhelmed as if a fire hose had been turned on them. Perhaps they could handle it after all, but *not right now*, it felt. These were eager, not to reject outright what Benjamin True was saying, but to put it off to a more convenient time, for this is how most people have decided to handle matters of fundamental

152

moral importance.

"I am reminded of Yahweh's frustration in dealing with Israel, for they were the same kind of people that you are. He said,

> All day long I have held out my hands to an obstinate people, who walk in ways not good, pursuing their own imaginations...[61]

"There's no such thing in the real world as rights without duty, but you imagine it so as you watch your own country fall apart."

He held up the Coin of Rights again, showing its DUTY side.

"Look what it says again in the small letters:

> Suffer not the law to be unjust, nor the rulers lawless.

"You have failed miserably on both counts. You have lots of laws that are unjust in various ways, and there is no question that the typical American politician is a lawbreaker. But the real problem here is not them; it's *you*. You not only elect and re-elect these people who have proven that they will violate their oaths of office, but you *want* them to violate those oaths. You *want* them to break the rules—to abandon the Rule of Law—because you want them to keep looting the treasury on your behalf. You are so greedy for the little you get that you hardly notice how rich these people have become from this business. You are no more fit than any other people on Earth to maintain an orderly society. It hardly bothers you at all that you are so unruly—that you would rather violate your Constitution than to amend it lawfully. You are indeed an obstinate people, following your own imagination—your own devices—and remaining rebellious to the constraints of reality. You reject the wisdom of the ages—the very things that so many intelligent and wise people invested in so dearly to learn. You don't see it as a treasure handed down to your generation, but as a bother and as a hindrance to your entertainment. You are consumed with yourselves, having little idea of the vast wealth of truth that surrounds you. You squander it, letting it waste away on your watch, to be discovered anew, perhaps, by some future generation who just might see the value in shunning your immoral choice of ignorance and initiating a new renaissance—one in which they will begin terribly behind because of your negligence in maintaining the wisdom of the ages on *your* watch.

"Most of you do indeed know what you're doing. Deep down inside, you are aware, if only a little bit, that you are making a huge mistake to be so negligent and unruly. You know it, but you've decided not to care—'for now', you tell yourselves. And with that, you put it off indefinitely as you watch your lives waste away year after year. You don't even care for your own children's sakes. Having them around just brings up the whole matter all over again, for their bright and curious faces should remind you that you, too—most of you—were born bright and curious, but decided not to live that way any longer. And so you're not able to embrace your children fully, for they represent something from which you have distanced yourselves. You won't deny yourselves for them. Nor will you do it for the sake of righteousness or honor or duty.

"No, you put it off, promising yourselves that you'll get back to it somehow, someday. You call it planning, but you let it turn into a lie as it becomes your protected habit to neglect such important matters. It's like the verse in the Robert Frost poem I quoted earlier tonight—the one about two roads diverging, and him trying to figure out which road to take:

> And both that morning equally lay
> In leaves no step had trodden black.
> Oh, I kept the first for another day!
> Yet knowing how way leads on to way,
> I doubted if I should ever come back.[62]

"When you put important things off, you know what you are like. You know you will probably never get back to it. Yet you put it off anyway. And that's when it becomes just another lie that you tell yourselves. You have learned how to be content with the mediocre and mundane— with the dysfunction and lawlessness and unruliness. Even as you gorge yourselves with entertainment, your lives are boring and unfulfilling. It's because you've missed the fundamental things—the matters of personal authenticity.

"When I lived here, I used to tell myself this:

> Life is short; why not do something extraordinary while we're here?

"Of course, I've tweaked that a bit since. Now, if I were still among you, I'd be thinking it this way:

> Life is short; why not **be** something extraordinary while we're

154

here?

I have since figured out that being a great person is even more valuable than doing great things. Anyway, the life I now live is not short at all and yet I *still* want to do extraordinary things. And so for you, why not put your house in order and keep it that way for the *first time* in history? Why not attain to that goal that your forefathers set but failed to achieve for any appreciable length of time? Isn't it about time somebody did? Or have you decided that it's impossible? And if that's what you've decided, why don't you have the diligence to go write yourselves a new manifesto and a new constitution that matches your sorry goals in life? Why not go ahead and put it in print that you want to steal every dollar you can from others who have worked for them? Why don't you write it down that you want a lawless government, that corruption is quite OK with you, and that you want the government to do for you the things that humankind have naturally done for themselves since the beginning of humanity?

"One reason you might not want to do that is that it would sting you to see your real values written in black and white. But another reason is that you don't want to put a new constitution to a vote because you don't think you could get it passed. As bad as things are, there are enough people with at least enough wisdom left to know that you had better hang on to whatever vestiges of the Rule of Law that you have left. But hanging on, however smart that may be, is simply not enough. Human life was never supposed to be about 'hanging on', about 'getting by', or about 'holding it together'. Life here is supposed to be successful and enjoyable and honorable. But in your greed and ignorance, you have put these thieves in charge of you, and then you wonder why things are not so good."

Benjamin True paused for a long breath, and as he did, the expression on his stern face lightened somewhat. Some even noted that he seemed to be smiling.

"Well, I'm going to do something for you tonight. And if you don't like it, you can always undo it. And as bad as things are, I do know that *some* of you are eager to make things better. Yes, *some* of you already have a pretty good idea of what I've been talking about all night, and you're willing to move on to the next level, if only you knew how to do it. Well, there are a thousand needful tasks if this mess is to be properly reformed, and I'm going to give you a gift. I'm going to help you take the first step right now. I know that when you get down, sometimes you just need a boost, so I'm going to give you that boost. And like I said, if you decide you don't like what we're about to do, you can always undo it later."

Chapter 15

The Committee of Five

Things had been tense in that darkened living room of the house on K Street. There had been much discussion throughout Benjamin True's performance so far, and while it might have been a rather heated discussion in any other group, this one had trained itself over the years to remain rather calm and clear-minded. Of course, most of the crises they viewed together on TV were of their own making, so that made this one different. Indeed, they were still a bit blindsided by this whole Benjamin True event, and couldn't figure out who was behind it, or what the motive might actually be. Interestingly, it did not occur to them to take it at face value.

They had already discussed the fate of their sniper, Lt. Dan Harriman, and were confident that he'd be successfully erased from existence once taken into custody by Capitol Police-after they had finally gained entry to the House Chamber. They would simply have Homeland Security approach the Capitol Police, demanding that Harriman be turned over to them as it was a matter of "national security", and the request would be honored. From there, DHS could easily make Harriman disappear for a time, and then later announce that he had had a heart attack, or had met some other deadly fate while in custody. The coroner, of course, would also be a DHS employee, so the coroner's report would naturally support the official claim, whatever it might turn out to be. And then that report's details would be sealed for several decades as this was, after all, a matter of national security.

It all afforded them yet another scrumptious opportunity to fabricate pretty much whatever story would suit them regarding the motives of this "renegade" Capitol Police officer. And they could pin it on whatever group they wanted. Perhaps it would be blamed on an international terrorist group yet another time, as this scheme seemed to be quite convincing to the American public again and again. Or perhaps they'd cook up some useful variation on the theme this time. It wasn't pressing; they had time. And, of course, they could count on the public not to look into the matter too closely, because they generally never do. Most of them are amazingly eager to believe such stories as they are put to them, having no idea that they would believe something different if only it were presented differently. [63]

But what about this Benjamin True guy? What was his game? All they knew so far is that he kept harping about the Constitution and about corruption—and more importantly, that he had got the Speaker of the House of Representatives in quite a compromised state. He wasn't exactly spilling the beans yet, but he had the lid well off the bean jar and was not terribly far, it seemed, from revealing any of a number of matters that the committee could not afford to have exposed.

And how were they going to finish that job, by the way? Having tried to kill the Speaker of the House might be a little harder to explain, but again, they had a little while to cook something up for that. The more pressing matter was how to keep him silent before he could share any details of the crimes he had already confessed to in general fashion.

As per an earlier discussion, Audra Blake had already put the video feed technician for the House Chamber on standby that they might give the order to cut the transmission at any time. But they had been waiting to see where this was really going, not wanting to create even more intrigue by cutting the feed unless they had to. Habitual conspiracy theorists, they well knew, tend to become extra excited when things like interruptions in communications happen.

And they already had a couple of assets outside on the Capitol lawn, just in case they should make the call to liquidate Benjamin True, provided he would exit the building at the spot he had earlier pointed out to everyone. Regarding this detail, they had strangely assumed he was telling the truth, having no reason to suspect otherwise, although they didn't buy his story about having "graduated" from humanity to the next level. There had been strangely little discussion among them as to whether True was the "real deal" or not. No one had any explanation for the various miracles he had performed so far, yet they still seemed to be working under the assumption that he was indeed mortal, which, to them, meant that he was killable. His fate, they were thinking, rightly remained in "to be determined" status.

"So, what about DuBois?" one of them asked. "What are we going to do with him? He's our biggest liability as far as we can see at this point."

"Well, we can't very well touch him until the House is open again," volunteered another. "Do any of you have a preference as to how to take him out when we can?"

"Probably best not to take another shot at him," said one.

"Maybe we should save the heart attack for him, and let Lt. Harriman hang himself in his cell. We can argue that Harriman was filled with remorse, and that DuBois had been overcome by all the stress. This also makes him a semi-martyr, and makes calls for a full investigation into his broad confession less likely to cause us much trouble."

The consensus on this question was agreeable for a few seconds, but then one of them second-guessed it.

"I'm not so sure that we can afford to risk anything further with DuBois still in play. Five seconds of choice words from him could put us in one hundred times the danger we now face. And we all know how hard it is to get the toothpaste back in the tube. Perhaps it's time we cut the video feed so as to get the public out of the loop. We can still watch the rest from here via the House's CCTV signal."

"How say you all?" asked the eldest of them.

"I'm not leaning hard enough either way to be adamant, so I'm fine with it if you all agree," pitched in another.

"I'm good with it. Let's cut it."

Nods from all around made it unanimous.

"Do it!" was the command to Audra Blake, who pulled out her cell phone, found the number for the House video producer, and dialed it.

"Hello?" answered the producer.

"Cut it."

"Roger that. Stand by; cutting it now."

159

With that, the producer in the tiny production room flipped a switch, and just like that, the broadcast would be terminated. "Done," he reported.

"If it's done, why am I still seeing the broadcast live?"

"Oh, there's a seven-second profanity delay built in. It should go dead any second now."

"Uh, not yet," observed Dominus after a couple seconds of pausing.

"Wait a sec; let me check." The producer switched on his TV and checked it on one station, and then another, and then a third. They were all still running live. He grabbed his stopwatch and the headphones with the live audio feed from the lectern mic.

In the headphones, he heard the words from Benjamin True just as they were being spoken in realtime, "you can always undo it later." Clicking the stopwatch on the word, later, he turned up the volume on the TV broadcast and waited for seven seconds, repeating the line to himself twice in a whisper to keep from forgetting it. "...you can always undo it later." Then at about six seconds, he heard the beginning of the line, and the end of it, and a pause afterward. He looked to the TV during that pause, and to his surprise, there was still live action on the screen, with Benjamin True taking a silent pause from his speech. He looked to his CCTV monitor, which showed the end of True's pause, and the resumption of his speech afterward.

"What the...?" he whispered to himself, picking up the phone to talk to Dominus. "We've got trouble. I cut the switch, but somehow, the feed is still live."

"I thought you said you turned it off!" snapped Dominus.

"I did! It's off, but it's still running somehow."

"You stop that feed ASAP, and keep me posted."

"Yes, ma'am."

Blake hung up, and the line went dead.

"He has cut the feed, but it's still working anyway," Audra Blake reported to the committee.

"Options?" asked the eldest of everyone there.

"If the feed won't die, then can we get the networks to switch to some other programming?" asked another.

"There are twelve or thirteen networks that usually carry the SOTU Address. That's eleven or twelve too many phone calls to make—too much explaining to do—and too many of our fingerprints on this. What else do we have?"

"Well, what if the networks all see something more important and switch over to that on their own?"

"Like what?"

"Well, it's still before nine on the West Coast. Say there was a mass shooting at a mall, or a bombing at a college basketball game. Every network would break away from SOTU for an event like that."

"That would certainly help dull the memory of this night so far. Can we do this, Audra?"

"Well, the shooting, I'm sure we can do. I have assets available, and I'm estimating they could deploy to a mall in L.A. County in just minutes. But the bombing would be more likely to provide a distraction on the scale we need, as it's simply not as commonplace as shootings are. I can give you a good answer in about five minutes if you're willing to wait. Or I can order the shooting right now."

"I prefer the bombing for the reasons Audra stated. I'm willing to wait five minutes for a determination," opined one of the five.

Audra Blake interjected, "One more consideration for you all is that mall security is a joke, but getting a bomb into a college basketball game will be a little tougher. I'll have to have a uniformed officer do that."

"Do you have the guy already?"

"Yes, it's the same guy, but in one scenario, he'll have to change into a uniform, and in the other, he won't."

"Gotcha. I vote for the five minutes to check on the game. We could probably get four or five times the casualties in that scenario, if not more."

They were unanimously agreed, so Dominus got to work.

Chapter 16

Congressman Dalvin Washington

In the House Chamber, Benjamin True took a deep breath and announced somewhat formally, "Would Congressman Dalvin Washington please stand up?"

Dalvin Washington was shaken. He had been elected to the House just two months back and had only been sworn in two weeks before. Had he been asked before the unusual events of this evening had started, he'd have been fairly confident that he had done nothing wrong as a Member of Congress, but he had never in his life been in a situation with more gravity than his present one, and found himself not too sure of anything.

Washington stood up, quite nervously, and as if he didn't already feel enough pressure, every head in the room turned his way with an audible rush. He didn't speak; he hadn't been asked to do that. He had merely stood as requested, forgetting instantly that he had genuinely been enjoying most of the speech thus far.

His seat was not on the center aisle where the president had entered, but near the aisle just to the left of that one, from the Speaker's point of view. He sat in the fourth row of regular seats, which is not to count the two additional rows of temporary seats that are brought in for the State of the Union Address each year. And his seat was the second from the aisle.

When Washington stood, Benjamin True nodded to him respectfully and with a slight smile, saying, "Congressman, Washington."

Washington nodded back.

"Congressman Dalvin Washington was sworn in just this session and has higher ideals than are normal for Members of Congress," True announced.

OK, that's not what I expected, thought Washington.

"Congressman, is it true that you submitted a resolution to the Clerk last week for consideration in the House of Representatives?"

"Yes, sir," answered Washington.

Benjamin True replied, "Well, I love your resolution, and I want to discuss it here tonight."

No words would come to Dalvin Washington's mind in response to this statement from True, but he certainly had a feeling of great relief. "Thank you, sir."

"Did you happen to bring a copy of it with you tonight?"

"No, sir. I'm sorry."

"No problem. I have one right here." True held out an empty hand, and suddenly it held a white paper document, to the great entertainment of some in the audience.

"I wonder if I might beg everyone's pardon for just a minute while I go down there to speak to the Congressman privately for a bit," said True. In an instant, he had simply disappeared from the rostrum and appeared in the aisle just in front of the row where Washington was standing, one seat in from the aisle seat.

Naturally, this shocked the audience, as this trick had not yet been performed for them.

Had Washington been just one row forward of his position, he'd have had a seat at one of four large wooden tables placed in the seating area of the House floor. The tables are used for committee presentations and such, and are about six chairs wide, with a few microphones atop each to facilitate members who want to speak to the assembly.

Benjamin True turned to the Member of Congress seated at the aisle on that row just ahead of Washington and said, "Perhaps we could work together here to facilitate a short conversation between me and the Congressman. Would you mind, ma'am, to stand up and to let Mister Washington take your place?"

"Not at all," she said, both quickly and agreeably. She was Jennifer Locklear, a fifth-term representative who didn't want to give Benjamin True any reason whatsoever to pay any further attention to her. She had enough skeletons in her closet to wreck anybody in Congress, and now that True was standing so close to her, she imagined that he could have heard her heart beating in fear in her chest.

Locklear was up in an instant and out into the aisle, where she waited for Dalvin Washington to step out so that she could take his place. When he did, however, the Congresswoman who was seated on the aisle beside him stood and shifted over to his seat, leaving Locklear the seat on the end.

Dalvin Washington found himself standing face to face with Benjamin True.

True stuck out his right hand and said, "Mister Washington, it is very nice to meet you."

They shook hands as Washington said, "It's my honor, sir!"

True leaned in close and whispered, "I love every word of your resolution, and I wouldn't change a thing. Now listen, we're going to vote on this resolution tonight, and while I wouldn't change a word of what you have, I'd like to add something to it. I've written a preamble to it and have added one section to the end. Would you please look this over and see if you find it agreeable?"

True handed him the document. It was two standard white sheets, stapled in the upper left-hand corner. The entire audience watched in rapt curiosity as Washington read the page-and-a-half resolution. Everyone was wondering, but no one spoke or even dared to whisper to a neighbor.

Washington, looked up at True and said, "It is beautiful! I love it!"

"So, you don't mind presenting this to the Clerk as an updated version of your resolution?"

"I'd be honored," replied Washington.

"Great! Now, you take out your cell phone and photograph this—both pages—then post it to your Facebook page right now."

"Sure, will do!" said Washington. He immediately got to work, using the committee table at which he now stood.

True had vanished again, and reappeared at the second-tier lectern. "Thank you all for your patience," he said to everyone in attendance. "Congressman Dalvin Washington has a bill for a joint resolution that this Congress needs to hear. I have asked the Congressman to post his resolution to Facebook so that everyone in the world may read it right now."

Turning to Dalvin Washington, True asked, "And did you post that resolution on your Facebook page?"

"Yes, sir. I did."

"You can all find him at Facebook by searching for Congressman Dalvin Washington." This statement immediately prompted many thousands of those watching on TV to find the Congressman's page on Facebook. Meanwhile, most of the TV news networks covering the event had posted Washington's name in the ticker at the bottom of the screen within just a few seconds of this introduction. And just like that, Dalvin Washington was big news.

"I want every American to see this resolution tonight, so those of you who are on Facebook need to do everything you know how to do to get others to see it, too. You need to like it and share it. You need to email it to all your friends. You need to call them. Whatever it takes to make sure it gets around very quickly."

To all in attendance, Benjamin True said, "When I went down to the well to speak with the Congressman, I suggested adding a preamble and one additional section to his resolution, and he agreed. And now I ask Congressman Washington to read his joint resolution."

Dalvin Washington stood and cleared his throat. Then he began to read from the paper that Benjamin True had left with him. "It reads:

Joint Resolution

Proposing an amendment to the Constitution of the United States providing for term limits for certain federal offices....

At the mention of "term limits", there were audible groans and a few boos from around the House floor, and Washington paused in his reading.

Benjamin True stepped in, addressing the assembly. "You will be silent as he reads, and if you will not do so voluntarily, you are well aware that I can make it so by my own will."

At this, the room fell voluntarily silent, and Washington continued to read:

> Resolved by the Senate and House of Representatives of the United States of America in Congress assembled (two-thirds of each House concurring therein),
>
> That the following article is proposed as an amendment to the Constitution of the United States, which shall be valid to all intents and purposes as part of the Constitution when ratified by the legislatures of three-fourths of the several States:
>
> "Article —
>
> **PREAMBLE.** *Whereas the sacred trust of public officers is to secure the public good, rather than to secure riches and power for themselves, and*
>
> *Whereas history shows that corruption in government is greatly facilitated by the lengthy tenure of those in office, and*
>
> *Whereas guarding against corruption in government is of greater importance than providing the brightest and best a long tenure in government,*
>
> *We the people of the United States amend this Constitution as follows:*
>
> **Section 1.** No person shall serve consecutive terms in the role of Representative, Senator, President, or Vice President. Nor shall any person hold any of these offices more than twice.
>
> **Section 2.** Any partial term served to complete the vacated term of another shall count as an entire term for the purposes of this Article. Any incumbent having served more than one term in the same office as of the ratification of this Article may complete the term already commenced as of that time, but shall not serve another.
>
> **Section 3.** No incumbent of any office named in this Article shall,

during his or her tenure, declare candidacy for, nor campaign for, any public office, whether federal, state, or local. Any incumbent already having satisfactorily filed for candidacy as of the time of ratification of this Article may proceed with such candidacy, provided the election for such office is no longer than two years future to the date of ratification. Violation of this section shall render the violator disqualified to be elected or appointed to any public office, whether federal, state, or local, for a period of ten years from the date of the violation.

Section 4. The Preamble to this Article shall be perpetually included with it, so as to instruct future generations in the wisdom we have gained."

"This concludes the text of the joint resolution," announced Dalvin Washington, who promptly sat down.

Benjamin True spoke from the lectern, "If ratified, an amendment to this effect would be a significant step in combating some of the corruption that has become business as usual in this government. By shortening the term, we shorten the amount of time that an incumbent is a sitting duck for the influence of those who want to steer the government for their own sinister purposes. So, it takes into view the common outcome of one's tenure in public office—which is corruption—and it fights against that tendency by shortening the term."

True continued, "It also has the effect of making it harder for the influencers to maintain their vast control over the government, for rather than corrupting one official and keeping him or her around for 20 or 30 years, there would a constant turnover, requiring them to expend many times the effort to keep control of the Congress."

Somebody from the Gallery called out, "We already have term limits; it's call *voting!*"

"And how's that going?" retorted True. "Is it working properly? Are the bad apples being voted out of the barrel? Of course not!"

A two-term representative from Oregon spoke up. "Why let us serve two terms, but not in a row?"

"This is to curb the nasty habit of the voters. It is common knowledge that incumbents have an inordinate advantage in an election. This is because the voters are cognitive/moral misers and slaves to the *Status*

Quo Bias[64] who don't give careful thought to their ways. It is simply easier for them to keep voting for the same senator or representative or president than it is to stop and give due consideration to which candidate would actually be best for the job. This is especially ironic since average approval rates for Congress are generally under twenty percent, and yet incumbents in Congress tend to get re-elected eighty or ninety percent of the time. And why is this? Well, the typical voter, disapproving of Congress, is really wishing that somebody else would fix things—that somebody else would go to the trouble of doing something new and different. But when it comes to his or her own vote, that voter is far more likely than not to vote for the same official that held the seat the last time. This is such a corruption of the idea of the responsible voter, but it's what kind of people you are on the average.

"And so here's a case where it's wise to protect the voters from their own negligence. Rather than trying to reason with them and hoping you can get through to enough of them, which is unlikely to do any good anytime soon, you simply remove the option of voting for the same person every time. Yes, if you like the person, you can have them back, but only once, and not right now.

"This also has the effect of letting things air out during this cool-down period. That is, those officials who have acted corruptly in office will be forced out by law, and then they have to wait at least a whole term before they can come back. This gives their opponents a whole term to expose any wrongdoing they may have done in the first term—quite like I have done with a few of you here tonight. Exposure generally tends to harm one's chances of future success, and the fuller the exposure, the fuller the harm.

"Now, as I said before, if it were wholly up to me, the rule would be that you get one term, and you're done. This government does not exist to give you a job, but to serve the good of the public. So you'd come up here and serve, and then you'd go home and do something else that's good for the world."

A voice from the back somewhere called out the objection, "But you'd be getting rid of the *good* ones, too."

"Ah," said True with intrigue in his voice, "you're voicing the mega-popular complaint that shows how screwy the common thinking is. First of all, the *really* good ones—the ones who will refuse to violate their oaths—the ones who insist on being honest, rational, and responsible in every way all the time—they are so rare as to be statistically insignificant. So, you're wrecking an amendment that could really fix a lot of things, based on a scenario that's so rare, you'd have a hard time naming a good incumbent.

"But beyond that, here's what's screwy about the way you think on such things. You think that a good public servant has but one proper task, and that that task is to serve in the government. But who is it who teaches the next generation back home how to come up here and do it right? Nobody. That's who. If someone comes up here and actually behaves properly while doing it, then the *greater* need thereafter is not to continue serving in that way, but to magnify that goodness by teaching many others back home to adopt the same virtues and skills. But almost none of you ever think of that. Instead, to you, getting to sit in one of the chairs up here is your sole concept of doing good. And then you wonder why it's so hard to find good public servants.

"Indeed, that super-rare Member of Congress who gets it right should be writing books, teaching others how to do it from A to Z and informing them as to what to expect. They should be giving seminars and making videos and such. It should become an extracurricular option for high schoolers to adopt in their spare time, and for college students, and for adults already in their careers. But there is currently no such program. So, a person who actually had a good track record in these matters could work in this area with near-zero competition, and could influence two generations at once. That's what a true public servant could do after holding an office up here in Washington. But can you name any such person who is doing this as I have described it? No, you can't.

"Now, I'm well aware of how this current Congress thinks. It's the same way that every Congress since 1789 has thought, only worse, because the corruption is now more widely grown and is now more sophisticated and systemic. You will think that this proposed amendment is a bad idea. You will see it as the end of your careers, and you will think that to actually vote for such a thing would be to voluntarily give up your careers. That will be your first instinct in this matter. But you need to give it some more careful thought.

"Some of you, as you have seen tonight, have been laid bare in your corruption, and your careers are already over, whether you've realized it or not. Indeed, after having the night to think it over, some of you will be resigning in the morning, hoping that there will be leniency for you if you go quietly.

"Almost all of the rest of you—with a precious few exceptions—are still quite vulnerable—and you know who you are. Your corruption is plenty bad enough to land you in jail for a long, long time—to destroy the power and wealth you have accumulated for yourselves, along with the vain house of cards in which you live, pretending that you are worthy of some honor just because you hold a title and enjoy the support of the corrupt voters who put you here.

"You are, most of you, treading softly with me because you fear being exposed tonight. You're sitting on the fence of indecision, struggling with the decision as to whether to touch a toe to the ground on one side or the other. On the one hand, you're scared to death of the exposure and you're thinking about getting out of government, but on the other, you're contemplating whether you could just keep the charade going, and that maybe you can go another year without getting caught.

"What you don't realize—and what is so hard for most humans to realize—is that the fact of your bad behavior is bad, whether you acknowledge it or not. Whether you will admit it or not, each of you is *already* found out, and the evidence against you is known to those who are not subject to some corrupt court whose judges can be bought. Whether other humans ever hold you accountable or not, you are still accountable for the reality of how you have lived your lives against the reality of what is right and just.

"You are gambling that you can get away with it for long enough to retire eventually and to spend out your corrupt days in wealth and peace. In this government, there are two elected officers in the Executive, 100 in the Senate, and 435 in the House. That's 537 of you, plus the nine appointed justices of the Supreme Court. That totals to 546 people, and almost every one of them a liar, cheater, and thief—a violator of his or her oath of office, and a domestic enemy of the very Constitution they swear to protect and defend.

"At present, there are seven of you who have not violated their oaths of office. All of them are first-term Members of Congress who just got here two weeks ago. And of those seven, four of them previously served in state government, where they violated the oaths they gave there. Of the remaining three, one of them is planning on violating his oath next week when a certain unconstitutional bill comes up for a vote, and the other two will be tempted again and again to compromise themselves.

It remains to be seen whether they have the will to remain righteous in office.

"Of the rest, there are more felony counts than can be counted in a week. These are things that *could* be known about these people, but again, 'who will guard the guards?' As it is, the guards up here look the other way and do not prosecute these crimes. And the people at home pretty much know that things are crooked, but as a rule, they don't insist on getting into it, because they simply don't care that much. And then there are a few who are willing to make a difference, but who can't figure out how.

"The scope of it all is quite shocking, however, for those who are actually willing to open their eyes. Here is the scope of the corruption; you need to see this."

There was quite a stir in the Chamber as the long second-tier desk behind which Benjamin True was speaking was suddenly covered with file folders—very thick file folders in many cases—detailing the criminal acts of the members of the government. There was a folder for each of the 546 members of the government. Three were empty, and the others ranged in thickness from just a few documents to many inches of documents. Some, in fact, were in multiple expandable files stacked atop one another, and all marked with the same incumbent's name. The longer the incumbents had been there, the taller their files, and the tallest one was over two feet in height.

"These files detail your crimes and corruption in office," explained Benjamin True. "Three of them are empty files, and all the rest have at least enough information to have you removed from office, for you have all—all but three of you—violated your oaths of office here in this present government—and those remaining four did it in their state governments before they got here.

"So, there it is in print," said True with a sweeping of his arms across the long desk before him.

Suddenly, the whole matter became a lot more real to a great many people. Those in the government were shocked and scared, as well as being partially stunned and without the means to wrap their minds around the whole matter at once. Some of their minds were simply flooded with thoughts like *I'm going to jail; I'm going to jail.* A few others decided to flee somehow, and some of them tried to think through how they might do it, while a couple of them actually stood up and climbed out to the aisles to run for the doors, not remembering that they would find them locked and inescapable.

In the Gallery above, the seriousness of the corruption seemed more real to most than ever before. They had come in having the common political biases that generally rule the populace, but True had done enough to get them to think a new way—at least for now. Most of them would find a way to shake it off once they got back home, of course, but for now, it weighed heavily on their minds.

Benjamin True turned around and asked Ward DuBois and Linda Surgeon, "Would you two please step down here to examine this evidence?"

The two stood and walked around the Speaker's desk, stepping down to the next level and behind the desk that True had commanded alone for most of the evening now. While the Speaker and Vice President got started, Benjamin True also motioned to the Clerk of the House, seated to the left of the Speaker's chair, and then to the Parliamentarian, who was seated to the right of the Vice President's chair, as well as to the Sergeant at Arms for the House, who was seated for the evening on the front row of the House, quite near the Parliamentarian. They all came to True as requested, and he said, "Would you each please perform a cursory examination of the evidence?"

These three also complied and joined in the examination in short order. Speaker DuBois and Linda Surgeon, of course, pretty much knew what they would find. DuBois knew that he was finished, and had known it for what seemed like a very long time since his earlier confession that night. Surgeon, on the other hand, still had a bit of fight left in her—in theory, at least, though she saw few options for actually doing anything to escape her situation.

The Clerk of the House, however, had generally just stuck to the business of helping to administrate the workings of the House, and he had not been personally involved in any of the corruption, though it was hard to remain completely oblivious to it while working around such people day in and day out.

And so it went with the Sergeant at Arms. He had recently begun his post and was determined to keep it "strictly business". His job was primarily to keep order, and he was not involved with the legislation in any direct sense. But still, he knew that things weren't right here.

The Parliamentarian had been in the house a long time. It was her job to advise the Speaker, in particular, on the rules of order, and her post was not to be political in any sense. Her personal mantra was "Just the facts", and she strove to remain disinterested in what the House might actually do. Rather, her job was simply to be sure that the way they did it was according to the rules of procedure.

After she had examined a couple of the smaller folders more conveniently near the top of the stack, the Parliamentarian decided to open one of the large expandable files, belonging to a long-time Member of the Senate. The desk top was covered, leaving no suitable workspace, so she attempted to move a large stack of individual files in order to make some working room, but she lost her grip and several of the files began to slip out of her hands. In an attempt to regain control of them, she lurched forward against the desk behind which they were all standing, and raised her hands even higher, trying to scoop them back into balance in her hands. It didn't work. Her attempt to regain control served instead to send the folders airborne. Many of them emptied their contents in a mess that not only covered the pile of files on the second-tier desk, but that even ranged as far as the longer desk below.

Among the documents were proofs of their crimes and compromises, as well as all the badness that had come about as a result of it all. There many papers, of course, but also a horde of 8x10 photographs. They landed, some on the desk below, some on the pile of Secret Service equipment that True had deposited on that desk much earlier, and the rest sliding off that desk and onto the blue carpet between the lowest desk and the seats on the House Floor.

Among the photographs exposed were several types of subject matter. Some were lewd photographs of the officials themselves, and some of them in lewd activities with yet other people. Others were of dead soldiers and dead civilians of foreign countries. Some were of dead children in hospital beds. There were pictures of ghettos and of polluted rivers and shut-down factories. There were photos of homeless people living under bridges.

And then there were the documents. There was the occasional news story, but most of it was original source material—things like deposit slips and receipts and bank statements—hard evidence of wrongdoing. There were death certificates and autopsy reports. There were CIA files on assassinations and on the overthrow of governments. There were scientific reports exposing how other scientific reports were fraudulent. There were records of election fraud and of payments made to people who would vote multiple times under assumed identities.

There were transcripts of conversations between politicians and media moguls. There were transcripts of conversations between politicians and the big-money players wanting them to steer things their way. There was evidence of protecting large industries that cause harm to people in various ways—through their products, and through the food or pharmaceuticals or other chemicals they produce.

It was all there, and the faces of the three non-politicians examining the folders were especially instructive. They were people whose jobs were to remain unprejudiced and emotionally objective, but their faces betrayed the disgust and shame they felt at seeing all this evidence of wrongdoing.

Meanwhile, William DuBois had pretty much stopped examining anything at some point in the exercise. Had anyone been watching him closely, they would have noticed that his pace of flipping through the files had slowed considerably compared to the other four, and that eventually, he had come to a halt over a single, thick file. He was overcome with remorse, and stood crying silently, with streams of tears flowing down his cheeks. The file he had been examining was his own.

Linda Surgeon had also slowed down, though she wasn't crying. She was more numb than anything. She had even quit trying to figure it all out. At this point, she was simply along for the ride, and she'd find out where this was all going when they all got there.

Benjamin True, who had stepped back to the side of the Speaker's desk, which was behind them all, to let them examine the files, spoke up to the five in front of him. "Would you five please tell the crowd whether these files do in fact comprise the evidence as I stated?"

They all stopped their activities and nodded in the affirmative.

"All right. Thank you for your help. Please return to your seats," said True. And they did.

Chapter 17

The Diversion

There were ten thousand police officers in the Los Angeles Police Department, and many of them moonlighted in various jobs. But Officer Pete Durance wasn't like them. His second job was actually his primary job. That is, he worked for Dominus, and the LAPD job was necessary to do what Dominus wanted done.

While driving his cruiser to the college arena, he texted Dominus, "Going to catch a BB game for a bit. Maybe you'll see me on TV!"

They had already discussed the timing, and Dominus took this call as a signal that the diversion would happen somewhere between ten and twenty minutes out.

On the campus, Officer Pete Durance pulled his cruiser up to the curb in a loading zone, got out, and locked the doors. He had a black nylon backpack slung over his right shoulder, and it was somewhat camouflaged against his black uniform.

Inside the bag were eight blocks of C-4 explosive, taped together, and wired to a detonating device that was made from a prepaid cell phone. At 1.25 pounds each, the eight blocks constituted enough explosive to clear a large house off its foundation. The resultant explosion would send gases expanding at a rate of several thousands of feet per second, causing massive destruction to nearly anything nearby. It would be deadlier, of course, had he filled the pack around the explosives with shrapnel, such as nails or ball bearings, but he didn't need to be lugging

177

around a bag that looked like it weighed 30 or 40 pounds either, so the ten-pound load would just have to do, and he'd maximize its effect by finding the best available placement.

Dominus had told him that they needed at least fifty dead, and that anything spectacular to look at in the aftermath would be a bonus. Durance figured he'd just have to improvise with all that; making it into the game was the primary challenge. And for that, all he needed was to find another cop willing to let slide with the rules to help a buddy out. The chances of this, he figured, were pretty good.

Durance walked the sidewalk to the main entrance of the sports complex. As he approached, he could see that there were four doors abreast going in, and four marked "exit", the latter being farther from him than the former. And between the sets of doors, there was a uniformed officer standing watch. Fortunately for Durance, there were still a fair number of fans trickling in so that the officer had more than just Durance to be concerned with. Just as Durance had begun to slip through the first door, the officer on guard did turn his way, but a nod from Durance was enough to get a nod in return, and just like that, he was inside.

He walked past the ticket booth and some bathrooms and spotted the first of two obvious doors into the gym itself. As expected, there was another uniformed officer at the door, standing just a couple of feet from the student who was tearing off ticket stubs. A quick glance down the way to the second door showed a second officer there as well. This door, therefore, was as good as any, Durance figured.

He approached the officer from the side, rather than going through the line. "What's the score?" he asked the officer.

"I don't know, but from the sound of it, we're winning. You working the game?"

"No, I'm off, but I come out here to work out in the fitness center, and I thought I might slip in and catch a few minutes of the game before I do."

"Have fun," came the reply with a nod. And just like that, Officer Pete Durance was in the gym.

The gym was fairly packed, which was good for Durance. And the scoreboard explained the excitement. It was 58 to 50 in the third quarter, with the home team leading. Durance had entered the gym through a door that was situated in one of its corners. Inside, he found himself in something of a descending tunnel on a diagonal path toward center court. He walked the 50 feet or so until the tunnel emptied, and he stood there to get his bearings. He had just walked under a section of seating, the rows of which ran at a diagonal to the court itself. There were just a few seats across its front row, and each successive row had more and more seats, until the rows got shorter once one got about half way up.

The first order of business was to look like a fan, so he identified the home team and waited for them to score. When they did, he cheered, along with what looked like a few thousand home-team fans. He took a minute or so, looking about at a casual rate as he pondered where best to put his bag. There was no obvious access to any space under the seats, so the first thing that came to mind was to be up in the seats someplace near the very corner where he was now standing. This way, the blast would reach more people.

He spotted a few empty seats about ten rows up and thought it suitable, so up he went, being careful to turn to watch the game on his way whenever the crowd seemed excited about what was going on. As he climbed the steps approaching those empty seats, however, he noticed more empty seats in the far corner ahead. This would put him at the very top of the seating, and while it seemed not as good in one way— that is, that the bomb would only have victims beside and below it, rather than both above and below—it would be more damaging having a structural wall right behind it to focus its blast inward toward the gym.

So, he changed his mind and climbed all the way up. As he climbed, he was able to think more about the physics of this situation. He began to examine the walls behind the seating, and noticed that there was a heavy column built into the wall every thirty feet or so, and the seating was right up against those columns. *Could I bring down one of those columns?* Atop each column, he noticed as casually as possible, was a long truss that reached clear to the other side of the gym. *What if one of those trusses comes down?*

He had been headed toward the column in the corner, but noticed that it was considerably larger than the other columns along the wall. *Too big,* he thought regarding the column in the corner. Besides, the wall to his left was topped by a single truss running along its every column. But the columns along the wall to the right each held the end of separate trusses that spanned all the way to the opposite wall. Removing one of those columns, therefore, would bring down the entire truss and the roof above it.

That's the one right there. He changed directions and made his way to the second column on his right, about thirty feet from the huge corner column. The seats at that height were sparsely populated, and nobody seemed to be paying him much attention, so he continued to climb, turning to catch the action whenever the crowd signaled that there was some.

The gym had hard plastic stadium-style folding seats, bolted to the floor and spring-loaded to fold closed when no one was occupying them. As he approached the column, he noticed that the empty seats in front of it were about a foot away from the wall, and that the column itself stuck out such that it touched the back of one of the seats. *Could I get any luckier?*

He swung his pack to the floor and sat down in the seat just shy of the column. He was careful to keep glancing at the game to keep up appearances. *These people won't notice you as long as you don't do anything obviously unusual.* He cheered when appropriate, but nothing too loud. And then began a quick exercise in thinking.

OK, if this column breaks, that truss comes down across this entire end section of seating. That's several hundred—maybe a thousand people. Oh, and if the column breaks, that also makes a big hole in this wall, which will look good for the TV cameras from the outside. And if the column doesn't break, all the people in the few rows in front of me will still be thrown forward and down the seats. Will I get at least 50? Maybe. Probably, if they're standing up. Not so sure if they're seated. Of course, the metal and plastic in these seats will make some pretty good shrapnel, too. What am I missing? Any down-side to this plan? I've got to get the bag under the seat, against the column, and I've got to arm it. Will set it off with the burn phone once I'm in the cruiser. Am I missing anything? What's this place going to be like once I walk out of here? How long until I'm back in the cruiser? Three minutes, best possible time? What's this place going to be like in three minutes? Are these people still going to be here? Yes, of course. Even if the game were over now, it would take more than three minutes for them to clear these seats—plus, the truss above is going to take out a few hundred if it comes down. OK, I don't see any problem with this. Arm the bag, push it under the seat and against the column, and wait for the crowd to stand up and cheer before I leave, so I won't be so noticeable.

He looked about to be sure no one was watching. Then having satisfied himself in the negative, he unzipped the front pouch of his bag to reach the small plastic control box that it contained. He switched it on and was met with the satisfying glow of the green LED. He zipped it back and looked up again to be sure no one was paying attention. Then he pushed the bag under the seat to his left, pushing it firmly against the column behind the seat. Then he sat back in his chair and waited.

Can't wait too long. Dominus said they were in a hurry. I need a big moment in the game.

Fortunately for Officer Pete Durance, the point spread had narrowed in the few minutes he had been here. It was now 62-60 and the crowd was getting louder. Then it happened. The home team intercepted a pass and made a dash for the far end of the court. This brought everyone, including Pete Durance, to their feet. And off he went, down the steps to the floor level.

When he reached the bottom, he decided not to exit through the same door, because it was best not to be seen again by the same cop if it could be avoided. He proceeded, therefore, down the end of the court, to an exit quite like the one he had entered. And from there, the trip back to the cruiser should be a snap.

Chapter 18

The Vote

The mood in the House was grave. There had never been any event like this one in the history of this government, of course, but no one was thinking that, except maybe some of the reporters. Most of those in government, however, were having trouble thinking about anything except how much in trouble they probably were. Few had remorse for the harm they had done to the citizens of the United States of America, and fewer still for their sins against the principles to which they so regularly had given lip service, but *many* had remorse for the predicament they were in. That is, for getting caught.

Benjamin True, who had been facing the audience from the second-tier lectern, turned around to speak privately with Vice President Linda Surgeon and Speaker William DuBois.

"Well, now it's time to get something done. I want you to vote on this resolution tonight."

"That's highly irregular," noted Linda Surgeon, looking to the Speaker for support.

"Yes, I don't think that's ever been done before," replied DuBois, still somber, "but it's not illegal as far as I know. We are in session and called to order, and there's surely a quorum present in both houses."

Surgeon had to concede to those facts, and besides, she didn't want to pick a fight with Benjamin True.

"Well, it's going to be tricky taking a roll call vote in this joint session," Surgeon noted.

"I don't think that anybody's going to want to stand out much on this vote," countered True. "Most everybody in this room is realizing—or *should* be realizing—that his or her career in politics is probably over, and I'm not thinking that many are going to want to be on record as having voted against this joint resolution. So, I think you can do it with just a voice vote."

Neither had any objection.

"So, it's a House bill," said True to DuBois. "What are you thinking, William? Why not just have the House stand in place and vote first, and then…"

"Wait," said Speaker DuBois. "Let me get the Clerk of the House over here." He turned to his left to gesture to the Clerk, who was already watching, and he said, "Linda, you might want to get the Secretary of the Senate up here, too."

"Good idea," she replied. Then she gestured to the Secretary of the Senate, who had been seated near the front row on the far right of the hall.

The two administrators approached the Speaker's desk, curious as to what might be going on.

"We're going to take a voice vote on this resolution," Benjamin True informed them both. "We know it's irregular, but we just need to work out the details."

The clerk spoke up. "Well, each house has a special form for bills—uh, sorry—joint resolutions—to be submitted on. So, we'll need that. And the House form will have to be signed by Congressman Washington, since he is the joint resolution's sponsor."

"OK," said True. "Here are the forms," he said, producing them from thin air and handing them to each administrator. "You'll see they're already filled out, except for Washington's signature."

True turned around to face the House and said, "Congressman Washington, do you have a minute?"

"Yes, sir," came the reply from Washington as he stood up. "Do you need me up there?"

"Yes," answered Benjamin True.

Dalvin Washington took one step into the aisle, and then he simply disapparated, and reappeared beside Benjamin True.

"Whoa!" shouted Washington in surprise, as he reached out a hand to the lectern to steady himself.

"Fun, huh?" asked True of the recent arrival on the dais.

"Yeah, but somewhat unexpected," he chuckled, still beside himself with surprise.

"Well, you can start preparing yourself for the trip back," replied True with a smile. "We just need you to sign your joint resolution, and then I'll send you back."

The Clerk handed Dalvin Washington the form and a pen.

"Thanks," said Washington, and he put the form on the second-tier lectern and signed it. He didn't have the presence of mind to realize that he had just signed this in front of many millions of viewers. He turned to True and said, "Are we going to vote on this?"

"That's the plan," said True. "So now, with your permission, I'll put you back in your seat. Or would you rather walk?"

"Oh, no. I'm not going to miss this. You can zap me ba..."

True's keen sense of humor had seen it coming, and he decided not to resist the urge.

When Washington suddenly appeared back in his seat in the House, he let out another "Whoa!", just as at first. This prompted laughs from the crowd, and Dalvin Washington's highly-entertained smile was just fun to behold—unless you happened to be one of the members of the United States Government who had a stuffed file on the desk in the front. Then it wasn't so funny.

Benjamin True looked back to the Speaker's desk and announced to the four there, "OK, I'm going to make a few more remarks, and then, Mister Speaker, you can take it from there. Is everybody good with that?"

They all nodded in the affirmative, then Benjamin True turned to face the audience once again.

"Much of the discussion tonight has been about the oath to support and defend the United States Constitution against all enemies, foreign and domestic. And much of that discussion has been focused on the domestic enemies—particularly, those here filling the floor of this House Chamber. But I've got something pretty serious to say to those at home, and you need to hear me."

"This oath to support and defend the Constitution is not just something for Members of Congress, or the Supreme Court, or for the president and vice president. No, it's an oath that many millions of Americans take for one purpose or another. The military takes it. Law enforcement officers take it. State employees in many states take it, and practically every elected official in every state, county, and city government takes it. There are now more people living who have taken this oath than who voted for President Hernandez in this last election. But America does not bear the character of a nation filled with so many people who actually *believe* in that oath. No, no, no, no. America is nothing like a country where many tens of millions of people had a deep and sincere concern for seeing the Rule of Law maintained under its constitution. And that means that most of you who have taken such an oath pretty much didn't mean it.

"It's on *your* watch that this generation is preparing to hand off this country to the next generation, even worse than it found it. Again, you are the ones who have let this happen. And it's time to come to your senses and admit the truth of the situation. It's time to finally do the right thing and make good on your oath for a change.

"But before we do, I also need to say something to those of you who have not taken an oath to support and defend the Constitution. There's *another* oath you have taken—almost every one of you—and it's one that *you* don't take very seriously, either. It's the Pledge of Allegiance. And I'll tell you right now that I don't like that Pledge. It says some things that simply aren't true, like about how this nation is 'indivisible', as if no state has a right to leave a voluntary union of states. That's like a brutish husband telling his wife that if she ever leaves him, he'll track her down and kill her. And I ask you, what sort of marriage is that?

"But I don't have time to get into everything that's wrong with the Pledge of Allegiance. Rather, my point is that you have taken it. And I'm talking to every school kid and everyone here who has ever been a school kid. Many hundreds of millions of Americans have taken that pledge, yet you're not living up to it. You pledged allegiance to this republic, but this republic is built on a Constitution. That's what defines what it is supposed to be. And yet in that Pledge, you say, every single time, that this is a place where there is 'liberty and justice for all'. Well, that's a lie. It is simply not the case that there is liberty and justice for all here. Indeed, I hold out this very assembly tonight as an example of over 500 officials who have denied certain liberties to the American people, and who have themselves escaped the very justice that you brag about in that Pledge.

"And how do these people get here? And how do they stay here? It's by the voting that you people at home do---you people who have recited that Pledge of Allegiance hundreds or even thousands of times. Do you see what kind of people you are? You'll say a thing again and again for decades, and never really think through what you're saying or what it means. Well, for you, too, it's time to make right on that Pledge.

"Right now, I want every one of you who hasn't done it already, to go to the Congressman Dalvin Washington Facebook page and like this resolution. And share it. And I want you to write a comment. You can say whatever you like, but I also want you to write, 'Upholding my oath' if you've taken an oath to support and defend the Constitution. And if you haven't, and if you've taken the Pledge of Allegiance, then I want you to comment, 'Upholding the Pledge." So, you go do that right now. Don't wait; do it right now."

"Congressman Washington?" called out Benjamin True.

"Yes, sir?"

"How many likes do you currently have on your joint resolution post?"

Washington took out his cell phone and navigated to his Facebook app. "Uh, OK, it says I have 1.3 million likes."

There was a gasp from the crowd.

"And how many shares?"

"Uh, about 260,000."

"OK, folks," said True to the audience at home. That's not enough likes or shares. Remember, you need to like it and share it right now, because this Congress is about to vote on this joint resolution, and you're going to want to make sure that they know that you insist on them passing it."

Representative Thomas Devaney rose immediately and called out, "Mister Speaker!"

"For what purpose does the gentleman from Alabama rise?" asked DuBois in customary style, now standing.

"I call for a point of order."

"On what grounds?"

"This is highly irregular, Mister Speaker, as no such thing is prescribed in the House Rules or in the Constitution."

"Your point of order is not well taken, sir. The Chair knows of nothing in the Constitution or in the House Rules to prohibit such action."

"Mister Speaker," rebutted Thomas Devaney, "we have had this uninvited guest for over an hour and he was never properly recognized by the Chair."

"If the Chair remembers correctly, no one rose on a point of order at the time his visit commenced. It is now too late to raise on objection to it," replied DuBois calmly and fairly.

"But we're basically under siege here! This is wholly irregular!" objected Devaney more stridently than before.

"Well, gee, Tommy," said DuBois, breaking decorum and unloading on Devaney with a sarcastic tone, "we're in a bit of a Constitutional crisis here, then, aren't we? It's not like there's a provision in Article I of the Constitution for what to do when an angel shows up at the State of the Union Address, now is there?"

There was a mixture of laughter and unrest at DuBois' reply. Devaney said nothing, and just sat down.

Senator Bertrand Earhart rose to object. "You can't lead a vote on this, sir! First of all, we're in a joint session, and it's against the law for us to take a vote. And besides that, you're not the President of the Senate, nor the Speaker of the House."

Benjamin True looked at him from across the room. "Senator Bertrand Earhart, have you not yet soiled yourself enough for one evening? Have you thought about what you're doing here? Do you really want your name to go down in history as one of the very few who dared to argue against this amendment? Do you really think you'll find the support of enough people after tonight's revelations that you can stay in your career as a corrupt politician?"

Earhart had no reply.

"Four point three million likes!" shouted someone from the Gallery.

Benjamin True addressed the whole crowd. "Before we move forward, let me tell you why I chose term limits as the one amendment to shoot for tonight. As you know, there are many topics that strongly divide your nation, but term limits is not among them. In fact, over 70% of Americans favor term limits[65], and that's true for Republicans and Democrats alike. It is the most extraordinary example of a great idea that almost everybody knows is a great idea, but that still doesn't get enacted. Now, that's mostly because the American citizen is, on the average, a negligent overseer of his own government, but it's also because they don't believe that this Congress will ever vote limits upon itself. But I think I have given a really good reason tonight for this Congress to do that very thing. I deliberately picked, for your first step of a thousand needful steps, an issue that neither side has to do any rethinking on in order to get it right. So, this is your big chance, America. If you really want to do something right for a change, you're not going to have a better shot at it than right now.

"Now, I had you save your phone batteries earlier for this time. Go ahead and turn them on and search for Congressman Dalvin Washington's page. See for yourself what the American public is saying."

Someone from the Gallery called out, "A comment here says, 'Can't we just hang Senator Bertrand Earhart?'"

Another read aloud, "Just send Earhart home and we'll take care of him from here!"

"This one says, 'I voted for Earhart, but never again!'" came another reader.

"Well, Senator," began Benjamin True, "Do you want to keep drawing attention to yourself?"

"But what you're suggesting is *illegal*!" objected the senator.

"Is it now? Would you kindly cite the law that says that a joint session of Congress may not take a vote?"

"I'd have to look it up, but I'm sure there is one."

"Senator, that's pretty much the same way you handle the Bible, and here you are doing it with the law. But you'll find no such statute, for there is none. So, either you are in egregious error, or in yet another lie. An honest man would shut up immediately, but you still have the will to fight."

"Well, you still have no authority to lead a vote. You are not the President of the Senate or the Speaker of the House!"

"But *I* am," said William DuBois as he stood, "and the Senator will please be seated." DuBois flipped the switch on his lectern that made it rise to its normal working height. Then he raised the microphone to its normal position and stood behind his lectern.

"I will not be seated," defied Earhart. "I will not sit quietly by and watch this government be taken over by someone who does not have the good of the people at heart."

"The Sergeant at Arms of the House will silence the senator," ordered Speaker Dubois.

At this, Sergeant at Arms Keith Everly rose from his seat at the first row of the extreme left of the House. This was not the customary seat of the Sergeant at Arms, for he normally sat along the rear of the rostrum in the lowest seat to the Speaker's right, just at the edge of the stone frontispiece. His seat for the evening was just a few steps from his customary place, and Everly ascended the rostrum to retrieve the silver and ebony mace that symbolized the power his office yielded. The mace sat in a green marble stand, just to the audience's left of the American flag that hung behind the Speaker.

Mace in hand, Keith Everly stepped back to the well of the House and walked around to the place held by the unruly and still-standing Senator Earhart. Everly raised the mace symbolically and commanded Earhart, "The senator will come to order and will be seated immediately."

"I most certainly will not come to order!" shouted Earhart. "Don't you all see what's happening here? Can't you see that this is a coup? This man is trying to undermine this very government, and we must resist him. This is *Satan* and we must resist him!"

Earhart's seat was in the section just to the right of the center aisle, from the Speaker's perspective. He was in the second row of regular seats, which put him in the fourth row on this occasion, as two temporary rows had been brought in to seat the Supreme Court. Earhart was in the middle of his row, which made things more inconvenient for the Sergeant at Arms.

"You are under arrest, Senator. You will shut your mouth immediately and step out to the aisle, or I will remove you forcibly," promised the Sergeant at Arms.

"You can't arrest me; I'm a United States Senator, and I have a right to free speech in defense of this country."

Senator Rudy Bergman had had enough of Earhart's mouth. They were longtime political foes, and he had always been put out by Earhart's cocky attitude. Bergman knew his own career was over, and had already decided to resign the next morning. He had little to lose, he reasoned to himself, so he thought he'd do something he had wanted to do for a long time.

Rudy Bergman turned around and said, "Shut up, Bertrand." Then he punched Bertrand Earhart in the jaw, knocking him out cold and landing Bertrand back in his own seat.

This brought lots of cheers from the hall as the Sergeant at Arms gestured to the two Senators beside Bertrand to step out into the aisle to give him access to the unconscious senator. Once the row was cleared on his side, Keith Everly stepped in to handcuff Earhart. Having the mace still in his hand, he asked Bergman, who was still massaging his stinging fist, to hold it for him. Bergman complied and the Sergeant at Arms handcuffed the limp hands of Earhart in his lap. Looking back to Bergman, Everly said to him, "Thanks for the help. You know, I've wanted to do that myself for a long time," he said with a wry smile.

"Yeah, you and me, both," replied Bergman.

"Heck, me too," replied another senator who had been close enough to hear the conversation.

Sergeant at Arms Everly lifted the unconscious senator into an impressive fireman's carry and took him out to the crowded area of carpet just in front of the rostrum. There he laid him down on the floor, atop the mess of photos and documents that had sobered the room so effectively before.

The excitement with Earhart had sparked lots of conversation, of course, and the hall was rather boisterous as Speaker DuBois rapped his gavel on its block. "The Congress will be in order," came the command, and things settled down.

Senator Bergman, still holding the mace, asked the senator to his left to let him out into the aisle. From there, he took the mace out to the Sergeant at Arms who had just turned to come for it. Bergman handed it off over two Secret Service agents, who were still seated, quite uncomfortably by now, on the carpet.

The Sergeant at Arms bent down to the agents while gesturing to Earhart's snoring body, "You realize he's right there under all your guns. If he gets rowdy, do you guys have it?"

"You bet," one of them answered.

DuBois addressed the assembly, "This joint session of the Congress is in session, and a quorum is present in both houses. The joint resolution is in proper from and is duly signed by its sponsor," DuBois continued. "Further, President Surgeon and I have agreed that the House will take a voice vote first, and should it pass the House, the Senate will address the question thereafter."

"The Chair will entertain a call for the previous question," stated DuBois.

"Mister Speaker?" called Dalvin Washington from the committee table at which he was now standing.

"For what purpose does the Gentleman from Iowa rise?"

Congressman Dalvin Washington wasn't certain of the terminology, but he didn't let that stop him. "Mister Speaker, I call the previous question so we can vote on this thing."

There was a little laughter from the floor.

"Second!" It was Congressman Randy Thomas, the "Doubting Thomas" who had earlier been treated to levitation by Benjamin True.

"The motion to call the previous question has been made and seconded. All those of the House of Representatives in favor of putting the question, say..."

"Mister Speaker?" The call this time was from Congresswoman Patti Spence of Mississippi.

DuBois rolled his eyes at the interruption, but stopped dutifully to entertain the congresswoman. "For what purpose does the

Gentlewoman from Mississippi rise?"

"For a point of order, Mister Speaker," said Spence, matter-of-factly.

"Say on," said the jaded DuBois.

"Mister Speaker, where should I start? This joint resolution has not gone to committee, it has not been debated, it hasn't had a second reading, and on and on."

"Your points are well taken," allowed DuBois. "The Chair will entertain a motion to suspend the rules." DuBois said this looking straight at Dalvin Washington. "For what purpose does the Gentleman from Iowa rise?"

Dalvin Washington, still seated, took it as a prompt, which it was. He stood up and said, "Mister Speaker, I move to suspend the rules and call the previous question."

"Second!" It was the Doubting Thomas again.

"Mister Speaker!" shot Congresswoman Patti Spence again.

"For what reason does the Gentlewoman from Mississippi rise?"

"For a point of order, Mister Speaker." This time she did not wait to be invited to say on, but barged ahead, "I mentioned several rules that were being violated, yet the motion does not state which of these rules is to be suspended. Further, the motion called for two items, and not just one."

"Your point is well taken," said the Speaker. Then, turning back to Dalvin Washington, he said, "Would the Gentleman from Iowa care to revise his motion accordingly?"

Dalvin Washington stood up. "Yes, Mister Speaker, I move to suspend —uh—any such rule as would preclude the House from voting on this joint resolution."

"Second!" said Thomas.

"The Chair puts the question of suspending any such rule as would preclude the House from voting on this joint resolution. As many as are in favor of suspending the rules, say `Aye'."

There was a significant rush of movement as the bulk of the House of Representatives stood at their seats and joined in a chorus of "Aye".

"As many as are opposed to suspending the rules, say 'No'."

Ten or twelve voices said "No," some of them shouting so as to inflate the appearance of a consensus. But it was useless. And it signaled more than mere uselessness, for it also signaled that there was insufficient opposition to the joint resolution to keep it from passing the House.

"The motion to suspend the rules carries by considerably more than the necessary two-thirds. Would the Gentleman from Iowa care to restate the motion to call the previous question?"

The Gentleman from Iowa was happy to restate the motion. "Mister Speaker, I move to call the previous question."

"Second!" chimed Thomas before Washington was even finished.

"The question is put to the House of Representatives on the Gentleman's joint resolution for term limits. As many as are in favor of adopting the joint resolution, say `Aye'."

As before, almost all of the representatives stood and sounded "Aye".

"As many as are opposed to adopting the joint resolution, say 'No'."

The urge to resist had gone out of the opponents to the joint resolution. Most said nothing at all, and didn't even stand up. One dared to vote, and said in a dejected monotone, "No."

There was an uproar of cheers from the Gallery as Speaker DuBois announced "The Ayes have prevailed. The joint resolution is adopted by the House." This declaration was punctuated by a single rap of the Speaker's gavel.

Not everyone in the Gallery was thrilled, of course, because many of them were deeply invested in the government seated beneath them. But those who celebrated did so enthusiastically.

The Speaker's gavel gave three loud cracks as he called "The Gallery will come to order."

As things were settling down, one spectator, waving an iPhone from the Gallery shouted, "Mister Speaker, there are eighty-seven million likes and seventy-nine million shares!"

"Glory Hallelujah!" was heard, though it was not obvious who had said it. And that expression seemed to typify the moment for many in attendance.

Meanwhile, the Clerk of the House handed the joint resolution to the Speaker, who signed it, and handed it back for the Clerk to certify.

Speaker William DuBois turned to Vice President Linda Surgeon and held out his gavel. "Madam President, you may preside over the Senate."

Linda Surgeon took the gavel and approached the Speaker's lectern just as the Clerk of the House handed her the freshly-certified joint resolution for the Senate's consideration.

Surgeon, looking quite tired and all business, struck the gavel and said, "The Senate will come to order. A quorum is present, and we will consider the joint resolution *Proposing an amendment to the Constitution of the United States providing for term limits for certain federal offices.*"

"One hundred and three million likes!" echoed a shout from the Gallery, creating an uproar.

Linda Surgeon found the number impressive, and it was fairly obvious that fighting this groundswell was not a wise move. But suspending the rules in the Senate was harder than in the House, because if only one Senator objected, the proposed rule change had to be put explicitly into writing, and had to be postponed until the following day. *Just get it over with*, she thought. *How can I just get out of here?*

Surgeon let the uproar continue, though by all rights, she could have called for an end to it. Her pause was rewarded by the next announcement from the Gallery.

"One hundred and nineteen million likes!"

Thank God, she thought. *That's almost as many as voted altogether in the last election.*

After that thought, Surgeon took a breath to address the Senate, apparently having decided in that briefest of intervals to position herself as the champion of term limits.

"It would seem that we are at quite an historic moment," said Surgeon to all assembled. "The will of the people is obvious, and the disqualification of this Congress is equally obvious. As many of you know, Rule V of the Senate Rules prohibits any immediate suspension of the rules if one member objects. In that case, the vote on changing the rules would

195

have to be postponed until the following day. But I would fear for the safety of any Senator who should dare to impede a vote on this joint resolution, for what I'm seeing on Facebook indicates that the public would be most disagreeable to anyone who would object to voting on this question."

"One hundred and twenty-eight million!" resounded yet another announcement.

"Holy crap!" exclaimed William DuBois under his breath. "That's more people than voted in the last presidential election!"

Linda Surgeon heard him.

"Pass it!" came a call from the Gallery.

"Pass it!" came another. And then they continued in rhythm.

"Pass it! Pass it!" echoed the Chamber as a few hundred from the Gallery quickly picked up the chant. And it grew as many Members of the House chimed in.

Surgeon cracked the gavel twice, calling "OK, OK, we know you want it passed, but we have to have order to get it done. So please settle down."

Her words were heeded somewhat, and when things had quieted a bit, the settling down seemed to accelerate.

"OK, the Chair will entertain a motion from the Senate to suspend whatever rules may exist as would hinder the Senate from taking a voice vote on this joint resolution immediately."

Senator Rudy Bergman was still rubbing his fist from time to time, and he still knew his career was over. Before him, over the heads of some of the members of the Supreme Court, he could still see the unconscious Bertrand Earhart lying on and in front of the reams of evidence against the Congress, and above that to the left stood Benjamin True, and yet above him stood President Linda Surgeon.

Bergman broke the ice. "I so move, Madam President."

"I second the motion," said another senator, whom Bergman could not see from where he stood.

"One hundred and thirty-three million likes! One hundred and six million shares!"

"Point of order, Madam President!" shouted Senator Michael Steen.

"Oh, God!" said Speaker DuBois under his breath in disgust.

"The Gentleman from Texas is recognized."

"Madam President, the motion as suggested by the Chair is so vague as to require that it first be interpreted before it can be put to a vote."

"Boo!" came a response from the Gallery, which was in short order joined by others booing. Somebody yelled, "Punch him, too, Rudy!" which suggestion raised much laughter.

Linda Surgeon would normally have nipped such unruliness in the bud, but tonight, it was in her favor. She had even cracked a smile at the call for Rudy Bergman to punch Senator Steen, and she wasn't the only one. Within just seconds, a cheer had developed from the Gallery, and had spread to the Members of the House: "Ru—dee! Ru—dee!"

This, of course, brought even more laughter because of the famous scene in the movie by the same name. Surgeon let the fervor swell as she watched Steen from the corner of her eye. She simply stood back a step from the lectern, gavel in hand, doing nothing to restore order.

Meanwhile, Senator Rudy Bergman was smiling, but did nothing to act on the calls from the crowd. It was, perhaps, he thought to himself, a nice way to end his career, though. *Perhaps history will be lenient with me.*

The *Ru—dee!* chant continued and the objecting Senator Steen, whose voice would no longer be heard over the crowd, simply sat down.

Then President Linda Surgeon stepped forward and said, "I put the question to the Senate, on suspending any and all such rules as would hinder the Senate from conducting an immediate voice vote on the joint resolution. All those in favor, signify by saying, 'Aye'."

There was a resounding "Aye" from everywhere in the House Chamber all at once. The Senate represented only a small fraction of all those in attendance, but it seemed that most of the rest had voluntarily voted with the Senate. Linda Surgeon thought about restoring order and taking the vote again, but she realized that the real test would be whether there would be zero votes against suspending the rules.

She cracked the gavel twice. "OK, listen, everybody; we have to hear the remaining vote." Noting little difference in the level of crowd noise, she cracked it again several times. "We have to hear the remaining vote."

The noise had reduced by over half, but the room was still unruly.

Linda Surgeon pounded the gavel several times more and said, "Now listen, if you want this thing done, you're going to have to get quiet. Otherwise, I will ask Mr. True to *make* you be quiet."

Benjamin True simply smiled and nodded to Linda Surgeon, saying nothing. The invoking of his name, however, appeared to be sufficient, and in just a few seconds, the room had become quite silent and orderly again.

"Thank you," said Linda Surgeon to the quieted crowd. "All those opposed to the suspension of the rules, say 'No'."

She waited two seconds and there wasn't a peep.

"The Ayes have it. The motion passes."

There was chaos again in the hall as cheers of every sort erupted.

Surgeon pounded the gavel again, and the room came quickly back to order.

"Now, please, everyone. I beg you, let's just get this done, and for that, I need you to be completely quiet and to stay that way until the voting is all done. Do you understand?"

The room grew completely quiet as there was much sincere nodding in reply to the President's plea. Almost everyone in the Chamber and the Gallery was standing in anticipation. People's hearts were racing as they hung on every word.

"And this time, I need the Senate, and *only* the Senate, to vote," she said, scolding the audience, many of whom looked downward in shame at the rebuke.

Except for the still-unconscious Senator Bertrand Earhart, who seemed to be sleeping quite comfortably, Senator Michael Steen, who had abandoned his point of order in the chaos, and Senator Jeanine Planter, who was still temporarily blind and mute, the entire United States Congress was standing. Even Speaker William DuBois, who had sat to honor Linda Surgeon's authority during the Senate deliberation had stood up, though he stayed a couple of steps behind her.

Surgeon continued, "The question is now put to the Senate regarding

the Joint Resolution *Proposing an amendment to the Constitution of the United States providing for term limits for certain federal offices.* All those in favor of adopting the resolution, say 'Aye'."

"Aye!" resounded from those forward rows where the Senate sat.

Then there was some shushing from those in the Gallery and from the Members of the House, many of whom were diligently intent on remaining quiet and orderly as requested.

The room reached utter silence as everyone awaited the next words from President Surgeon.

"All those opposed to adopting the joint resolution?"

One agonizing second of silence passed. And then another. And then came what was perhaps the most amazing sound ever made in the history of the US House Chamber. The unconscious Senator Bertrand Earhart let out a booming snort as he began to snore.

The House and Gallery alike exploded in laughter. And so did America.

Linda Surgeon leaned into the microphone and declared, "The Ayes have it. The joint resolution is adopted!"

Chapter 19

My Gift to You

It was nearly 2:00 a.m. when Benjamin True turned to face Linda Surgeon and William DuBois, who were both still standing. He said, "I'd like to say a few final words before I depart."

They both nodded in agreement and took their seats.

"Please be seated," True instructed the crowd over the continuing exultations.

The crowd complied, each of them struggling in his or her own way to grasp the meaning of what had just happened.

"Well, you've done it. You have passed a proposed amendment that will be sent to the States for their legislatures to ratify—or not. I helped you do it, and this was my gift to you, because like I said, sometimes you just need a boost. And now, before I leave you, I want to give you some things to think about."

True pointed to the wall on his left, above the Gallery seats and nearer the rear than the front of the room. "In just a few minutes, I'm going to float right through that wall, and down Pennsylvania Avenue, just as I promised earlier. Again, I will travel down that road for as long as there are people there to see me. You can get plenty of pictures and video to satisfy yourselves that this is not all some elaborate hoax. But to all of you I say this: tonight should be an event to spur you to thinking, and not to shutting down.

"First of all, you must understand that liking an idea or a principle is a far cry from putting it consistently into practice. If I were to ask the average American whether it's good to have a government that is fair and just and righteous, he or she will surely say, 'Yes!'. But it is in this way that most people fool themselves. They think that just because it generally sounds good to them, they are all for it. The reality of the matter, however, is that they are not *all* for it, because if you really want a fair, just, and righteous government, you have to invest yourselves in a lot of work to make it that way and to keep it that way. And this is what I believe Ben Franklin was talking about when he said that:

> It is easier to build two chimneys than to keep one in firewood.[66]"

To follow his metaphor, if you really want to keep all these chimneys—justice, the Rule of Law, responsibility in government, and so forth—you're going to have to cut and split and carry a lot of logs. And you'll have to shovel a lot of ashes, too—and sweep that chimney clean from time to time. That's simply how reality works.

"But what if you don't *like* this real world into which you were born? What if you don't like how reality works? What if you hate it that there are real-world consequences to the choices you make? What if you hate it that reality never takes a break—that it's always turned on? What if you hate it that certain things simply must be searched out, thought through, and figured out—and that not all facts are easily discovered and understood? What if you resent the fact that life takes work? What if you would rather not be responsible for yourselves? What if you would rather pretend that someone else owes you all the things you need, and that it's *their* fault when you are needy? What if you hated to correct yourselves when you are in error? And what if you deeply resented anyone who would point out any of these things about you?

"What if you had inordinately invested years of your life in the cause of being angry over the misdeeds of other people? Or what if you had built a sense of identity around being the victim of some manner of oppression under which you suffer, or believe you suffer? What if you had learned to take all criticism as 'persecution'. And what if it had become your habit to do the very things that you condemn in others, and to tell yourselves that when *you* do it, it's OK because it's 'for a good cause'?

"These are the behaviors and the ways of thinking that plague this country. These are the cracks in its foundation that make it impossible for this Union ever to build itself into an authentic representation of the high ideals that were set for it in the Declaration of Independence and the Constitution. Indeed, these are the very things that keep its *people* from being authentic representatives of the ideals that they themselves will claim at first blush to be good ideals.

"What keeps you so predictably from the truth is your own resistance to it. Suppose that God himself were to set a time to come to the Earth for the purpose of solving every problem, answering every question, and settling every mystery, dispute, and argument. An event like that would upset the world considerably. It would call the bluffs of most humans, exposing the fact that very few are actually interested in knowing and understanding everything. Indeed, most don't *want* to know. They fear the upheaval and embarrassment of being proven wrong on so many points, and they avoid the work of having to set things straight in their minds. And each one has got his or own identity built around his or her own peculiar combination of beliefs and knowledge.

"That's what you are generally like, and there are precious few humans alive who have got themselves to the point of being even ninety percent cleansed from such low schemes of thinking. But here's the great, great news: You have a *choice* in this matter. It is not predetermined. Nor is a previous bad choice—or even a *string* of bad choices—irreversible. Indeed, I like the way that Thomas Paine put it:

We have it within our power to begin the world over again.[67]

"I think that Mister Paine was exaggerating a bit, of course, as the whole world is not your business. But you certainly have it within your power to begin your own culture over again, just as each one of you can do the same with his or her own self. In fact, success in the former task *requires* success in the latter.

"But don't deceive yourselves. What you have done here tonight is just the beginning of a single repair upon your government. It counts for nothing if the States don't ratify this amendment. And that reality is just a glimpse of the bigger picture. That is to say that getting term limits into the Constitution is just one needful step, and there are a thousand others after that. Sure, celebrate your victories as you go, but do not succumb to fatigue and lie to yourselves that your work is done when it is not. Indeed, that is the kind of screwy thinking that has got this country where it is today. This is exactly the bad habit against which you need a full-scale revolution.

"If you want to have a country that lives up to the high ideals that your forefathers put on paper, then you're simply going to have to learn to think better, and you've going to have to give up a lot of your hobby and entertainment time in order to get it done. And so, I leave you with a two-tiered choice: The first choice is this: *From here, you can do what is easy, or you can do what is right.* And having made that choice, you become qualified to face the second choice, which is the thing upon which your success or failure will all depend: *You can do what is right only sometimes, or you can do what is right all the time.*

"Now listen to me. Where is the Archivist of the United States?"

Robert Dickens stood up from his chair in the aisle to the extreme right of True's lectern. "I'm here."

"I want Mister Dickens to be making his way up here while the Speaker, Clerk, President, and Secretary make sure that this joint resolution is duly signed and certified in every respect."

Dickens began walking to the rostrum.

"The Archivist," continued Benjamin True, "is the one charged with forwarding exact copies of this joint resolution to each of the fifty states so that the state legislatures can vote on whether to ratify the Amendment."

Robert Dickens approached Benjamin True's position, leaving a few feet in between out of some mixture of respect and fear.

"Now, Mister Dickens, can you send this out to all the states tomorrow?"

"Well, that's faster than we usually work, but yes, I can probably get that done."

"And you will send out the *exact* wording of this proposed amendment, without changing a jot or tittle?"

"Yes, that's my job," said the archivist.

"Well, I hope you'll pardon the offense, but there has been monkey business with such things in the past, and we'd hate to see it happen again now."

"Understood," nodded Dickens.

"And when should the States expect to receive them?"

"I will send them Express Mail through the United States Postal Service, so they should have them by Thursday, or Friday in the case of the more remote states."

"Very well, Mister Robert Dickens. Now that the whole world knows your name and your face, I'm sure there will be lots of people expecting you to do just as you have said," said Benjamin True with a kind-but-assertive smile.

Benjamin True turned back to face the audience and the main camera. "Now, you at home—you don't need to wait for your governors to get this proposed amendment. No, you need to be on the lawns of your state capitol buildings first thing tomorrow morning. And you need to stay there until they have ratified it. And one more thing: you make sure that they vote on this amendment *exactly* as it is offered. No monkey business, and no editing. If at least 38 states don't all ratify the exact same document, word for word, letter for letter, as approved by this Congress tonight, it doesn't count.

"And know this. There are currently billions and billions of dollars being made off of the corruption that thrives here in this town. If you oppose that corruption too much, the corruption mongers will come after you. It will get ugly, and I won't be here to thwart them like I did tonight. Tonight, I stopped a double assassination attempt in this Chamber and an attempted bombing at a certain basketball game in Southern California."

There were gasps and murmurs of curiosity. "You'll probably want to look into that," he said dryly.

"So, that's about it," said True. "You won't be able to fix this government unless you fix yourselves first. In fact, the need to fix yourselves is so great that you'll have a hard time overestimating it. Your moral and cognitive dispositions are, in fact, the means by which they gain such an advantage over you. It is quite difficult, however, to scam a person who strives to be honest, rational, and responsible all the time.

"So, learn how to think right, and then learn the character to do it all the time. Then fix your families. Then fix your churches and schools and cities and counties and states. And then you'll finally be in a spot to have a righteous Union of States. If you can achieve it, that's great. And if you can never get enough who are thinking right at once to get much changed around here, then those of you who have done it right will still have succeeded in fixing yourselves. And that should be your non-negotiable goal in life.

"And now I leave you with the words that had become my main theme when I lived here: Life is short; why not do something extraordinary while we're here? Indeed, why not be something extraordinary while we're here?"

Benjamin True picked up his tricorn hat and put it on his head. Then he rose up above the lectern at which he had stood most of the evening, and began to float northeastward, toward the spot in the wall he had previously indicated.

The crowd stood, some stunned, and some applauding. "Are you ever coming back?" one of them shouted.

"I doubt very seriously that I shall ever return. But you have what you need to do as well as you please," he replied.

He floated over the desk loaded with file folders, and over the pile of Secret Service gear. Then there was the handcuffed Senator Bertrand Earhart, who was just coming to and wondering what all had happened.

As he continued moving, Benjamin True looked to his left, where Senator Jeanine Planter was now standing and still unable to see or to speak. She was clinging to the arm of a male senator, who stood to her right, and could be seen to be trying quite franticly to communicate something to him. He, in turn, was waving to get Benjamin True's attention, and alternatively pointing to the troubled Senator beside him.

True nodded to acknowledge the signaling, and just like that, Senator Jeanine Planter regained her sight and speech.

Benjamin True then floated fairly near to Congressman Dalvin Washington, who had clasped his hands together in a show of gratitude and mouthed the words, "Thank you!" through the din of the room.

With a hearty smile, Benjamin True returned a "Thank you" and a nod of his own.

Then, as he neared the railing of the Gallery, True reached in his pocket and withdrew the Coin of Rights. He made sure that young Tom Peterson was watching him, as if there were any chance that he would not be, and then he tossed him the coin as he floated nearby. Tom caught it in amazement, knowing instantly what it must be.

"You are awesome!" shouted Tom Peterson. Moved by his deep respect for Benjamin True, he called out, "Thank you so much!" and smiled the biggest smile of his life.

Tom's grandmother was very proud of her grandson. With her arm around him, she also thanked Benjamin True has he approached the wall through which he would pass. And then, just as he had said, he was gone from the House Chamber.

Chapter 20

Pennsylvania Avenue

Benjamin True passed through the various walls between the House Chamber and the exterior of the United States Capitol Building, emerging on the westward side of the Capitol into the cold January air. From here, he paused and beheld the classic view of the National Mall on the clear winter night. Looking due West, he could see the lighted Washington Monument, and beyond that, the Lincoln Memorial, the former being a mile away, and the latter, twice that far.

Beneath him and several feet away on the veranda stood one of many Capitol Police Officers posted along this side of the building. The officer held an M-4 rifle, but was signaling no aggression toward Benjamin True, who was floating several feet above his head. He did, however, radio in information of his position and his sighting of the intruder. The call came back, "Roger that. Do not engage. Repeat. Do not engage."

This order came as a relief to this particular officer, though another might well have been disappointed not to have the chance to engage a target. The officer spoke to True. "I heard your speech on my phone, and I loved it."

True said, "Thanks," as he continued to look down the Mall before him.

Noticing True's concentration on the view, the officer said, "So, what do you think of the Mall?"

"Well, naturally, I don't think like most of you here do. I, for one, wish they'd take down these two idols." True gestured down the Mall to the Washington Monument and Lincoln Memorial, and then continued, "How ironic it is that these two men, in particular, should become practically deified in this culture. They were the most instrumental of any Americans ever in letting the corrupt bankers get a foothold in this government, and yet they are praised the most. Even inside on the ceiling of this Capitol's Rotunda, there's a painting of Washington[68] supposedly being received into heaven, welcomed by the lesser *elohim*[69]. And did you know that the Lincoln Memorial down there calls itself a 'temple'[70]?"

"No, I didn't know that," replied the officer.

True paused a moment, and then shaking his head, he asked, "Why must they always make monuments to men, rather than principles?"

"I never thought about that."

"Well, it's vanity. That's why. People like power much more than they like principle. It's so empty. So vain. They praise their corrupt public heroes, with hardly a chance of achieving such grand status themselves, yet they could all become champions of principle in their own right. The one thing that *is* within their grasp, they forgo for a counterfeit substitute."

True looked down at the officer, who had found himself in a much deeper philosophical conversation than that for which he was well equipped, and said kindly, "Well, I suppose I should be moving along. Nice talking with you." With that, he began to travel forward, slightly to the Northeast.

"Yeah, you, too," said the officer, amazed at the chat he had just had.

Benjamin True floated across the westward portico beneath until he had cleared the fountain and the steps. He landed on the snow-covered lawn, just beside a very wide sidewalk leading in the exact direction he intended to go, thinking he might enjoy the walk down Capitol Hill to the street level below. He stood still for a moment on the Hill, looking down to the crowds assembled at Peace Circle, which was over a hundred yards away. He took a deep breath and reflected with a smile, *Well, I did it, and it was beautiful!* He was deeply happy and peaceful. *And now I suppose I must brace myself for the experience ahead. This should be quite interesting!*

There might have been spectators here on the lawn, but since the entire Capitol had been on lockdown, the grounds would long since have been cleared of any visitors. Had it been warm weather, he would have gone barefoot to enjoy the walk in the grass, but this was still good as it was, as it reminded him of his walks on the family farm in his previous life.

As he walked, he sang a hearty tune with a strong beat just right for walking. His voice was deep and well-suited for this song composed in the Dorian mode:

> *What sort of souls are we?*
> *Righteousness and Justice*
> *Shine the light by which we'll see!*
> *Righteousness and Justice.*
>
> *Come, let us reason how*
> *Righteousness and Justice*
> *Can solve what ails us now.*
> *Righteousness and Justice!*
>
> *Tyrants laud with lying tongue*
> *Righteous and Justice.*
> *By it they would have us hung*
> *While their own sins dismissing.*
>
> *Unruly fools say it's no good—*
> *Righteousness and Justice.*
> *But when someone steals their food,*
> *They're suddenly all for it!*
>
> *On this Earth, there's work to do*
> *To keep things as they should be.*
> *The sluggard wishes this weren't true*
> *And never grasps what could be.*
>
> *Fools suppose that someone else*
> *Ought to cure what ails them.*
> *They'll complain, but will not act,*
> *Then wonder why that fails them.*
>
> *Reality is always on;*
> *There's no way to escape it,*

Save in the world of make-believe,
Where fools pretend to shape it.

Good hearts will dare no wrong--
Not for any purpose.
Diligence, their daily song,
Guides them on their way.

Believe you nothing false,
Nor teach it to another.
Thus, will you guard your heart
And guard that of your brother.

Effort is no enemy
To body, mind, or morals.
The wise embrace it and are freed
From needless strife and quarrels.

When you're wrong, correct yourself.
Righteousness and Justice.
Love your brother as yourself
In Righteousness and Justice!

Do unto others as
You would have them treat you.
Never do another wrong and
You'll have friends to greet you.

How good when brothers dwell
In this way together.
It has been always thus,
And shall it be forever! [71]

Benjamin True's aim was Peace Circle, which was at the bottom of Capitol Hill, along 1st Street NW, where Pennsylvania Avenue continues northwestward toward the White House, after having been interrupted by the Capitol grounds over which True was now walking. Peace Circle was where the crowds began, and he had been able to see them there since he exited the Capitol, even though the street lights weren't very bright. As he neared the bottom of the Hill, his song complete, he lifted off again to clear the barricades and police officers stationed at the sidewalk at the perimeter of the Capitol grounds. He would stay aloft so as to make himself visible to as many as possible. Floating above the crowds, of course, would also make navigation down the packed street more manageable.

Peace Circle was filled with spectators and mobile news crews, all of whom were anxious to get an early view of the approaching visitor. They stood all around the Peace Monument, a 44-foot-tall white marble memorial to those officers, seamen, and marines of the United States Navy who had died in the naval battles of the US Civil War.

What this city really needs is some more monuments to the glory of war, True thought to himself sarcastically.

As he approached, the clamor of the crowd became substantial. Nearly all, it seemed, had smart phones aimed his direction and recording video. News reporters shouted questions, as their videographers shot live video feeds back to their networks. "Do a miracle for us!" shouted one bystander.

"Do you mean, 'other than flying'?" asked True, making a point that was missed by the one asking. He simply kept on going, now floating about ten feet higher than the tallest heads in the crowd.

He stopped at the Peace Memorial, and went around to its northwestern side. Atop the monument were two sculpted figures, one was "Grief," whose head was laid on the shoulder of the other, "History," who held a stylus and tablet.

Pointing up to the sculpture, which was several feet higher than his current position, Benjamin True asked the crowd, "Does anybody here know what the inscription up here on History's tablet says?"

No one knew, which was no surprise to True. Someone did, however, have enough curiosity to call out, "Tell us!"

True replied, "It says *'They died that their country might live.'* But like so many other things in this town, that's a lie. This memorial is to those who died that the United States might conquer the one-third of its states who had just voluntarily and peaceably left the Union to form their own country. They had left over unfair tariffs that crippled the South and benefited the North. Tariffs, mind you, that were started by Alexander Hamilton and continued under Abraham Lincoln, who finally brought Hamilton's dream of total despotism to reality.[72] Lincoln conducted a coup, and turned a voluntary Union of states into a mercantilist oligarchy from which no state would ever be free to leave again. And this, of course, gives a whole new meaning to the term, 'slave state', now, doesn't it? Lincoln's war only became 'about slavery' in its second year, when that cause began to seem politically useful to Lincoln."[73]

"And do you see that statue way over there?" True was pointing southeastward to a much larger set of statues about a hundred yards away. "That's Grant, who, as Lincoln's highest general, committed total war against the seceding states until they were conquered in 1865, and then oversaw the lawless occupation of those conquered states until he was rewarded with the presidency himself just a few years later. Interestingly, Grant himself had been a slave owner. Few know it, but as I said, that murderous war only became 'about slavery' *after* it started. In fact, on March 2, 1861, after 7 of the 11 Confederate states had already seceded, the US Congress passed a proposed amendment to the Constitution, stating:

> *No amendment shall be made to the Constitution which will authorize or give to Congress the power to abolish or interfere, within any State, with the domestic institutions thereof, including that of persons held to labor or service by the laws of said State.*[74]

"Now, if you ask me, that's an awfully strange amendment to make just before a war that it supposedly going to be fought to end slavery. No, that war was fought to start a *new* kind of slavery in which the states and their people become the property of the Federal Government. And there stands General Grant's statue, front-and-center to the Capitol for all to see. It is a symbol of this government's utter dominion over what is now called 'one nation', and 'indivisible.'" Benjamin True's mood was solemn and stern.

"I want one o' them gold bars!" shouted one lady in the crowd below.

Benjamin True just shook his head and continued northwestward down Pennsylvania Avenue. Generally, his speed was not very fast—perhaps the same as one walking quickly would have maintained, though walking quickly on this crowded street would not have been possible. He did, however, slow down and even stop on occasion, as the various conversations warranted.

One man stopped him and said, "Sir, I heard your speech on the radio. It was hard to take it all in, but I'm just feeling sick about George

Washington and some of the other early leaders who behaved badly. I never knew that."

"You wouldn't know, because you grew up in this hearsay culture—this meme culture—this textbook culture where you learn and teach, not by examining the source documents, but by textbooks, wherein you study what *someone else* wants to tell you about the source documents. Ironically, you don't even know if the textbook authors have studied the source documents themselves, or whether they have just copied information from yet other textbooks!"

"I never thought about that," said the man.

"You should ponder it at length," the angel counseled him. "Really, what makes you think that George Washington or Thomas Jefferson—or Abraham Lincoln, for that matter—should be any different from the politicians of today? Do you really think that these men were divine beings?"

"Well, no, I guess not."

"Of course, they weren't. But you live in a system whose leaders don't want you asking questions. They don't want you looking into matters deeply, so they keep making these men out to be bigger than life, and America keeps falling for it.

"These men were breaking free from King George, which was their right," True continued, "and they wanted to justify their secession to the king and to the world. Well, some of their rhetoric reached for the stars, even beyond the extent to which their actual, daily convictions would reach. That's why you get statements such as where the Declaration of Independence says, 'all men are created equal.' Most of the founders thought that sounded pretty good to them—especially since King George was not treating them as equals. But they did not give much thought to it as it regarded how they, themselves, were treating the slaves. And even if there had not been any slavery, the way they treated the *citizens* did not always hold up to that paradigm of equality. Just think about how Washington's bank deal caused all that financial loss for everybody because of the inflation he knew it would bring. He got suckered into that because of his lust for an increase in the value of lands he already held.

"No," True told the man, "these were normal men with normal moral dilemmas. Sure, some of them generally behaved better than others and had a higher level of thinking than others, but when they got things wrong, it was pretty much the same old sort of wrongdoing from which you all suffer at the hands of others today."

"Wow! You've given me a lot to think about!" said the man.

"Well, nice to meet you," said Benjamin True with a nod. Then True continued on his way.

Just as he began to move again, True noticed a reporter and videographer quickly approaching from the South side of the street. "Mister True—Julie Hastings of WMSM-Washington—you sure stirred it up tonight with lots of controversial subjects! Would you care to comment?" She pointed her microphone at the floating angel above her.

"I'll tell you this much, and then I must be getting along. The way I see it, there are two main kinds of controversy. First of all, there is that controversy which comes about between honest, rational, and responsible people, disagreeing or debating over matters such as understanding, taste, or priorities. That kind of people debate so as to establish the truth of a matter. Then secondly, you have the controversy that comes about between those who take an honest, rational, and responsible approach to reality, and those who would rather avoid reality on the matter in question. The latter sort debate so as to *avoid* the truth of a matter. If I raised any controversies tonight, I believe you will find almost all of it to be of the second type. And if anyone is complaining about the things I said, it is highly unlikely that they are the sort who are not interested in the truth of the matters I raised."

Just as the reporter brought the mic back to her own face to continue with a follow-up question, True began to move along, and said politely, "And with that, I'm afraid I must be going now. Goodbye."

As he continued along Pennsylvania Avenue, there was an impromptu group singing, "This little light of mine..." and beyond them a way was another news team, whose reporter held up her microphone and shouted to True, "Are you a Russian spy?"

True, who simply kept moving, said, "Uh, no," in a tone that showed that he was put out by the stupidity of the question.

Then came a request from a man in his sixties. "Can you heal me?"

True paused in the air, examining the man's appearance for a moment. "Sir, there's nothing wrong with you that couldn't be fixed by eating real food and cutting out the toxins you now ingest. Mankind survived for a long time on this planet just fine, eating the real food here—those, at least, who had good access to it. And now that most of you don't grow your own food, or even know who grows it for you, you eat this counterfeit food that makes you sick."

"So, you won't heal me?"

"If you won't heal yourself, sir, even knowing how, what good is there in doing it for you? You have a reality problem."

The man stood silent and convictionless as he watched Benjamin True continue to float away.

A few feet farther, a street preacher, strangely disinterested in the spectacle of the floating visitor, was making the most of his proximity to yet another news crew, who were busy filming his preaching against the backdrop of Benjamin True's approaching figure. The preacher was busy insisting to those in earshot that, "Unregenerate man is woefully limited by the sinful nature he inherited from the Fall! He is morally bankrupt! Desperately corrupt!"

Benjamin True floated nearby, and said, "A question for the preacher, if I might?"

"Go ahead," invited the preacher.

"On this question of the so-called sinful nature and moral bankruptcy, tell me, what human deed would be so virtuous as to make it simply impossible for an 'unregenerate man'—as you put it—to do?"

To the surprise of the few that were paying attention, the preacher simply ignored the question. He began to pray aloud, "Great Father God, please help us to discern between what is merely interesting, and what is truly of core importance as we navigate this dark world."

Once again, True shook his head with a sarcastic smile, and said, "Yeah, I couldn't think of an example, either." He simply kept moving.

"Did my wife make it to heaven?" asked another bystander.

"Sir," said True in a sympathetic tone, "I did not come here to reveal to you anything you cannot already know."

The man was crushed. "It's just so unfair that we cannot know."

"Is it?" asked True. "That is the nature of the world into which your lives have been set. It is the greatest mystery to every human: what lies beyond. And each one gets his or her turn to find out, Mister Libman. When I was awaiting death, I didn't run from the topic, as many do, but I embraced it. It made me want to live all the better."

"Anyway, as to your wife, you can bet that whatever the outcome, her judgment was just and merciful, because that's what God is like."

The man, surprised that True would know his name, was thankful, but sad.

"Live your life, sir. You can bear up," True said. And then he moved on.

Yet ahead on the sidewalk was a hotdog vendor who had come back out after hours, anticipating making some extra money from this unusual crowd. True saw the vendor and his cart, and surprised those nearby by landing there. The crowd was tight, but they managed to clear out a space big enough to park a car in as they yielded to the otherworldly presence of Benjamin True.

"Are those brats you're selling?" asked True of the good-natured vendor.

"Best brats in town. All natural, organic, gluten-free, and non-GMO, as are the buns!" boasted the vendor.

"I've always wanted to try one," said True.

"Well, you'll try one on the house!" Two seconds later, the vendor was handing Benjamin True a brat on a bun. "You can choose your condiments there."

"What should I choose?"

"Whatever you like."

"OK, what would you put on your own?"

"Ah, you want it done *right*!" said the smiling vendor, reaching for True's brat. He fixed it as he would his own, with mustard, sauerkraut, and grilled onions. Then he handed it back to True, who took a bite without hesitation.

"This is excellent!" said True as he was still chewing. "Thanks so much for the treat!" he said to the vendor. After taking his time to enjoy two more bites, he said, "I don't mean to be rude, but I should skip the rest of this and get back on my way." True was looking for what should be done with the remaining half of his brat.

"Oh, no problem. I understand completely," said the vendor as he took the brat from True and tossed it into his trash bin.

A lady from the crowd stepped forward and questioned Benjamin True, "Wait, how did you do that? Angels can't eat!"

"Oh?" he replied with a smile.

"No, and they don't have real bodies."

"Oh?"

"No, they have spiritual bodies."

"I see," said True, looking the lady straight in the eyes, and knowing exactly where she was getting the idea of 'spiritual bodies'. "Perhaps you should re-study that passage of scripture[75], taking particular note that the word 'body' has a specific and literal meaning, and wouldn't be there at all if the passage meant what you think it means. And regarding whether angels eat food, well, you should look into that for yourself, rather than taking someone's word for it."

"Well, I should be going," True told them all. And turning back to the lady, he held out his hand to shake hers. "Nice talking with you."

She shook his hand, obviously noting in the seconds that followed that it certainly seemed to have been a real and tangible thing.

True lifted off the ground again, merely by willing it, and continued along his northwestward parade route.

"That was really something tonight!" shouted a fan to Benjamin True as he passed over. To this, there was some applause and whistling from others in the crowd.

True kindly smiled and nodded in response and continued moving. As he continued a few more feet, one man was approaching as quickly as he could, pushing his way through the crowd until he arrived just in front of True. The man dropped to his knees and bowed his head, with his hands outstretched before him.

"You must not do that," True told him sternly.

The man did not move, and True instructed those by him, "Help him up; I am no one to be worshiped; I am myself but a glorified human, and am myself under the same authority as are you all."

As True continued to move along, the prostrate man was helped to his feet. The parade had now run several blocks, and the crowd continued for as far ahead as the eye could make out. The route passed several government buildings, including the National Archives Building, where the originals of the Declaration of Independence and the Constitution for the United States are kept. There were fancy hotels and embassies and all manner of other places along the way.

And there were the people. They were as varied in their personalities as in their appearances. Many of them had some remarkable qualities. For one, it might be kindness and compassion, and for another, personal discipline. There were those with keen senses of humor, and some, like the hotdog vendor, who were extremely winsome and affable. Some of them were deeply invested in various sorts of knowledge. Some had learned language very well, and some had invested themselves in the various arts. Some of them were pretty good parents in one or more respects, and had successful families to show for it. Some of them were diligent and faithful employees, and others among them held those same qualities as bosses, truly taking care of their employees. Some were concerned with the deeper things in life, and some had a reverence for history. Some were marvelous physical specimens whose bodies were amazingly fit to serve in all the ways the human body was designed to serve humankind. There were among the crowd some teachers who cared, some students who cared, some cops who cared, some government employees who cared, and so forth.

Benjamin True loved this about humans—how they were generally free to decide to invest themselves in good things. Indeed, he had enjoyed that freedom in his own lifetime, and had gained his own unique set of skills and knowledge and habits. Like practically everyone else who grows up in a careless culture, True had been free first to decide just how honest, rational, and responsible he wanted to be in life. And having faced that question where many avoid it, he had had to learn just how to achieve the level he had chosen in principle. And then, he had had to wrestle with how *often* he wanted to be honest, rational, and responsible. And like everyone else who sets a goal for him- or herself on the higher end of that gradient between dishonest and honest, Benjamin True had had to spend a few decades unlearning the various biases and disinformation that one picks up merely by virtue of living in a culture filled with them.

Things were certainly different now in some ways than before, but not all that much. No, people were still prone to follow social norms without giving much thought to them. They were still prone to overestimating their own knowledge, wisdom, and skill, and to underestimating how much evil there is in the world.[76] They were still prone to mental laziness and to moral laziness, too, which, of course, is the driver of mental laziness. And they were still prone to that ever-present plague upon the Earth, hypocrisy. It was the hypocrisy behind which so many attempted to shield themselves from both effort and accountability. This was the protection under which seemed to thrive the two standard departures from reality: the error, and the lie.

Yes, it had always been thus, and these hordes along the street tonight were all part of that same human tradition of aspiring to some form of goodness while swimming otherwise in a sea of moral and cognitive compromise. If only they would fully commit to goodness, then they could unfetter themselves from all that hindered them, including those persistent cognitive errors by which the scoundrels and tyrants have them so well entangled. But few ever seem to figure out that to be good is to be what humankind was designed to be, and that to be anything less is a low-minded substitute for authenticity. They find the effort required for being good to be too costly. Yet at the same time, they do not complain that the effort required for staying warm and well-fed is not worth it. No, they take a far more pragmatic view of their subsistence than of their morality—as if the thriving of the body were more important than the thriving of the person inside it. Then, having cleft themselves in two between body and soul, they have further put off the work of the body more and more—the good work for which it was designed, and on which it depends in part for its health.

And that's where this generation was different, for never had there been so much commerce and public policy aimed at easing the natural work of humankind—at turning them into something other than that for which their natural design had so suited them. By and large, they had traded the natural work of actual subsistence for the physically-less-demanding work of the various corporate careers that had become so prominent. They had traded the natural activity their bodies needed for a paycheck, with which they could, they believed, trade for the goods and services they believed would satisfy them. Yet in this, they grew less and less healthy every year, and even began to fool themselves that their decline was—as they were told—the mere and natural result of aging.

They had traded off the real food that their own ancestors had either grown or bought from local neighbors. They had traded it for counterfeit foods sold under the great brand names—brands to which they had also traded off their own buyer-beware thinking in return for the promise of convenience. And this trade-off led to yet another: they traded their health for a life of chronic sickness, as their weakened bodies, inflamed within by counterfeit foods and the various toxins that made the production of that food more profitable for the producers, revealed symptom after symptom. And yet again, they traded the obvious cure of correcting their eating for the promise of the long-term pharmaceutical prescription, to which they would financially enslave themselves for life. And without thinking, it was in this way that they had traded their final years at home for painstaking years in hospitals and nursing homes.

All this, of course, is because they, at least on some topics, and at some times, were willing to trade good thinking for bad and reality for unreality. They had traded the wisdom of the ages for the whim of the moment. It rarely occurred to them that since they all lived in a real world, perhaps the best policy would be to adopt a way of thinking that was itself based deliberately upon reality.[77] No, few would ever do enough thinking to figure that out. And fewer still, to go after actually putting it into practice. That kind of thinking was exceedingly rare, though practically everybody had the necessary faculties for doing it.

And those were the sorts of people filling Pennsylvania Avenue along this parade route. They were the sort over which Benjamin True celebrated their virtues and accomplishments, while regretting their persistent shortfalls. No one falls so short as the one who never tries. And no one tries so little as the one who never thinks. And no one thinks so little as the one who grows up being *told* what to think about everything, rather than being taught how to do it for himself. And that's what most of these people were like, to some extent. Only a very few of them had figured out that they could—and should—do their own thinking as a rule. Few would ever experience the epiphany that one's own thinking is the true, natural, and rightful domain of every human— that it is a space inviolable by anyone but oneself—that it can be made impeccable by one's own caring and learning to do so—that in one's own freedom of thought, each of us is truly the supreme ruler with the latitude to choose as exactingly as we please between reality and unreality, truth and falsehood, caring and apathy, good and evil.

Few of them ever came to see themselves truly as they really were. They were consumed with their own lives, and rarely got their hands around the fact that they were each overlapping lifespans in a sea of others who would come and go, just as they would themselves. They preferred, many of them, to see themselves as somehow more innately special than this, as if simply existing on the Planet Earth were itself a sign of personal merit. They would rarely figure out that the much better measure of their worth lie in the investment of what they might make of themselves while they are here. Benjamin True's incessant appeal to the question, "what kind of people are you?" would slip right through the minds of most without ever getting snagged on anything before it had found its way back out again. And so would his philosophy that, "Life is short; why not be something extraordinary while we are here?"

As he passed over the crowds, which were—in these various regards—both strangely beautiful *and* strangely dull, Benjamin True knew that not one in ten thousand had already discovered the bulk of such things about what it means to be human, and that fewer still had the disposition to put such fundamental ideas to the test. But here they were, and he had done them the service of telling them the truth—of providing them with a glimpse of the fact that maybe, just maybe, some higher view of life and its promise can and should exist on this Earth—even that such view could *prevail* upon the Earth. He hated that so many had settled, in the name of God, no less, for believing that they were, by their very nature, less capable than they actually were—less capable than they had each been created by that very God. That was ironic, indeed, yet so few would ever realize it, for this idea of "the curse" was just too savory for so many.

Benjamin True stopped as one lady, obviously making a beeline for him, began to hold up a pointing finger in front of her own scowling face.

"I just think it's wrong!" she said, wagging a disapproving finger toward his face, which was suspended several feet above her, "It's wrong that you would stoop so low as to engage in so much judging tonight. It was utterly shameful and it was ungodly!"

Benjamin True looked at her for a moment and said, "I have something for you right here, Ma'am." He tipped himself forward, so as to be able to hand her something, and on his way down, an 8x10 photograph appeared in his hand.

"What is it?" she asked angrily.

"Oh, it's a photograph of you angrily pointing a finger at me and telling me that I'm in the wrong—over 'judging', of all things."

She took the photo from him and glanced at it quickly. "Yeah, what's the point?"

"The point is that you are not thinking about what you're doing—I hope. Because if you do realize what you're doing, and you're doing it anyway, that's even worse."

"What in the world are you talking about?" she demanded.

"Ma'am, you are demanding that I quit judging, yet you yourself are judging me as if judging were itself a wrongful act."

"Well, it is wrong. Jesus said it himself: 'Judge not,' he said."

"Ma'am, in the passage to which you are referring[78], you have conveniently recited his words only up to the comma, and have omitted the several paragraphs that follow, including the parts where he makes it plain that people are indeed to judge by a fair standard, and that they should be prepared to be judged themselves by the same standard by which they choose to judge others. Because you quit reading when the incomplete passage grew to a length that suited you just fine—two words—you seem to have missed where in the same passage, Jesus expected his followers to be able to judge a *lot* of things accurately. For example, they were to judge the difference between a 'speck' and a 'plank'. They were to judge what is 'holy' and who is a 'dog' and what is a 'pearl' and who is 'swine'. They were supposed to be able to judge the difference between 'bread' and a 'stone', between a 'fish' and a 'serpent', between a 'narrow gate' and a 'wide gate', between 'destruction' and 'life', between a 'false prophet' and a real one, between a 'ravenous wolf'... 'in sheep's clothing' and a real sheep, between 'grapes' and 'thorns', between a 'vine' and a 'thistle', and between 'good fruit' and 'bad fruit'."

"And there's one more thing in that passage," he continued. "They were supposed to be able to judge rightly as to 'lawlessness'. And lawlessness, ma'am, was the general subject of my entire appearance in the Capitol tonight."

Her face was still hardened.

"Here's something you should know about how God thinks, ma'am. The proverb says:

> He who justifies the wicked and he who condemns the
> righteous are both alike an abomination to the Lord.[79]

"You had best stop condemning those who do good, ma'am, and especially, you had best stop doing it in the guise of proclaiming what is supposedly godly and not."

The woman stomped off without a word.

"Sir?" called out a man in his forties.

Benjamin True continued forward, but at a slowed rate, so as to give the man a chance to catch up to him.

"Sir," said the man, now walking along the street that was True's course, "Why won't the government just do right, and quit lying, cheating, and stealing?"

"Well, it is written:

> To turn away from evil is an abomination to fools."[80]

"Hmmm," pondered the man for a couple of seconds. "OK, so how come my friends think I'm nuts when I speak up about all the lying, cheating, and stealing, like you did tonight?"

"Again," True stressed to the man, "*to turn away from evil is an abomination to fools.[51]* They have decided to love lying, cheating, and stealing as a way of life for themselves, so they think you're an idiot for giving those things up voluntarily. It's really that simple. And if you were to decide to be honest, rational, and responsible yourself in every way all the time on all matters, then there's one more thing you should keep in mind."

"What's that?"

"It's this proverb:

> An unjust man is an abomination to the righteous, but one
> whose way is straight is an abomination to the wicked.[81]

"The point is that you're always going to be an abomination to *somebody*—either to the righteous, or to the wicked. There will always be strife between the two. And those who aren't *feeling* that strife have

225

got themselves in a very bad place. They have secluded themselves from righteous people, and taken shelter in the company of other wicked people."

The man stopped dead in his tracks as True kept going. "Yeah, uh, thanks," he said, still getting a handle on a fact that was yet to him profound.

After another block or so of this unusual parade, with a sea of smart phones and reporters documenting it all from the street below, Benjamin True came upon a married couple in their thirties, who called out, "We loved the word problems! Do you have any more of them?"

"Sure, why not?" said True in good humor. "Here's one:

> A certain lily pad in a lake begins to double in size every day. On day 30, it grows to the size of the full lake. On what day was it half the size of the lake?"[82]

"Oh, that's easy;" said the husband, who looked at his wife and asked, "You got it?"

"Umm, I'm thinking it would be day fifteen, right?"

The husband greeted her answer with a big smile and a high-five. "Nailed it!" he congratulated her.

"Oops," said Benjamin True. "You should think through that one some more. The error you have made is in failing to understand what sort of problem you are trying to solve before you start stabbing at solutions. This scenario presented to you is not an arithmetic progression, where the lily pad grows by a fixed amount, again and again, with each passing day. But that's what you thought it was, so you simply divided the 30 days by 2 and got the wrong answer of 15. The scenario is rather a *geometric* progression, where the lily pad doubles in size every day, so the difference in the actual amount grown from one day to the next is not constant. If the lily pad is the same size as the lake on day 30, then to find when it was only half that big, you need to reverse the process of doubling every day. When you do that, you see that it must have been half the size of the lake only one day before it reached the full size of the lake. So, the correct answer is Day 29."

"Oh," called out the husband in perfectly shameless mirth. "I see! You got us both with that one!"

His wife laughed along, amused at their error. "You got any others?" she asked.

"OK, I'll give you one more, and then I should be moving along."

"Oh, great! I love these!" the husband exulted.

"Alright," said True. "For this one, there's a visual, so look over here to my left." He pointed to a building on the South side of Pennsylvania Avenue. It was the Wilson Building, and it housed the executive offices of the Mayor and Council of the District of Columbia. With the wave of a hand, Benjamin True caused a very large image of four cards to appear on the building.

"OK, do you see those cards?" he asked them.

"Yeah, they're huge!" the woman laughed.

"Alright," said True. "This is a fact about the cards on the building: *Each has a letter on one side and a number on the other.* Remember, that's a fact. I guarantee it's true, and it's not in question."

"Gotcha!" said the man.

"OK, now, here is a rule about these cards that needs to be tested: *If a card has a vowel on one side, it has an even number on its reverse.* So, the question for you is this: *Which card or cards must you turn over in order to test whether this rule is true or false?*[83]"

Again, the man jumped in first. "OK, OK, OK, let me see. You said each card has a letter on one side and a number on the other, right?"

"Right."

"So, then what rule are we testing?"

"The rule you are testing is that: *If a card has a vowel on one side, it has an even number on its reverse.*"

"Hmm. If a card has a vowel..." he was thinking "...then it has a number on the other side. Hmm. OK, well, the card with the A on it has a vowel, since the A is a vowel. So, we need to turn that one over to see if it has an even number on the back side. And, umm, the card with an 8 is an even number, so we need to turn it over to be sure there's a vowel."

The man's tone was not certain, and Benjamin True said nothing to settle the matter prematurely.

"Yeah, so I'm going with the A and the 8. They have to be turned over to test the rule."

"And what do you say, ma'am?" True asked the wife.

"Hmm, do I have to say something different?"

"No, you can say whatever you like."

"Well, I like the A and 8 answer, too, so I'll go with that."

"OK, you both said A and 8. Is that correct?"

They both nodded.

"Well, you are half right," announced True.

"Oh, which one of us?" asked the man.

"You both answered the same," True pointed out.

"Right. So, which one of us got it wrong?"

Benjamin True was amused and decided to explain graciously. "When I said you were half right, I didn't mean that half of the pair of you were right, but that the answers that you both gave were half right—meaning that one of the two answers you gave is right, and the other is wrong."

"Oh, I get it!" announced the man, pleased with this new understanding.

"So, what part is right and what part is wrong?"

"Well, you were right about the A card. To test the rule, you definitely need to turn that card over. And if it didn't have an even number on the back of it, then you'd know the rule is false."

True paused to be sure the couple was still with him.

"Right, so what were we wrong about?" asked the man.

"Well, let's see. You were right about the A card, so the one you got wrong would be the 8 card."

"Oh!" said the man. "Why is that one wrong?"

"You made an error in your logic. It's an if/then problem. That is, if vowel, then even. Do you get that?"

"Yes", the man said.

"OK, well, you need to know that if/then statements don't necessarily work in reverse. And that's your error. It doesn't matter what the 8 card has on its back side because the rule tells us nothing reliable about what an even card would have on its reverse."

"Oh, I see," said the man. "Well, thanks for explaining it to us."

"I'm not done yet," said True.

"Oh," said the man, "well, please continue."

"There's one more card that you should have wanted to turn over. It's the 5 card."

"Why's that?"

"Because if the 5 card has a vowel on the back side, then there's a violation of the rule, for any card with a vowel should have an even number on the reverse, and 5 is not an even number."

"Oh, that's really complicated!" said the man with a smile.

"Yeah," said his wife.

"Yes, over 90% of people miss this problem. And it tests one's understanding of some of the more basic rules of logic. So, it's quite troubling that so many in this culture do so poorly with logic, and yet they don't seem to be alarmed at the situation."

"Oh, you're sure right about that, Mister!" said the man solemnly.

"Yes," agreed the wife. "Thank you so much for coming to help those people learn to think better. God bless you!"

With that, the couple walked away and True overheard her saying to her husband, "Isn't it so sad that the people don't understand those problems? I just think somebody should help them."

Benjamin was still shaking his head at this cluelessness when he was approached quite warmly by a man who obviously had something to say. "Hello, Mister True, is it?"

"Yes, Benjamin True at your service!"

"Mister True, I wanted to thank you for coming tonight, and to tell you that I have really learned something from your example?"

"Oh?" questioned True.

"Yes," said the man. "I had wrongly assumed something about heaven. I had assumed that unlike here, everybody there would be made perfectly into the same sort of person."

"Oh? What do you mean?"

"Well," the man explained, "here in the church, we have people who are more drawn toward the intellectual side of thinking and those who are more drawn to the spiritual side. I am the spiritual sort myself, and not the intellectual sort, by the way. Anyway, it's really fascinating to see how God gives us both kinds of people in our fellowship. But I had been thinking that when God makes each one perfect in heaven, he would see to it that everybody gained that special spiritual maturity, and would move on from the intellectual side of things—not that that's bad, mind you, but it just isn't as mature."

"So please do explain to me," queried True, "just how it is that you have learned something from my example tonight."

"Oh, yes!" said the man, excited to share his epiphany. "It's very obvious that you yourself lean pretty hard toward the intellectual side, and not the spiritual side. I mean, all this talk about thinking logic and such. Well, I'm ashamed to say it, but I had just assumed that God would perfect *everybody* in heaven so that they would be fully spiritual, but I see that I was wrong about that, and that God is just as tolerant and gracious about people's weaknesses in heaven as he is of people here in the church."

"And you figured this out all by yourself?" questioned True.

"Yes."

"I see. So, you think that it's unspiritual to use your mind?"

"Well, I wouldn't put it exactly like that."

"Let's not mince words here," challenged True. "It's pretty clear from your statement that you think that you are more mature than I am— more 'spiritual'."

"Again, I wouldn't put it that way."

"But if you did, it would be honest, at least, for that is clearly what you think. So let me test your concept of spirituality with a few questions. Tell me this first: Who gave you your hands?"

The man was a little lost at this question. "Uh, my hands?"

"Yes, who gave you your hands?"

"God did, I suppose. Is that where you're going with this?"

"Yes. God gave you your hands. Now, does he expect you to use them, or not to use them?"

"Uh, to use them, I guess."

"Are you really guessing, or is that your true belief?"

The man still looked a little lost.

"Let me help you out here," said True. "Do you go around every day questioning whether you should use your hands or not? Or do you rather default to using your hands anytime it appears that there's a need for them?"

"Oh, I use them all the time."

"Right, and do you ever feel guilty about that, like you're sinning somehow to use them?"

"Well, no. I guess not."

"Are you really guessing again, or do you just use the word 'guess' the way that most people use the word 'think'?"

"Sorry, I *think* not."

"OK," continued True. "So, you use your hands that God gave you, and you use them every day, and you don't feel guilty for using them."

"Right."

"And why not?"

"Why don't I feel guilty? Is that what you mean?"

"Yes, why don't you feel guilty about using your hands?"

"Well, why should I? What's wrong with it? Didn't God give me my hands for my own use?"

231

"Indeed, he did!" said True. "And now you understand the way I think about the human mind. Didn't God also give you your brain?"

"I guess—uh, I mean, I suppose he did."

"Yet in the case of the brain, you think that it's a sin—or at least an immature act—to use it? Tell me, sir, why is that?"

"Well, it's in the scriptures that thinking is bad."

"Oh? Would you care to cite the passages you have in mind?"

"Well, the one about the carnal mind comes to mind[84]," explained the man.

"So tell me, is your mind carnal?"

"Aren't all our minds carnal?" defended the man.

"You tell me, sir. Tell me why Paul would instruct them to be made new by the renewing of their minds.[85] If they had no choice but to be carnal, as you seem to assume, why did he instruct them to do better? Why did he talk about training in righteousness[86] and training in godliness[87] and training themselves by the constant use of discernment[88]?"

"Well, you're not going to like this, but Paul was more on the intellectual side himself. He was just saying it the way that *he* saw it."

"And *you* know better, of course," said True with a skeptical tone.

"I wouldn't put it like that."

"Of course you wouldn't, because that would make you look arrogant, and you'd rather not appear arrogant, even if you are."

"Look," defended the man, "I didn't come to pick a fight with you, but I can see that I've done it. Paul also wrote, in one of his more spiritual moments that knowledge puffs up, while love builds up.[89] I think he knew that he had a real struggle with intellectual pride, and that he was constantly battling it. Some passages he did better on than other ones."

"Oh, my!" reacted Benjamin True. "Would you care to tell me, then, how you know the difference between what Paul got right and what he got wrong?"

"Well, it's all spiritually discerned."

"I thought you might say that," said True. "You're making two huge errors here, both of which come from not making good use of the mind God gave you. First of all, you're interpreting Paul's letter to the Corinthians in a way that makes zero sense in light of the rest of his teachings. He was fighting the very sort of presumption from which you yourself are suffering. They had this silly saying that 'we all possess knowledge'[89], when, in fact, they did not have knowledge in all matters. That sort of 'knowledge', he told them, was puffing them up. And he went on to put another nail in the lid of that coffin. He told them that the one who merely *imagines* that he knows a thing does not yet *really* know it.[89]"

"But that's your intellectual spin on it all, sir," defended the man. "Really, I hate to rebuke you, but it's obvious that you don't understand that these things are all..."

"Spiritually discerned[90]," interrupted True, speaking over the man as he finished his sentence. "Yes, I knew exactly what you were going to say. You're now referring to 1 Corinthians 2, from which you will surely argue of yourself that 'we have the mind of Christ'[90]. What you don't understand is that Paul was speaking of himself and his own apostolic team. It was *they* who had the mind of Christ, and not the Corinthians. Indeed, was this very letter not written to rebuke them for their bad thinking? Had Paul truly been telling them that they all had the mind of Christ already, there would have been no need whatsoever to appeal to them that they get their thinking right."

The man was silent, and deep in reflection.

"Look, you're making an error that is woefully common," True continued. "It is the error of assuming that the apostles were not in a special role, but an ordinary one, and that everything that was true of them is also true of you. You go home and think this one through. Go read both the letters to the Corinthians and follow the whole we/you stream of thought. There's a lot of it, by the way. But you find that trail and follow it, and it'll lead you right into some really big surprises about some bad assumptions and you and millions of others are making about what the Bible actually says about you."

The man was sober, and somewhat somber. "Well, I'll look into what you're saying, but I must confess that I'm skeptical."

"The risk here," counseled True, "is that your skepticism—your bias —will keep you from seeing the pattern that's right in front of your nose. In just an hour or two, with all the electronic Bible tools you have these days, you could easily find enough evidence to suggest very strongly that God wants humans to be cognitively active, and to be so consistently, responsibly, and diligently. There are lots of passages—even ones that are quite familiar—that are frequently overlooked and ignored as Christians rush to shut down their minds. Tell me, do any of these one-liners sound familiar?

Come now, and let us reason together, says the Lord. [91]

Give careful thought to your ways. [92]

The first to plead his case seems right, Until another comes and examines him. [93]

Stop judging by mere appearances, but instead judge correctly. [94]

So a man should examine himself... [95]

For as he thinks in his heart, so is he. [96]

Purify your hearts, you double-minded. [97]

A double minded man is unstable in all his ways. [98]

...do not be children in your thinking. Be infants in evil, but in your thinking be mature. [99]

Do not think of yourself more highly than you ought, but rather think of yourself with sober judgment. [100]

Those who consider themselves religious and yet do not keep a tight rein on their tongues deceive themselves, and their religion is worthless. [101]

But the seed in the good soil, these are the ones who have heard the word in an honest and good heart, and hold it fast... [102]

...do not deceive yourselves... [103]

If anyone imagines that he knows something, he does not yet know as he ought to know. [104]

if we judged ourselves rightly, we would not be judged. [105]

Let no one deceive himself.[106]

... the mature...have their powers of discernment trained by constant practice to distinguish good from evil.[107]

Test yourselves to see if you are in the faith; examine yourselves![108]

Do not merely listen to the word, and so deceive yourselves. Do what it says.[109]

"Does any of that sound familiar, friend?" True asked him.

"Most of it does."

"Then you have been doing the very thing that last verse tells you not to do. You have been deceiving yourself by not doing what you are told, and pretending that your disobedience is acceptable to God. You have adopted a twisted sense of what 'spiritual' means."

"But I got my beliefs straight from the Bible," the man objected.

"No," corrected True, "you got them from your faulty *interpretations* of the Bible.[110] If I may be blunt, your mindset about the Bible is simply foolish. You think that whatever you think it means is what it means, and that you couldn't possibly be wrong about any of it, because the Holy Spirit is giving you all the right answers. You think to yourself—although you'd never say so out loud—'If I were wrong about this, I'd know it.' But you have no clue how wrong you are, and about how many things, because you have got that kind of mental work shut off in your mind."

"Mister True," pleaded the man, "logic is simply not the answer. The Spirit is the answer.

"Just what do you think logic is? How do you define that word?"

The man, who had been fairly eloquent so far, was taken aback at the question. He stammered and stuttered, and eventually came up with, "It's a worldly system of thinking that relies on human intellect rather than on God and his Spirit."

"Well, your bias on this matter is very clear," True shamed him. "Here's a much better way to think about what logic is: Logic is a set of thinking rules, none of which anybody has ever been able to disprove in the last couple thousand years of debate on the topic."

"Well, that's a novel definition, don't you think?" the man challenged.

"Is it? If your definition is such the standard, how come it wasn't readily on your lips the moment I asked you to define the term? How come you had to process it, rather than just having it memorized? The fact of the matter is that you have spent most of your life opposing something that you don't even understand well enough to give a definition for it. And how dull is that? It would gall you to have someone demonstrate for you that God and Jesus, as quoted all throughout the Bible, are impeccably logical, for you think that is a bad thing. Don't you?"

"Again, I'm not saying it's bad; I'm just saying it's not the most spiritual way."

"Oh, so you're accusing the Holy Spirit of being illogical? You're accusing the Holy Spirit of Yahweh with operating outside the limits of impeccable thinking?"

There was no answer.

"Friend, you just told an angel that you think you're more spiritually mature than he is, and that you think you're more mature than the apostle Paul was—not in so many words, but that is the unmistakable meaning of what you did say. And you just admitted to recognizing a long list of passages that make it quite obvious that God expects believers to be honest, rational, and responsible in their thinking. Obviously, you have not thought this through. And the obvious reason for that is that you think that thinking is bad. You've got yourself in one of the worst traps there is. You go home and think about what I've told you. Search it out and see if what I've said to you isn't the truth."

The man nodded in agreement, averting his eyes from True.

"Well, if you'll excuse me, I should be getting along," said True. "Goodbye."

The man nodded again as the angel continued his slow flight along Pennsylvania Avenue. As True moved across the crowd, still considerable in its size and density, and still filled with news crews anxious for every second of sensational coverage they could get, he noticed a very old man making his way carefully down from the curb to the paved street. The man looked upward every few steps, bracing himself with his cane, and anxious to keep track of True's whereabouts, in hopes that he would not miss the chance to speak to him. When at last he caught

True's eye, he waved to him. True waved back and gave a gesture to suggest that he would come to the man, who stood patiently next to the curb he had just descended.

The crowd made way for the angel to touch down just in front of the man. Benjamin True held out his right hand to shake, and said, "Hello, sir, my name is Benjamin True."

"I am very pleased to meet you, Mister True," said the man as he reached out to shake True's hand. He was careful to look the angel in the eye, as he hooked his cane handle into his trousers pocket so as to free up his left hand, which he also used to shake True's hand. "Thank you for coming over to me, sir. As you can see, I am far from agile these days."

His speech was slow, but quite deliberate and poised. "My name is Ernest Mansfield, and I came out here to tell you that I realized tonight, during your speech, that I have been a fool all of my life. I thank you for the many rebukes in your speech. You pegged me well for the fool that I am. I got caught up early in the idea that my party is better than the other, and I never stopped to realize—like you said tonight—that the party I chose is itself corrupt enough to ruin this nation on its own."

True continued to listen patiently as the man spoke, still holding True's hand in both of his own.

"I am ninety-eight years old, and I have been a sucker for this partisan trap *all my life.*" Those last three words got to the old man as he spoke them. He began to sob, dropping his head forward.

Benjamin True put his left hand on the man's shoulder and remained quiet, trusting that the man needed no help to express himself.

"I don't know how long I have left on this planet, but obviously, my days are short," Ernest Mansfield continued, gaining more control over his emotions. On my way over here, I laughed at myself that it should take me ninety-eight years to learn such a simple lesson. But at least I've learned it now, and I can correct myself from here forward."

The angel smiled at him and said, "Yes, you can!"

"Well," continued the man, "I won't keep you any longer, as I'm sure you have many more people to see. I came out here to pay my respects to a man who dared to tell me the truth, and I've done it. And so I bid you good night, sir."

"I am very glad to have met you, and I thank you for coming to find me. May your time from now on be more fruitful than you would imagine! Good night to you, as well, Ernest Mansfield."

Each nodded to the other, and Mansfield finally loosed his grasp on True's right hand. As the old man turned slowly back toward the curb, the pony-tailed soldier lifted once again to a height well above the heads of the crowd and turned northwestward again.

Benjamin True's parade went as far as the White House and beyond, with the streets still being fairly crowded up to that point, and more people showing up all the time. Along the way, he was asked who was going to win the Super Bowl, and more than once about the winning lottery numbers. He was met with smiling faces and cheers, and by those paralyzed with fear. He was met by the tough guys who acted as if their very souls might fall apart if they should abandon their hardened scowls even for a second, and he was met by those with various questions—many of them superficial or based on erroneous understandings—and a few really good ones that he regretted he didn't have time to answer.

He had many admirers here, even though many who admired him had not understood much at all about his State of the Union Speech. No, they liked him just because they took a fancy to like him for whatever reasons, however arbitrary they may have been. No further justification for it was necessary to them. At this point, they really didn't *care* to understand him, because that's just what some people choose to be like—woefully incurious about the important matters of life. Precious few as there were, however, Benjamin True did see some brighter ones among them, and these were the ones that made it all worth it to him. He had such hope for their success.

Chapter 21

Sky Creedmoor

Sky Creedmoor had worked late in his Culpeper, Virginia auto repair shop, as he had had a big job that was running slightly behind. But there was more to it than that. He occasionally enjoyed the quiet and solitude of the nighttime hours and had long had a habit of listening to meaningful things while he worked. This night he had planned, of course, to listen to the State of the Union Address while he worked, and that was the secondary activity that had become his primary motivation in being there after hours on this particular night. In fact, he had been holding this State of the Union ritual for years in his shop in this small town in Northern Virginia.

The town of 19,000 people was founded in 1759, and had been surveyed by a young George Washington. It lay just over 60 miles southeast of Washington, DC, as the crow flies, or about 70 miles by road. In good weather and in non-peak traffic, one could drive the distance in under ninety minutes.

Sky Creedmoor's shop was at 207 N. Main Street, just one block East from the historic courthouse in downtown Culpeper. His house, however, was just across the Rappahannock River at Kelly's Ford, about a 20-minute drive from his shop in Culpeper. He and his small family owned a modest house on 5 acres here, where they could enjoy the natural setting and the relative seclusion.

His wife and son were home on this night, though his son would normally have been in the shop with Sky to hear the State of the Union

Address. He had had a bad cold for a few days, however, and was at home in bed, his mother enjoying the quiet evening to herself.

Sky had been told more than once that he wasn't exactly a "normal mechanic," which epiphany usually struck people either after getting into a conversation with Sky, after surveying the contents of the bookshelf in his office, or, perhaps, after noting that he didn't normally listen to the radio as do many other mechanics, but most of the time to podcasts or lectures on any of a number of topics. And if he did happen to have music playing, there was no telling what it was going to be. One day it might be The Manhattan Transfer, and some other day, Harry Connick, Jr., or the Bulgarian State Radio & Television Female Vocal Choir, or Flatt and Scruggs. And then, for two weeks straight, it might be all Barbershop quartets and choruses all the time. And then after that, he might not listen to any music for weeks because he simply had other things on his mind. Sky's problem was that there were just not enough hours in the day to learn everything that needed learning. And learn, he did—constantly.

Depending on whom you asked, and on *when* you asked them, you'd have been informed that Sky was "very serious" and "very funny" and "very nice" and "very judgmental". He was a "genius" and also an "idiot". He must have been a "Liberal" and he must have been a "Conservative". One man had puzzled over Sky Creedmoor thus: "He sure has a lot of ideas of his own!" At hearing about this, Sky had wondered aloud, "Well, whose ideas am I *supposed* to have?"

He had spent a few decades playing mythbuster to the world's persistently erroneous beliefs. He had studied as time had allowed in religion and politics and history. He was a fan of the sciences and was something of an engineer/inventor himself, which sometimes came in handy in his mechanic work. Sky's son, who was 13, had been soaking it all in for years. When he was four, he'd come to Sky on many evenings and say, "Hey, Dad, can we talk about the government?" And Sky would tell him this or that about the corruption, as well as about what it was *supposed* to be like and why. And Sky enjoyed watching his son grow up without the common misconceptions that so many others not only grew up with, but would never figure out for the errors and lies that they were.

Most generally, over his 51 years, Sky Creedmoor had become a problem solver. And in the most recent years, he had been trying to learn just why it is so hard to get people to change their minds when they are wrong about something. This question had eventually led him to the field of cognitive science, where he had become convinced of the evidence that humans are far less rational than they think they are—and even more importantly, than they *could* be. And then, of course, came the necessary struggling with his *own* state of rationality, as he learned of the cognitive errors that are common to all humans. As he read of the thinking errors common in the society, he discovered to his own dismay, that he was prone to many of those errors himself. But he had been brave enough not only to wrestle his own self-view into reality, but to learn to avoid many of those errors most of the time. And for his success in being willing to see himself accurately, he loved the observation by Daniel Gilbert:

> If you are like most people, then like most people, you don't know you're like most people.[111]

Sky was OK with that—that is, that he was prone to cognitive vulnerabilities and tendencies, like everyone else, and that if he were going to be a cognitive success, he'd have to work at it. Having a myth-busting avocation, he understood, would have made it easy for him to be a conceited *besserwisser*, so he strove to keep himself in check, and he chose to do so by memorizing and repeating an epiphany he had read on a blog somewhere:

> I am most likely wrong about many things.[112]

Lots of people found that idea somewhat unconventional—which it was—and even a little bit unsettling, Sky had noticed. Others found it novel and interesting, and might even say it from time to time in a tone that made them sound humbler than they actually were. But Sky was different because he actually believed it. He was completely sure that there must still be beliefs in his mind that had not yet been properly vetted. And how could he know *how many* such things yet remained? And further, even though he was now much more careful than before to vet new things before believing them, he still forced himself to realize that even now, he might not be getting everything just right. His life, therefore, had become something of an exercise in cognitive vigilance. He still made errors, of course, but especially in the more important matters of life, his errors were generally less serious and certainly rarer. And he liked it that way pretty well, as it seemed to be working for him, even though it took much more work this way. This is what kind of person he had chosen—and was still choosing—to be.

By the time 9:00 rolled around, Sky had long since had the radio tuned in to the best station, and his hands and face were already greasy from his work. Listening to the State of the Union Address was not something he looked forward to with any sense of patriotic romanticism, as he had in his youth, for he had long since figured out the artifice and scheme, and was rarely taken in by the rhetoric anymore. But he did listen out of a sense of due diligence. He was a citizen, after all, and the direction of the country was important, even though things were rarely as they were advertised to be.

By about 9:17, however, Benjamin True had descended upon the State of the Union Address, piquing Sky Creedmoor's attention like no other event he could remember. In the first few seconds after True's spectacular appearance, Sky heard a radio announcer break in to say, "Some manner of disturbance has broken out in the State of the Union Address. We continue with our live coverage."

It was then that Sky Creedmoor ran to his office and turned on the TV. He quickly found the event running live on one of the news channels, and began the struggle of both listening to the speech and catching as many of the tickers at the bottom of the screen as he could. "BREAKING: Intruder at SOTU!" A few seconds later, the ticker said, "State of the Union Speech Interrupted." And after a few seconds more, it said, "INTRUDER: 'Benjamin True'."

Sky immediately fumbled for the "Record" setting on his TV remote as he stood watching. As he stood there wiping his hands on a towel without having bothered to find any GOJO®, it never occurred to him to sit down. *Who is this man? What's he up to? Is this some sort of hoax?*

The longer he watched, the more obvious it became to Sky that this didn't *look* like a hoax. It lacked the telltale signs of a hoax so far, as far as he could tell. But more than that, there was some real substance to this man's bearing and his speaking. His appearance, his character, his expressions—they all seemed so real, so believable. And this man sounded like a mythbuster himself.

When things had settled down a bit in the House Chamber, Benjamin True had announced that when he was done, he'd be leaving the House and floating down Pennsylvania avenue to the northwest. Sky Creedmoor had a large map of Virginia, as well as one of the District on his office wall, but he didn't need to consult it. He knew exactly how to get there, and how long it should take, provided the snow that had been falling for the last two hours wasn't going to get crazy.

If Benjamin True were going to head northwestward on Pennsylvania Avenue, that would put him going by or around or through the White House somehow, and then continuing to the northwest on Pennsylvania to where it ends on M Street NW in Georgetown. *Of course, I have no idea how long he's going to keep talking in the House. I suppose I could miss him if he finishes soon. But if he's going out to be seen by the masses, there's going to be a boatload of people out there. That's going to take a while, so I have a chance of getting there on time. And I'm not going to risk missing this.*

Sky Creedmoor cranked up the volume on his shop TV so that he could keep listening while he went outside to start his car and get its radio tuned in to a suitable station. When he had done that, he grabbed his coat, hat, and gloves, made sure he had his smartphone. Then he did something for which he had thanked himself innumerable times in the past. He planted his feet and forced himself to think through where all was going, what he was likely to encounter there, and what he should have with him. He double-checked the trunk to be sure that his go bag was there. Upon seeing it, he decided to put it in the front seat and immediately checked to be sure his two spare cell phone batteries were in it and charged. They were.

Why am I doing this? Do I just want to see him for myself? Or can I actually talk to him? Where along Pennsylvania should I try to intercept him? Oh, plug in your phone, Sky. Wait, you have to lock the shop before you go, Sky. And what about Dewey? He can't miss this, but he's too sick to come. And I really need Anne, too, but she's got to stay home with him. Plus, it's an extra half hour to stop by the house to get them.

These thoughts were hard enough to manage in a hurry, of course, and especially while listening to the most amazing event ever to happen in this country. As various events in the House Chamber were drawing screams and other loud reactions, Sky realized that the radio just wasn't going to cut it. He pulled over and found a video feed on his phone. After watching it for a few seconds, he realized that he was now in a dilemma between watching and driving and decided that he'd somehow manage to do both at the same time. *I cannot miss this. Are you an idiot? You are NOT going to watch a video while driving through the snow at night. I had better call Anne. I'll call her once I'm on Highway 15 and will explain it to her then. Wait, no, I need to be sure she's watching this speech now.*

He pulled out of his shop's parking lot and dialed his wife's cell. "I'm not in danger, but I'm in an emergency and I can't talk more than ten seconds. Turn on the State of the Union Address immediately, and wake Dewey up because he needs to see this, too. I'm going to see this man. Leaving the shop now. We'll keep in touch via text messages as I'm able. Love you. Gotta go. OK, bye."

As he continued to listen, sneaking a peak from time to time, Sky realized that he was generally believing his eyes and ears and that his own mind was resonating with the words of Benjamin True. *Could this be the real deal? I have got to talk to this man—or whatever he is.* And off he drove toward the White House, or thereabout.

Chapter 22

The Meeting of the Minds

Benjamin True was now northwest of the White House, well over a mile and a half from the Capitol Building where his parade had begun, and still on Pennsylvania Avenue. It was just after 4:30 a.m. and the ordeal had turned into the biggest night-time event ever in the District. Crowds were now thinning, but even so, a couple of mobile news crews were still present. One had managed to follow along his parade route, somehow or other, crawling along in their compact car through the crowd behind him. The other had simply intersected Pennsylvania Ave from a side street.

The waning crowd still were taking videos and pictures. True had lost track of the number of selfies that people had taken with him over their shoulders. And they were still asking questions. Far fewer had anything to say to him, he had noticed. The most frequent thing said to him was, "Thank you," and other similar expressions. After that, it was, "I'm a Christian!" Most of those who told him this seemed to expect some manner of instant camaraderie—some smiling acknowledgment and approval on account of the confession. But most quietly found it at least a little unsettling that he did not respond as they had imagined he would. They had a hard time grasping that he was not as impressed with their confessions as they were, but that he had meant what he had been saying all along—that his concern was in what kind of people they were, as opposed to what kind they *thought* they were.

Benjamin True looked at the waning crowd ahead and thought that about another block and a half would do it, so he continued on, as he had said he would do, with the two news crews in tow. They were hoping that yet another spectacle would occur so they could get the "scoop", just as they had when they had earlier captured the giant images of cards that he had displayed on the side of the city executive office building. He had generally avoided interviews with the media, though he was asked several times along the route.

In this final block and a half of his parade, little of particular note happened, except that one of the two news cars had overheated, putting a stop to its progress. As the awaiting crowd had thinned, there was now more room for people to follow along behind as he continued to float above the street. As the last of the onlookers got their photos and videos, Benjamin True simply vanished.

Those nearest to him were startled by his disappearance. "I guess he's gone," said a man to his wife.

"Funny that he would just go without saying anything," she replied. And the two turned to walk back to their apartment, which was a few blocks away.

Likewise, most of the crowd began to disperse immediately. It was over seven hours since this whole ordeal started, so obviously, many were exhausted. A few of them lingered to reflect on the event, however, because that is what some people choose to be like. But most were gone quickly. Among them was the second news car—the one that had not overheated. It simply turned right at the intersection where True had disapparated, and accelerated away into the night, along with the hum of its engine. Its crew would deliver their footage to the station as soon as possible.

Just as True had vanished, however, a lone bicyclist had been turning the corner yet another block ahead, and was headed southeast, toward the spot from which True had disappeared. The bicyclist was Sky Creedmoor.

Sky had come to Washington in his car, of course, but had had considerable difficulties along the way. He was just a few minutes away from home when he discovered that the roads were icy for about ten miles. He even slid off the pavement at one point, but was able to get back on the road after several minutes of maneuvering. Then there was a stretch of severe blowing snow in the ten miles or so between Warrenton and Gainesville. Visibility was so poor he had slowed to under 30 miles per hour, and felt he was pushing his luck even at that low speed. The worst of the snow and ice was over by the time he reached Washington, which was quite a relief, as he was running considerably later than he had anticipated. Even so, as soon as he had crossed the Potomac River on I-66, near the Lincoln Memorial, he took the E Street NW exit and promptly had a blowout.

This is all kinds of bad! What am I going to do now? I'm not a mile from the White House, so I guess I'm humping it from here.

He pulled off the road and parked the car. He grabbed his go bag, which was a backpack, and put it on his back as he began to walk eastward to 18th Street NW. Benjamin True had long been on the street, he had learned from the live news feeds on his smart phone, but it was difficult to know where he was at this exact time. To further complicate the matter, Pennsylvania Avenue is interrupted by the White House, and there are several paths one could take to get around the White House and back onto Pennsylvania. The last landmark he had recognized in the video was the northern fence of the White House, which would have put the angel on H Street NW. Sky assumed, therefore, that True would take the most direct path, and just follow H Street westward until it intersected with Pennsylvania.

As he continued to hike northward, the streets became more and more crowded with pedestrian traffic. It was obvious that something was indeed going on. As he reached Pennsylvania Avenue, he asked a man whether the angel had gone by yet, and the man told him *no*. Sky Creedmoor then ran the next block to H Street, where more people were waiting, and he asked another the same question. He got the same answer, "No."

Sky was quite tired, given not only the very late hour, but his ordeal in getting this far from his shop in Culpeper. It was at this point that Sky managed to buy a bicycle from a guy in the crowd. It cost him $200 in cash, and he noted as he rode away on it that it was worth every bit of $20. But it was still better than walking. He had poor success riding the bike eastward down H Street because of the crowds. He tried the sidewalk, which was a little bit better than the street, but still had quite a hard time getting to the next block eastward. That intersection was with 17th Street NW, and upon asking, he learned that Benjamin True had turned South there to pick meet up with Pennsylvania Avenue at the first opportunity, rather than to take the more efficient route along the road he had just pedaled.

Creedmoor looked southward along 17th Street and could see that while many were just standing there, there was also a fairly obvious parade of people who were apparently following Benjamin True at a snail's pace.

There's no way I'm going to catch up with him through that crowd. I'm going to have to head back the way I just came—like it wasn't fun enough the first time!

He reasoned that if the crowds were still on the street, Benjamin True would still be out there somewhere, because True had promised as much. So, he set a course westward along H Street, and found it still quite difficult to travel, though the crowds has thinned a little as word had spread that True had taken another route. Creedmoor took H Street westward all the way to where it intersects with Pennsylvania. The crowd was denser here, and he asked a lady whether True had yet passed. This time, the answer was *yes*, so he moved one block north so as to be able to advance faster westward by avoiding the crowds. This strategy had problems of its own, however, as Pennsylvania runs diagonal to the grid. The result was that Sky's path was in a sawtooth pattern at times. And to make matters worse, the "yes" lady's answer about whether the angel had yet was *wrong*, which fact Sky would not discover until after several more minutes of bicycling. How anybody could have been wrong about such a simple matter is a puzzle that Sky would never figure out.

It would have helped if he could have monitored the news as he rode, but he had forgotten to bring his ear buds and his Bluetooth headset alike. Holding his phone to his ear while riding was simply impractical, so he had decided simply to search until he found Benjamin True. Needless to say, it had been a difficult night for the exhausted Sky Creedmoor, who was riding about Washington DC on a bike in January, in the snow, looking for an angel he had seen on TV.

Sky eventually made his way ahead of the parade, however, and emerged on Pennsylvania Avenue just one block west of this floating man in a Continental Army Uniform. And just as he had turned the corner, having barely laid an eye on Benjamin True from a block away, he saw him disappear.

Just like that, he was gone.

Sky Creedmoor quit pedaling and put on the hand brakes, coming to a full stop in that practically-abandoned block of the street. He got off the bike and stood there, crushed at what he had just witnessed.

"Had you come to see me?" came a voice from above and behind him.

Sky was so startled that he fell over trying to turn around as fast as possible. He landed on his rear in the street and found himself looking up to the floating Benjamin True, who, it seemed, had apparated to a spot under which Sky had just ridden.

"I haven't been that startled in a long time," said the panting Creedmoor, shaking his head and smiling. He was still winded from bicycling.

Benjamin True touched down to the ground and walked over to the grounded bicyclist. He reached out his right hand and said, "Let me help you up."

"Thanks," said Sky Creedmoor, accepting the help and getting to his feet.

The two stood face to face.

"Benjamin True," he introduced himself, putting a proper hand forward for shaking.

"Sky Creedmoor," Sky returned the gesture in kind. "That's a nice uniform you have there."

"What, this old thing?" True smiled.

Sky smiled back, recognizing the old joke. "Hey, uh, I think I heard almost everything you said tonight, and I don't know where to start. As far as I accurately know myself, I think I agree completely with you on everything I heard. I've been studying on these topics for years, and I found your speech to be very amazing and very true."

"Thank you," said True, still smiling.

"I have so much to say to you and to ask you, but I don't know how much time I can get with you."

"Well, we'll see about that. What's the first thing on your mind?"

Creedmoor was still a bit winded from his ride, but was thrilled that he was being taken seriously. "OK, let's see. You said in your speech—I think you were talking to Senator Earhart—you said something like, 'Don't get me started about the churches.'"

249

"Right, I said that," said True.

"Well, I'd like to get you started about the churches," said Creedmoor with a smile that wasn't too apologetic.

Benjamin True smiled in return. "That's funny," he said, appreciating Creedmoor's sense of humor. "I'm afraid I didn't come to address that topic in detail, however."

"Then can we talk about the Bible?"

Benjamin True seemed truly disappointed. "I'm sorry, but this visit just isn't about the Bible, either—although that would make for some great conversation. I will tell you one thing, though, but first, I think that it would be good if we were to sit down."

"That would be great;" said Sky Creedmoor, "I am quite tired."

"Well, there's that, but then there's the fact that some talks deserve a reflective posture." True looked around at the sidewalks on either side of the street and found no benches. "Now, that's funny," he said with a smile, "you can't hardly spit in this town without hitting a monument of some sort, but when you need something practical like a bench, there's none to be had!"

Sky knew immediately that he liked this guy.

"Well, I think this will do just fine," said the angel, as he deftly pointed a finger to the sidewalk, where a beautiful slatted park bench suddenly appeared just under a street lamp."

"Whoa!" said Creedmoor in surprise. "That's quite a trick!"

"Thanks," said True as he gestured toward the bench. "Shall we?"

"Yes, thanks!" Sky righted his bike and pushed it to the sidewalk, where he laid it down again, the bike having no kickstand. "Hey, that's awfully fancy for a bench!" he said, admiring Benjamin True's finely polished handicraft. "That's not Macassar Ebony is it?"

"I see you know your exotic woods well!" said True, impressed.

"Oh, not very, but I did sell Steinway Pianos in what now seems like a previous lifetime, and that was one of my favorite woods."

"Well, do join me on my bench, and we'll get back to our excellent conversation."

As Sky Creedmoor sat, the angel noticed that the news crew a block away had spotted them. The cameraman and reporter were walking toward them, and were about a hundred feet away.

"That's close enough," True told them, holding out his right hand in typical *Stop!* fashion. Sky could see that the pair stopped moving forward immediately, being unable to advance any further, but not being frozen. The news team set up immediately from where they were, with the reporter talking in her mic while the cameraman captured her report with True and his guest seated on the bench in the background.

"My, you certainly do have some powers!" he told the angel.

"Yes, it's an amazing upgrade, this heavenly body! Now, where were we? Oh, yes, I was going to tell you one brief thing about the Bible. Most people handle the Bible pretty much like they handle the Constitution. That is, they adopt opinions about it—even really strong opinions—without ever really doing the work necessary to understand it deeply. Some of them tell themselves they love it even though they don't understand what it really means. And among them are many who actually *reject* some of its teachings, even in the name of loving those teachings. And they have no idea just how flimsy and arbitrary and twisted their views about the Bible are. They are clueless that if the Bible had been presented to them differently than it is typically presented by these careless preachers and writers, they'd have a very different outlook on it.

"Just like the Constitution was written at a higher level of thinking than that to which most are accustomed, that is doubly true of the Bible. And this makes it a book that is filled with traps for the cognitive/moral miser. They don't want to expend the effort on understanding it accurately, so they just latch onto whatever they *want* to make of it, and off they go, ignorantly supporting and even promoting ideas that the authors and God himself never would have supported in a million years. And some, of course, stand opposite these people, ignorantly opposing it without understanding it, either.

"Well, it's quite the same as with politics, Sky; it comes down to what kind of *people* the believers are. The more authentic the person, the more he or she will figure out about the Bible—or the Constitution, I should add. And the ones who are *wanting* to be lied to and misled will never understand what should be made of it."

Sky Creedmoor, still amazed to be sitting on a bench with an angel, simply nodded in agreement, disappointed that they couldn't get into it, but pliable enough to go along with the wisdom and the agenda of his new mentor. "OK, well, I'm sad that we can't discuss those things at length. I'm assuming, however, that the government is a fair topic for conversation?"

"Yes," nodded Benjamin True.

"OK," said Sky with a diligent tone. "Well, all the way here, I decided what I would ask if I could only ask you one political question." Before he could finish this sentence, Creedmoor's expression changed. He cocked his head to one side and rolled his eyes in acute frustration. "Oh, great! Here I am finally talking to you, and I've forgotten what question I was going to ask you!"

"It'll come back to you," True calmed him. "You obviously have a lot on your mind."

"Oh, yeah. I remember it now. OK, you mentioned in your speech that the term limits were just the first step, and that there were a thousand other needful steps. So, I'm wondering, what would come *next*?"

Benjamin True was obviously pleased with this question. "Mister Creedmoor, look down there." True pointed to the southeast along the street, toward the Capitol Building, which could no longer be seen from this spot. "I've passed over a million people tonight, and not one of them has asked me that question."

Sky recoiled slightly at this news, but True intervened before Sky could make too much of it.

"Don't get me wrong; it's a *great* question. But I want you to let that sink in for a moment. Not one of all those people asked me that. And that means, of course, that they simply aren't thinking the way you are thinking. And why do I tell you this? It's because you need to understand that you should not assume that anybody else in this country is going to be thinking well about certain things. You can't afford to think that somebody else will get to it and will take care of it."

"I understand," said Creedmoor, feeling quite sobered by the occasion.

"Yes, you do understand on principle, but you need to understand it even better. You just can't count on the American public to take care of business as it should."

"OK," said Creedmoor, opening his mind to understand it further.

"There are about six million people who live here in Metro DC, and *one* of them came out here to ask me that question," said True, pointing at Creedmoor. "Are there others who might have thought of the same question themselves? Sure, there are a few—a very *small* few, I should add—but how many actually came out here to look into it?"

"One?" asked Creedmoor.

"Yes, one. So, what does that tell you? What would the facts in evidence suggest about waiting around for somebody else to have your same idea and to run with it the way it needs to be pursued?"

"I knew things were bad, but I had not yet calculated anything of the sort. If I were to take one in six million as the ratio, then figuring for all 340 million of us here, that comes to what? 50 or so?"

"It's higher," corrected True. "It's around 56."

"Are you telling me that there are only about 56 people in this country who would come here to ask you that question if they could?"

"Having the question pop into one's mind is rare enough, but actually coming here to seek out its answer—that is a behavior that's exceedingly rare," answered True. "You'd be lucky to find one person per county who would even *think* of the question."

"Wait, there are what—3,141 counties—right?"

"Right."

"And you don't think that every county has at least one person who is tuned in enough to ask such an obvious question?"

"No, I don't, and yes, it's that bad. There are a great many complainers, but very few deep thinkers—very few problem solvers who actually find some promise in thinking through the big picture of what ails the country and coming up with some viable solutions. Sure, there are lots who have their own ideas about this or that, mind you, but very few are actually trying to work the *whole* puzzle with an eye toward substantial reform. So that makes you a fairly rare animal, Mister Creedmoor."

Sky Creedmoor felt a little slow on the uptake, but he thought he was understanding True's message to him. It seemed to be a compliment and an encouragement wrapped up into one, but it also made him feel as if he had been punched in the stomach. *Fewer than 3,000 in this whole country? No wonder it's so hard to find friends who are interested in really discussing all this!*

"So, you're wanting to know what should come next?" True asked.

"Yes," said Creedmoor, shaking his head quickly to try to restore himself to his full senses. "Please tell me."

"Well, it depends on how you want to tackle things. You could take on a strategy to 'strike while the iron is hot', of course, pushing for other popularly-supported amendments as soon as tonight's amendment gets ratified—if it *does* get ratified. Maybe you could build some momentum that way, but the big challenge is that you'd have to find a way to *organize* such efforts. It's not like you can have an angel pop in to help out on every amendment, so who's going to spearhead all that?"

"Right," said Sky Creedmoor, his head spinning.

"Of course, such a strategy can only be so effective, because only a few needed reforms are popularly supported at this time. Don't get me wrong; you could certainly build some momentum after getting tonight's amendment passed, and considerably more if you can get a second one passed. And that would be worth a lot. But that's going to run out quickly, whether the number you can get passed is two or ten. The people will quickly long for a rest, even if it is grossly premature. Most people will always want to feel at rest, even when resting is a really bad idea. So, for the *rest* of what's needed, you'll have to change the way a lot of Americans think first.

"So, instead of going after further amendments, you could opt for going after changing their thinking first, and then get into the actual business of reform later, once you've got somewhere. That strategy, of course, runs the risk of letting the iron grow cold. Or, you could try to tackle both at the same time. This all is up to whomever will be doing the work, of course, so it's not my decision. No matter how you approach it, though, your toughest task will be in getting Americans to step up and actually *do* the work."

Sky pondered a second and said, "What approach would you take if you were me?"

"Well, I'd try to tackle them both at the same time. The emotional momentum of that sense of getting something done is worth a lot—and it's not just emotional, but actual; they will have actually accomplished something needful. And while you can only expect to get so much done without a big shift in the way that Americans think, a few of the things you *could* get passed sooner than later are not insignificant in the impact they could have on curbing the corruption. And at the same time, every change you succeed in making will be helpful in influencing the people to think differently."

"OK, like what?" asked Sky Creedmoor. "What are some of the things that stand a chance of getting passed—things that the people could get behind without having to change their thinking in a major way just yet?"

"Well, I'll give you one example to ponder. You might stand a decent chance on an amendment that prohibits any member of Congress from voting on any bill that he or she has not certified in writing that he or she has read first."

"Yeah, that's a good one!"

"It should also require that a proper quorum for taking a vote must be counted, not from those present, but from those present who have certified that they have indeed read in its entirety the bill in question. Oh, and it will need to set forth what happens to those who lie about having read the bill."

"Yes, that's exciting!"

"It would certainly cut down on a lot of the corruption you're seeing now, with members of Congress not doing their own jobs as diligent legislators, but merely rubber-stamping the bills their masters give them. Oh, and speaking of their masters, another simple amendment that might have a chance is to require that every piece of legislation must disclose all its authors and their addresses and occupations. The American people deserve to know who writes these bills, because when there's a ghost writer, they are often representing the ones that stand to benefit the most behind the scenes."

"This is all very good. What else?"

"Well, let's talk about the big picture some."

"OK, please go ahead," said Creedmoor.

"Tell me, regarding my speech tonight, did you agree with me when I said that the US Constitution is not perfect?"

"Oh, yes, I've figured that out several years ago. I think it's pretty good, but it's not perfect."

"Right. Me, too. So tell me, what is one of its most fundamental faults?"

"Well, it certainly has some intentions that should have been fortified more heavily to make it harder for the bad guys to twist its intent, but it seems to me that one of its biggest weaknesses is that it presupposes in most places that sufficient will would exist among the citizenry to enforce its measures."

"Ooh, I like you!" said True, smiling from ear to ear. "You are exactly right! Being just a document, the Constitution cannot enforce itself; it takes *people* to do that. And it doesn't have enough tools in it to provide much help to those few who see the wisdom in keeping it in force—especially since they are so far outnumbered by those who don't. And, of course, nothing in the Constitution can *force* the people to be great citizen-overseers of their government. After all, virtue is wholly voluntary, and can be forced on no one."

"Yes, I see that," said Creedmoor, still reflecting studiously in case there were something here beyond the obvious to be grasped.

Benjamin True went on, "OK, I'll go on, and you stop me if I lose you. Now, the framers did nothing to see to it that Americans would grow up being *taught* the things they need to know in order to be effective and righteous overseers of their own government. The assumption was that the families and churches and the schools would take care of that, but those institutions, more or less, have been left on the doorstep like a gold bar, and have long since been snatched up by those who don't want Americans overseeing the government, but who want to have control of it for their own sinister purposes. Many of them give the *appearance* that they're preparing the next generation to take over, but the work they are doing is unsatisfactory and deliberately compromised.

"Being an American," True continued, "is like inheriting a great mansion. Anybody can inherit it simply by virtue of being born here, but where does one find the character necessary to maintain that mansion? That character is not included in the inheritance; one must supply it himself."

Creedmoor reflect with a smile, "Hmm, character not included. That reminds me of my reading about the now-debunked *standard economic model*, by which it was long assumed—quite wrongly—that consumers generally act rationally in their own interests?"

"Exactly," answered True.

"Ha!" said Creedmoor, smiling as he continued to work the thought through. "I guess I knew that already in its parts, but I had not put the whole of it together in this way before. It's simply not a given that the American citizen will act rationally in his or her own best interests when it comes to overseeing the government."

True answered him, "Right! They need help learning to think and act rationally in such matters. And there's something more. The grand assumption of the founders was that the American people needed the freedom to oversee their government *because they wanted the job*. But the truth was that the citizens didn't really want that job—not many of them. And so, the role of overseer has been left out on the doorstep like another gold bar. It has long-since been snatched up by those who want to oversee the country for their own ulterior motives. And those players promise the citizens that they'll watch over the government *for* them, and that all the citizens need to do is to vote and pay taxes."

"Yeah, I get that," said Creedmoor. "And the people, of course, are generally suckers for that because they are cognitive/moral misers who don't like to do the heavy lifting."

"You got it!" congratulated True.

"So, what needs to happen here?"

"Well, do you see any way to fix the government without fixing the people?"

"Hmm, no. Well, unless we're thinking about finding a wise and benevolent dictator who will be upright on behalf of the people, so that they can afford the luxury of living in negligence. But that doesn't really fix the people, which is what you asked about."

"Right," confirmed True, "and good luck finding such a dictator, anyway. You won't find one in ten thousand of that level of character, and one in a hundred thousand who also has the required knowledge."

Creedmoor nodded in obvious agreement. "And even if you found one, you'd have the age-old problem when it turned out that his or her heir was not of high character."

"Exactly," said True, smiling again at how fun it was to talk to a human that had done so much good thinking already. "So that brings us back again to the need to fix the people."

"OK, but I've long puzzled over what percentage of them we have to fix to make it work? I know you can never fix them all. So how do we best leverage the support we *can* get?"

"That's a great question. You can do it with a fairly small percentage of the population, provided they can keep their doctrine pure, and that you can give them the tools they need. Let me explain.

"Look at how many people don't get involved in politics at all. Those people aren't helping your cause, but at least they're not actively hurting it much, either. So, don't worry about them just yet. And you definitely don't want to 'get out the vote' where this crowd is concerned, because they don't know anything, and are not apt to vote wisely."

"Yeah, I just figured that out a year or so ago—about getting out the vote, that is. And boy, does *that* fly in the face of conventional political wisdom!"

"So that leaves two groups you need to be aware of. One of them is definitely striving against the Constitution—and they constitute a big problem. They are the ones who openly call for disobedience to it at times. That's really bad, of course, and you don't want to 'get out the vote' in that crowd, either. Believe it or not, however, they are not the *biggest* problem."

"Oh?" questioned Creedmoor.

"No, the bigger problem comes from those who *think* they're completely for the Constitution, but who still support and profit from various practices of disobedience to it. A lot of those folks are the sort who believe that compromise is a good and necessary thing in politics— that it's somehow the 'fair' way to do political business. They'll let the lawless crew win a victory from time to time in a trade-off that they reason is 'for the greater good'. But this is hogwash, because doing the wrong thing is never for the greater good. In fact, it's one of the stupidest ideas in all of the world, that in order to get along with one's unruly neighbor, it's only 'fair' to let him have his unruly way from time to time."

"I agree," said Creedmoor.

True continued, "Imagine a medical team in the emergency room operating on this principle of compromise. Imagine the surgeon having to do harm to the patient, not because it was best, but because it was politically expedient, he thought, in order to get the rest of the team to do what the surgeon thinks needs to happen. You'd have a team that successfully removed the bullet, but that didn't give enough blood to the patient because of budget cuts, or that removed a perfectly-good ear, too, for some crazy motive that has nothing to do with the reason the patient is in the emergency room in the first place."

""I never really thought of it that way, but it makes lots of sense. And that definitely sounds like how our government operates," agreed Creedmoor.

"That's because it's filled with opportunists, who are not there to do good, but to find every excuse they can find to do as they please. OK, so to move on, I'm sure you've figured out by now that getting somebody to express their enthusiasm for a good idea is a far cry from getting them to lift a finger to fight for it. If you raise a flag for honesty, for instance, you'll find a lot of liars who will salute it, and they will never even realize that their lives are not characterized by the principle they are saluting as good."

"You're making it sound worse, rather than better," Creedmoor said with a slight smile.

Benjamin True nodded in agreement. "Things are very bad. You live in an epidemic of dishonest, irrational, and irresponsible behavior. That is the cognitive fashion in the United States. And at the end of the story, it turns out that there simply aren't any shortcuts to making things right."

"I was afraid you'd say that. But really, I know and fully accept that you're right. I've been working on all this for years—trying to figure out how it can be really fixed—as opposed to the fluff that most of the activists are after."

"Do you know that starfish story?" True asked him.

"Do you mean the one about the boy trying to toss all the starfish back into the surf from where they washed up on the beach in a storm the night before?"

"Yes, that's it. As you know, an old man tells him, 'There are too many; you'll never make a difference.' But the boy, who happened to be holding one of the dying starfish at that moment, says, 'Well, it'll make a difference for *this one*,' and he tosses it back into the surf."[113]

"Yes, I see your point. There will always be those who will be separated from what is right—lots of them, like those starfish on the beach—so any model of government that requires the majority of the citizens to be righteous and diligent is going to fail."

"There you go," True assured him. "And fortunately, you can run a country pretty well with much less support than 100%. But you're fooling yourself if you think you can just wave a flag a bit and get enough people to shape up as a result of it."

"Naturally," said Creedmoor. "So, are you telling me that governmental reform needs to come to a standstill until some massive reform of character can be accomplished?"

"Not completely, but you're definitely going to reach a point very quickly where there are indeed some things that America must fix before she can fix anything else. You'll be limited in what you can get done, because people of corrupt and/or untrained minds simply won't put up with the effort required to maintain a righteous government—not until you can change the way they think. Indeed, they cannot currently agree even on what would *make* for a righteous government in the first place! So, in the meantime, one important thing to be working on is to give the good thinkers some better tools with which to leverage their influence."

"How do you mean," inquired Sky.

"Well, again, it's not ultimately the more important side, you understand, since the most important thing is to help individuals get their own thinking on straight. But there are a few people here who are pretty much ready to get started, and they could be getting to work sooner than later on some reforms. I'll tell you about that in a minute, but first I want to tell you about something else that you know already, though not as well as you need to know it."

"OK, tell me," invited Sky Creedmoor.

"When you've helped one person to adopt Reality-Based Thinking [114], you have achieved success in your basic mission. That's it. You're done.

You've proven the concept to him or her. You've achieved the core mission. And from there, it's just a matter of doing it again and again until you have reached a critical mass of Realitans[115]—if you ever can—who will have the collective influence to fix the government, too. But you are doomed if you get this mixed up—if you get to thinking that fixing the government is the primary goal. Saving the individual starfish is the goal, for the only thing that *really* matters about a country is what kind of people comprise it. And you'll never fix the people by fixing the government. You mark my words: you'll never fix the people by fixing the government. In fact, I don't even think that corrupt people have any *right* to a righteous government?"

"Hmmm," wondered Creedmoor.

"They don't deserve it, and they can't maintain it. And they will corrupt it and drain its coffers dry. And if they get a righteous government anyway, by some stroke of luck, it may help *some* of them in some indirect way to become better people, but most of them will simply bask in the light of the good government, and continue their corruption as they please, enjoying rights for which they will always refuse the accompanying duty. So you must never lose sight of the fact that helping the people be better is the real goal—even as you keep doing what you can to improve the government."

"OK, I get that, and I will see to it that it stays always on my mind. Now, regarding giving the good guys more leverage in repairing the government, please tell me what you're thinking," asked Creedmoor.

"Well, the term limits proposal that was just passed is a big one—assuming it gets ratified. It helps the good guys by automatically getting rid of the bad guys in office sooner than later. It also helps the good guys by giving them a whole term at least between the bad guy's first term in office and a possible second term. This way, they have time to get the word out as to the bad behavior that the bad guy exhibited while in office the first time. It also helps the good guys by lightening their load. No longer do they have to convince dull voters that the incumbent is not a good choice, for that choice is now removed as an option, and the status-quo-loving voters simply won't have the option of supporting the status quo anymore."

"It's even more genius than I had yet understood!" said Sky.

"Yes, it's brilliant. And if this had been enacted from the beginning, things certainly would have gone better so far. Now, we already discussed an amendment that makes each legislator certify that he or she has read a bill before being allowed to vote on it."

"Right."

"Well, that one helps the good guys, too. No longer do they have to work so hard to convince their legislators not to support this or that, because many of those legislators will not be allowed to support bills they haven't read—and who's going to read a 2,500-page bill, really?"

"Not many, that's for sure."

"Right. Not many at all. So it changes the game significantly. As it is right now, the good guys need some real teeth to go after the one who does wrong, rather than just to wait for his term to expire, and amendments like this would help them considerably. Do you remember how I told you that you'd have to decide what happens to a legislator who lies about having read a bill?"

"Yes."

"How about including in the amendment a provision by which such liars would be immediately removed from office upon being found guilty of the same?"

"Sweet! But good luck getting the Congress to impeach its own."

"Ah, but you don't have to settle for the status quo on that. As you point out, impeachment and trial is now in the hands of the corrupt Congress, so you're asking the guards to guard the guards—which, naturally, isn't working very well. But you could include in such an amendment a provision that allows others to adjudicate these cases of perjury. For instance, each state legislature certainly should have a right to impeach and try any Member of Congress from that state who would lie about having read a bill before voting on it. And in addition to that, any District Attorney in the district from which the Member of Congress was elected should be able to file charges of perjury upon finding probable cause that the Member had lied about it."

"Dang! I see the 'teeth' you're talking about," said Creedmoor.

"Right. And think about what all happens from such a change. It also renews the waning principle of States' Rights—which should be an inviolable fundamental of a Union of States—and it renews at least a little bit of the right of the People to oversee their own government effectively. In fact, on this count, the People end up stronger and with more power than in the beginning. And it's not with more power to do harm, mind you, but to do good."

"That could actually turn into something much more important than just getting the Congress to read the bills," observed Creedmoor.

"Exactly, because once you establish the principle that the Congress ultimately serves at the pleasure of the States and the People, then you can expand that right of oversight to other things besides whether they read a bill before voting on it or not."

"OK, I see how you're thinking here. This is good and it helps me to understand just what we might do. Do you have any other examples of what we might try?"

"Well, if you spent a Sunday thinking about what I've told you so far, you'd come up with several other examples that would not be all *that* hard to get implemented. So, I'll cut to the chase and give you a tougher one that you can't get done anytime soon because the American people just aren't morally ready for it."

"OK, what is it?" invited Sky Creedmoor.

"OK, let me set the stage for you before I get to the specific strategy. Tell me this—and I want you to be thinking in a big-picture philosophical way on this question: by what three processes do people generally get themselves separated from reality and truth?"

"Well, I've been thinking about this long and hard, but I only have two processes in mind, and not three. I think that when people get off in the weeds in their thinking, it's either because of the error or the lie."

"Very good," said Benjamin True, obviously pleased with the reply. "And the third process I had in mind isn't a process in the same exact way. Rather, it is the act of not thinking at all. That is, it's going with what they've 'always heard,' or going with tradition or the status quo. It is giving in to habit."

"OK, I see where you're going now. You're describing basic cognitive miser behavior."

"Exactly. So, that's one of the three processes. But now, to address the other two that you identified correctly: In the error, the person accidentally finds him- or herself believing a thing that is untrue. It's because of some misstep in the thinking process. And the error is responsible for a great deal of loss and strife in this world."

"Indeed!"

"The lie is even worse. In that case, a person who knows the truth has decided to reject it and to believe something else instead—or worse, to pass it on to others in order to get them to believe it."

"Right," agreed Creedmoor.

"Well, the not-thinking, the lie, and the error work together to devastating effect. The person who is prone to errors may not realize the lies that another is perpetrating against him. His own lack of learning and of discipline makes him vulnerable to those lies. Indeed, he may not even realize very strongly when he's lying to *himself*. So, if you want to make America resistant to the lies of scoundrels and tyrants, you've got to teach them how to think, of course. You've got to get the schools to teach thinking fundamentals like they never have before, even in past decades when they were better at it than they are now. That helps take care of the *error*. But besides that, here's what I'm really getting at in this particular part of our conversation: What can be done about those *liars* in particular?" True paused to let the question sink in.

"I'm listening. Please say on."

"Look at how many bills are titled one thing when they are in fact quite the opposite. And look at how often politicians make a promise knowing full well they never intend to keep it. And look how many so-called 'justifications' and 'rationalizations' for bad acts of government are not genuine."

"Yeah, that's pretty much business as usual."

"Right," continued True, "and look how this happens with the corporations, too. Look how much unfair advantage they gain by lying."

"Yes, fraud and misrepresentation is a major plague on this country."

"Right," said True, "and it needs to be stopped."

"But we already have all kinds of laws against it."

"Sure, you do, but who's going to enforce them? Corrupt officials? And even when one lying politician or corporate executive does get slapped with a penalty of some sort, they all know it's the exception. They just write it off like somebody getting struck by lightning because they know that prosecution for such is very rare."

"What are you suggesting," asked Creedmoor.

"It's profoundly simple, but what I'm suggesting is that it needs to be illegal for anyone to tell a lie under color of office, whether that is an elected office, an appointed office, *or* a corporate office. All three hold positions of public trust, and all three need to be accountable to the public for their bad behavior. Any such office holder convicted of telling a lie under color of office needs to be snatched out of office forthwith, and prohibited from ever holding any such office again—whether they reform themselves or not."

"Wow!"

"Remember the scripture:

> Now it is required that those who have been given a trust must prove faithful. [116]

"Why should anybody who has been given a trust by the public be tolerated by the public when violating that trust?" asked True, as he patiently watched the scope of it dawn on Sky Creedmoor's face. "Those gold bars have to be protected with the highest diligence. Otherwise, you're going to have the systemic corruption that you have. And further, any corporation that shows a track record of such lies, no matter how many executives they hire to tell those lies for them, simply needs to be dissolved and its assets sold to the highest bidder, with the proceeds going into the public treasury."

"But the shareholders would lose their investments if we did that."

"Yes, they would," said True, sensing Creedmoor's trouble with the concept. "Do you remember the Coin of Rights from my speech?"

"Yes."

"Well, this is that same principle. If you want to have the *right* to be a member of a corporation—to own stock in it—to profit from its revenues—then do you not also have a *duty* to see to it that that corporation behaves righteously?"

"OK, I'm really embarrassed that I had not figured that out yet. You're obviously right."

"Look at how many millions of investors there are in American companies who gain their profits through the fraud and misrepresentation of the corporations in which they invest. America won't accept what I'm about to say, because her heart is hard, but this is every bit as corrupt as a Member of Congress supporting some unconstitutional or unethical scheme by which he or she can illegally grow rich. There is no difference whatsoever in principle, but only in the amounts by which each is unjustly enriched."

"I can't argue against that," admitted Creedmoor. He paused for a moment to reflect, and then thought out loud, "But wait a minute. If we're going to start prosecuting politicians and corporate officers who lie—and corporations that lie—that's going to make for a huge increase in court cases and expenses. Who is going to pay for that?"

"Let's start with the question of who would *want* to pay for that."

"Well, people who want to see a righteous society would want to pay for that," answered Creedmoor. "Uh, those who wanted it *and* who were the sort to put their money where their mouth is."

"That's it. Again, it's the Duty side of the Coin of Rights. Of course, this country would save lots of money if it were to break the stranglehold of the lying corporations and politicians, so it would come out ahead in the long run. And besides that, the more prosecutions there were under such an amendment, the greater the deterrent to the lying, so the demand on the courts wouldn't stay all that high forever."

"Again, I can't argue with any of that. You're right on every count."

"Yes, the corporations are much too big for their britches. The going legal mantra is that they have the same rights as people, but that's a lie; in actuality they have super-human rights, and are allowed to do things that no person could get away with doing. If the American people were responsible and reflective, they'd figure this out and put a stop to it, but that's not what kind of people they choose to be. So, the corporations continue on in their inordinate influence over this society and its government alike.

"For example," True continued, "how in the world did any American ever think it was a good idea to let corporations make contributions to political candidates? How does that even remotely seem proper? If anything in the world has 'conflict of interests' written all over it, *that* certainly does. So, it needs to be flatly prohibited that any corporation could ever donate money to any politician for any cause—including any charity the politician may run."

"Yes, that would be good," said Creedmoor. "It would keep the mega-corps from having undue sway over the decisions of government. And it would...." Something dawned on Sky Creedmoor. "Hey, political parties are corporations!"

"Yes, they are," said Benjamin True as he enjoyed watching Sky think it through.

Sky Creedmoor went silent for a few seconds, thinking. "Yes, they most certainly are," he said, as a grand smile washed across his face. "If they could be shut down for lying, that would completely break the chokehold that this stupid and unconstitutional 'two-party' system has on American politics—and if they could no longer contribute money to candidates..."

"It's not just a stupid system; it's sinister. But you're right; it would certainly go a very long way. And if you could get that passed, the scope of reform that it could facilitate would be hard to understate."

"It's brilliant!" said Creedmoor, still wrapping his mind around its implications.

"You must understand, however, that this would be an attack against one of the primary *tactics* of corruption—not on the corruption itself, for that lives in the human mind, but on one of the main ways they put it into practice. So, the pushback against such an amendment would be immense. Again, you'd first have to have a public that cared a lot about it if you're ever going to get that one passed. And that would mean a lot of people being willing to do things that might well undermine their personal financial statuses. Think what happens when the company you've worked for ten years gets liquidated for habitual lying. Or when the investment you've been earning a little on the side from every year goes south because its officers were lying. This is going to cost people in ways they can see immediately, and good luck getting them to look down the road to what a better society it could make—to the ways it would pay off for the in the long run. As it is right now, America is just too heavily invested in her own corruption. So again, what you need is to find a way to inspire Americans to adopt an unhypocritical spirit of reform. They need to become the sort who won't satisfy themselves with token measures, and who won't congratulate themselves too early with vacuous celebrations."

Sky Creedmoor looked at him with a deep sadness. "So, are you telling me that it's practically impossible?"

"No, that is not at all what I'm telling you. What I'm saying is that you need to forget about chipping away at these branches, and really go after the root of the problem."

"The bad thinking and bad morals, that is?"

"Right. You've got to make good thinking and good morals fashionable. Make it attractive to people as much as you can, without lying or cheating in order to do so."

"OK, but every time I correct somebody—wait, that's not right—*almost* every time I correct somebody on politics or religion, they refuse the correction. Even the ones who *say* they see my point and who say they agree generally go right back to what they were believing and saying before—they just stay away from me so that I can't see them doing it."

"Yes, many people are incorrigible because of their bad thinking habits. They are the sort who, if they could read a conversation like you and I are having, would fail to realize just how much it is slamming their *own* bad behaviors, and who would choose to focus instead on the bad behaviors of others. All they see is what is immediate. That is, they feel the immediate sting of being corrected, and they decide they're not having any of that, no matter how much it might actually help them down the road. Or they feel the immediate rush of satisfaction when they give into that drive to 'just do something' to solve a problem, but they won't look down the road to see the bad long-term consequences of what they propose to do. Just look at how they like and share religious and political memes on Facebook. They take a notion to like something, so they want to share it right now. Do they make sure it's true first? Nope. Do they vet the quotes that supposedly came from George Washington or Abe Lincoln or Albert Einstein? Nope. They just pass them along right now because right now it suits them to do so. They don't think about what it would mean later, down the road, when millions of people have come to believe something false, just like they have themselves. It's very foolish, and it protects them from making the changes they need to make. So in this way, they are quite incorrigible. But not *everybody* is. Some of them, who might really like to become righteous in their thinking, are still stumbling over their own errors, lies, and biases. They get defensive against the very people who could help to set them straight."

"So, what do I do?" asked Creedmoor.

"Well, first let's talk about the really big picture, and then we'll talk about vacuum cleaners."

"OK, I'll bite," said Creedmoor.

"Do you remember when I started my speech proper tonight, and I warned everybody that my perspective would be different from theirs?" asked True.

"Yeah, I think so."

"Well, let's talk about that. Look down here at the street," he said, pointing down to the snowy street on which they stood. True began to motion with his finger in the air, and as he did, black lines, as black as coal, began to form figures on the snowy slush at their feet. First formed was a rectangle, and then inside that rectangle, True wrote the words, *Corrupt Culture*.

"First, let's talk about your human perspective. You all come into the world into this box—into this culture where so much of what one hears is false, and in which there is lots of lying, cheating, and stealing going on. No matter how good or bad each of you may want to be, you're born into a greater culture that's quite corrupt. Maybe you're born into a family that's better than average or worse than average. But either way, you have to decide for yourselves whether you are content to live in that corruption, or whether you're interested in thinking outside that box, trying to imagine a better way."

Benjamin True drew a lengthy arrow out and away from the right-hand side of the *Corrupt Culture* rectangle.

"Now, when somebody here starts thinking outside that box, and especially when they start *doing* things outside the box, naturally, they think of it as *Progress*."

The word, *Progress*, appeared above the arrow, and Sky Creedmoor nodded to signify that he understood.

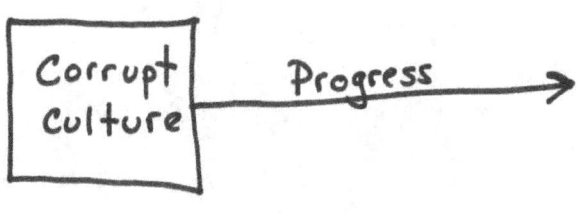

"Well," continued True, "that's pretty much the human perspective on things. That's the perspective I had when I was here—more or less. But since then, my perspective has changed considerably. I now live in a culture that is perfect."

True drew another box on a line beneath the first box and arrow he had drawn. In it, he wrote, *Perfect Culture.*

"Now, when *we* think about getting outside of *our* culture's box," he said, drawing an arrow, this time to the left of that new box, "we don't think of that *Progress*, of course; we think of it as moral *Compromise*."

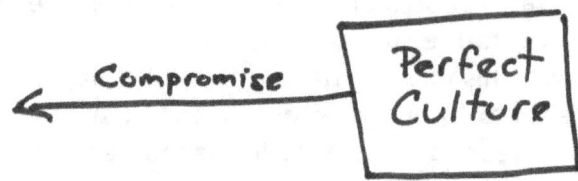

"To most of you down here, if you get outside your cultural box, foraging into this middle ground..." True waved his finger around the *Progress* arrow, "...you tend to only see what you're doing from your own perspective, and naturally, you think of it as good. And don't get me wrong; it is certainly better than to stay inside the corruption box. But what most of you never stop to ask yourselves how a perfect culture would see your business. So, you'll take one step outside that box and think to yourselves, 'Ah! Look what progress we've made!' and you don't keep pushing and stretching and searching for better because you're just so quick to want to seek out rest from the struggle. Or worse, because you're not really interested in a wholesale, sustainable reform, but are only interested in relieving some acute ailment that you just can't stand anymore.

"So, most of you get stuck on this line between the two boxes. You don't really keep moving toward perfection as a rule. Rather, you want to plant yourselves as soon as possible in a new spot, from which you will refuse to move until some new crisis forces you to make more adjustments. That's what the cognitive and moral miser does—the bare minimum for now."

Sky replied, "Well, I knew about the cognitive/moral miser part already, but I'm not sure I'm really getting what you're saying about this Perfect Culture box."

"Oh, I'm not done yet," True assured him. Pointing to the *Perfect Culture* box, True said, "Where I live, everything was fixed a very long time ago, as we simply don't live in corruption like this culture here does. For us, one step outside this box would constitute a major emergency, where in your culture, things getting worse in step-by-step fashion is just business as usual."

"You got that right!" sounded Creedmoor.

"So, it's a real stretch for you all to think like we do. It's not impossible, mind you, but it's hard because you've never lived in a culture like that. So, if you're going to figure it out, you're going to have to burn a lot of mental energy in reasoning and imagination. This is highly-reflective work, and you, of course, live in a decidedly non-reflective culture."

"You can say that again."

"If you all reflected more, you'd easily see ways to make things better—to make your *selves* better—and you'd easily see the that it's worth it to do so. You'd see the need for all manner of improvements that you have it within your power to make. But as it is, you live in a rat race with lots of noise and distraction, and with plenty of bad examples from those who have chosen not to care about the cesspool of corruption. And this is pretty much everything you need to make reflection seem undesirable, and to make it harder to do. With you all, it's as if *what you see here is all there is*[117]—as if it were inconceivable that life could get much better than this."

"And that explains the difference in my mindset and the mindsets of all those people in the House Chamber tonight, as well as all these on the street, too."

"Well, I suppose I spend more time reflecting than most, Mister True, but I'm none too impressed with myself right now, and you sure have got me feeling like a stranger and exile, desiring a better country."

Had anyone else been overhearing the conversation, they might have missed Creedmoor's allusion to a Bible passage, but it was not lost on True. Sky had alluded to a passage about the great heroes of the faith throughout the Bible times[118], and about how they were all looking forward to a heavenly afterlife, as opposed to how most on Earth simply do not concern themselves with that sort of thing.

"Well, you just keep longing for that country, Sky, and not only longing for it, but reasoning as to what it must be like there. That's one of the secrets to authenticity, by the way. Using yourself and your current status as the benchmark to judge how your own life is going—that's really dull and short-sighted. But the person who measure him- or herself against perfection—that's the one who can really get somewhere!"

Sky Creedmoor seemed a little lost in the moment, but not agitated. He was calm and focused, and seemed to be emotionally keen, rather than emotionally dull, as so many get when faced with conversations that stretch their limits.

"So now let's talk about vacuum cleaners," suggested Benjamin True.

"Huh?" questioned Sky.

"If you recall, I had said I wanted to talk about the really big picture, and then about vacuum cleaners."

"Oh, yeah. OK, I'll bite. Tell me about vacuum cleaners," said Sky, preparing his mind for another adventure.

"OK, we were going to talk about how best to help people, so let's pretend that you're a vacuum cleaner salesman going door to door to sell your vacuum cleaners. And at each house you visit, you go on and on about how much hidden dirt there is in their carpets, and how it's really nasty, and how you can go in there and demonstrate to them just how nasty their houses are, and how they can even hire you to come in and do the first nasty cleaning for them."

Creedmoor wondered where this was going.

"Based on your knowledge of typical human behavior, how well is that sort of marketing approach likely to work?" True asked.

"Not well; most people won't endure that sort of embarrassment without shutting you out. I've proven that again and again. They just don't have the character to face their errors honestly and rationally."

"True, indeed," said True. "Would you be *wrong* in telling them the truth about how bad their mess is?"

"No, of course not."

"Right. But it wouldn't be effective with most people."

"Right," said Creedmoor.

"So, that's one approach, and in my little story here, *you* get to be the dummy who tries that approach," said Benjamin True with a wry smile. "But *I'm* a vacuum cleaner salesman at a vacuum cleaner store. And in my store, people who are already interested in vacuums show up, and I show them all about hidden, nasty dirt—*in general*—and about what our vacuum cleaners can do to get it out. So, more of them will buy my vacuums than will buy yours, many of them not yet realizing yet how nasty their own houses *really* are, but they buy them on principle. And then they take them home, and they use them there. And the point is that they clean up their *own* messes at their own pace, discovering the extent of it for themselves, more or less. You don't have to do it for them; they do it themselves. They figure out how nasty their houses are all on their own, having been taught what generally should be looked for. It's their discovery, for the most part, and not something that is forced upon them."

"Please keep talking," invited Creedmoor as he tried to let it all soak in.

"You've got to get yourself into a position where people won't shut you out as soon as they hear you mention this or that philosophical position that you hold. For example, if a guy introduces himself as a Baptist preacher, he has just turned off every Catholic in the room. Or the minute he announces he is a Democrat, he has just shut down every Republican in the room."

"OK, I get that," replied Creedmoor.

"Good, so you have to avoid that as much as you can. You need to get yourself into a position where you can talk about *thinking* and about *character* without politicizing it or religious-izing it. And you know what I mean by using that made-up word."

Creedmoor nodded and smiled. "Sure, that works."

"And, of course, you want to avoid making use of ridicule and name-calling, and things done purposely to incite one's opponents to disgust."

"I'm glad you said that!" said Creedmoor. "I've been noticing for years how even the most popular of political pundits and talkers in this country stoop to base behavior like that. They'll talk about how to deliberately aggravate the 'other side', as if this were a useful activity for winning people over, but all it does is to create the backfire effect, and they just dig in and double down because they feel persecuted."

273

"You have made a very good observation. And you would do well to consider whether that tactic is an error, or a *deliberate* strategy to keep people divided."

"Yeah, I've wondered about that."

"Well, it's some of each. Some of them are just immature, but others know for a fact what they are doing, and they do it deliberately as part of their mission. And it plays on the baser instincts of their audiences, many of whom buy into it and practice the same themselves. They think that by listening to these shows, they're really taking it to the next level intellectually, but there's a lot of low-level mindwork going on there, and it's really counterproductive. It's really no wonder that your country is as divided and disgusted and offended as it is. It's not an exercise in higher thinking, but in lower thinking."

"You sure got that right!" agreed Creedmoor.

"Well, when you learn how to avoid giving needless offense, that's where you're going to be the most effective. And with every starfish you can get back into the water of right thinking, *that* is the fulfillment of your *real* goal. It doesn't just 'make a difference' for that starfish; it makes a *huge* difference!"

Sky Creedmoor grew suddenly still, and a solemn expression came over him. "You know, I have the feeling that that is exactly what you are doing for *me* right now—making a huge difference."

Benjamin True smiled at him. "Perhaps, but look how I'm doing it; mostly, all I'm doing in your case is to affirm the things you already have pretty-much figured out."

Creedmoor smiled and raised an eyebrow, pondering True's confidence in him. "Perhaps," he admitted.

"And one more thing: the old man in the starfish story, however much he may have seemed like a killjoy, was indeed right; there are too many starfish for one boy to rescue. This is why you need a plan by which starfish are not only rescued one by one, but by which at least the sharper ones among them are taught to rescue yet other starfish. I know that model is a little challenging in this particular story, because after all, starfish don't have hands and legs, and could do little to save each other. But it's just a metaphor for humans, and humans are quite capable of setting their thinking straight if that's what they choose to be like. And they're capable of helping others, too."

"Yeah, I've thought about that."

"Well, keep thinking on it, because it's crucial. This is one point on which many activist causes fail: they don't successfully convert their converts into converters. It's one thing to get Billy to quit doing whatever bad activity he has been doing, or to start doing something new, but there may be a couple hundred million people just like him, and you don't have time to get to them all. So, what you need to learn to do is to teach Billy how to help others, too. And if even only one in ten of those people who listen to you decide to become teachers, too, then you're really onto something. And you'll find that there are indeed some people out there who want to become exactly that. They will thrive on it, but you've got to help them be authentic through and through, and keep them from hypocrisy and double standards. I say that because nothing sours a sermon more than knowing that the one preaching it is a hypocrite. If you want to kill a message, just put it in the hands of a hypocrite, and he'll do more damage than it would do to simply discontinue the message altogether."

"OK, that's a lot to think about. It'll take me a while to reflect on all that."

Benjamin True shifted his weight and took a deep breath. "I see that you know yourself pretty well—how your mind works and all—and that's good." True smiled at him again, and continued, "Well, I'm very glad that we got to talk about all these things. It was the best talk of the night by far."

As Benjamin True stood up, Creedmoor quickly stood, too, and objected, "No, you are *not* leaving me here! We just got started. Do you realize how many years I've gone, having just my wife and kids to talk to about these things?"

"Having a wife and kids who are interested in talking about these things is a *lot*."

"Yes, but..." Creedmoor made himself pause, and then started in with a quieter tone. "Yes, it is a lot, and I am very grateful for it. I think I'd be insane without my wife and kids." A tear dropped to his cheek.

"You're OK," Benjamin True assured him, obviously understanding things yet unspoken.

"Yes, I'm OK," Sky said softly. Then his tone hardened somewhat. "But this doesn't make any sense. I've worked all these years to learn the pittance that I've learned, and now you come and affirm the course I'm on, and give me even more wisdom on the subject, but now I'm supposed to just go back to my stupid mechanic shop and fix stupid cars for a living when I'd rather be learning and helping people with things that are a lot more important than water pumps and tune-ups?"

Benjamin True didn't reply, but was obviously pondering something.

Sky Creedmoor continued, "I don't mean any disrespect to you, Mister True, but did you really think through this visit? Is *this* the intended consequence of it?"

By this time, Sky's cheeks were awash with tears, as he continued to plead his case.

"Come on, give me *something*. You've gotta give me something more to go on than just this short talk. You've pretty much come down here and verified for me a bunch of things that I had already figured out *must* be the truth, but here you are, *proving* a lot of it for me. And that just tortures me. OK, OK, yes, it's great to have learned more, and to have had some things verified. Yes, that's very wonderful, and I'm very thankful for it. But look, it's going to take me years and years to work all this into any sort of useful and effective form. And I'm not funded for this, and I don't have a team of thinkers already lined up to help with it. And you've already been thinking about it for a couple hundred years."

Sky Creedmoor felt bolder now. He looked at Benjamin True and pleaded, "Please. Give me something more to work with."

Benjamin True was still contemplating, and Creedmoor could see it in his eyes, so he waited patiently. Silently. And then, after many seconds had gone by, Benjamin True began to speak.

"You should know, my friend, that you are much more advanced in your understanding than I was at your age. I think you even know more at this point in your life than I did at the *end* of my lifetime here. This should encourage you. I'm very sorry that this conversation must be so short. But I think that in the coming days and years, as you reflect on it, you will realize that it has done more for you than you now think it has. Anyway, I think you'll be able to make good use of *this*," he said, as he produced a large manila envelope from nothing and handed it to his new friend.

Sky Creedmoor was intrigued. He slid a thick document part-way out of the envelope and read the title.

"Wow," he whispered in amazement. "Just WOW!" He took a long breath, and then another. "OK," he said, and suddenly, he was a different man inside, it seemed. Maybe not forever, but for now. What he had seen had changed who he was for now. And he was at peace.

"And I think you should have this, too," Benjamin True told him, as he handed over yet another document. This one was a typical #10 business envelope with a letter inside. It was addressed to the proprietor of the Babcock Theatre in Billings, Montana. The envelope was not sealed, and Sky Creedmoor emptied its contents, which consisted of a single page—a handwritten letter, which Sky read to himself right then and there.

He finished the letter and folded it back without a word, stuffing it into the envelope and slipping that envelope down into the larger one. From the little bit he had read, Sky Creedmoor knew instantly that he held two treasures in his hands.

Embarrassed, Sky told him, "You know, I have to admit that I've thought from time to time about giving this crazy quest to fix the nation, and just trying to live a good life with my family in my remaining years."

"I know what you mean. I kept going back and forth on that question, too—when I was still alive. But I do not now regret those efforts I chose to pursue. Not *all* of them, anyway, though some of them were pretty dumb in retrospect! But I helped a lot of people back then, and with the communications and research technology you now have—and with your love for whatever is the truth of a matter—you can do even more good than I did.

"Now, I want you to reflect on this in the hours and weeks that follow," continued Benjamin. "Think about everything I said to the people tonight, and you'll realize that not one word of it was something that they couldn't have learned or figured out for themselves. It was not my intent here to reveal any secrets to humankind; that was not the service I aimed to provide—although those who are ignorant of these things will assume that a lot of this is new information from on high. Yes, I freely admit that getting all the evidence of the corruption of all the politicians like I produced tonight—that would be quite beyond the reach of the average Joe, but it's not like they don't already know that such corruption is rampant in government and in the corporations."

"I agree," answered Sky. "We have movie after movie about the corruption in our government, so it's not like it's a secret."

"So, what I did tonight—the way I served the people—was mostly in showing them how to *care* about what kind of people they are and what kind of people are running their government. But it's only a beginning. Don't you think for one second that much societal good will come from tonight without a massive follow-up effort. And while what I'm saying is true about the governmental reforms that need to happen, what I'm *really* talking about right now is about teaching the public to be better citizen overseers of the government. To build that value proposition to any effective size, you'd have to have the public, private, and home schools teaching virtue, whether they want to do it in the name of religion or on the merits of virtue itself. And you'll have to have them teaching sound reasoning, which is itself a part of virtue. That'll be a tough fight, because so many Christians have been taught to avoid good thinking like it's some sort of a sin. So don't overestimate what I did tonight. Like I said all along, it's just a start."

"From my perspective, you did a *lot!*"

"And so will you, if you like. It's up to you," replied the angel. "There are about 800 kernels on an ear of corn, and if they all get planted, that one ear can make 800 more just like itself. If you were to help 800 more people decide to think right, and to learn how to do it, that would be a *huge* return for your life. That's no rule for you, of course; it's just an example. Perhaps in your case, you can reach fewer than 800. Or perhaps, much more than that.

"The hardest part of it for you will be to get people to start thinking their *own* ideas through, and to reassess their *own* habits. They're quick to criticize others, but slow to correct themselves. Even some of the wiser ones among them hold to several ideas that aren't nearly the great ideas they think *they* are. Most of the popular ideas simply won't work in the real world, or will cause so much trouble by way of unintended consequences that they're not worth pursuing. It all comes down to getting *individuals* to rethink what kind of people *they* are themselves.

"Again, you can try to change the big picture status of the country if you like—and you have no idea how much success to expect from such a campaign—but even if you never get one law changed or one corrupt government initiative canceled, you can still help lots of individuals get their own thinking in order. That's all for *you* to manage; it's for *you* to decide how much is enough for you to go after personally, and how much is too much. But do yourself a favor, and don't go looking for shortcuts to change the government without changing the citizens. That is a fool's errand."

Sky looked concerned. "I have no funding to speak of, and any substantial campaign of the sort you are suggesting will take lots of money, so what do I do about that?"

"Well, an established activist or pundit could help a lot, if you can find one who is willing to become a true Realitan[115]. Most of them are examples of what I call the 'incomplete activist'."

"How's that?" asked Creedmoor.

"Well, whatever the main thrust of their activism, regardless of whether it's actually good or bad, almost everybody in that business is also doing harm. Whether it's by accident, or on purpose, while they're promoting their main cause, they're also causing at least as much trouble as they're trying to stop. They'll be gloriously correct about one point, and quite wrong on another. Or gracious in one matter, and intentionally irritating on another. We already talked about this part, but just go to a search engine and see how often you find things like 'how to piss off a conservative' or 'how to piss off a liberal'. The outcome of this is quite predictable, and very damaging. It makes people of low character dig in to their bad positions, rather than to reason their way out of it.

"But anyway, if you could convert the thinking of a player at that level, that could be a real boost to you, though it may cause them to lose their jobs and to have to find another way to stay in the public arena. Otherwise, you'll need to find one or more donors who will put their cash behind the cause if you really want to get anywhere—on a national scale, that is. Barring all that, your only hope of getting the message out is in putting it in such a way that it resonates so strongly with enough people to 'go viral' as they say, without you having to push it by advertising.

"All that aside, however, the main thing is this: You be sure that *you* stay honest, rational, and responsible in *all* matters, *all* the time. That's the missing ingredient in this culture—the sincere drive toward total authenticity. So you keep *your* thinking right, and from there, help others as you're able. Never get suckered into saying or writing something you don't know to be true, and never get lured into compromising your own soul just to win a larger audience. And never try to trick, manipulate, or deceive your audience into doing right. The goal is for them to be right through and through, and not just to behave for right now in whatever way suits your immediate goals for them. If you cheat like this, you'll be wasting their time, whether you ever figure it out or not. It simply will not work. Do you know the line from James, where he says:

> And if anyone does not stumble in what he says, he is a mature man " [119]

"Yes," Sky confirmed.

"Well, how many figures on the national stage do you know who strive to be impeccable in *everything* they say?

"That would be pretty rare. It seems that in every speech or monologue or debate, I hear inaccuracies and biases from pretty much all the speakers. I've even written to a few to correct them, in years past, and hardly ever find one willing to correct him- or herself."

"Right. Either they just don't care, or they are too ignorant to know they *should* care about every detail of their message. So with every speech, the good they try to do is undone by giving their enemies plenty of fodder by which to discredit or dismiss them. And it's not just their enemies that cause harm to their causes; their own fans eat it up and repeat it as fact without checking it out for themselves. Such an enterprise is not about authenticity, but about something else.

"But as for you, you see to it that you avoid doing that. You be a complete man, and never stop learning better, no matter how popular or influential you become. There are two worlds, my friend, and the next one is not made for those who don't care if they're wrong. When you make a mistake publicly, you admit it and correct it publicly.

"The road of authenticity has always been narrow, and it's always been the case that only a few find it. While that number certainly goes up somewhat when there are authentic teachers available, you will never have the majority of a society adopt personal authenticity as a way of life. Anyone who is pandering to a 'big tent', rather than striving for personal authenticity, and the authenticity of his or her followers, is on the wrong road. And one of the easiest ways to discover this is to observe whether the leader truly adopts the Self-Correction Ethic[120] in *all* matters. That's the distinguishing characteristic that you want. That's the leader who is responsible to reality. So you be sure that *you* keep discovering and correcting your own errors, no matter how advanced you become."

Sky Creedmoor nodded with a look that seemed to Benjamin True like he understood. "Yes," said Sky, "even now, after all these years of learning, *I am most likely wrong about many things.*[121]"

"That's what sets you apart, my friend," Benjamin True told him. "It takes a lot of courage to look at life that way. And you must understand that the average human is going to be scared of you. Many will reject your calls to higher thinking because they're scared that the process will reveal what they've known all along—that they are not as authentic as they like to think. They would rather think of themselves as authentic than they would to do the work required to make it actually so. And among them are some who would rather pull you down than to rise to the call themselves. It's all quite ironic. But you are certainly right that you are indeed most likely wrong about many things—even as far along as you are. And as long as you embrace that, you'll certainly find some others who will embrace it, too, once you teach it to them. You are well on your way! And I'm afraid I must be on my way, too."

Knowing there was no way to grasp the richness of this encounter all in one moment, Sky Creedmoor just shook his head in resigned amazement. "What can I say to you?" Sky asked Benjamin, with a tear in his eye.

"What can I say to *you*?" replied Benjamin, with a dear smile.

There was silence, and then Sky asked, "And you're not coming back, are you?"

"Anything could happen, I suppose, but I doubt very seriously that I shall ever return."

"But I can see you again, right? I mean, later, when I'm done here?"

Benjamin True smiled the biggest smile yet, and with an assuring nod replied, "Oh yes!"

Sky paused to take in that glorious thought, and was immediately saddened yet again. "You know, I just met you, and it's already obvious that I'm about to lose the most amazing friend I ever had."

Benjamin True smiled at him. And Sky Creedmoor smiled back. And just like that, Benjamin True was gone.

AFTERWORD

The character, Benjamin True, is a literary device that I created in hopes of finding a way to set this important discussion in some new and intriguing light that might just inspire a substantial percentage of our cognitively-tired society to give the matter some fresh consideration. I avoided, in *almost* every instance, having True speak for God, and had him quote scripture instead, working on the assumption that the things that were true of God's opinion when those passages were penned or spoken would still be true now. I leave it to my audience to figure out whether I have got this right in each case.

Of course, the character, Benjamin True, is the product of a shameless and thinly-veiled attempt to put myself on the soapbox. He's my big chance to play out the sorts of things that I would say myself, if by some inconceivable magic, I were to find myself giving the State of the Union Address. His wisdom, if that's what it is, represents a better way than what is commonly believed, and many of those whom he corrects (but not all) in the story are people who believe things I used to believe before I (finally!) vetted them for myself.

And that brings us to the character, Sky Creedmoor, who, when we meet him, is busy with the work of vetting, questioning, and imagining solutions to our problems. I created Sky to represent my own quest for knowledge, understanding, and authenticity. His meeting with Benjamin True embodies my longing for someone far in advance of my own wisdom and knowledge, who could quickly set me straight as needed, and point me in the right direction from his or her own place of profound understanding. Interestingly, having written the character to be like me—having framed his journey in this world—makes me want to be even more like Sky. That is, to live all the more deliberately in pursuit of authenticity. I could wish that we all could be like Sky, and that we could all happen upon a Benjamin, but truly, I think it is likely enough for a Sky Creedmoor to know a couple of others like himself. If my experience in this world is any indication, such people are very rare, yet as it happens, I live with two of them! And this makes me one of the most fortunate people on this Planet Earth.

Regarding using Benjamin True as a literary device, I was critical of the concept in the beginning, and I still am. While many believe that God is indeed intervening in American politics, I do not. (This is because I see no evidence of it, nor any promise in the Bible that such would happen.) Nonetheless, I have Benjamin True tell everybody that God does not think it wise to intervene in American politics, and then turn right around and announce that God allowed him to come here anyway! It is to him inexplicable, and it would be inexplicable to me, too, except that I wanted to write this book, so I simply made the story happen as required to make it work. It is, after all, a thought experiment in what God—or someone who knows him intimately—might think about our political business.

To be fair to myself, God does not send Benjamin True with a message, but to speak for himself. And while I cannot be certain that I have got it right regarding what a godly and interested, long-term onlooker like True might say, I hope that the exercise is useful to the reader who wonders at the same question. It has most certainly been useful to *me*, and if I have got something wrong, and if the reader can demonstrate that to me, I will correct myself further and be a better person for it.

Perhaps I should note for the record that to a large extent, I have taken my own advice in this book, inasmuch as I have not made it into a laundry list of political and religious items in need of reform. I chose instead to go after the corruption, which I believe to be the heart of the matter. So, rather than to point out what all is wrong with everything America is currently doing, I have set forth the basics in hope of persuading as many as possible to put these principles to work themselves, and figuring out the particulars as they go.

While I'm not sure whether I'll be able to keep up with the feedback or not, I do invite you to contact me at jack@thinkulusmedia.com.

ACKNOWLEDGMENTS

This book is a result of the journey of my life so far. Its lessons range from those timeless basics my parents and sisters taught me, to what I learned in school and church, and then on to those deeper lessons that one only learns by searching them out for himself. I have searched and searched and am not nearly done yet. Yet in these more recent years, I have partnered with my wife, Kay, who is also a life-long learner, and whose companionship has enriched my journey beyond description. And from that union came our son, James, whose emergence as a thinker in his own right has never been so obvious as in the evolution of this novel. His part in its development, like Kay's, has proven so needful as to make it hard to imagine having written it without our daily discussions about its various parts and pieces. Whether I would have ever written this without their partnership is highly doubtful, for their presence in my life has a great deal to do with who I am and what I have chosen to be.

I could go on and on with acknowledgments to those friends who have taught me needful things along the way, even daring to correct me when I have needed it—which kindness, by the way, is far too rare in this world. So once again, I offer my thanks to our dear friend Michelle Lancaster, who dared to correct me all those years ago on a blockhead political belief I held. Not only did I learn the point in question, but I learned, more importantly, that I was in need of *more* learning. Indeed, if I had been wrong about that, then what else?

In the bigger picture, I am very grateful for the wisdom of the ages, which I would study full-time if I had the leisure to do so. Included in all that are many recent works in cognitive science, over twenty-five volumes of which I have read in recent years in my quest to figure out why we are so apt to persist in correctable errors. The three authors most influential to me in this search are Keith Stanovich, Daniel Kahneman, and Dan Ariely.

Also adding significantly to the contemporary grasp on the wisdom of the ages is Michael Heiser, whose scholarly (and prolific) work on the Ancient Near Eastern writings (including the Bible) is the most useful of which I am aware. He does full-time what I can only afford to do as an avocation.

The idea for the Coin of Rights was mine, but I solicited lots of help developing the concept for the coin itself. Many thanks to you all for your help, and especially to Garrett, who endured the long process of getting the coin's design just right.

My deepest gratitude also goes out to Jim Foos, my friend since college, whose role in my life as the occasional sounding board is invaluable, and whose encouragement went a long way in the writing of this book.

Naturally, I must thank my cousin and life-long outdoor adventure partner, Chris Pelham, not only for his expert advice regarding the sniper sequence, but also because I dare not write a first novel without paying homage to Chris in it somehow! Thanks also to my competitive shooting friend, Tyrel Lynn, for his advice on this same topic.

Finally, thanks are in order for those who helped with the biggest-yet-least-glamorous tasks of all. That is, to my wife, Kay Pelham, and to Michelle Lancaster, both of whom helped with the editing, and to Garrett Bibb, my friend of many decades, who not only helped with the cover art and Coin of Rights, but pulled me up the steep learning curve of Adobe InDesign, in which program this book was formatted.

It is a blessing to have such friends in this life.

OTHER WORKS BY JACK PELHAM

Obviously, this novel begs for some sequels, which I do have in mind to undertake if this present work should prove popular enough. In the meantime, however, here are other books and projects of mine that may interest you. And you can always check the latest at thinkulusmedia. com

Benjamin True Souvenirs and Promotional Items. You may purchase elegant replicas of the Coin of Rights, as described in this book and pictured on its back cover. Also available is *The Song of Benjamin True* and various items such as tee shirts and bumper stickers. Visit thinkulusmedia.com.

Reality-Based Thinking: *How everyone—including you—can think better*. This nonfiction book mixes what is classically called *epistemic rationality* with the paradigms of honesty and responsibility, making for a sustainable and high-functioning philosophy of life. This book seeks to avoid politics and religion almost completely, and focuses solely on the aspects of good thinking for its own sake. It should be available in early 2018. See details and ask to be notified of its publication at realitybasedthinking.org. Also see my website: realitybasedthinking.org

Society for Reality-Based Thinking. This fledgling society exists to promote RBT, and at present, consists merely of a Facebook page that publishes memes every day or so. As we build our audience, we'll roll out a membership plan and begin fundraising to take the promotion of the RBT message to the next level. facebook.com/Society-for--Thinking

What The Bible Says About Thinking: *Exploring one of the most neglected topics in Christianity* This nonfiction book scours the Bible for any evidence of how God expects righteous people to think. And there is a *lot*! The format is unusually simple, consisting mostly of categorized excerpts with occasional notes by the author. The point of it is to provide for the reader a quick survey of what all the Bible says and suggests about what is good and bad thinking. If you thought the dialog starting at the bottom of page 234 in this present novel is useful, you'll love this book. It should be available in late 2018 or early 2019.

RECOMMENDED READING

The following works I highly recommend for your consideration regarding the principles highlighted in this novel. With the exception of only three books on this list, I have read them all in their entirety—and some of them, more than once!

AMERICAN HISTORY

The Ascent of George Washington: *The hidden political genius of an American icon*, by John Ferling. 2009.

Hamilton's Curse: *How Jefferson's arch enemy betrayed the American Revolution—and what it means for Americans today*, by Thomas J. DiLorenzo. 2008.

How Alexander Hamilton Screwed Up America, by Brion McClanahan. 2017

Lincoln Unmasked: *What you're not supposed to know about Dishonest Abe*, by Thomas J. DiLorenzo. 2006.

The Real Lincoln: *A New Look at Abraham Lincoln, His Agenda, and an Unnecessary War*, by Thomas J. DiLorenzo. Reprint edition. December 2, 2003.

Overthrow: *America's Century of Regime Change from Hawaii to Iraq*. By Steven Kinzer. 2007.

BIBLE

The Bible

The Unseen Realm: Recovering the Supernatural World View of the Bible, by Dr. Michael Heiser. 2015.

The Naked Bible Podcast, by Dr. Michael Heiser. nakedbiblepodcast.comt

COGNITIVE SCIENCE (General Audience)

Reality-Based Thinking: *How everyone—including you—can think better*. By Jack Pelham. Should release in early 2018.

What Intelligence Tests Miss: *The Psychology of Rational Thought*. By Keith Stanovich. 2009

Thinking, Fast and Slow. By Daniel Kahneman. 2011.

The (Honest) Truth About Dishonesty: *How we lie to everyone—especially ourselves*. By Dan Ariely. 2012.

Predictably Irrational: *The hidden forces that shape our decisions*. By Dan Ariely. 2009

The Marshmallow Test: *Mastering self control*. By Walter Mischel. 2014.

How Customers Think: *Essential insights into the mind of the market*. By Gerald Zaltman. 2003.

SWAY: *The irresistible pull of irrational behavior*. By Ori Brafman and Rom Brafman. 2008.

Reality Therapy: *A new approach to psychiatry*. By William Glasser, M.D. Paperback edition. 1975.

The Day America Told the Truth: *What people really believe about everything that matters*. By James Patterson and Peter Kim. 1991.

50 Great Myths of Popular Psychology: *Shattering widespread misconceptions about human behavior*. By Scot O. Lilienfeld, Steven Jay Lynn, John Ruscio, and Barry L. Beyerstein. 2010

COGNITIVE SCIENCE (Academic Audience)

Rationality and the Reflective Mind. By Keith Stanovich. 2010.

The Rationality Quotient: *Toward a Test of Rational Thinking*. By Keith E. Stanovich, Richard F. West, and Maggie E. Toplak. 2016.

PHILOSOPHY (General Audience)

The 7 Habits of Highly Effective People: *Restoring the character ethic*. By Stephen R. Covey. 1989

Reality-Based Thinking: *How everyone—including you—can think better*. By Jack Pelham. This book should release in early 2018.

.

ENDNOTES

CHAPTER 1

1. United States Constitution. Article II. Section 3.

CHAPTER 2

2. Luke 6:46 New International Version

CHAPTER 3

No endnotes in this chapter.

CHAPTER 4

No endnotes in this chapter.

CHAPTER 5

3. "The Road Not Taken." Robert Frost, 1920. Mountain Interval, Henry Holt and Company, New York, NY.

4. United States Constitution. Preamble.

5. Letter from Thomas Jefferson to William Stephens Smith. 13 November 1787. Quoted in Padover's Jefferson On Democracy

CHAPTER 6

No endnotes in this chapter.

CHAPTER 7

6. Letter from Thomas Jefferson to William Smith. 13 November 1787. https://www.loc.gov/exhibits/jefferson/105.html

7. Letter from George Washington to Jabez Bowen. 9 January 1787. https://founders.archives.gov/GEWN-04-04-02-0428

8. Letter from George Washington to Thomas Stone. 16 February 1787. You may locate and read this letter with a free trial subscription at: http://rotunda.upress.virginia.edu

9. Letter from George Washington to Thomas Jefferson. 1 August

1786. You may locate and read this letter with a free trial subscription at: http://rotunda.upress.virginia.edu

10. Letter from Attorney General Edmund Randolph to George Washington. 12 February 1791. You may locate and read this letter with a free trial subscription at: http://rotunda.upress.virginia.edu

11. Letter from Thomas Jefferson to George Washington. 15 February 1781. You may locate and read this letter with a free trial subscription at: http://rotunda.upress.virginia.edu

12. Annals of Congress for 2 February 1791. https://memory.loc.gov/cgi-bin/ampage?collId=llac&fileName=002/llac002.db&recNum=333

13. Letter from George Washington to Alexander Hamilton. 16 February 1791. You may locate and read this letter with a free trial subscription at: http://rotunda.upress.virginia.edu

14. *Opinion on the Constitutionality of an Act to Establish a Bank*, by Alexander Hamilton. 23 February 1791. You may locate and read this letter with a free trial subscription at: http://rotunda.upress.virginia.edu

15. United States Constitution. Article II, Section 1, Clause 8.

16. Hamilton's Curse: *How Jefferson's arch enemy betrayed the American Revolution—and what it means for Americans today,* by Thomas J. DiLorenzo. 2008. Pages 29-30.

17. "Disgusted to see the federal district placed so far South, northern senators ominously deferred the request. For the first time ever, Congress withheld one act to pressure the executive into signing another. To avoid a setback fateful to the Potamac, Washington approved the bank. Within hours of getting what it wanted, the Senate obligingly modified the federal district's boundaries."
Founding Friendship: George Washington, James Madison, and the Creation of the American Republic. Stuart Leibiger. 1999. Page 136.

18. The Ascent of George Washington. John Ferling. 2009.

Bloomsbery Press. New York. Pages 294-295.

19. First of Men: A life of George Washington. First edition. John Ferling. 2010. 393-394. Oxford University Press.

20. An act to amend "An act for establishing the temporary and permanent seat of the government of the United States." Certified on 3 March 1791. See an image here: https://www.loc.gov/resource/rbpe.2170010p/

21. "...his search for the best site of the capitol was so transparently dictated by his self-interest that it aroused whispers at the time, though no one dared speak out. The president made a public display of conducting a supposedly dispassionate exploration for the most advantageous location."
The Ascent of George Washington: *The hidden political genius of an American icon,* by John Ferling. 2009. Page 295.

22. John Adams to Dr. Benjamin Rush. August 14, 1811. Pg. 345 of Old Family Letters. Old Family Letters: contains letters of John Adams, all but the first two ... Nabu Press. 2010.

23. The Ascent of George Washington: *The hidden political genius of an American icon,* by John Ferling. 2009. Pages 294-295.

24. Murray N Rothbard, A Histoy of Money and Banking in the United States: *The Colonial Era to World War II*. Page 69.

25. Chapter 5, United States Code. Section 3331.

26. Chapter 28, United States Code. Section 453—Oaths of justices and judges

27. This idea is known as The Golden Rule, and is stated by Jesus in Luke 6:31. The idea was not new to the Earth when Jesus spoke it, however, as multiple ancients had previously stated similar axioms. For a list of similar sayings in the ancient world, see: https://en.wikipedia.org/wiki/Golden_Rule

28. "The skills of judgment and decision making are cognitive skills that are the foundation of rational thought and action, and they are missing from IQ tests."
What Intelligence Tests Miss, by Keith Stanovich. 2009. Page xii.

"The mistake they make is assuming that all intellectual deficiencies are reflected in a lower IQ score." Ibid. Page 2. "It is ludicrous for society to be so fixated on assessing intelligence and to virtually ignore rationality when it is easy to show that the societal consequences of irrational thinking are profound." Ibid. Page 3.

29. This is the Bat and Ball Problem, from the Cognitive Reflection Test. Frederick, Shane (2005). "Cognitive Reflection and Decision Making". Journal of Economic Perspectives. 19 (4): 25–42.

30. This is commonly known as the *Jack, Anne, and George Problem*, and is taken from the work of Hector Levesque, who is a computer scientist at the University of Toronto.

31. Reality-Based Thinking (RBT) is the name I have chosen for my general philosophy of thinking, which stresses honesty, rationality, and responsibility as a sustainable way of life. I am currently developing this philosophy and will soon publish a nonfiction book entitled Reality-Based Thinking: How everyone—including you—can think better. See also realitybasedthinking.org and facebook.com/Society-for-Reality-Based-Thinking-567591796640229/ .

32. Haggai 1:5b

CHAPTER 8

33. From Martin Luther's Account of the Hearing at Worms in 1521 (excerpts) (Second hearing, April 18, 1521) Sources: H.C. Bettenson, *Documents of the Christian Church* (1903), based on Luther's *Opera Latina* (Frankfurt, 1865-73); Roland H. Bainton, *Here I Stand: A Life of Martin Luther* (1950)

34. Calling All Curs. 1939. The Three Stooges. https://www.youtube.com/watch?v=ScGPRsHSkaE

35. This "for a good cause" excuse I learned from the research of Dan Ariely. It is stated succinctly enough in the following footnote of his:
"*Based on these results, we could speculate that people who

work for ideological organizations such as political groups and not-for-profits might actually feel more comfortable bending moral rules—because they are doing it for a good cause and to help others."
The (Honest) Truth About Dishonesty. 2012. Harper. Page 232.

36. Albert Einstein: The Violinist. 1980. Peregrine White. http://astro1.panet.utoledo.edu/~ljc/Ein_violin.pdf Further details provided personally to me by Janice Harsanyi, who was the singer at the dinner, and who later was my voice teacher at The Florida State University.

37. The term "cognitive miser" was coined in 1984 by Susan Fiske and Shelley Taylor. It is a theory of human cognition that compares human thinkers to the traits of a miser or spendthrift That is, we tend to resist spending much effort on our thinking unless we are forced to. The idea is a generalization used to explain human behavior as a whole, but individuals can certainly become health cognitive spenders, expending more and more effort to greater and greater effect.
For a general discussion of cognitive miserliness, see the article here: https://en.wikipedia.org/wiki/Cognitive_miser

CHAPTER 9

No endnotes in this chapter.

CHAPTER 10

No endnotes in this chapter.

CHAPTER 11

38. This quotation is commonly attributed to Sir Edmund Burke, but such attribution is dubious. See here: http://quoteinvestigator.com/2010/12/04/good-men-do/

39. Some argue that the US has been at war over 90% of its years, but this all depends on what one counts as war. Regardless, a few minutes spent perusing the list of armed conflicts is adequate to get the point here. See a list here: https://en.wikipedia.org/wiki/List_of_wars_involving_the_United_States

40. John Adams, *Novanglus* Essays, No. 7.

41. Frequently misattributed to Sir Winston Churchill.

42. I coined the term *Realitan*, which is defined thus:
realitan — (ree-AL-uh-tun)
1. noun — a person who deliberately "lives in" reality as a sustained way of life; more specifically, a devoted and authentic practitioner of Reality-Based Thinking.
2. adjective — pertaining to or consistent with Reality-Based Thinking or a lifestyle thereof. (Example: He eventually abandoned his irrational position and took a realitan view of the problem.)
From: English "reality" and "-an", the suffix denoting a resident.
NOTE: Realitans are rare on the Earth. They are not perfect; they still make mistakes. They maintain a consistent attitude of full responsibility for their thoughts, however, and correct themselves when their errors become obvious.

CHAPTER 12

43. Statute 1. 1789. https://www.loc.gov/law/help/statutes-at-large/1st-congress/c1.pdf

44. Declaration of Independence. 1776. Thomas Jefferson

45. Declaration of Independence. 1776. Thomas Jefferson

46. *John Adams,* Letter to Zabdiel Adams. 21 June 1776.

47. *James Madison.* Speech to the Virginia Ratification Convention. 20 June 1788.

48. "The Way to Wealth", an essay first published in 1758 as a preface to Franklin's *Poor Richard's Almanack.*

49. *Benjamin Franklin.* Speech to the Constitutional Convention. 28 June 1787.

50. *John Adams.* Letter to the Officers of the First Brigade of the Third Division of the Militia of Massachusetts. 11 October 1798.

51. *2 Thessalonians 3:10*

52.   *Benjamin Franklin.* The American Weekly Mercury, February 18, 1728/9. The Busy-Body, No. 3

53.   *Attributed to John Witherspoon (one of the signers of the Declaration of Independence). Source unknown.*

54.   *James Madison.* Federalist No. 57, February 19, 1788.

55.   The Linda Problem. Tversky, A. and Kahneman, D. (1982) "Judgments of and by representativeness". In D. Kahneman, P. Slovic & A. Tversky (Eds.), *Judgment under uncertainty: Heuristics and biases.* Cambridge, UK: Cambridge University Press.

56.   This is Jack Pelham's Self-Correction Ethic. It is a central paradigm of Reality-Based Thinking

CHAPTER 13

57.   1 Timothy 6:9 ESV

58.   The reader should examine this list of supposedly documented CIA conspiracies, and particularly the item titled "Conspiracy Theory" Conspiracy. I have not vetted this list, but after a brief examination, find it worthy of such attention. https://www.reddit.com/r/conspiracy/wiki/locc
Also useful is the YouTube video entitled The Conspiracy "Theory" Conspiracy. https://www.youtube.com/watch?v=PuQTtw_nLoA&ab_channel=KnowMoreNews

CHAPTER 14

59.   Juvenal, from his Satires. Satire VI, lines 347–8. Late First, or early Second Century, AD.

60.   Benjamin Franklin. *Speech to the Constitutional Convention.* 28 June 1787.

61.   Psalm 65:2. New International Version

62.   "The Road Not Taken." Robert Frost, 1920. Mountain Interval, Henry Holt and Company, New York, NY.

CHAPTER 15

63.   "...cognitive misers allow their attention to be focused by others. Cognitive misers let the structure of the environment determine how they think The miser accepts whichever way the problem is presented and thinks from there, often never realizing that a different presentation format would have led to a different conclusion." Keith E. Stanovich. <u>What Intelligence Tests Miss: The psychology of rational thought.</u> 2009. Page 88.

CHAPTER 16

64.   Status Quo Bias is a routine of thinking by which one prefers things as they are, even if it would be better if things were different.

CHAPTER 17

No endnotes in this chapter.

CHAPTER 18

65.   Surveys in recent years are consistent with Benjamin True's claim that over 70% of Americans favor term limits. See these various polls:
1. (2011) http://m.rasmussenreports.com/public_content/politics/general_politics/september_2011/71_favor_term_limits_for_congress
2. (2016) http://www.rasmussenreports.com/public_content/politics/general_politics/october_2016/more_voters_than_ever_want_term_limits_for_congress
3. (2013-2017) https://www.isidewith.com/poll/313812228#

CHAPTER 19

66.   "The Way to Wealth", an essay first published in 1758 as a preface to Franklin's Poor Richard's Almanack.

67.   Thomas Paine. Common Sense, conclusion. The Complete Writings of Thomas Paine, ed. Philip S. Foner, vol. 1, p. 45. Originally published in 1776.

CHAPTER 20

68. The Apotheosis of Washington.
    https://en.wikipedia.org/wiki/The_Apotheosis_of_Washington

69. *Elohim* is a transliteration of the Hebrew word, מִיהֹלֱא, and is often translated as either "God" or "gods". Like our English word, sheep, *elohim* carries a plural form, but may refer to either a singular or plural subject, as determined by the context. Psalm 82 is the most useful passage in illustrating this, as it shows Yahweh (to whom it refers as "*elohim*") being "in the midst of" other gods (calling them *elohim*). Yahweh was not the only *elohim*, yet no other *elohim* was like him. For a scholarly review of this, see the work of Dr. Michael Heiser here: http://drmsh.com/the-plural-elohim-of-psalm-82-gods-or-men/

70. The inscription above the statue of Abraham Lincoln at the Lincoln Memorial reads, "IN THIS TEMPLE AS IN THE HEARTS OF THE PEOPLE FOR WHOM HE SAVED THE UNION THE MEMORY OF ABRAHAM LINCOLN IS ENSHRINED FOREVER"

71. This is The Song of Benjamin True, by Jack Pelham. Music for this song is available at thinkulusmedia.com.

72. Regarding Hamilton's tariff and Lincoln's continuation of it, I recommend the entire 209 pages of Hamilton's Curse: How Jefferson's arch enemy betrayed the American Revolution—and what it means for Americans today, by Thomas J. DiLorenzo

73. For a concise discussion of this point, see Thomas J. DiLorenzo's Lincoln Unmasked: What you're not supposed to know about Dishonest Abe. 2006. Three Rivers Press. Pages 24-25.
    For more on the shocking truth about Lincoln, I recommend this entire book, as well as the other famous book by the same author: The Real Lincoln: A New Look at Abraham Lincoln, His Agenda, and an Unnecessary War. Crown Forum; Reprint edition (December 2, 2003)

74. This is the Corwin Amendment, passed by Congress on March 2, 1861. https://en.wikipedia.org/wiki/Corwin_Amendment

75. English Standard Version (emphasis added). *1 Corinthians 15:40 There are **heavenly bodies** and earthly bodies, but the glory of the heavenly is of one kind, and the glory of the earthly is of another. 41 There is one glory of the sun, and another glory of the moon, and another glory of the stars; for star differs from star in glory. 42 So is it with the resurrection of the dead. What is sown is perishable; what is raised is imperishable. 43 It is sown in dishonor; it is raised in glory. It is sown in weakness; it is raised in power. 44 It is sown a natural body; it is raised a **spiritual body**. If there is a natural body, there is also a spiritual body.*

76. *The thoughts expressed here by Benjamin True are inspired in part by this excerpt from Daniel Kahneman:*
"Most of us view the world as more benign than it really is, our own attributes as more favorable than they truly are, and the goals we adopt as more achievable than they are likely to be. We also tend to exaggerate our ability to forecast the future, which fosters overconfidence. In terms of its consequences for decisions, the optimistic bias may well be the most significant cognitive bias. Because optimistic bias is both a blessing and a risk, you should be both happy and wary if you are temperamentally optimistic." Thinking, Fast and Slow. Daniel Kahneman. 2011. Farrar, Straus, and Giroux. Page 255.

77. This thought is the fundamental kernel of this author's philosophy of Reality-Based Thinking.

78. Matthew Chapter 7

79. *Proverbs 17:5, English Standard Version.*

80. Proverbs 13:19, English Standard Version.

81. Proverbs 20:9, English Standard Version.

82. This is the Lily Pad Problem, slightly edited for inclusion here. From the Cognitive Reflection Test. Frederick, Shane (2005). "Cognitive Reflection and Decision Making". Journal of Economic Perspectives. 19 (4): 25–42.

83. This is the Wason 4-Card Selection Task. https://en.wikipedia.

84. Romans 8:7 (KJV) *Because the carnal mind is enmity against God: for it is not subject to the law of God, neither indeed can be.*

85. Romans 12:2 (ESV) *Do not be conformed to this world, but be transformed by the renewal of your mind, that by testing you may discern what is the will of God, what is good and acceptable and perfect.*

86. 2 Timothy 3:16-17 (ESV) *All Scripture is breathed out by God and profitable for teaching, for reproof, for correction, and for training in righteousness, that the man of God may be complete, equipped for every good work.*

87. Titus 2:12 (ESV) *training us to renounce ungodliness and worldly passions, and to live self-controlled, upright, and godly lives in the present age,*

88. Hebrews 5:14 (ESV) *But solid food is for the mature, for those who have their powers of discernment trained by constant practice to distinguish good from evil.*

89. 1Corinthians 8:1-3 (ESV) *Now concerning food offered to idols: we know that "all of us possess knowledge." This "knowledge" puffs up, but love builds up. 2 If anyone imagines that he knows something, he does not yet know as he ought to know. 3 But if anyone loves God, he is known by God.*

90. 1 Corinthians 2:12-14 *Now we have received not the spirit of the world, but the Spirit who is from God, that we might understand the things freely given us by God. 13 And we impart this in words not taught by human wisdom but taught by the Spirit, interpreting spiritual truths to those who are spiritual.14 The natural person does not accept the things of the Spirit of God, for they are folly to him, and he is not able to understand them because they are spiritually discerned.*

91. Isaiah 1:18 ESV

92. Haggai 1:7 NIV

93. Proverbs 18:17 NKJV

94. John 7:24 NIV

95. 1 Corinthians 11:28 HCSB

96. Proverbs 23:7 NKJV

97. James 4:8 ESV

98. James 1:8 KJV

99. 1 Corinthians 14:20 ESV

100. Romans 12:3 NIV

101. James 1:26 NIV

102. Luke 8:15 NASB

103. Jeremiah 37:9 NIV

104. 1 Corinthians 8:2 ESV

105. 1 Corinthians 11:31 NASB

106. 1 Corinthians 3:18 ESV

107. Hebrews 5:14 ESV

108. 2 Corinthians 13:5 ESV

109. James 1:22 NIV

110. I call this cognitive bias "Interpretation Neglect" and define
     it thus: *The tendency to forget that one's belief in a matter
     does not stem directly from the evidence, but from one's own
     interpretation of the evidence. This bias does not allow for the
     possibility that the interpretation itself could be in error, and
     assumes that anyone challenging the belief must be taking issue
     with the evidence itself*

CHAPTER 22

111. Daniel Gilbert. Stumbling on Happiness. Vintage. March 20,
     2007.

112. Pelham's Law of Cognitive Error

CHAPTER 23

113. *This story is attributed to Loren Eiseley, and appears in various forms, sometimes under the title "The Star Thrower". See more here:*
https://www.goodreads.com/author/quotes/56782.Loren_Eiseley

114. See endnote #31 about Reality-Based Thinking

115. See endnote #42 about Realitans

116. 1 Corinthians 4:2 NIV

117. "What You See Is All There Is" (WYSIATI) is a cognitive bias, or as some might see it, a cognitive default mode for the human brain. Simply put, it is the working assumption that, "if there were more than what meets the eye, I would know it." The phrase and the acrononym, WYSIATI, were coined by Daniel Kahneman. For details, search the term in the index of Kahneman's book, Thinking, Fast and Slow. 2011.

118. Hebrews 11:13-16

119. James 3:2. The Greek word translated as "perfect" by many Bible versions of this passage is τέλειος (*teleios*). It is generally defined as *mature* or *complete*, in the sense that something described as *teleios* is everything he or she was intended to be.

120. "Self-correction is the rightful duty of all humans." This *Self-Correction Ethic* is a fundamental paradigm of Jack Pelham's philosophy of Reality-Based Thinking

121. Pelham's Law of Cognitive Error.

www.ingramcontent.com/pod-product-compliance
Lightning Source LLC
Chambersburg PA
CBHW071107250626
47159CB00002B/630